The PHANTOM TWIN

LISA BROWN

:01

First Second
New York

THANK YOU...

To all my brilliant readers: Nilah Magruder, Kate Maruyama, Shannon May, David Serlin, Laurel Snyder, Mariko Tamaki, and Michelle Tea. To Vera Brosgol and Raina Telgemeier for comics advice and hand-holding. To Laura Park for the pen nibs. To LeUyen Pham for above and beyond technical and stylistic help. To Kori Handwerker for expert flatting. To the fabulous folk of First Second: Andrew Arnold, Mark Siegel, Rachel Stark, and Calista Brill. To Charlotte Sheedy, of course. And to Daniel Handler, to whom I am completely and utterly attached.

First Second

Copyright © 2020 by Lisa Brown

Published by First Second
First Second is an imprint of Roaring Brook Press,
a division of Holtzbrinck Publishing Holdings Limited Partnership
120 Broadway, New York, NY 10271

Don't miss your next favorite book from First Second!
For the latest updates go to firstsecondnewsletter.com and sign up for our enewsletter.

Library of Congress Cataloging-in-Publication Data is available.
Hardcover ISBN: 978-1-62672-925-4
Paperback ISBN: 978-1-62672-924-7

Our books may be purchased in bulk for promotional, educational, or business use. Please contact your local bookseller or the Macmillan Corporate and Premium Sales Department at (800) 221-7945 ext. 5442 or by email at MacmillanSpecialMarkets@macmillan.com.

FIRST
EDITION

First edition, 2020
Edited by Calista Brill and Rachel Stark
Cover design by Andrew Arnold and Molly Johanson
Interior book design by Molly Johanson
Color assistance by Kori Michele Handwerker
Photo on page 204 by Century Flashlight Photographers, Inc.
Printed in China by RR Donnelley Asia Printing Solutions Ltd., Dongguan City, Guangdong Province

Inked with India ink and a vintage metal nib on Aquabee paper and colored digitally in Photoshop

Paperback: 10 9 8 7 6 5 4 3 2 1
Hardcover: 10 9 8 7 6 5 4 3 2 1

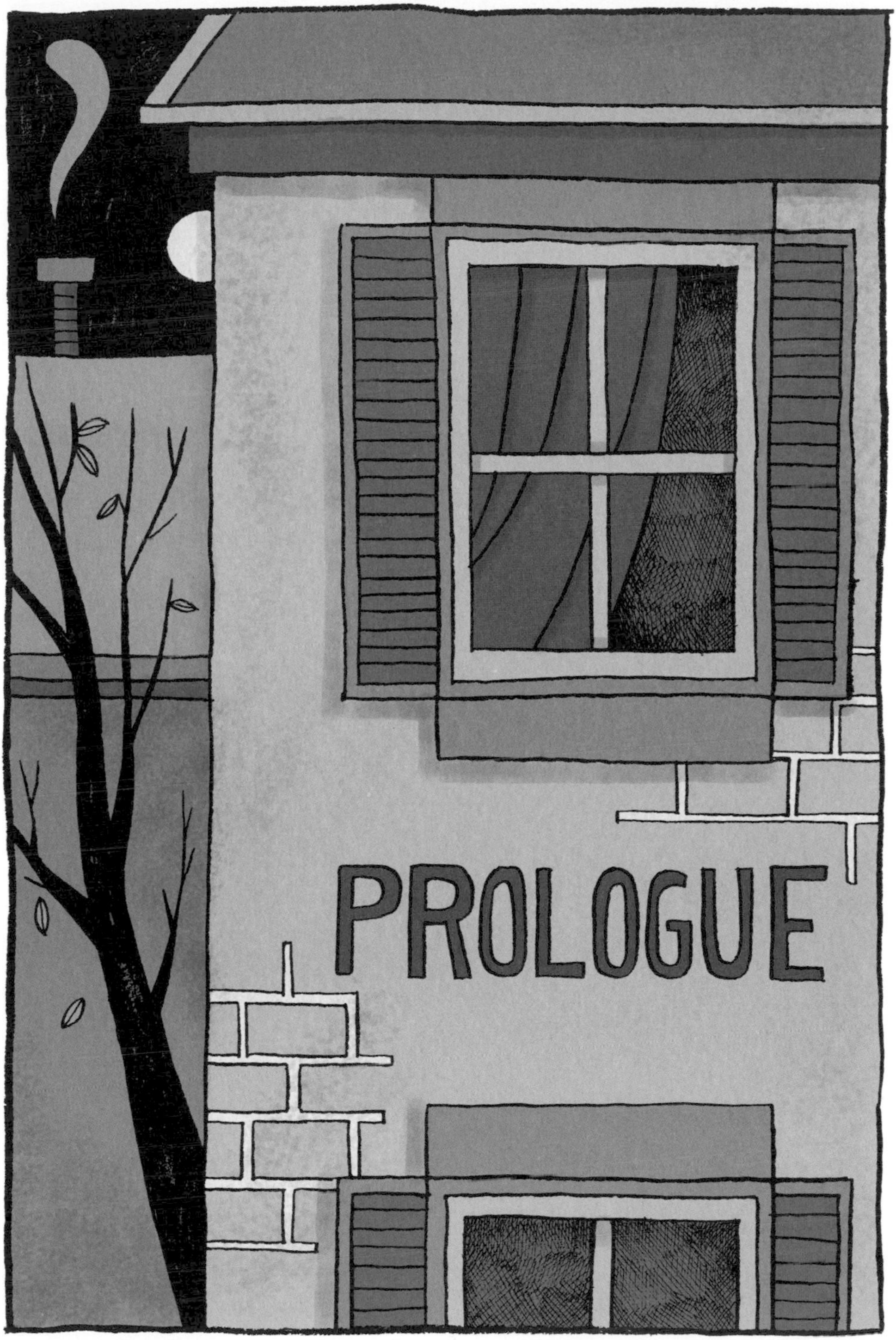
PROLOGUE

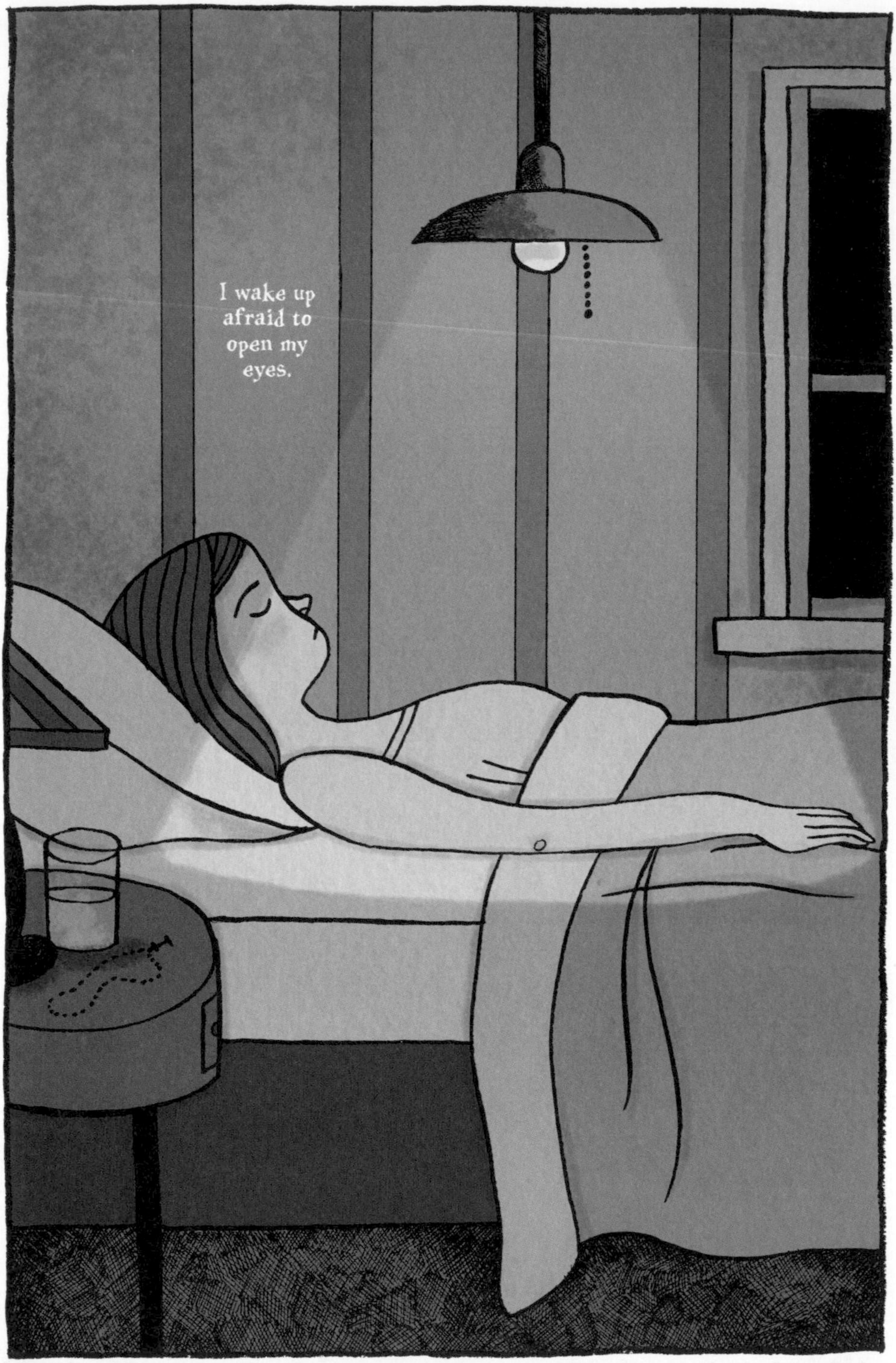
I wake up afraid to open my eyes.

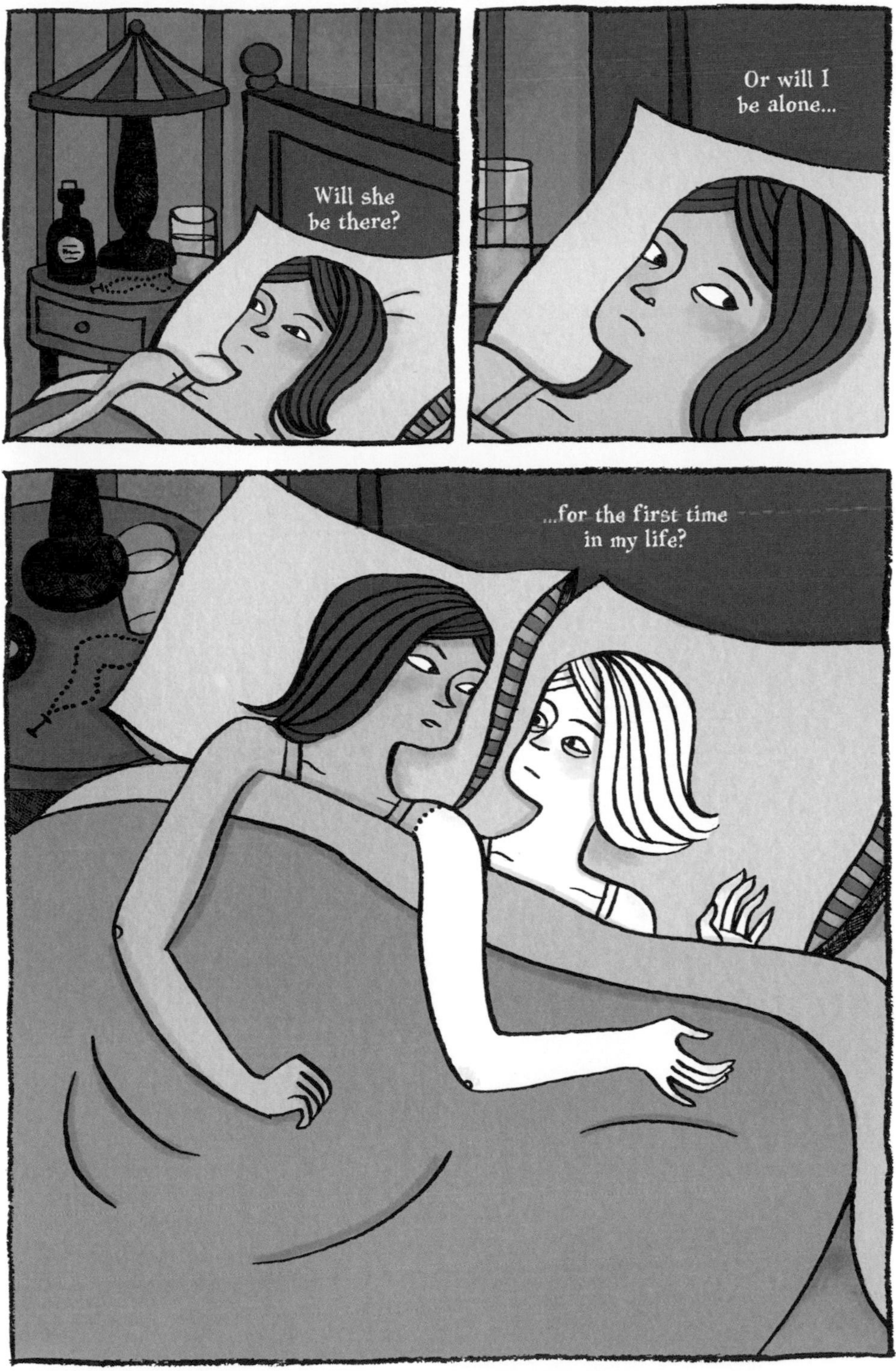
Will she be there?
Or will I be alone...
...for the first time in my life?

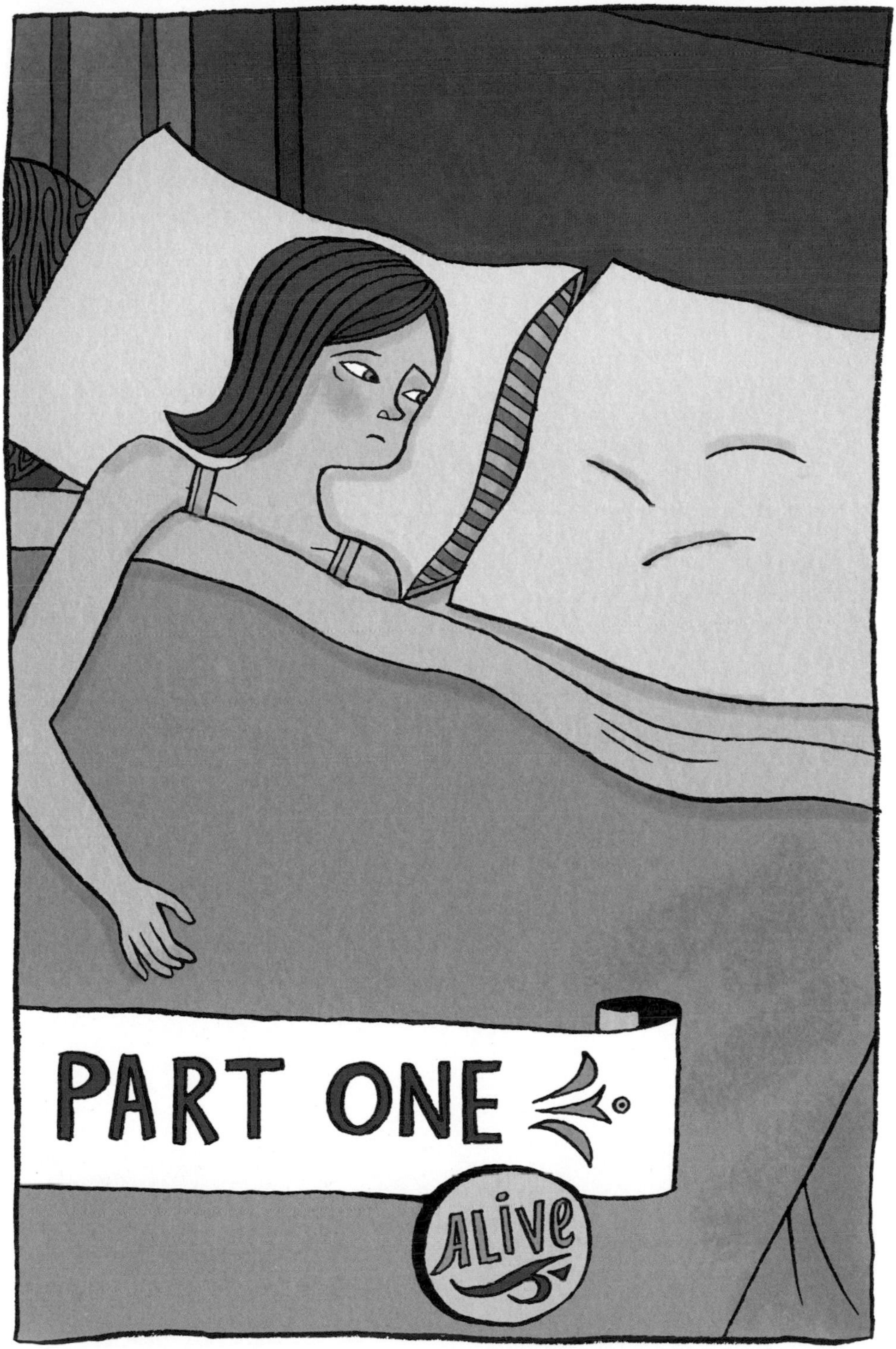
PART ONE
ALIVE

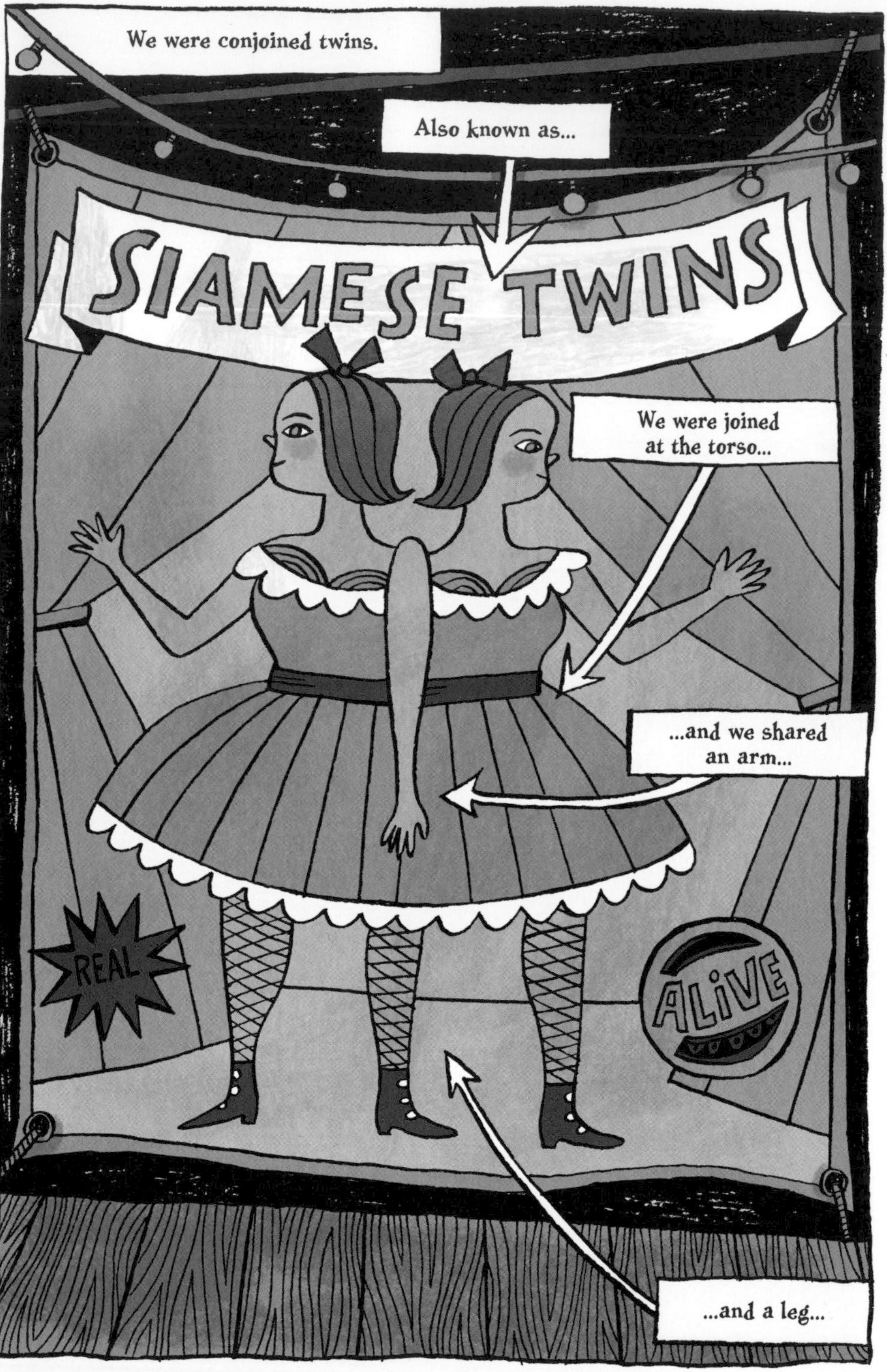

We were conjoined twins.
Also known as...
SIAMESE TWINS
We were joined at the torso...
...and we shared an arm...
REAL
ALIVE
...and a leg...

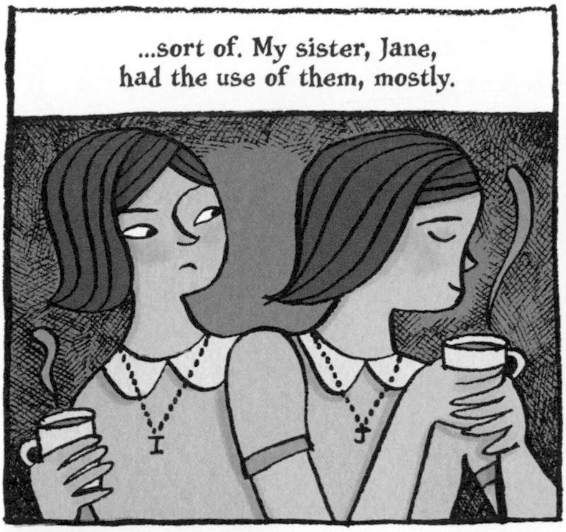
...sort of. My sister, Jane, had the use of them, mostly.

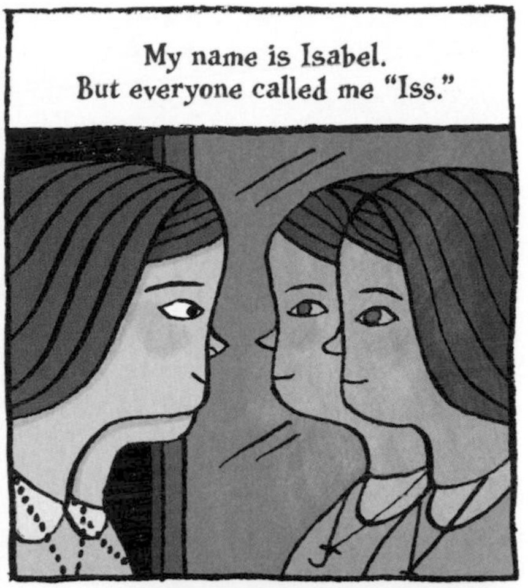
My name is Isabel. But everyone called me "Iss."

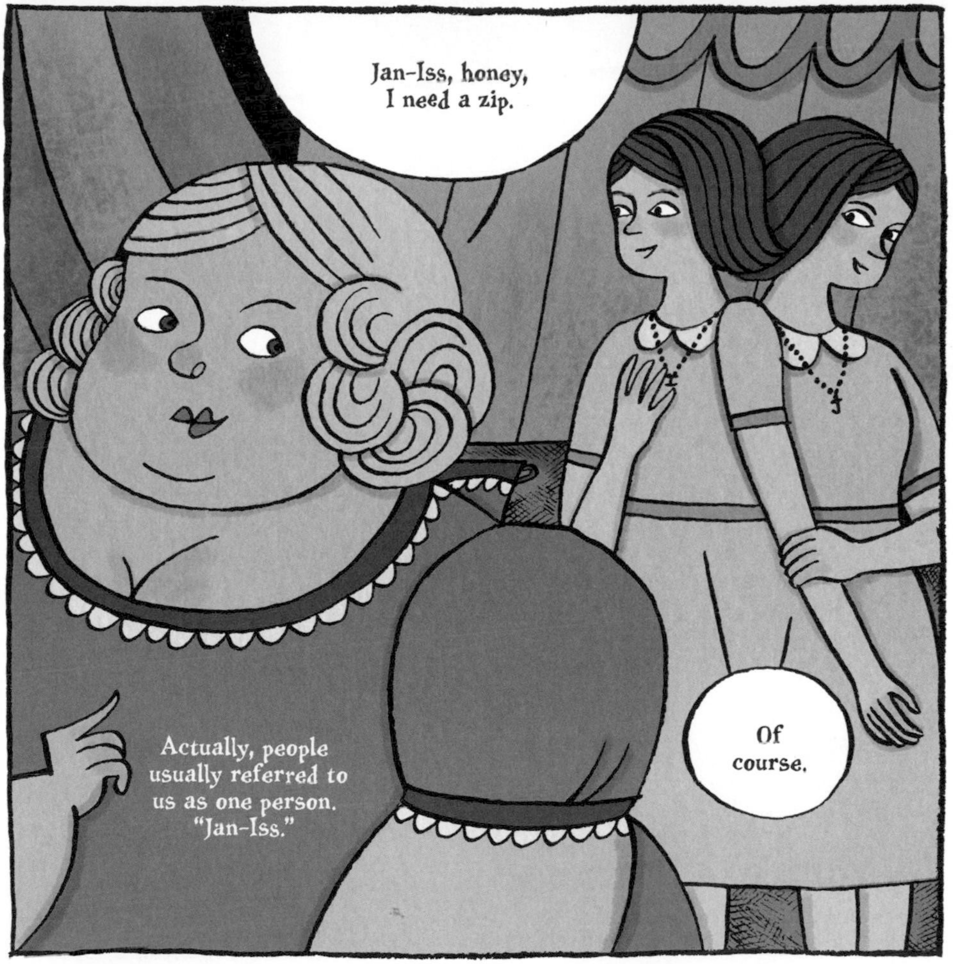
Jan-Iss, honey, I need a zip.
Actually, people usually referred to us as one person. "Jan-Iss."
Of course.

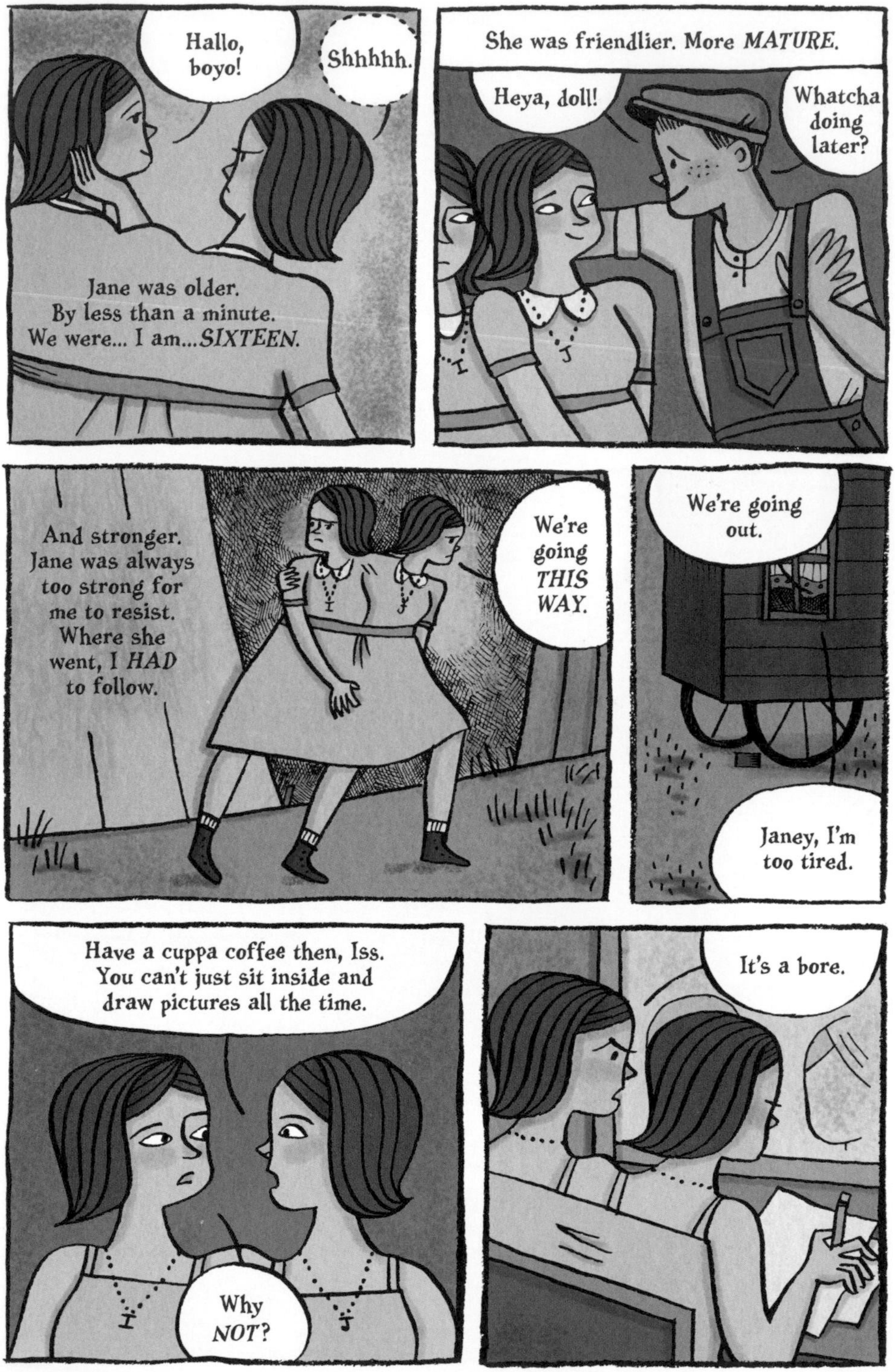

Hallo, boyo!
Shhhhh.
Jane was older. By less than a minute. We were... I am...SIXTEEN.
She was friendlier. More MATURE.
Heya, doll!
Whatcha doing later?
And stronger. Jane was always too strong for me to resist. Where she went, I HAD to follow.
We're going THIS WAY.
We're going out.
Janey, I'm too tired.
Have a cuppa coffee then, Iss. You can't just sit inside and draw pictures all the time.
Why NOT?
It's a bore.

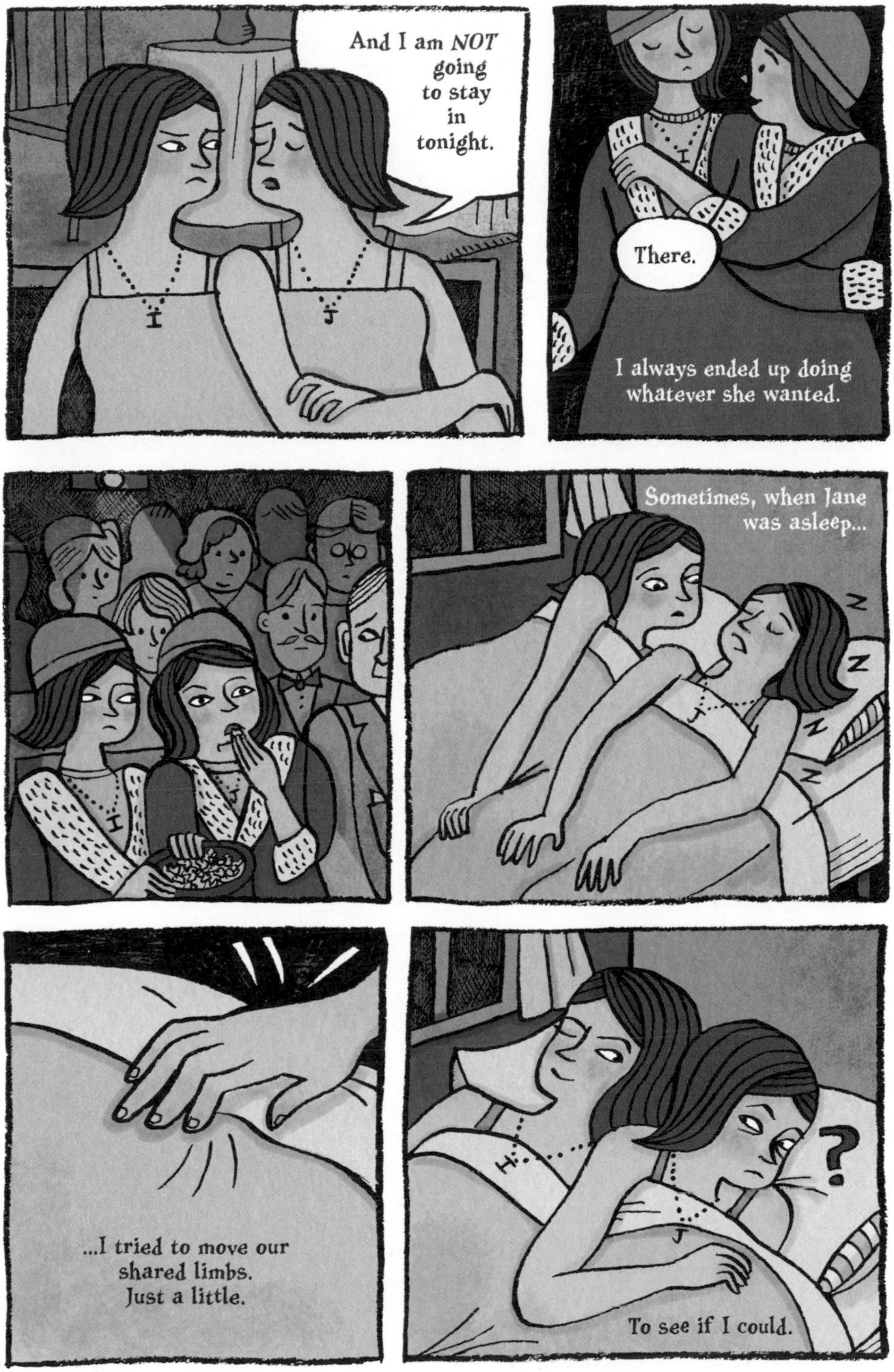
And I am NOT going to stay in tonight.
There.
I always ended up doing whatever she wanted.
Sometimes, when Jane was asleep...
Z
Z
Z
Z
...I tried to move our shared limbs. Just a little.
?
To see if I could.

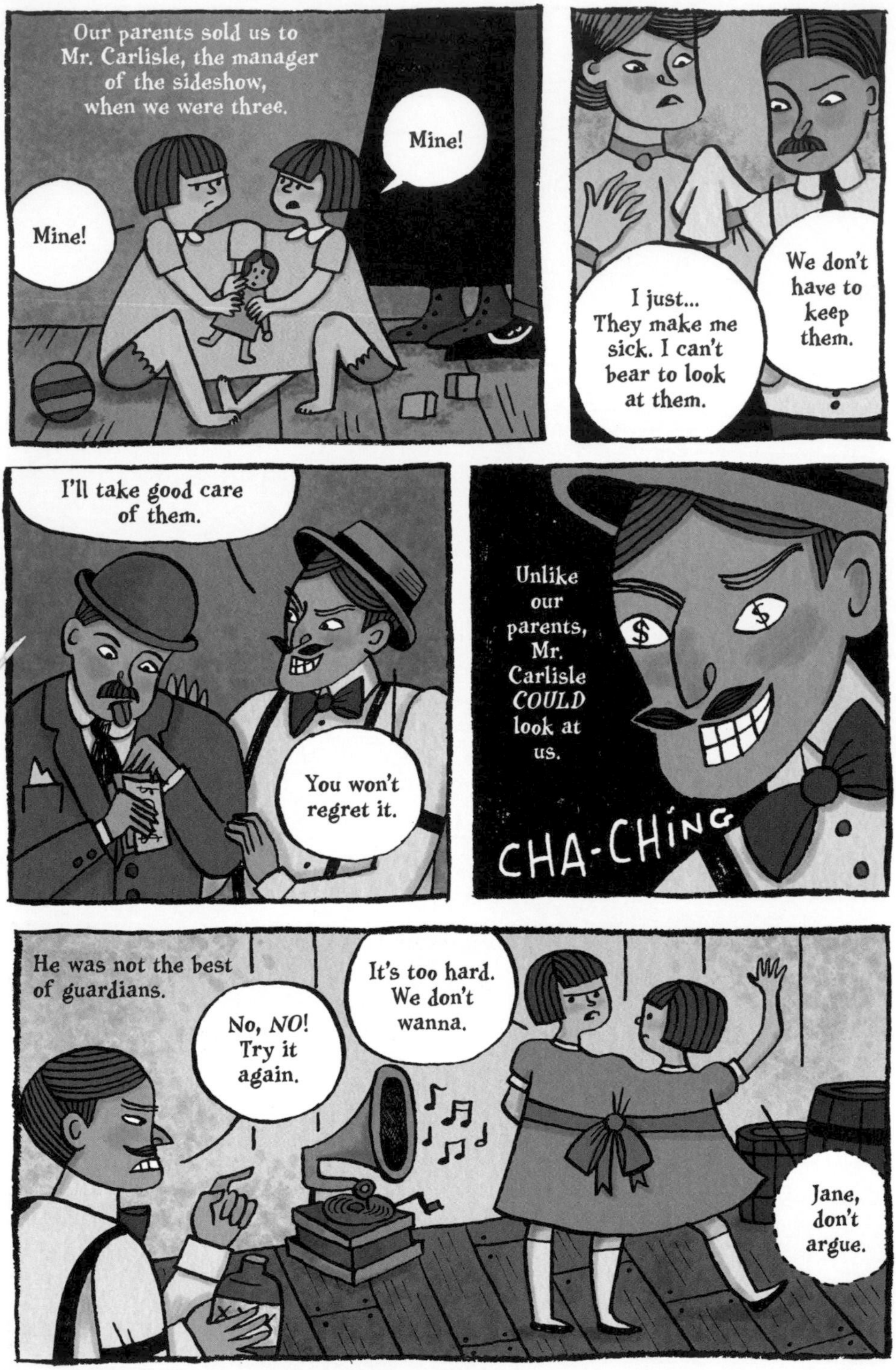
Our parents sold us to Mr. Carlisle, the manager of the sideshow, when we were three.
Mine!
Mine!
I just... They make me sick. I can't bear to look at them.
We don't have to keep them.
I'll take good care of them.
You won't regret it.
Unlike our parents, Mr. Carlisle *COULD* look at us.
CHA-CHING
He was not the best of guardians.
No, *NO*! Try it again.
It's too hard. We don't wanna.
Jane, don't argue.

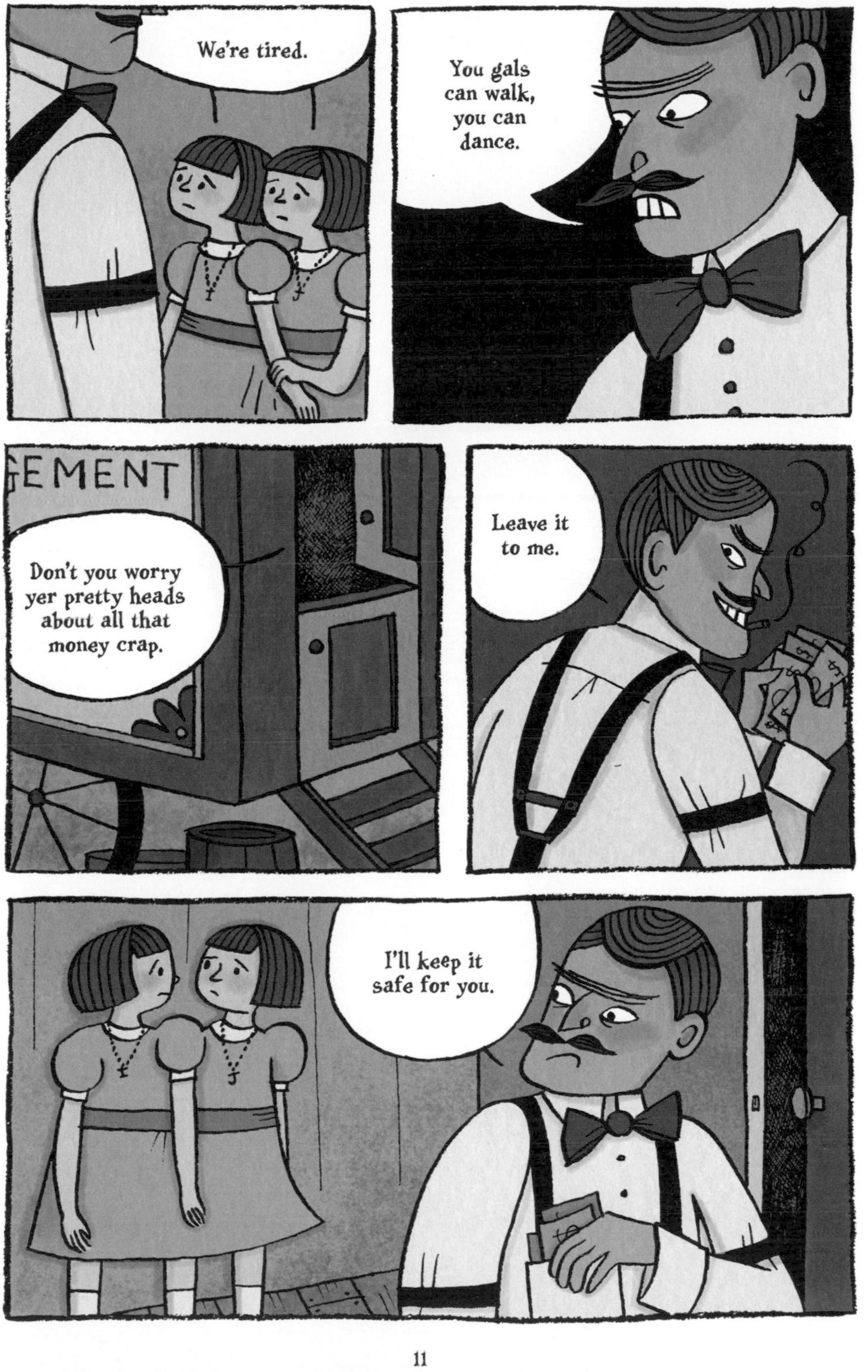
We're tired.
You gals can walk, you can dance.
Don't you worry yer pretty heads about all that money crap.
Leave it to me.
I'll keep it safe for you.

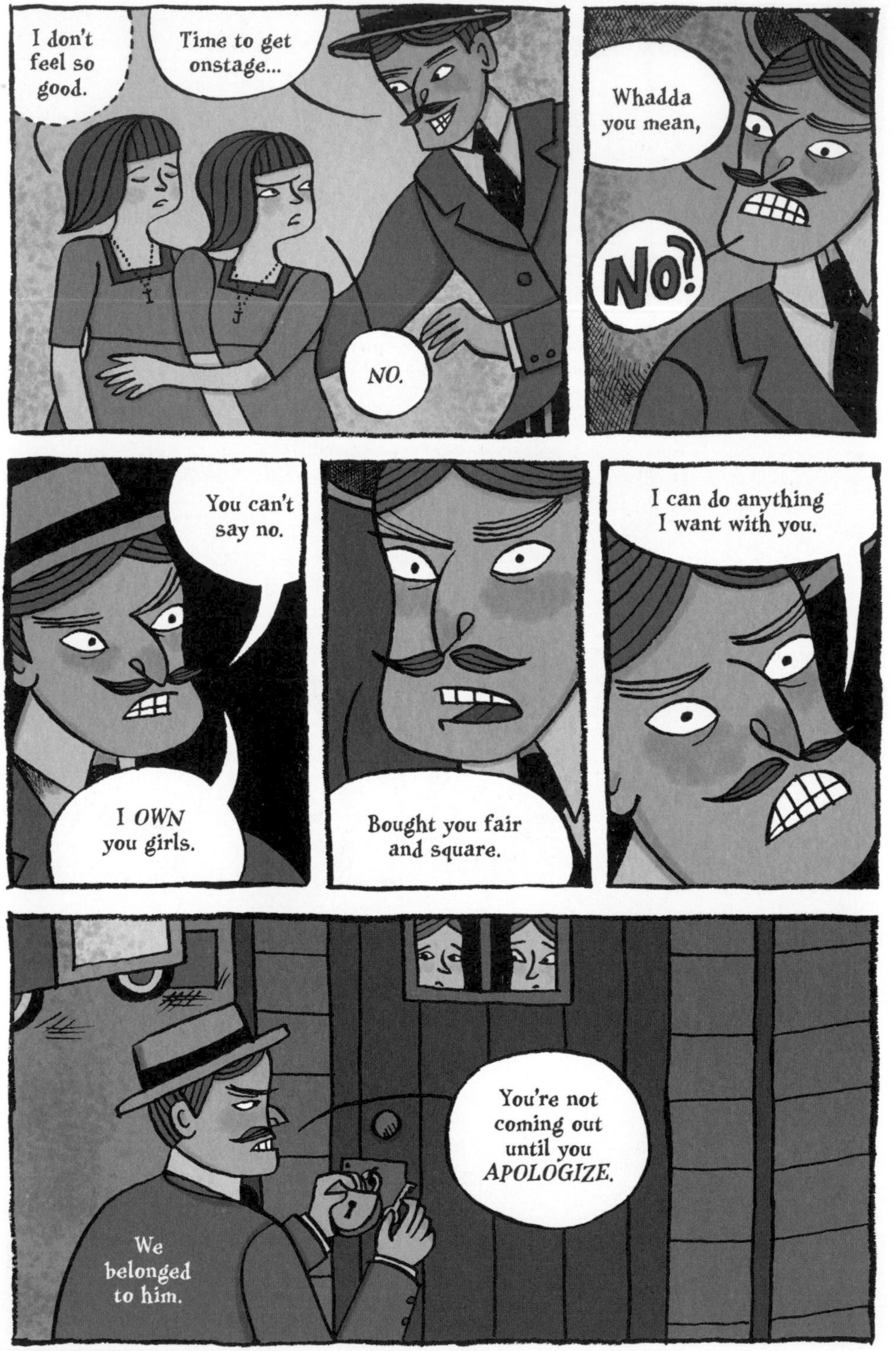

I don't feel so good.
Time to get onstage...
NO.
Whadda you mean,
NO?
You can't say no.
I *OWN* you girls.
Bought you fair and square.
I can do anything I want with you.
You're not coming out until you *APOLOGIZE.*
We belonged to him.

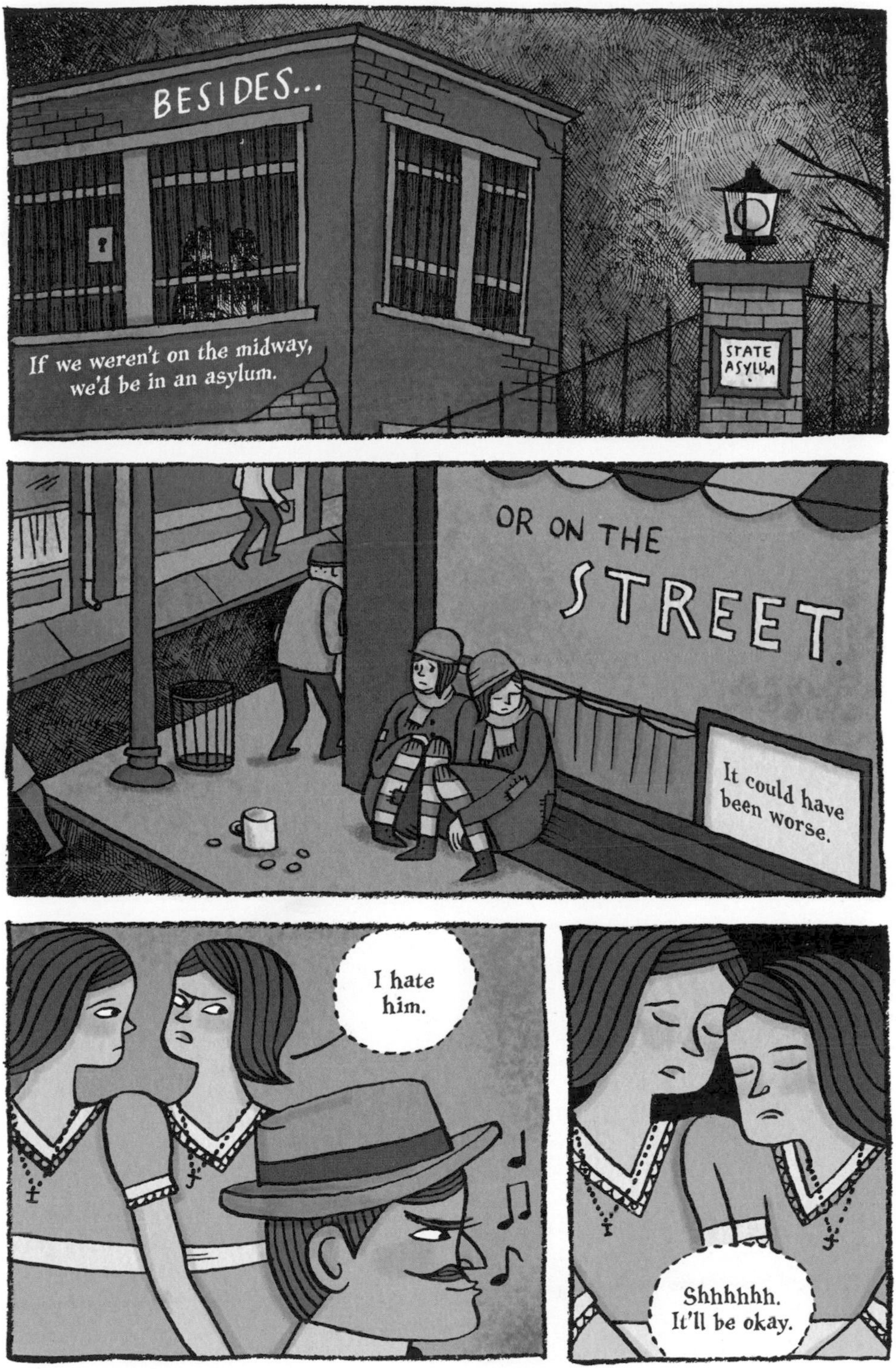
BESIDES...
If we weren't on the midway, we'd be in an asylum.
STATE ASYLUM
OR ON THE STREET.
It could have been worse.
I hate him.
Shhhhhh. It'll be okay.

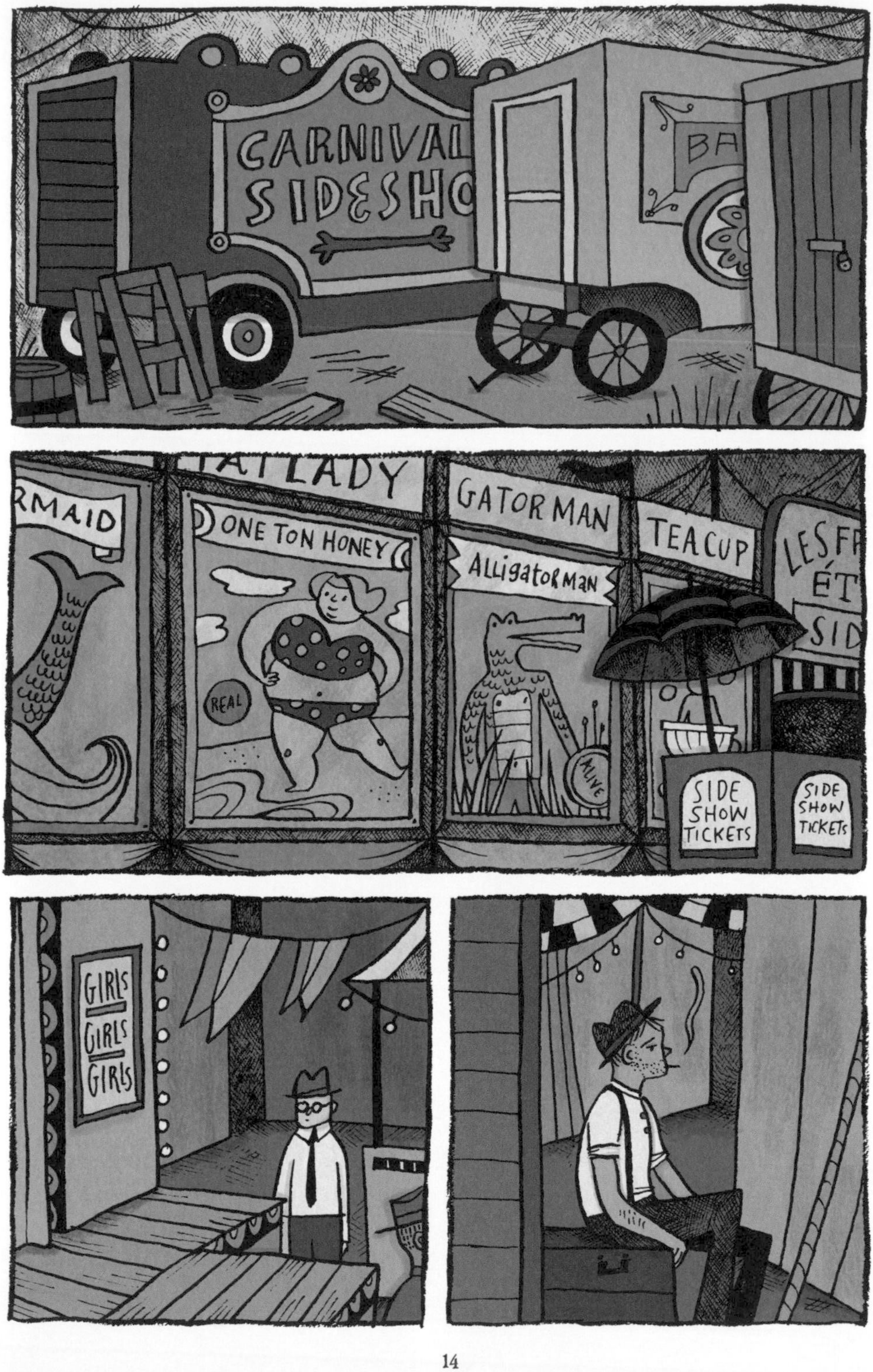
CARNIVAL SIDESHO
BA
RMAID
ATLADY
ONE TON HONEY
REAL
GATOR MAN
ALLIGATOR MAN
ALIVE
TEACUP
LES FR
ÉT
SID
SIDE SHOW TICKETS
SIDE SHOW TICKETS
GIRLS
GIRLS
GIRLS

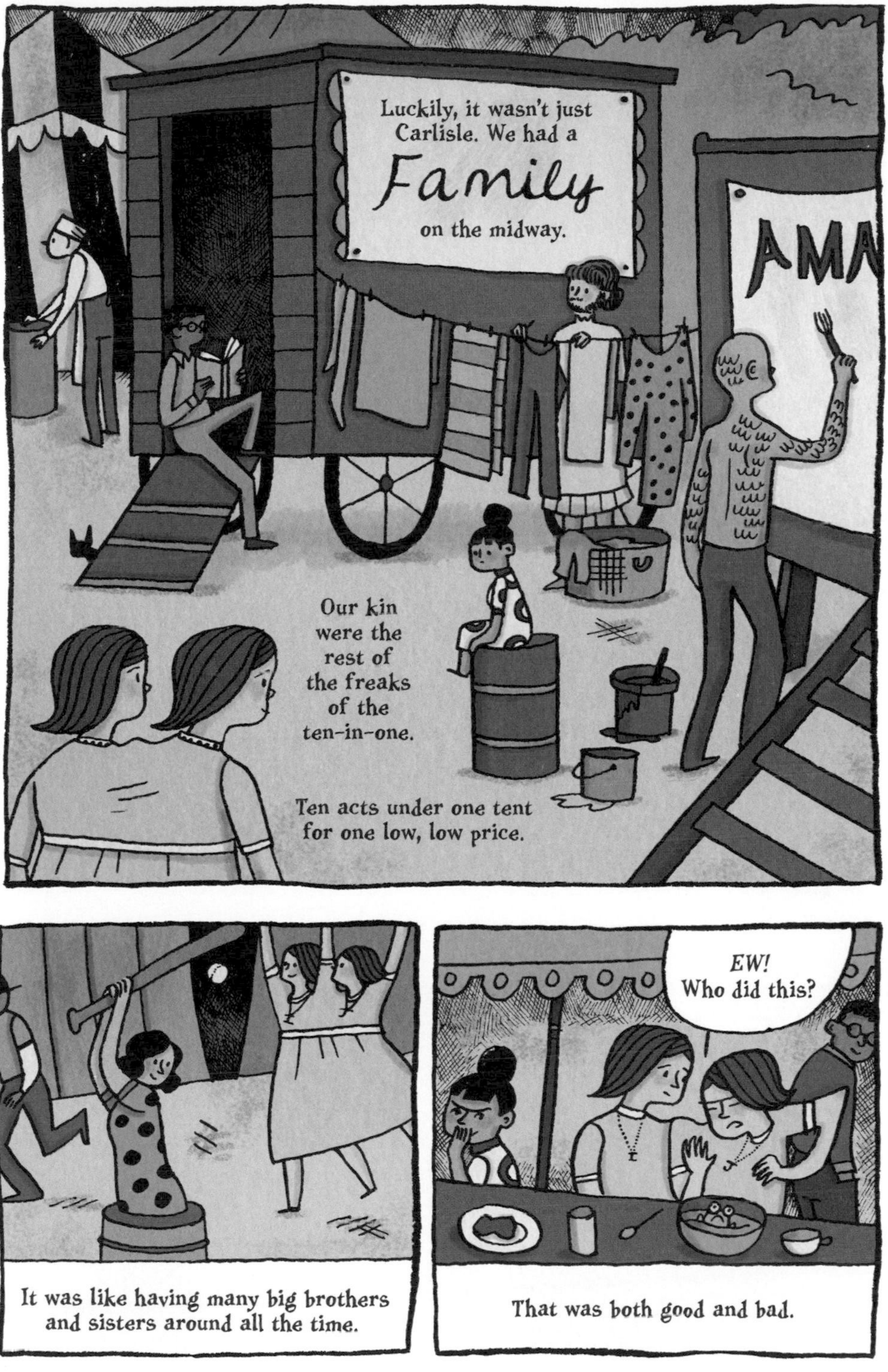
Luckily, it wasn't just Carlisle. We had a
Family
on the midway.
AMA
Our kin were the rest of the freaks of the ten-in-one.
Ten acts under one tent for one low, low price.
It was like having many big brothers and sisters around all the time.
EW! Who did this?
That was both good and bad.

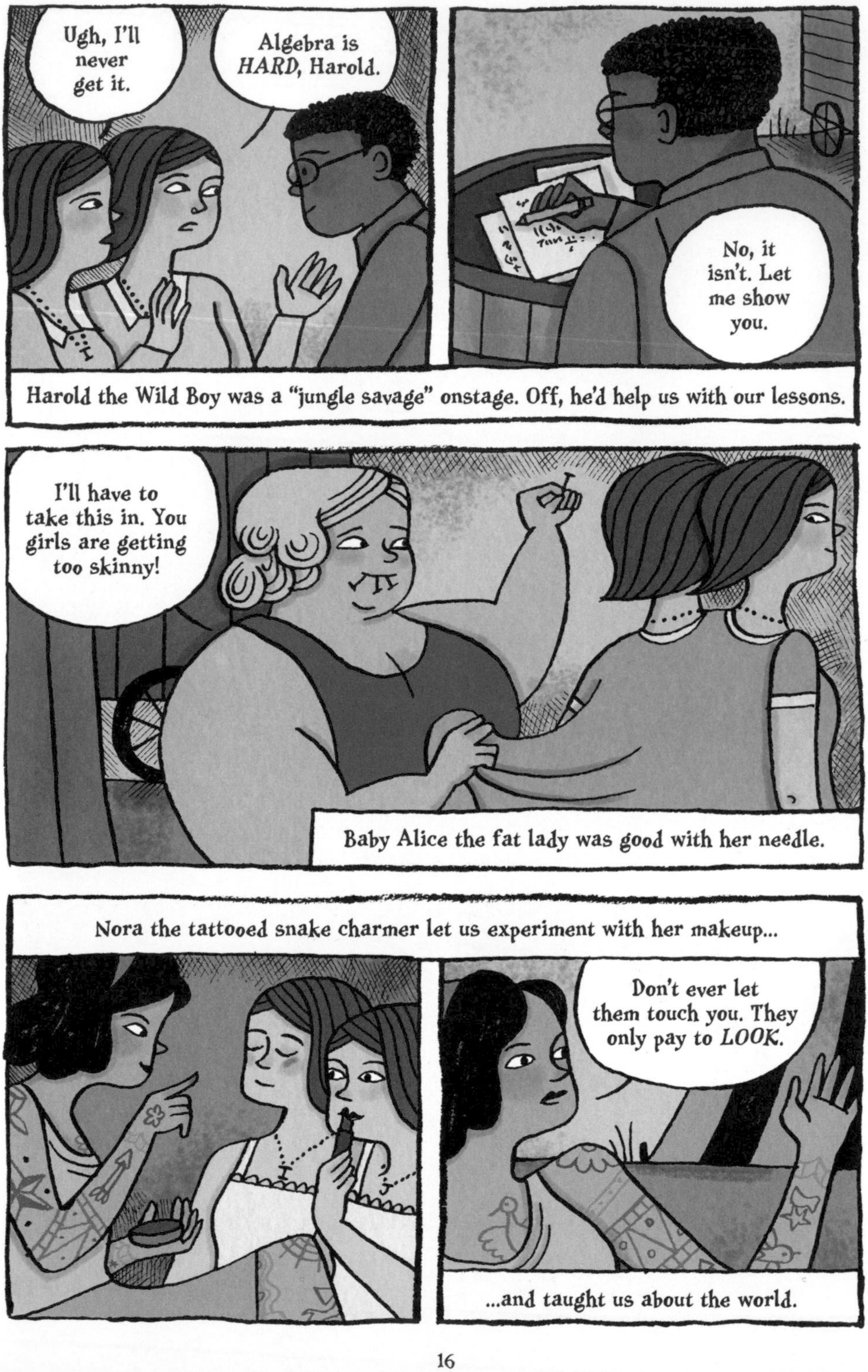
Ugh, I'll never get it.
Algebra is *HARD*, Harold.
No, it isn't. Let me show you.
Harold the Wild Boy was a "jungle savage" onstage. Off, he'd help us with our lessons.
I'll have to take this in. You girls are getting too skinny!
Baby Alice the fat lady was good with her needle.
Nora the tattooed snake charmer let us experiment with her makeup...
Don't ever let them touch you. They only pay to *LOOK*.
...and taught us about the world.

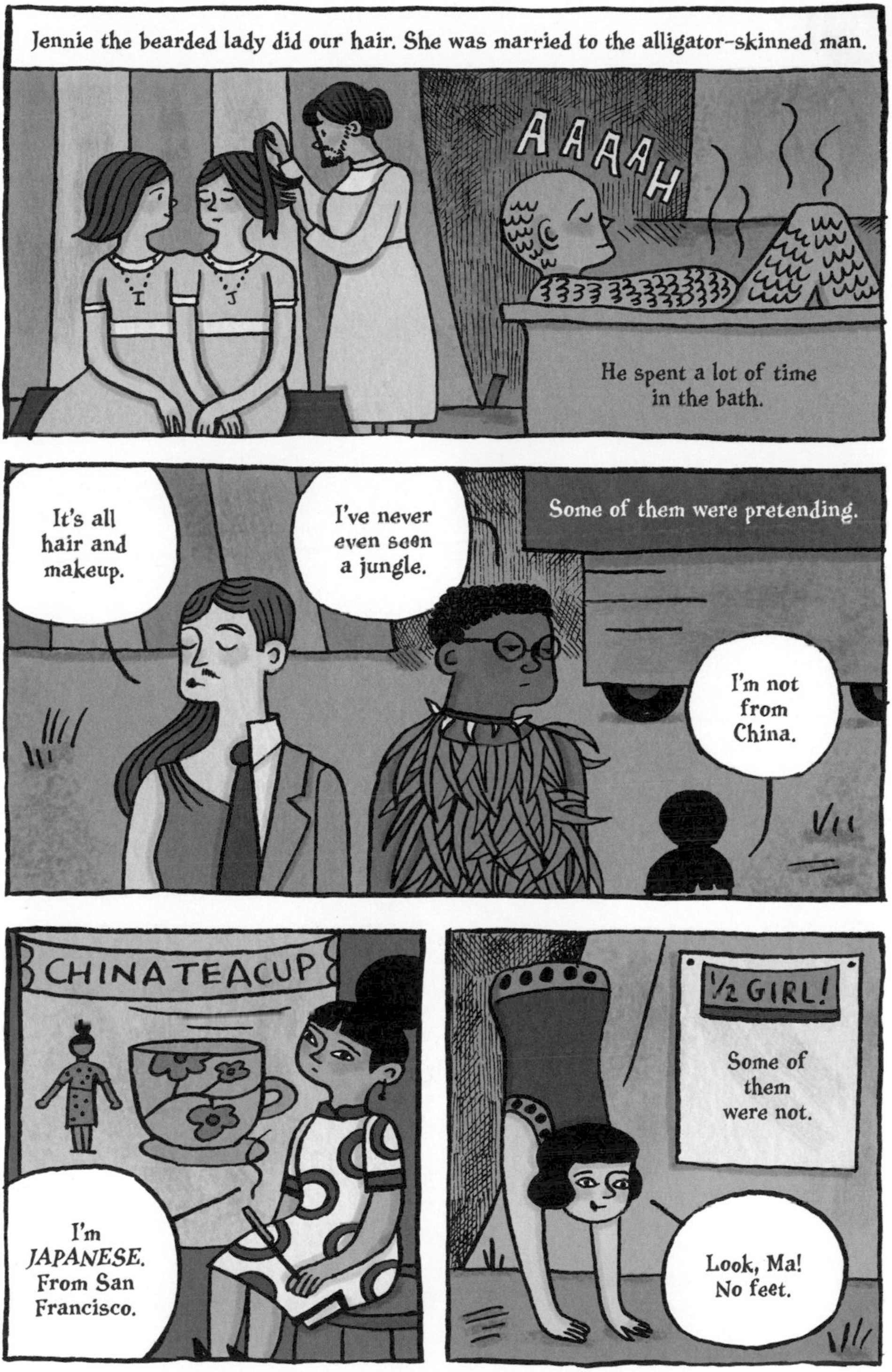
Jennie the bearded lady did our hair. She was married to the alligator-skinned man.
AAAAH
He spent a lot of time in the bath.
It's all hair and makeup.
I've never even seen a jungle.
Some of them were pretending.
I'm not from China.
CHINA TEACUP
I'm *JAPANESE*. From San Francisco.
½ GIRL!
Some of them were not.
Look, Ma! No feet.

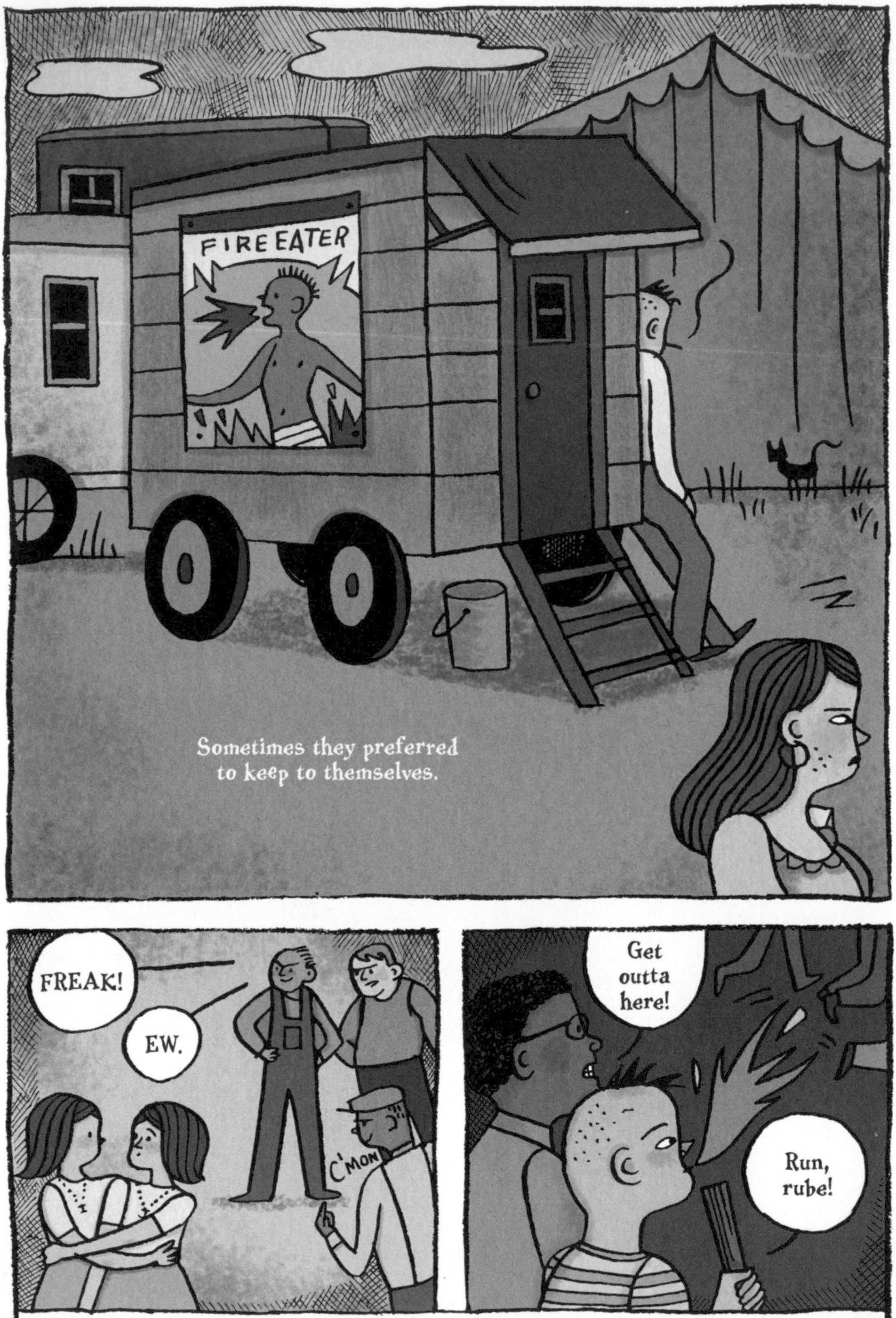
FIRE EATER
Sometimes they preferred to keep to themselves.
FREAK!
EW.
C'MON
Get outta here!
Run, rube!
But we could always count on them when we were in a pickle.

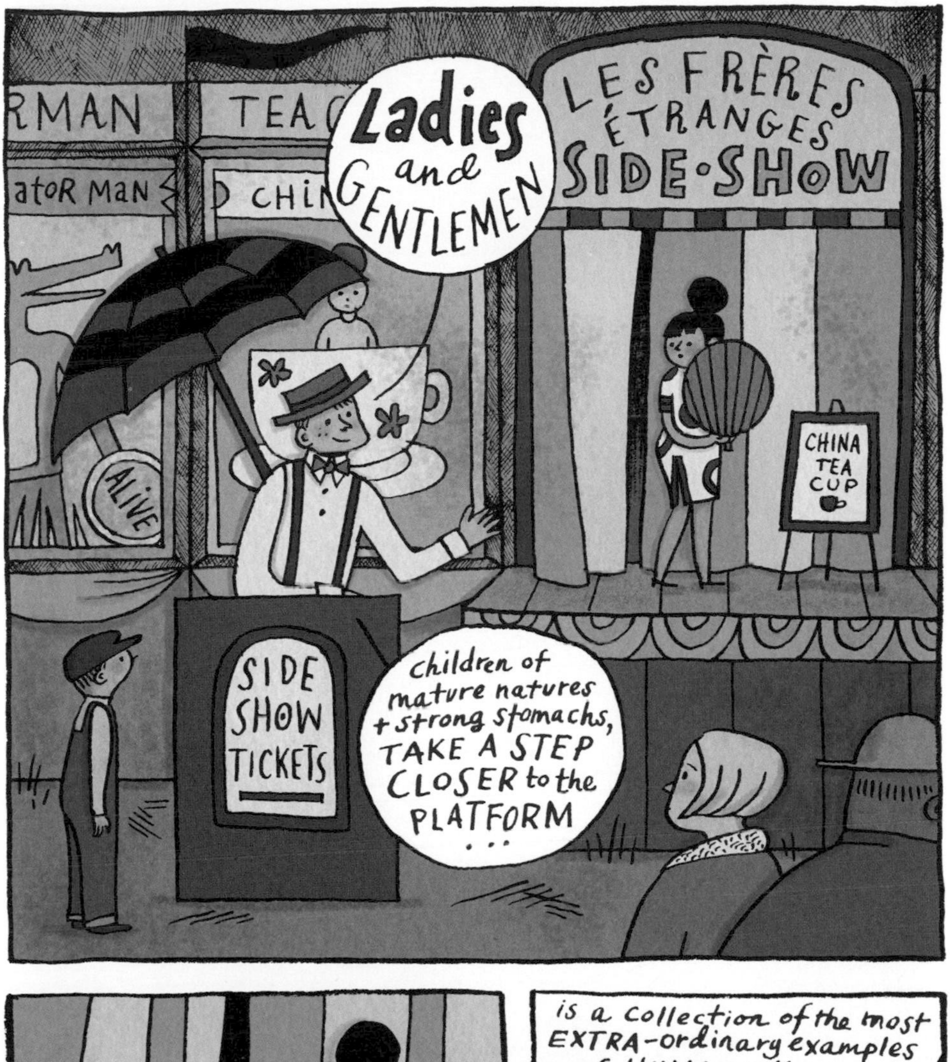
RMAN
TEA
ator MAN
CHIN
ALIVE
Ladies and GENTLEMEN
LES FRÈRES ÉTRANGES SIDE•SHOW
CHINA TEA CUP
SIDE SHOW TICKETS
children of mature natures + strong stomachs, TAKE A STEP CLOSER to the PLATFORM ...

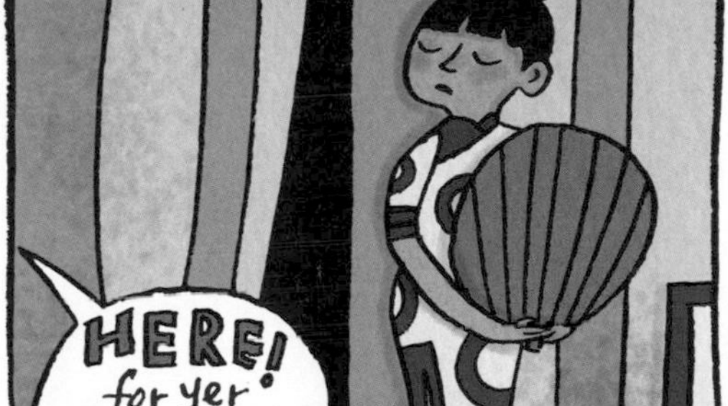
HERE! for yer Education + AMUSEMENT

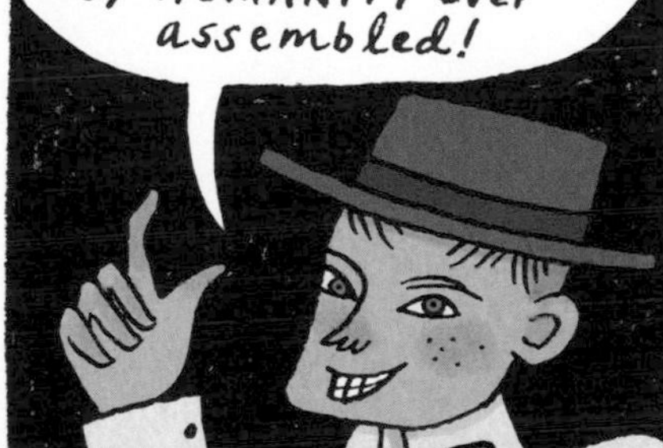
is a collection of the most EXTRA-ordinary examples of HUMANITY ever assembled!

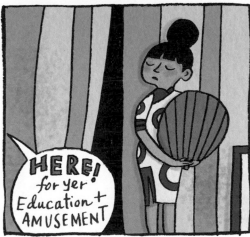

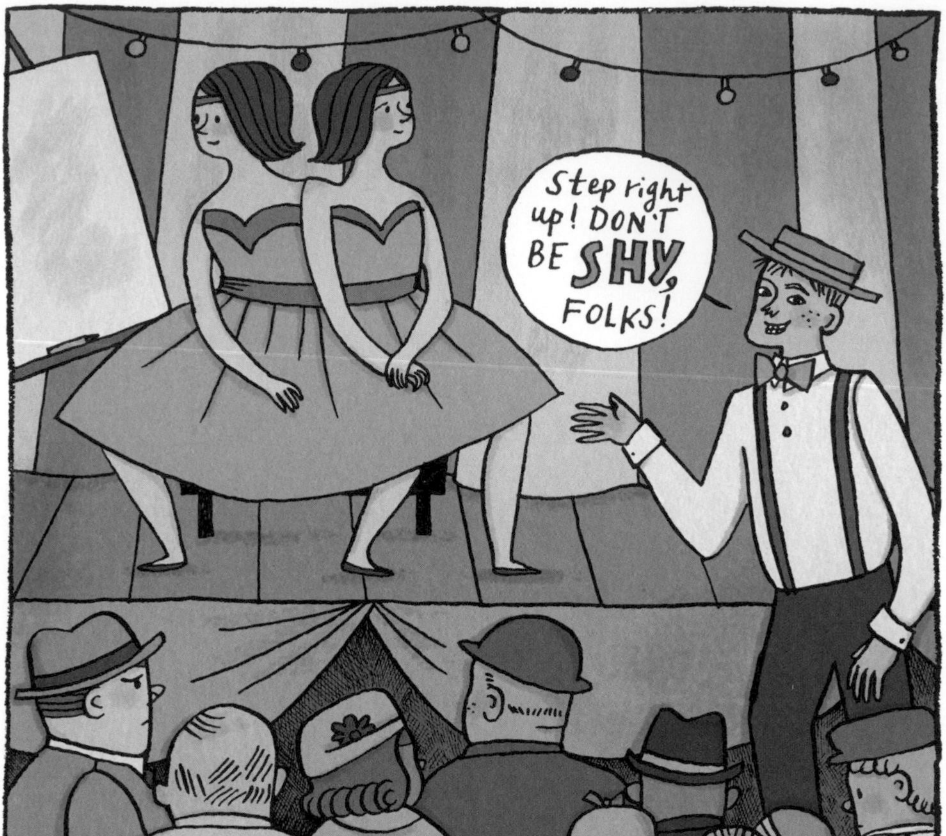
Step right up! DON'T BE SHY, FOLKS!
On the midway, we weren't disgusting. We were The Talent.

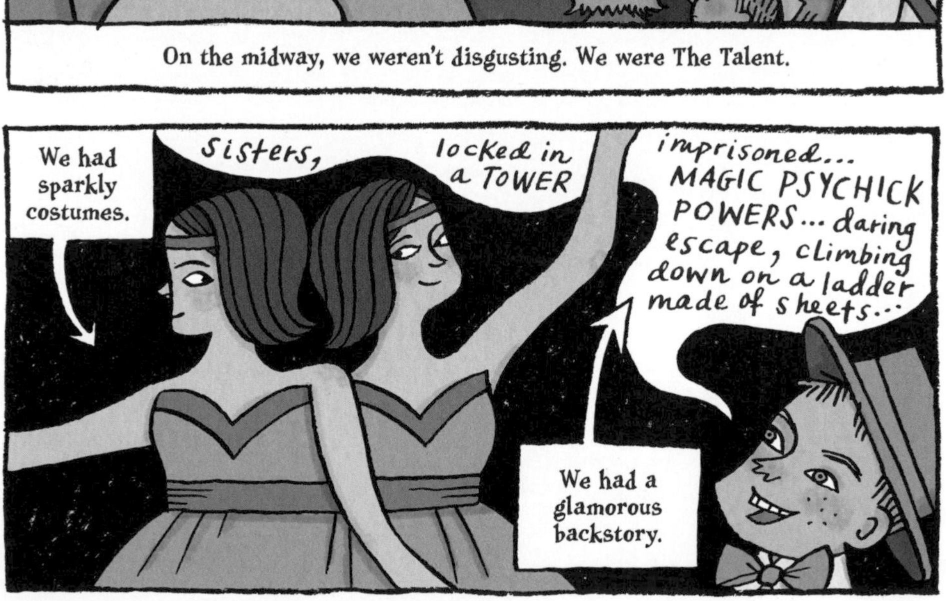
We had sparkly costumes.
sisters,
locked in a TOWER
imprisoned... MAGIC PSYCHICK POWERS... daring escape, climbing down on a ladder made of sheets...
We had a glamorous backstory.

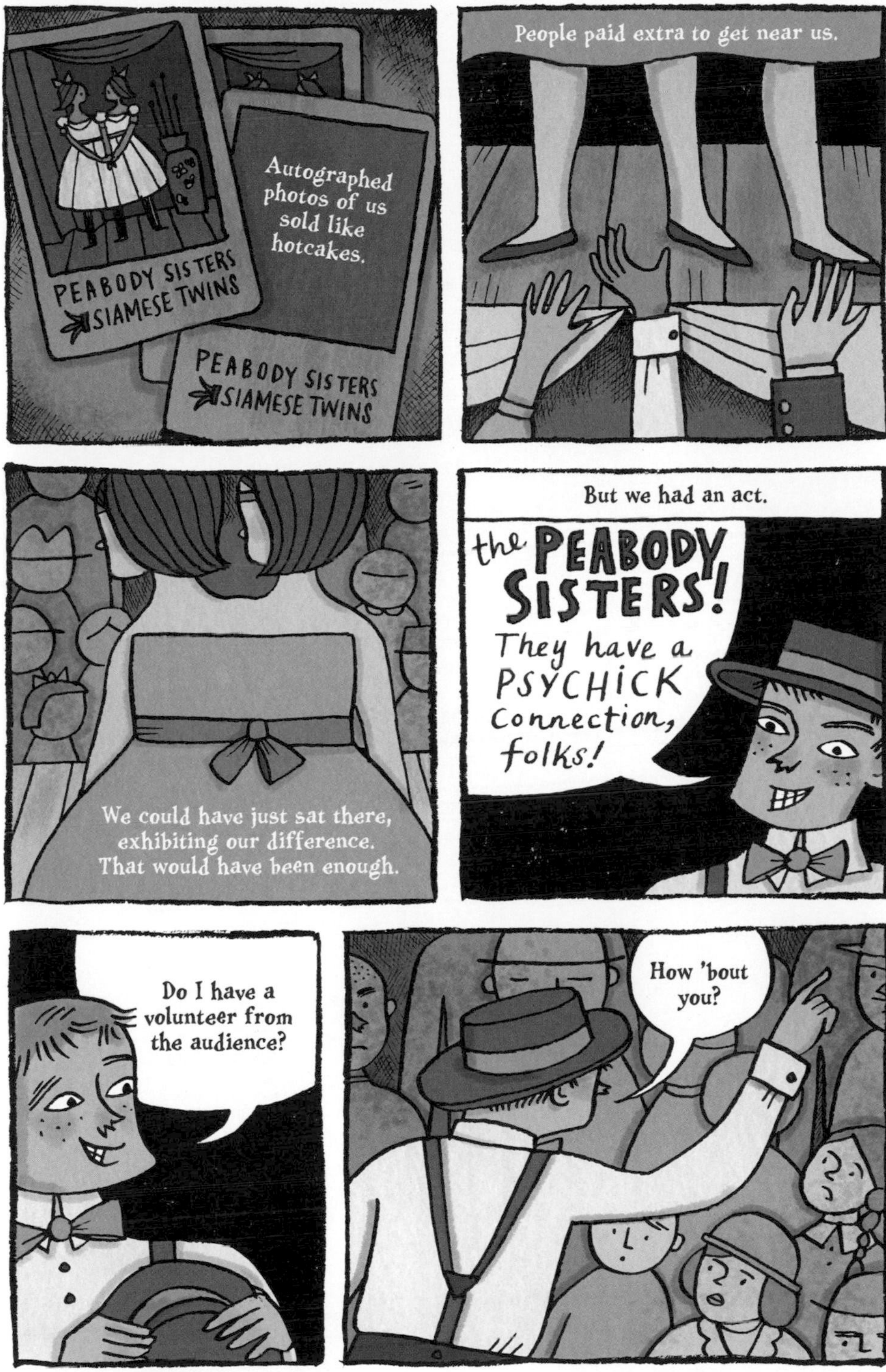
PEABODY SISTERS SIAMESE TWINS
Autographed photos of us sold like hotcakes.
PEABODY SISTERS SIAMESE TWINS
People paid extra to get near us.
We could have just sat there, exhibiting our difference. That would have been enough.
But we had an act.
the PEABODY SISTERS! They have a PSYCHICK Connection, folks!
Do I have a volunteer from the audience?
How 'bout you?

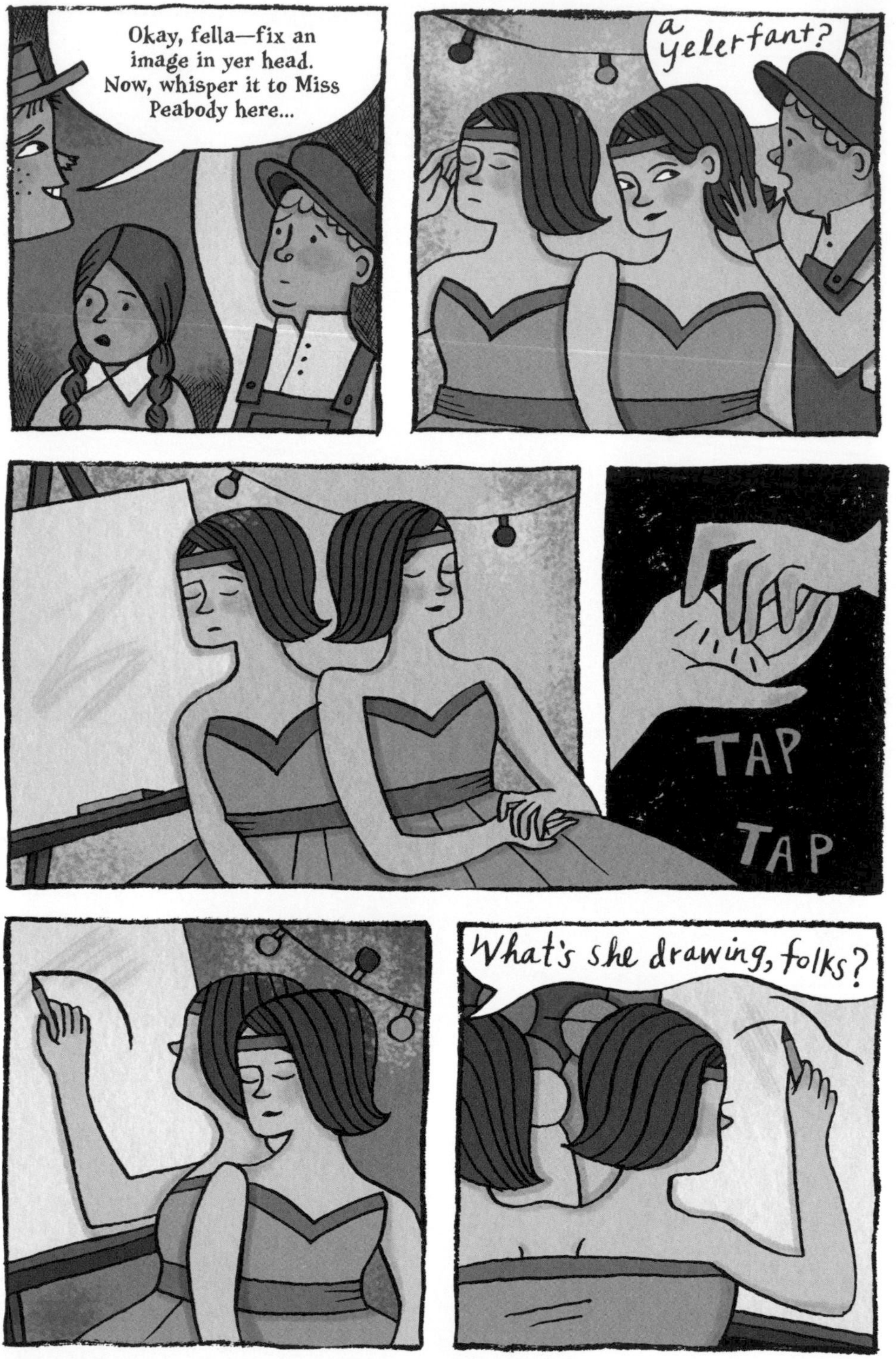
Okay, fella—fix an image in yer head. Now, whisper it to Miss Peabody here...
a yelerfant?
TAP
TAP
What's she drawing, folks?

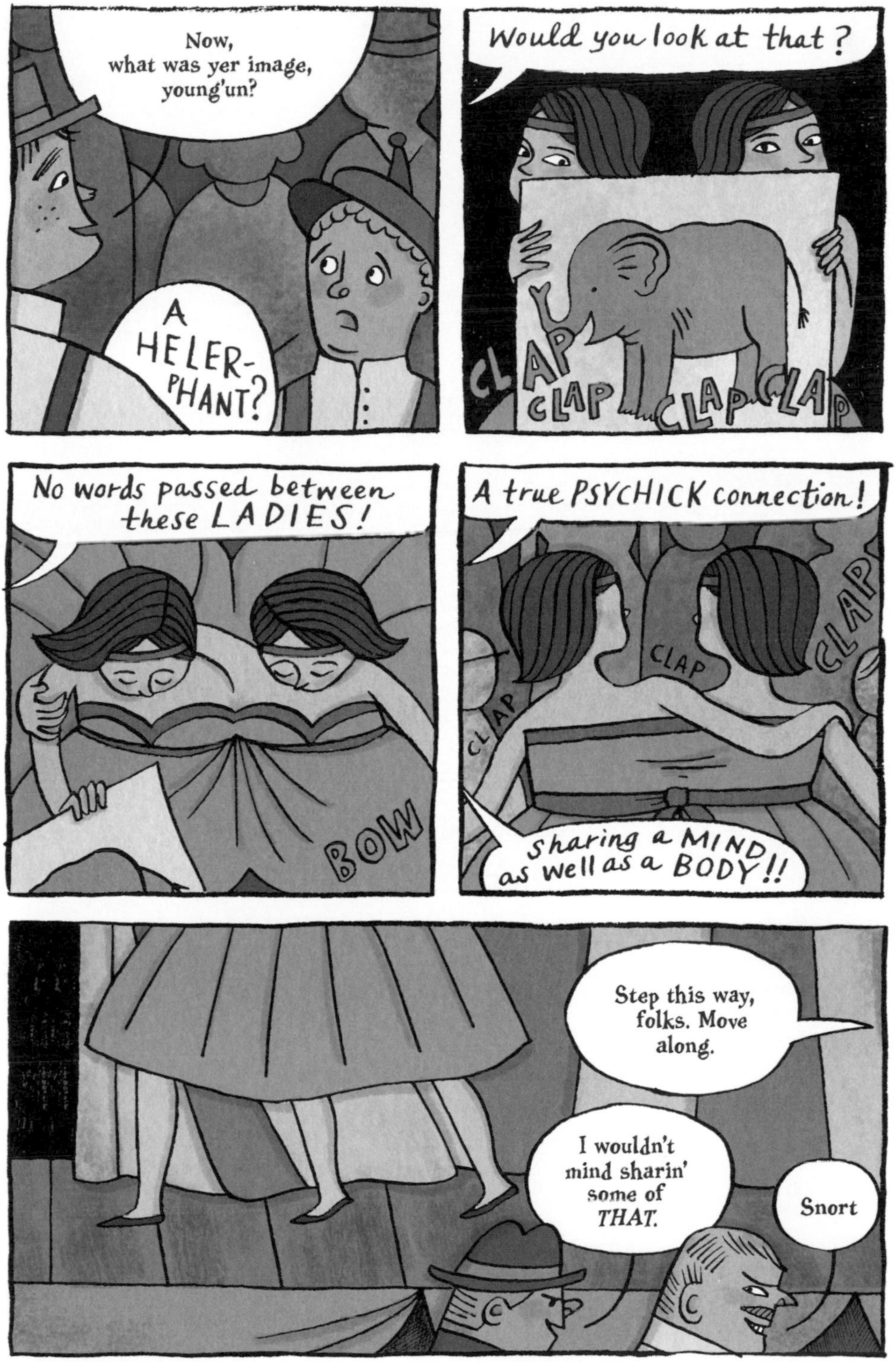
Now, what was yer image, young'un?
A HELER-PHANT?
Would you look at that?
CLAP CLAP CLAP CLAP
No words passed between these LADIES!
BOW
A true PSYCHICK connection!
CLAP CLAP CLAP
Sharing a MIND as well as a BODY!!
Step this way, folks. Move along.
I wouldn't mind sharin' some of THAT.
Snort

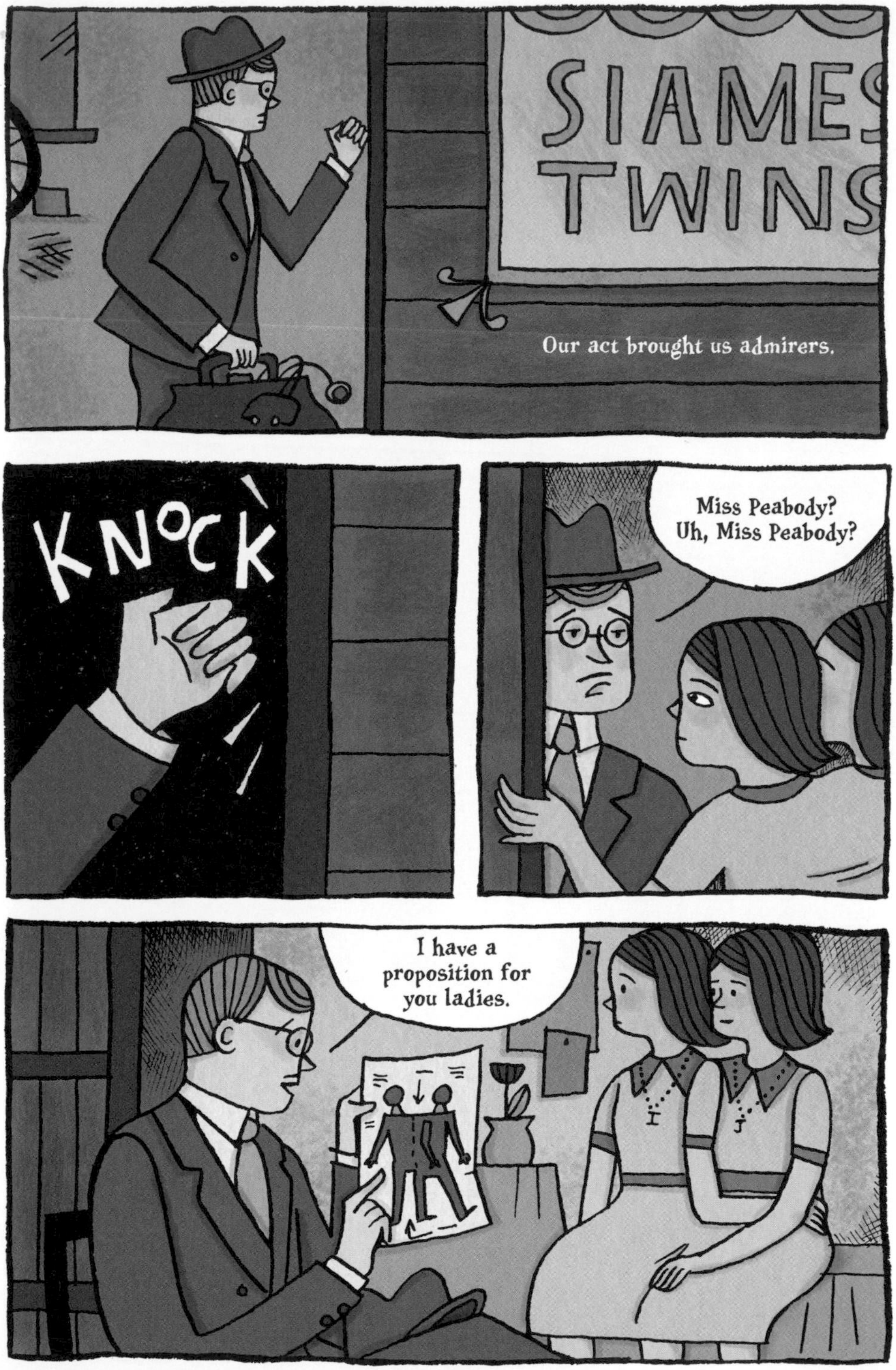
SIAMES
TWINS
Our act brought us admirers.
KNOCK
Miss Peabody? Uh, Miss Peabody?
I have a proposition for you ladies.

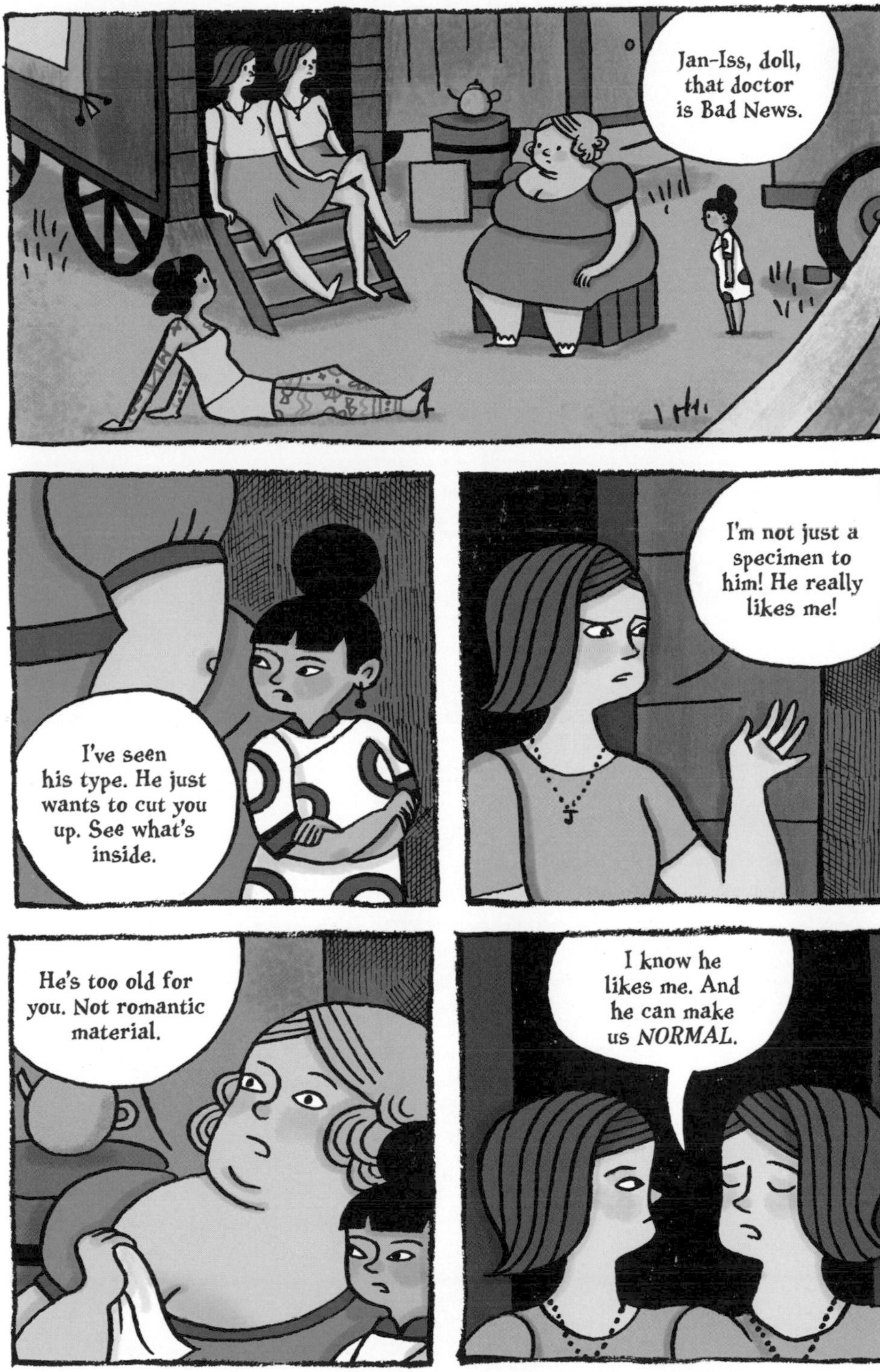
Jan-Iss, doll, that doctor is Bad News.
I've seen his type. He just wants to cut you up. See what's inside.
I'm not just a specimen to him! He really likes me!
He's too old for you. Not romantic material.
I know he likes me. And he can make us *NORMAL*.

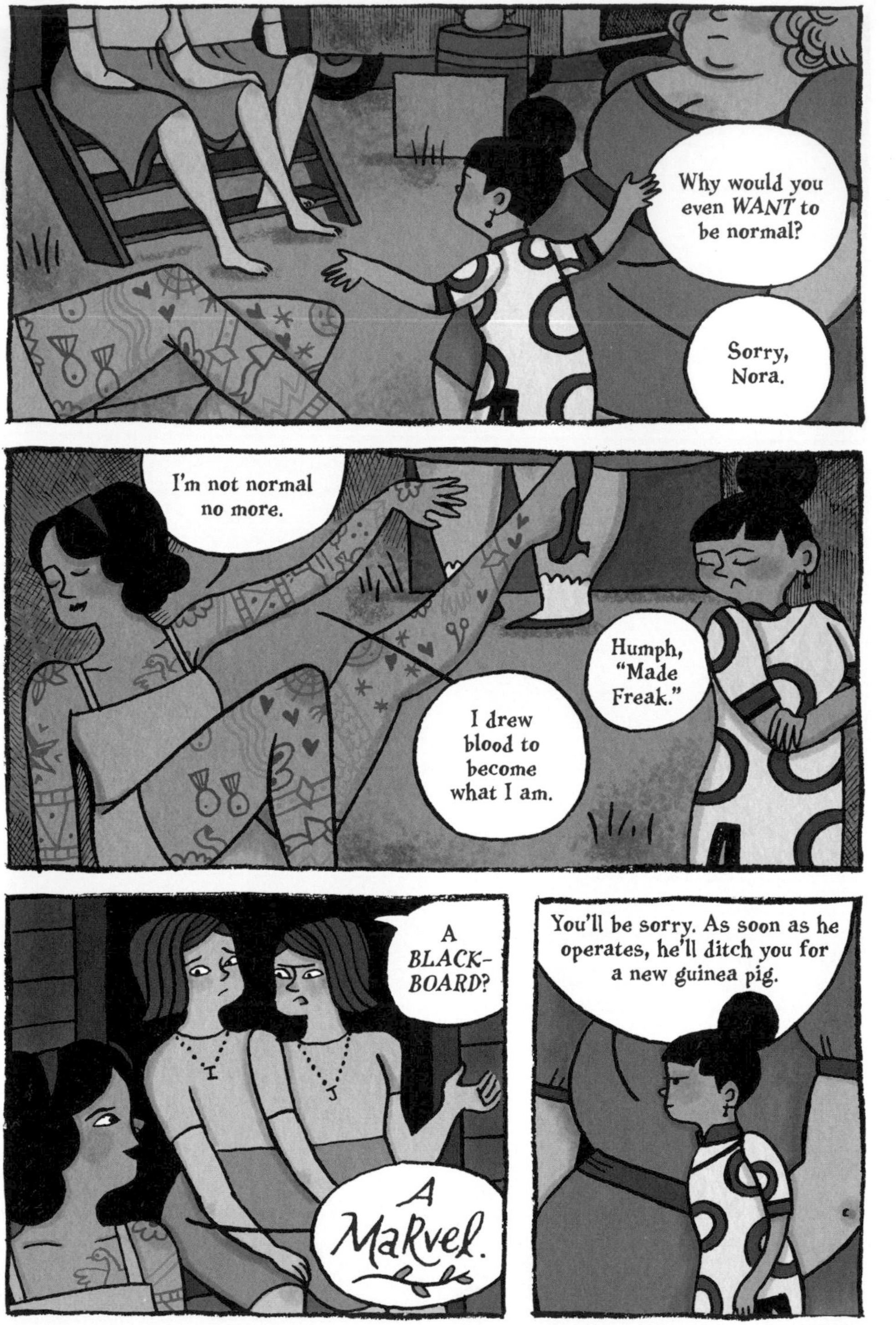
Why would you even WANT to be normal?
Sorry, Nora.
I'm not normal no more.
I drew blood to become what I am.
Humph, "Made Freak."
A BLACK-BOARD?
A Marvel.
You'll be sorry. As soon as he operates, he'll ditch you for a new guinea pig.

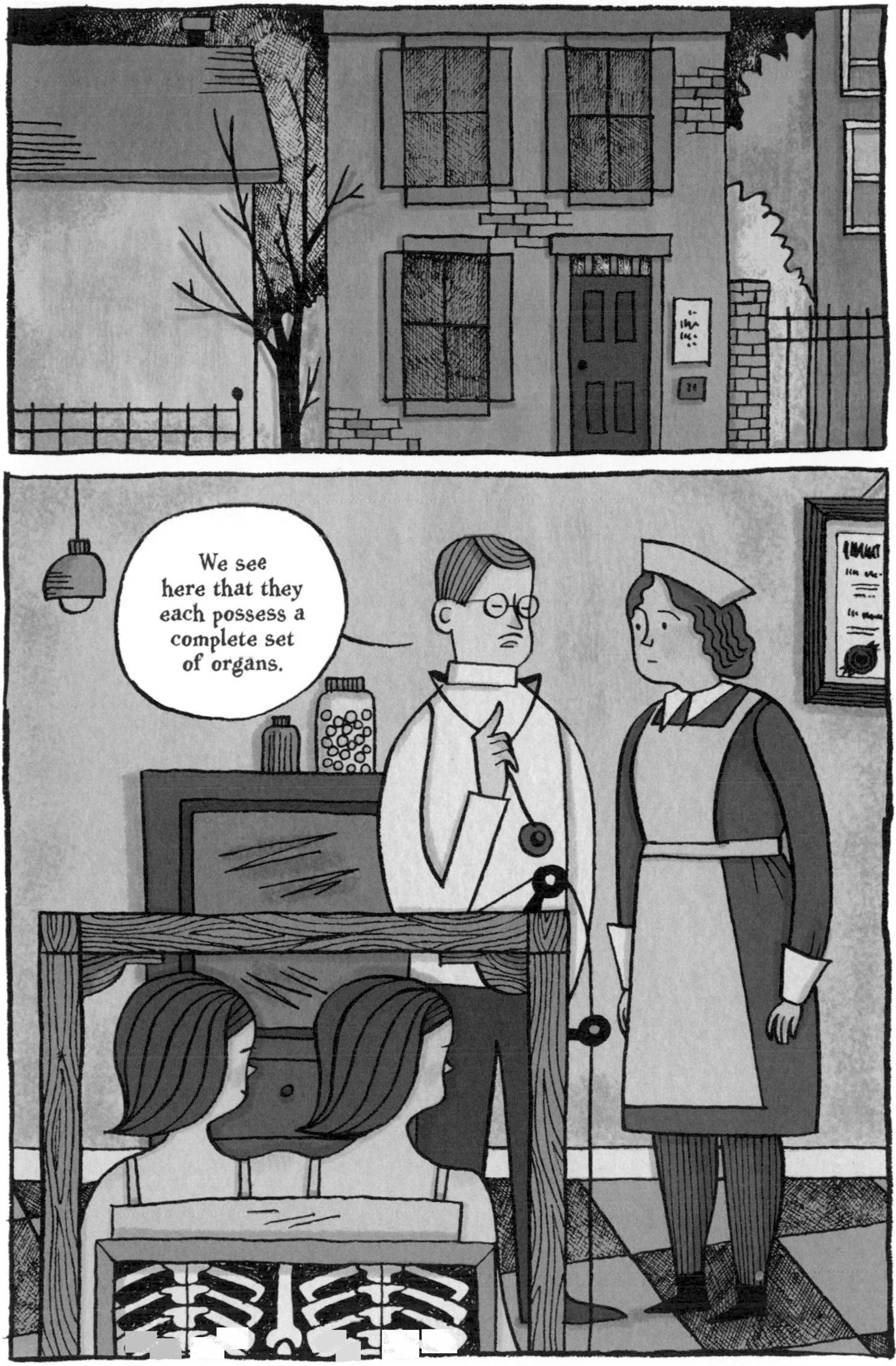
We see here that they each possess a complete set of organs.

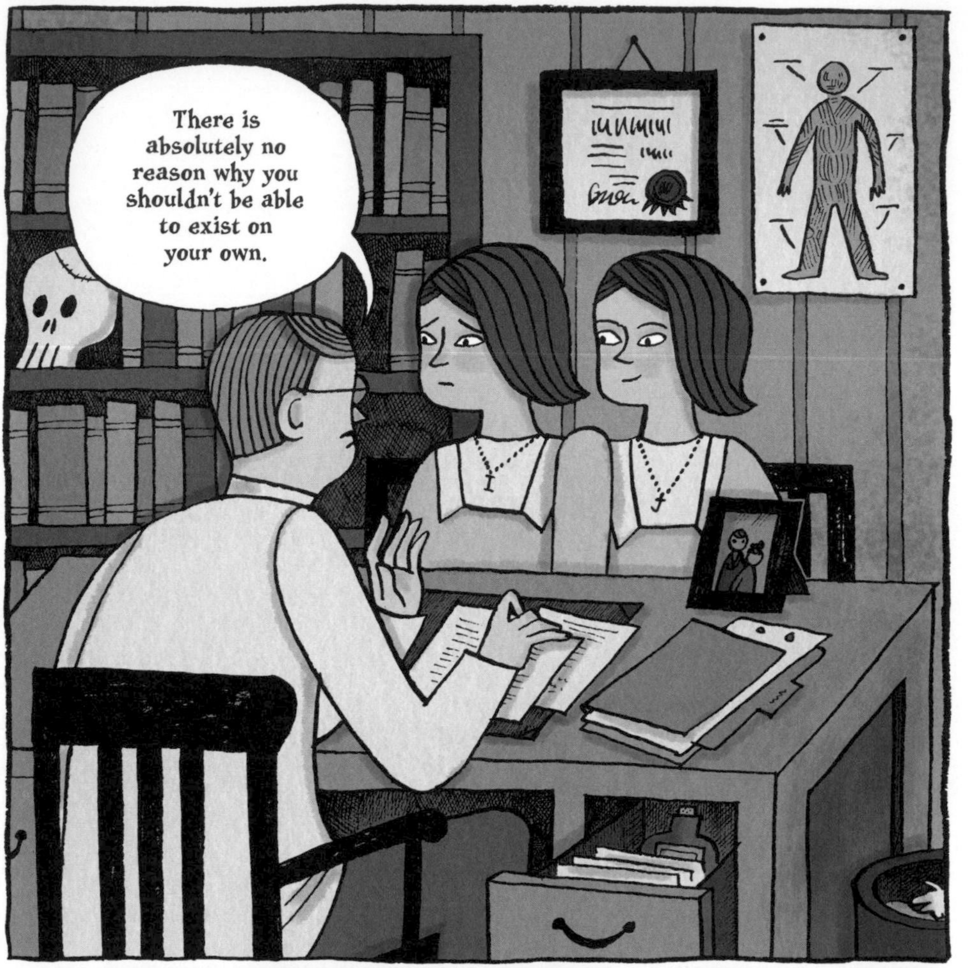
There is absolutely no reason why you shouldn't be able to exist on your own.

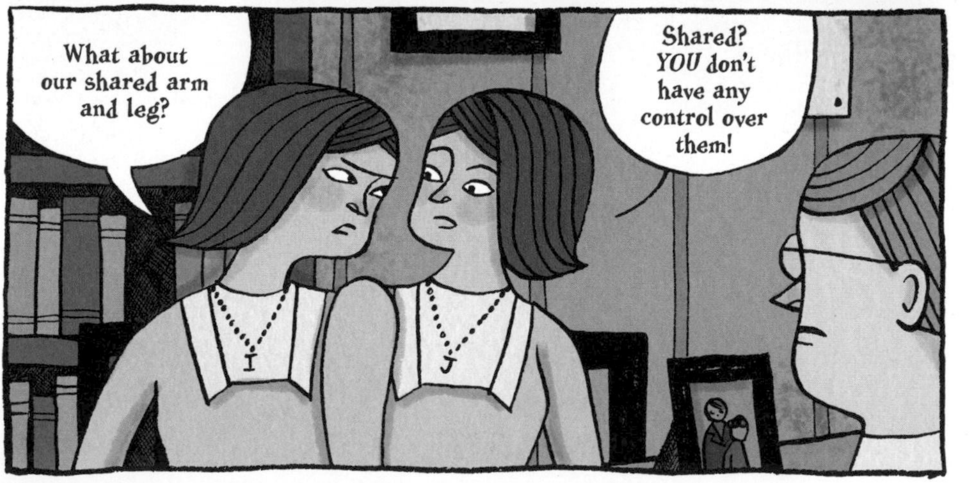
What about our shared arm and leg?
Shared? *YOU* don't have any control over them!

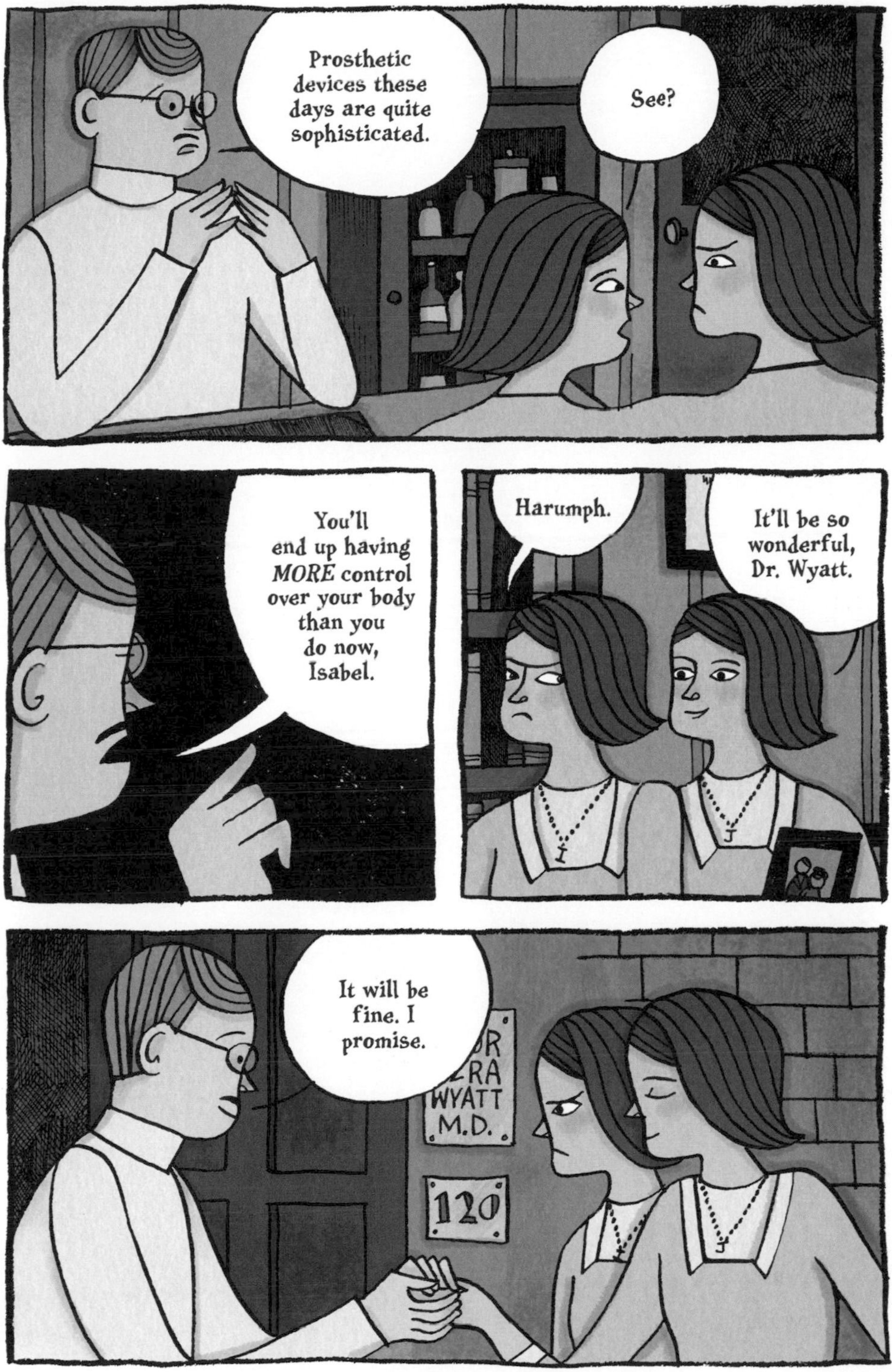

Prosthetic devices these days are quite sophisticated.
See?
You'll end up having *MORE* control over your body than you do now, Isabel.
Harumph.
It'll be so wonderful, Dr. Wyatt.
It will be fine. I promise.
WYATT M.D.
120

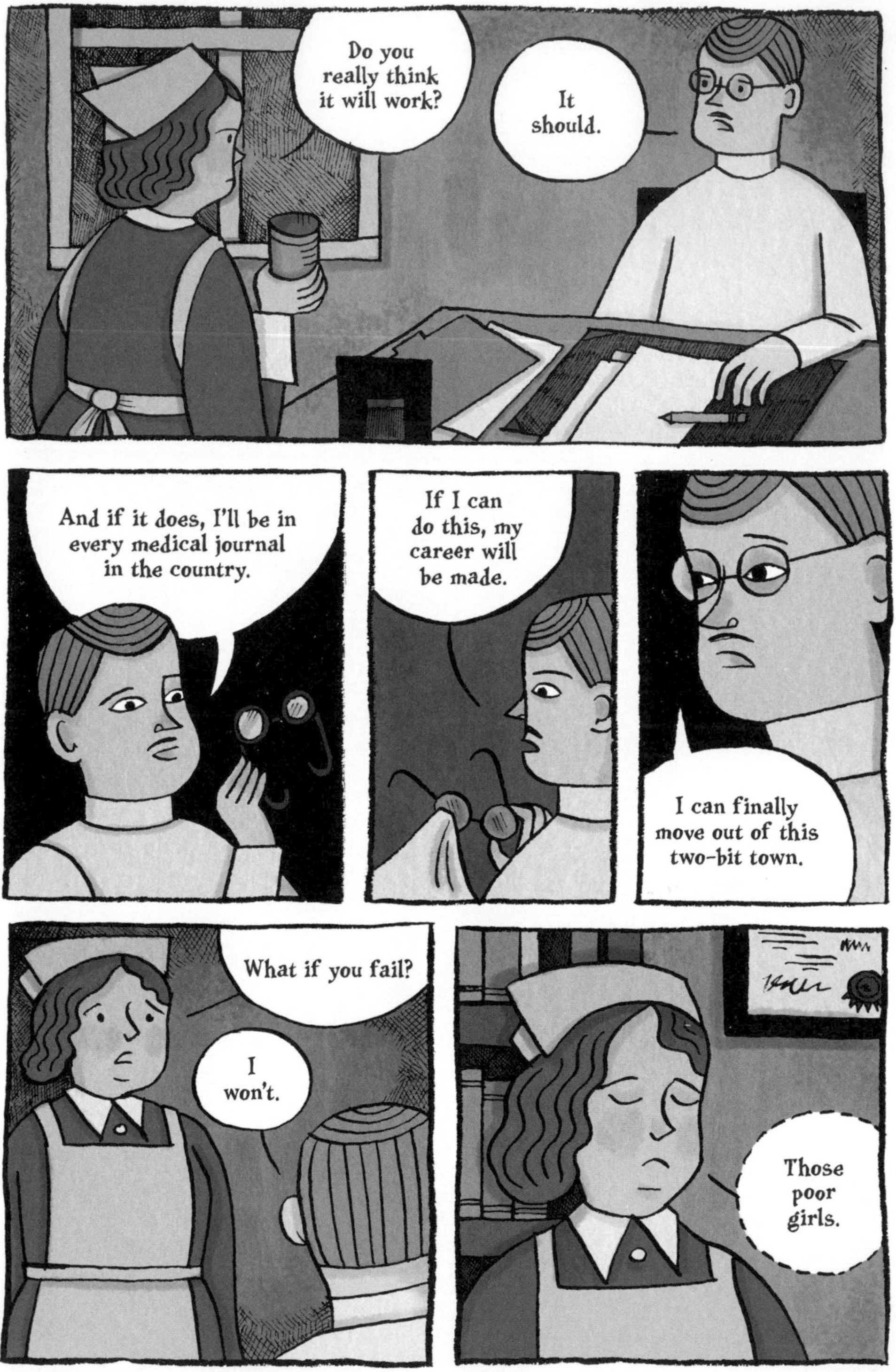
Do you really think it will work?
It should.
And if it does, I'll be in every medical journal in the country.
If I can do this, my career will be made.
I can finally move out of this two-bit town.
What if you fail?
I won't.
Those poor girls.

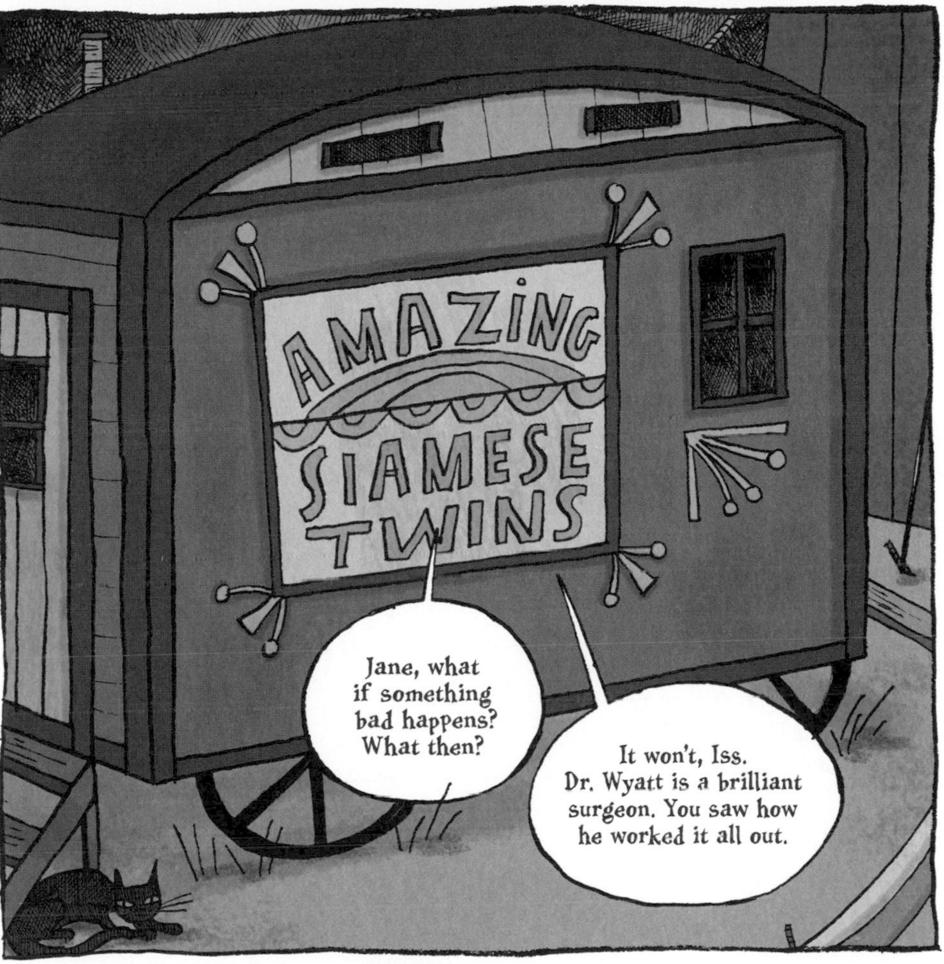
AMAZING
SIAMESE
TWINS
Jane, what if something bad happens? What then?
It won't, Iss. Dr. Wyatt is a brilliant surgeon. You saw how he worked it all out.

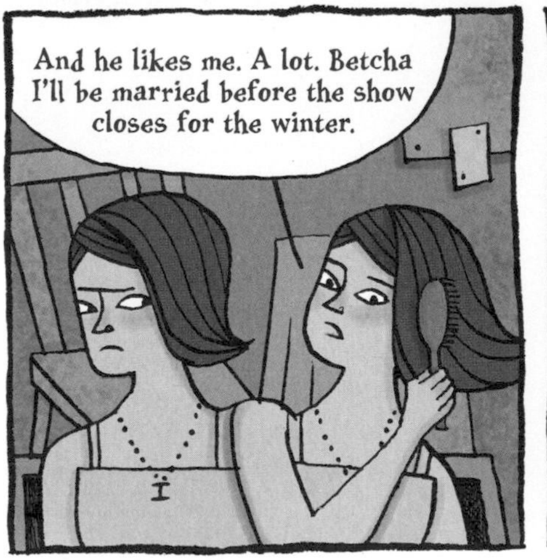
And he likes me. A lot. Betcha I'll be married before the show closes for the winter.

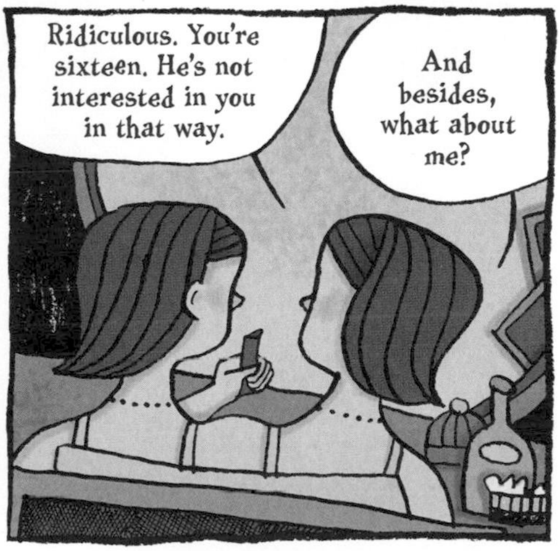
Ridiculous. You're sixteen. He's not interested in you in that way.
And besides, what about me?

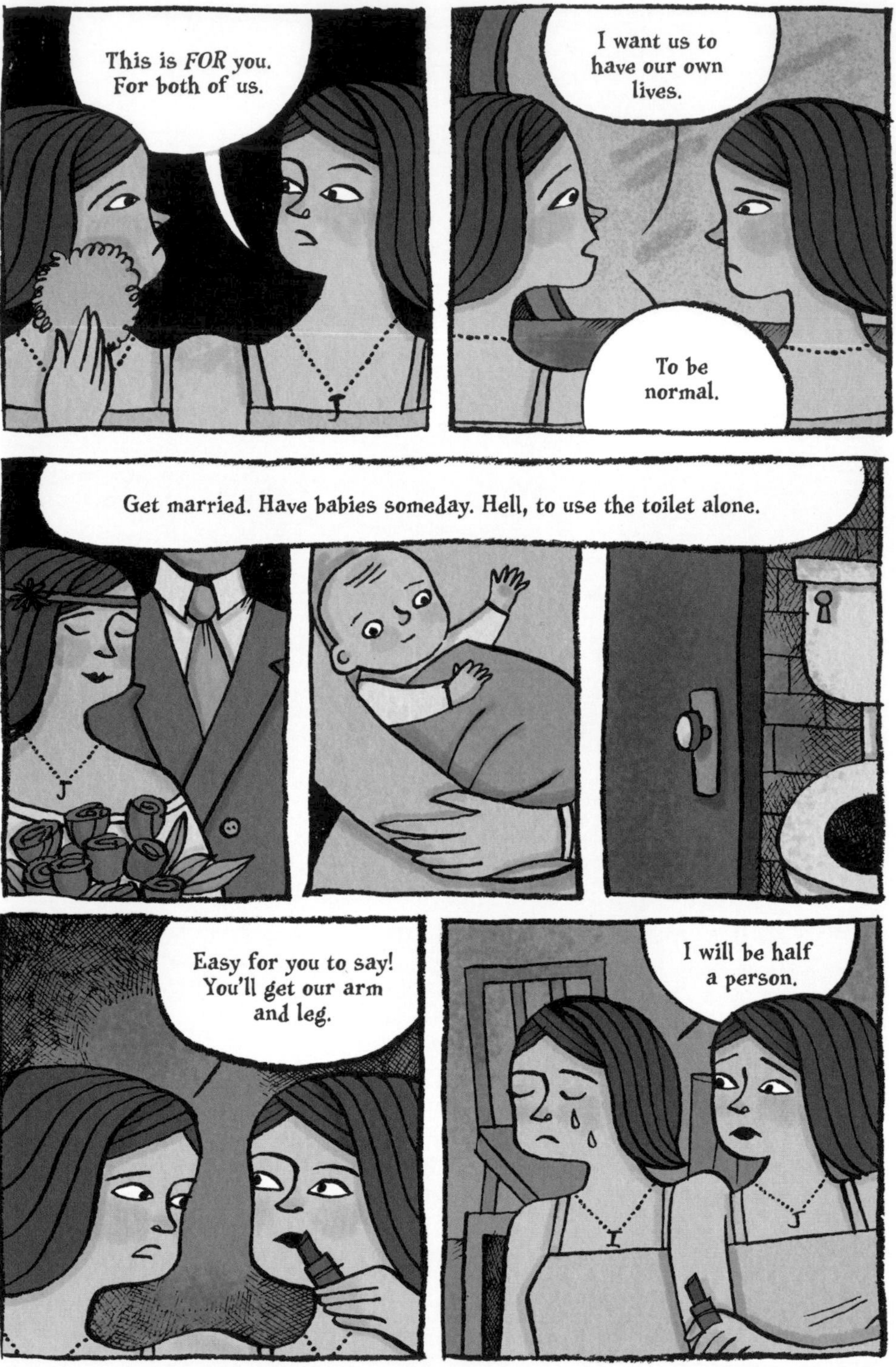
This is *FOR* you. For both of us.
I want us to have our own lives.
To be normal.
Get married. Have babies someday. Hell, to use the toilet alone.
Easy for you to say! You'll get our arm and leg.
I will be half a person.

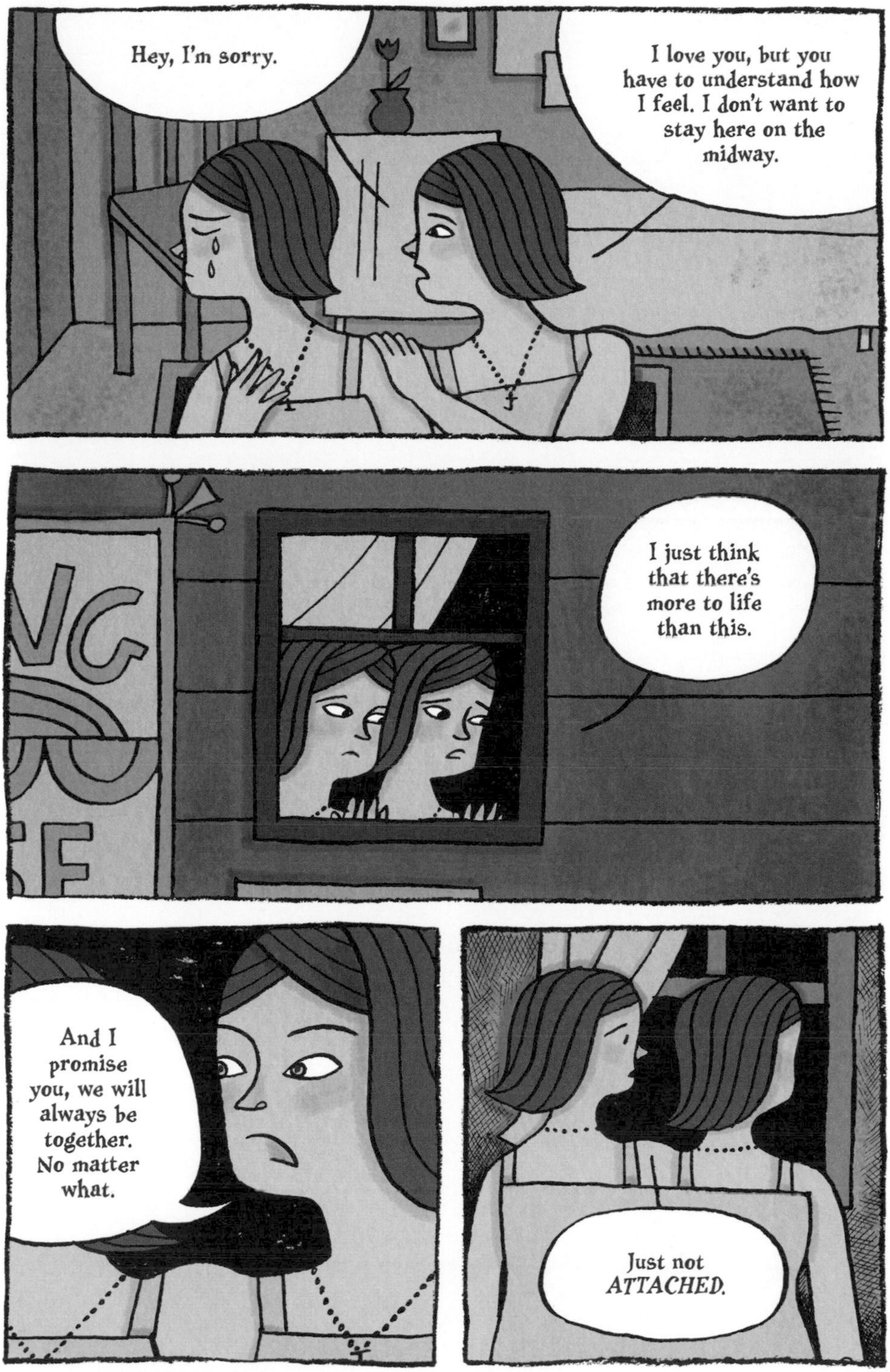
Hey, I'm sorry.
I love you, but you have to understand how I feel. I don't want to stay here on the midway.
I just think that there's more to life than this.
And I promise you, we will always be together. No matter what.
Just not *ATTACHED.*

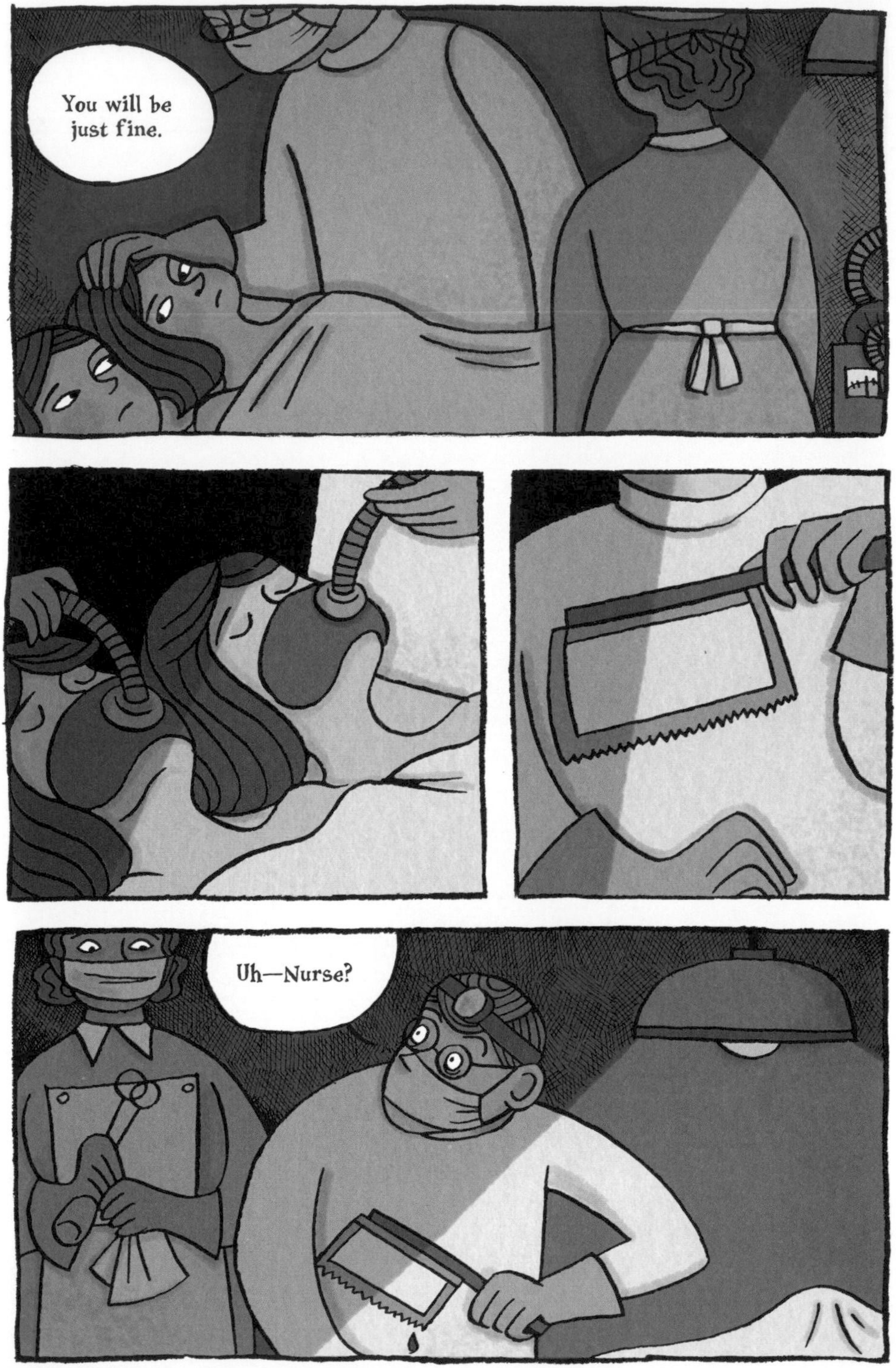
You will be just fine.
Uh—Nurse?

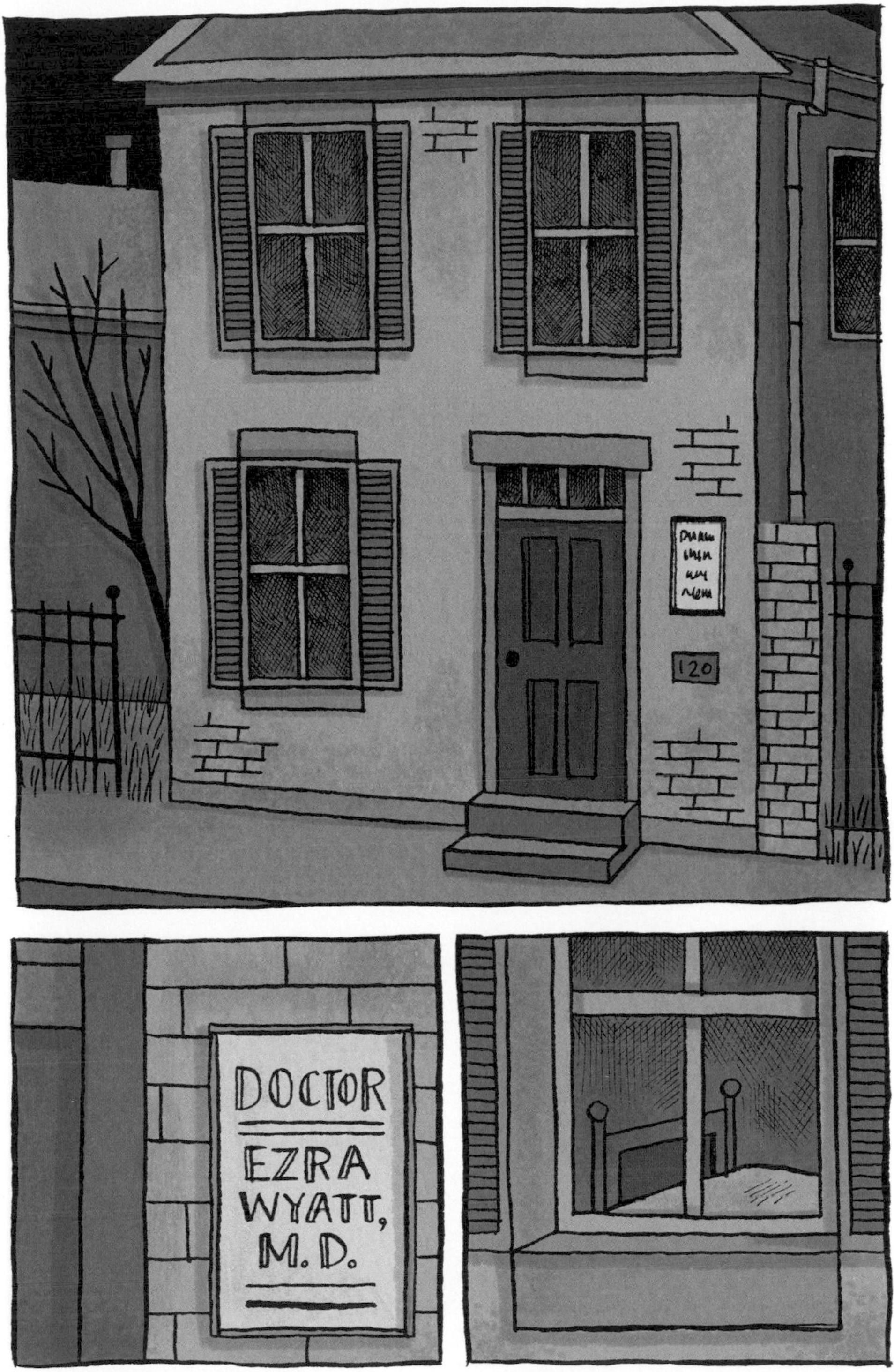
120
DOCTOR
EZRA
WYATT,
M.D.

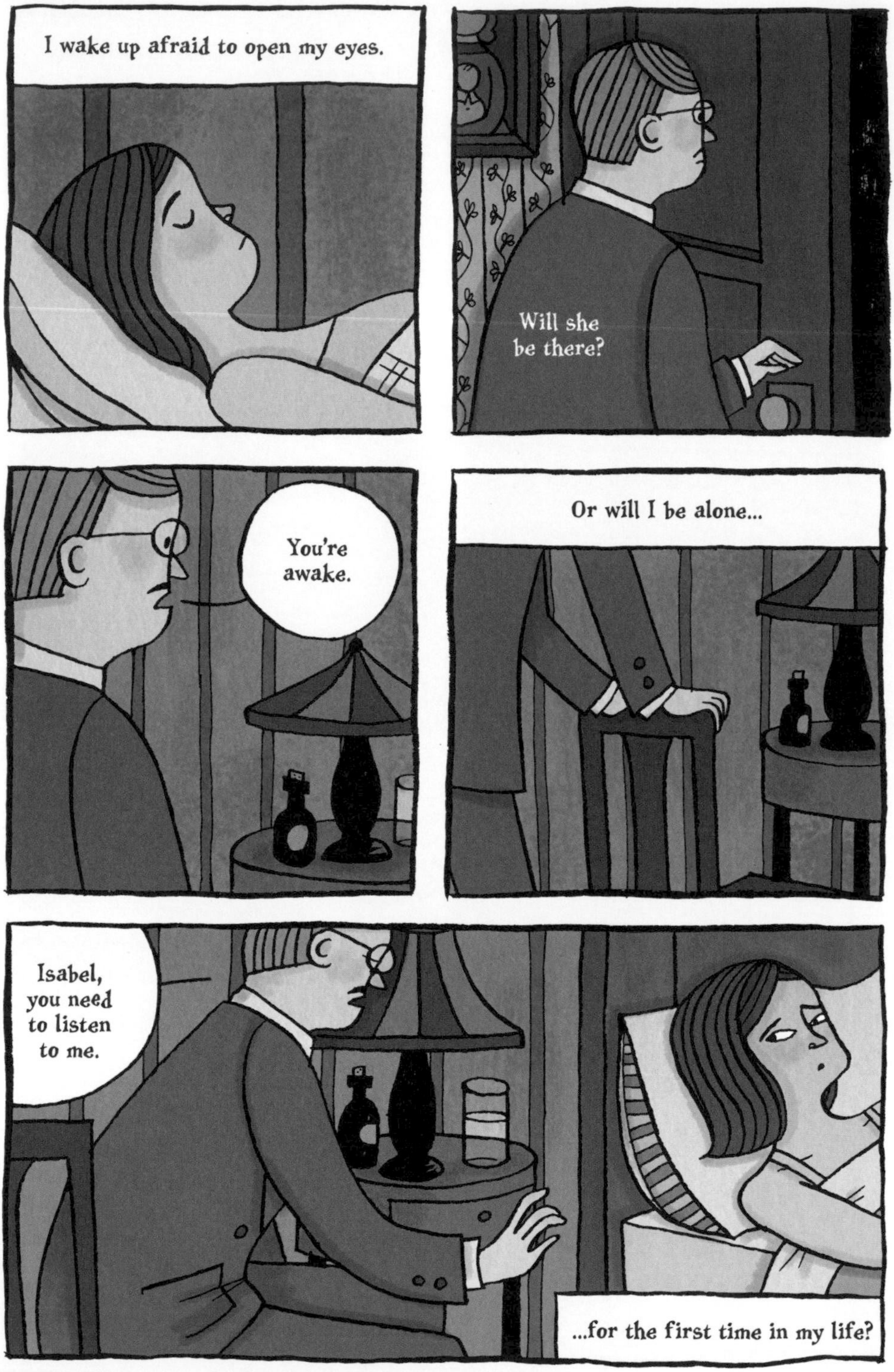
I wake up afraid to open my eyes.
Will she be there?
You're awake.
Or will I be alone...
Isabel, you need to listen to me.
...for the first time in my life?

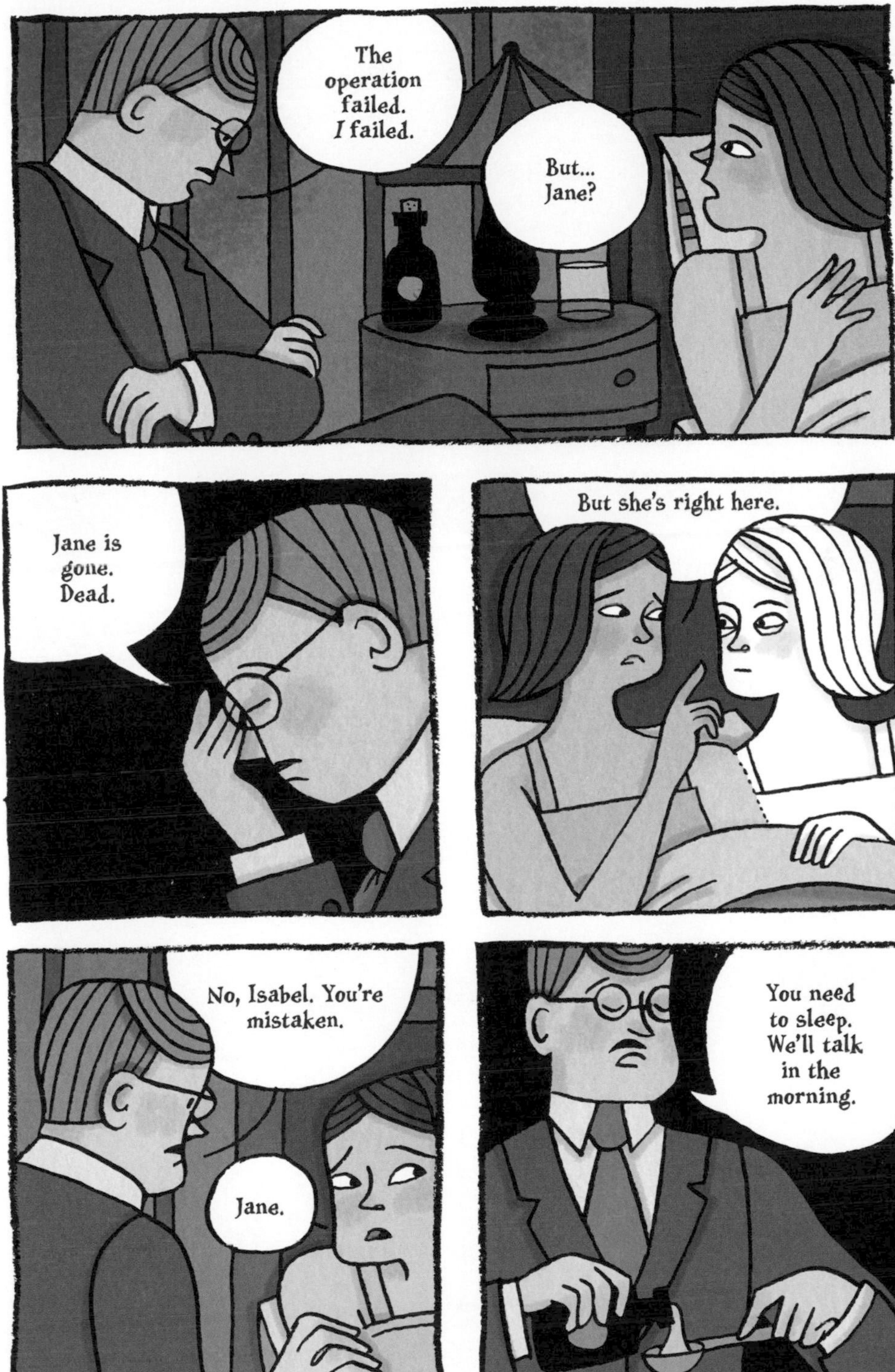
The operation failed. *I* failed.
But... Jane?
Jane is gone. Dead.
But she's right here.
No, Isabel. You're mistaken.
Jane.
You need to sleep. We'll talk in the morning.

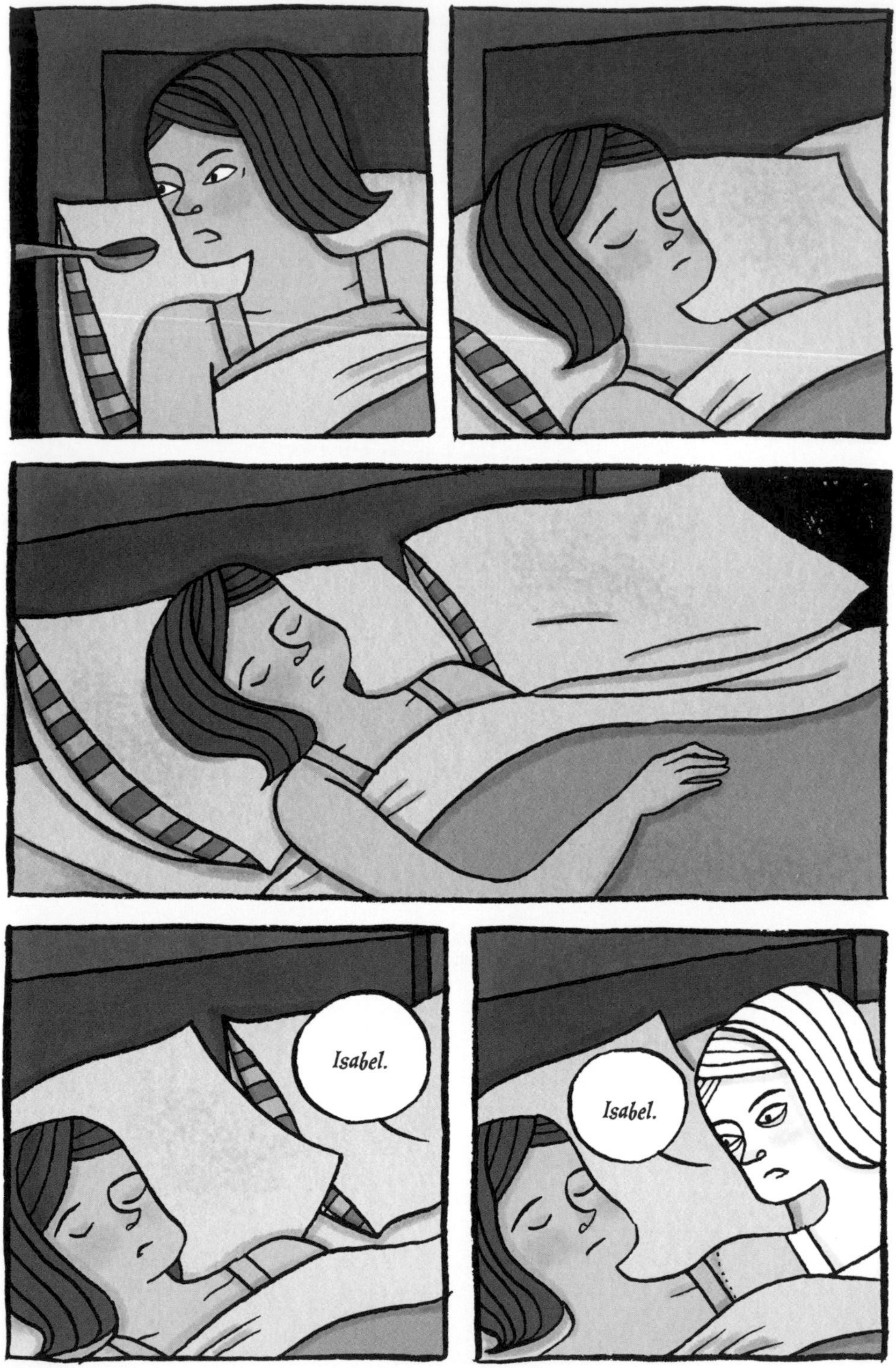
Isabel.
Isabel.

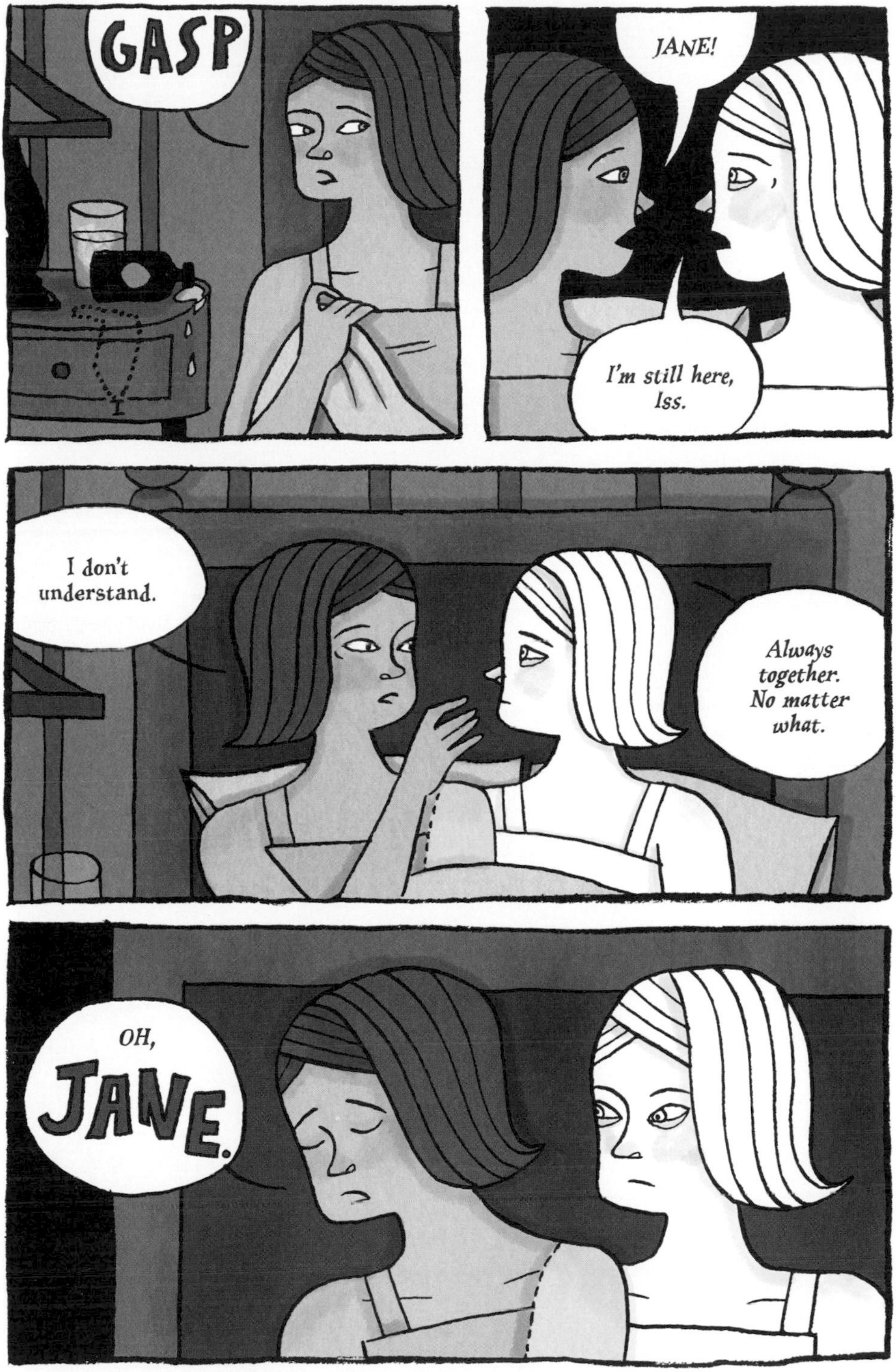
GASP
JANE!
I'm still here, Iss.
I don't understand.
Always together. No matter what.
OH, JANE.

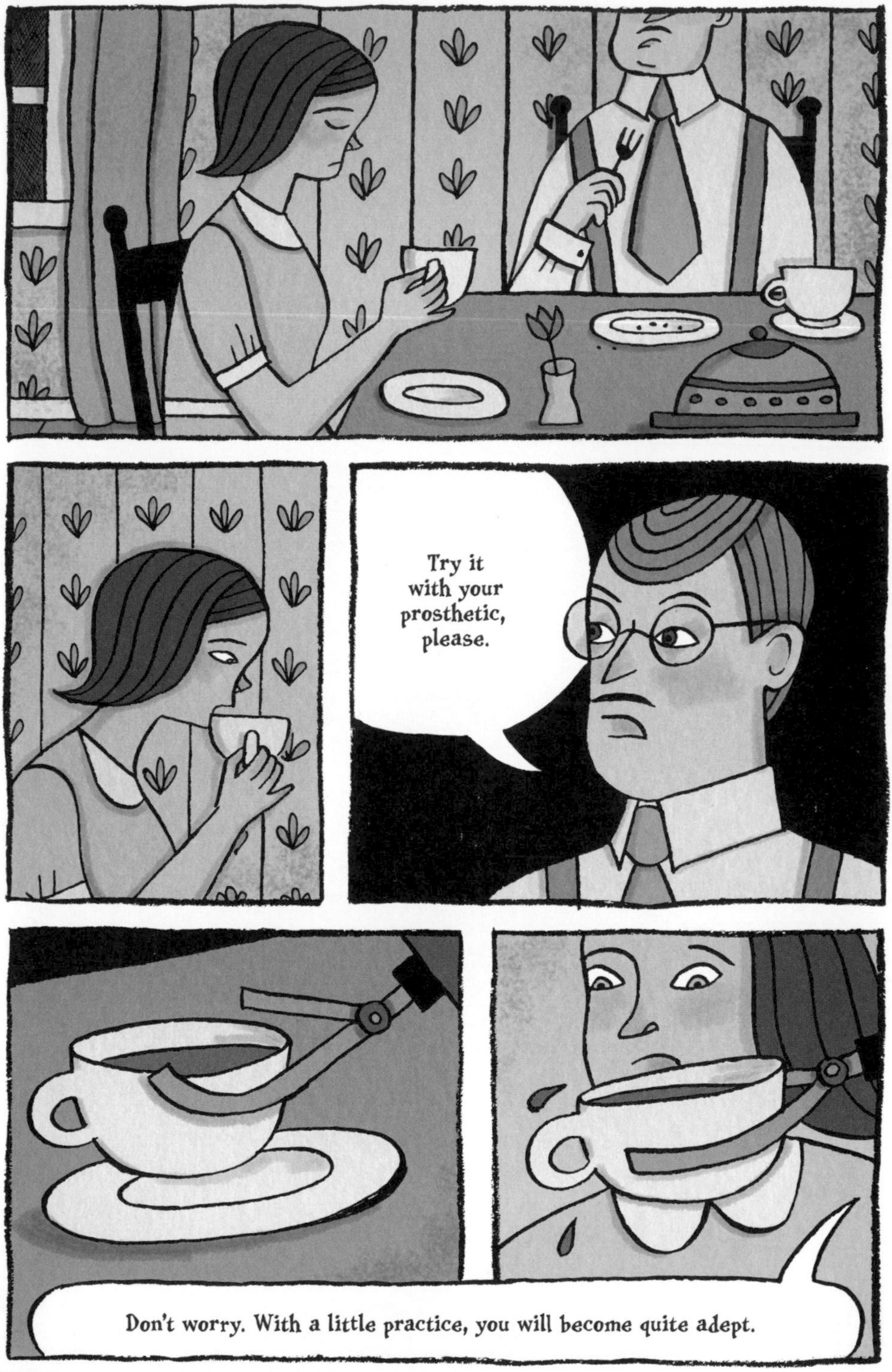
Try it with your prosthetic, please.
Don't worry. With a little practice, you will become quite adept.

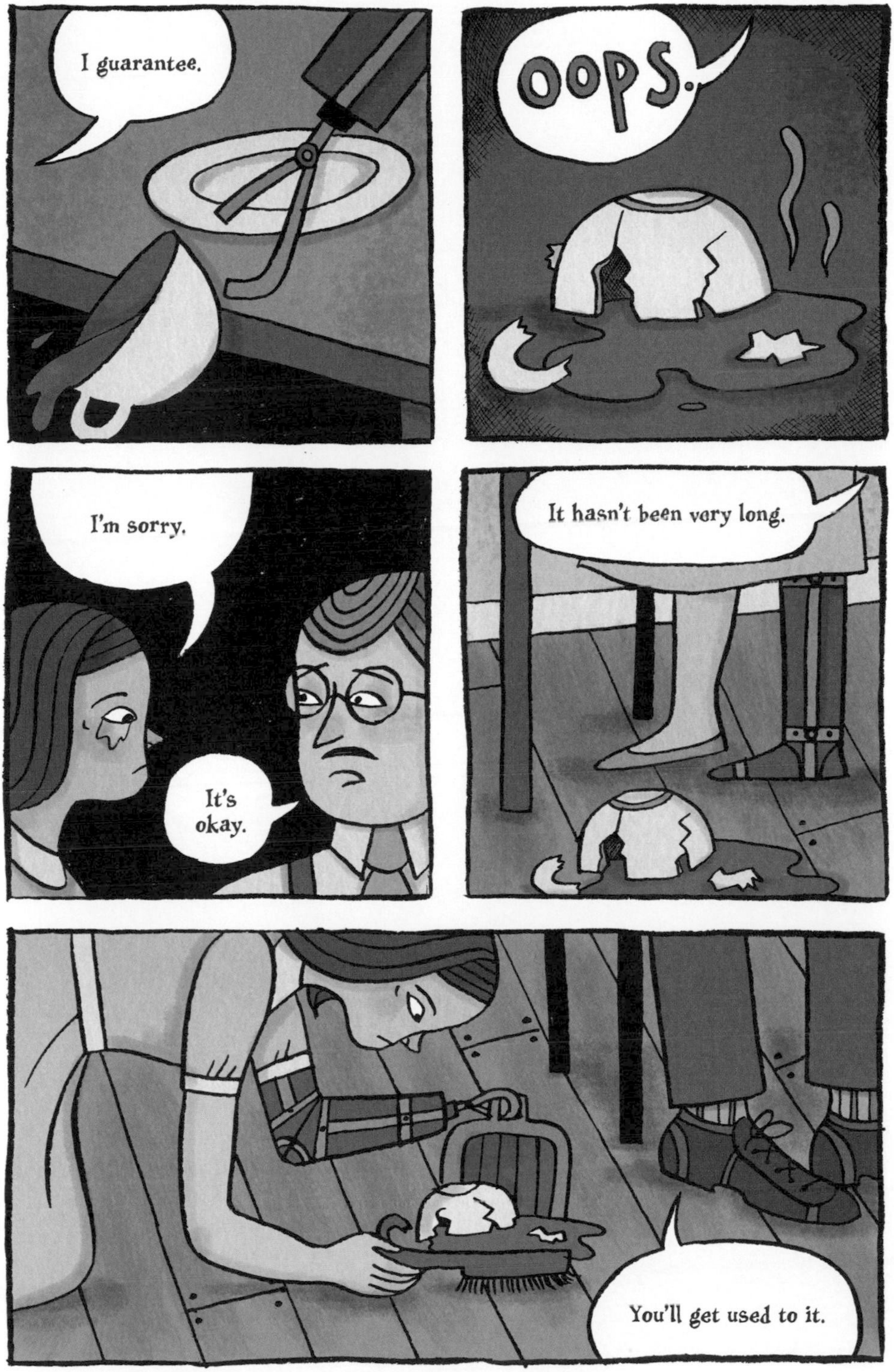
I guarantee.
OOPS.
I'm sorry.
It's okay.
It hasn't been very long.
You'll get used to it.

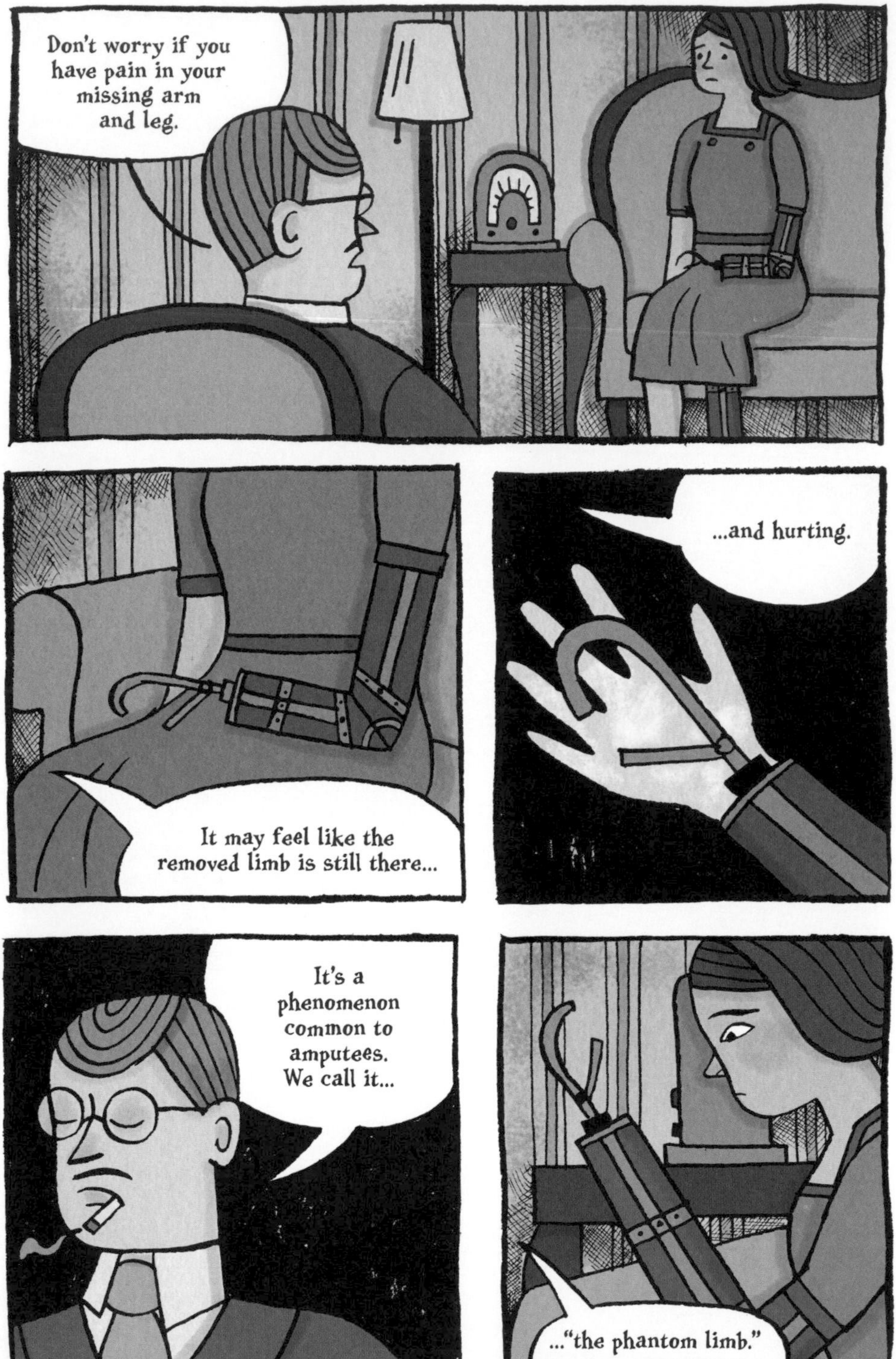
Don't worry if you have pain in your missing arm and leg.
It may feel like the removed limb is still there...
...and hurting.
It's a phenomenon common to amputees. We call it...
..."the phantom limb."

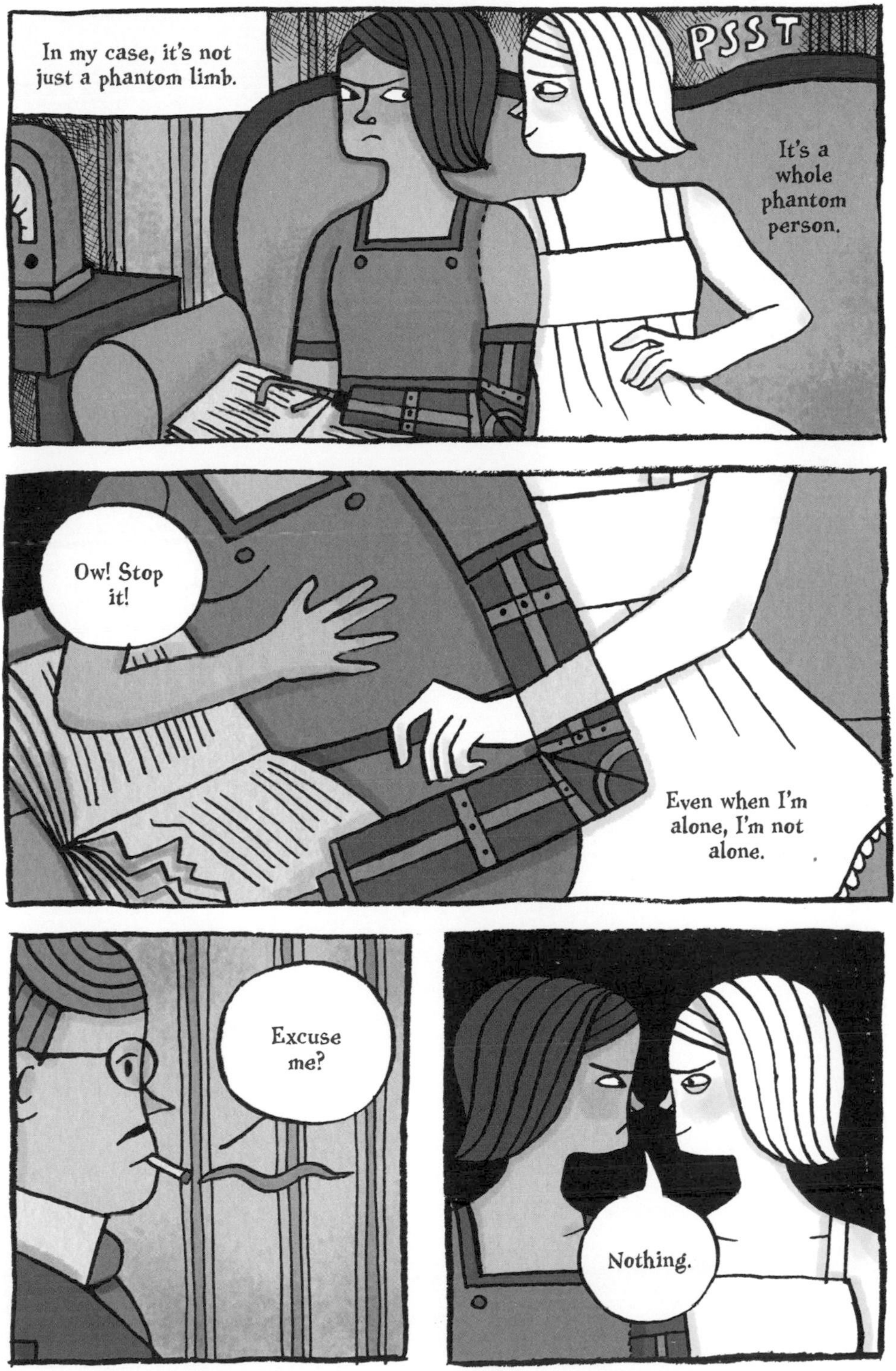

In my case, it's not just a phantom limb.
PSST
It's a whole phantom person.
Ow! Stop it!
Even when I'm alone, I'm not alone.
Excuse me?
Nothing.

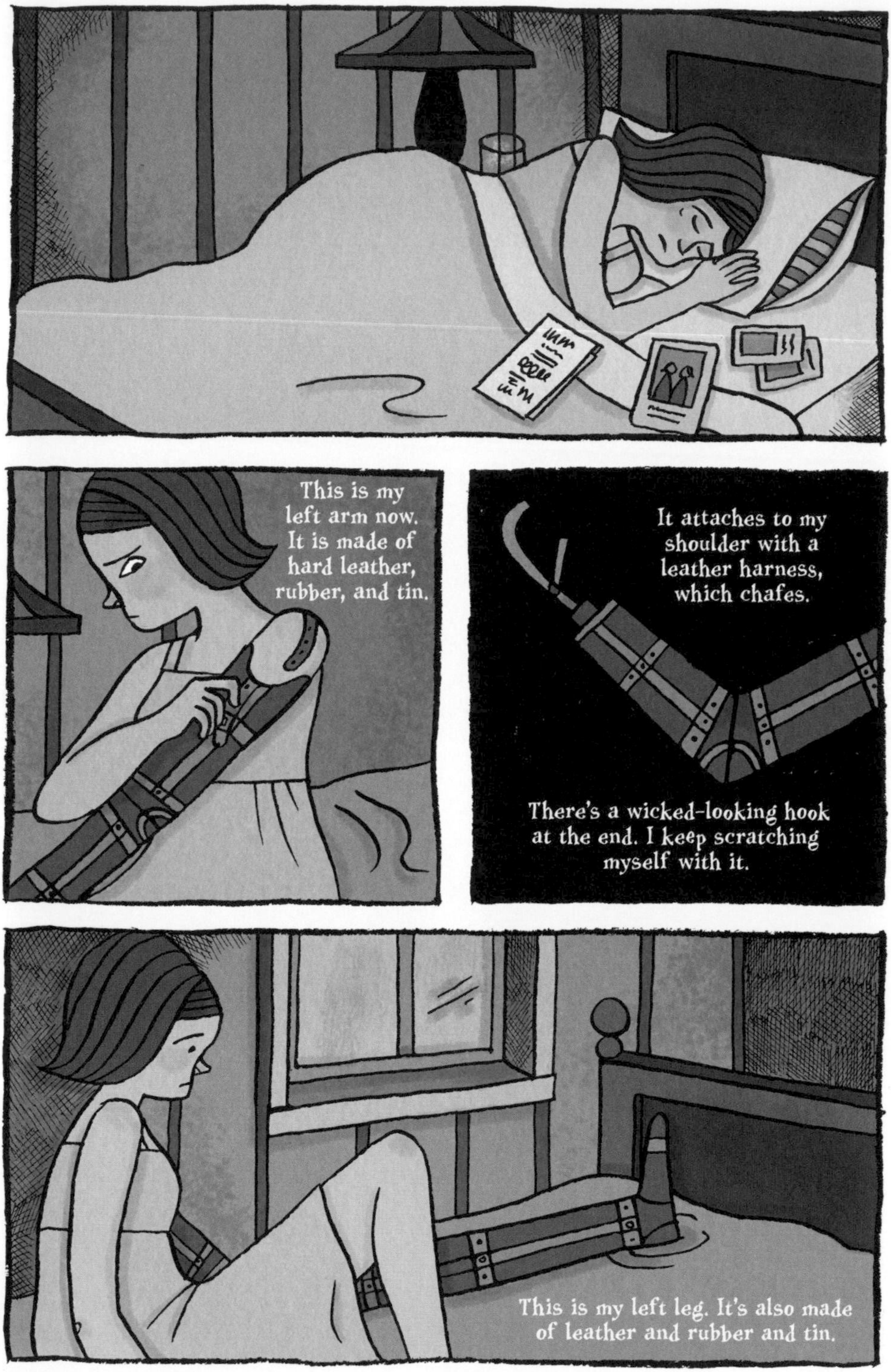

This is my left arm now. It is made of hard leather, rubber, and tin.
It attaches to my shoulder with a leather harness, which chafes.
There's a wicked-looking hook at the end. I keep scratching myself with it.
This is my left leg. It's also made of leather and rubber and tin.

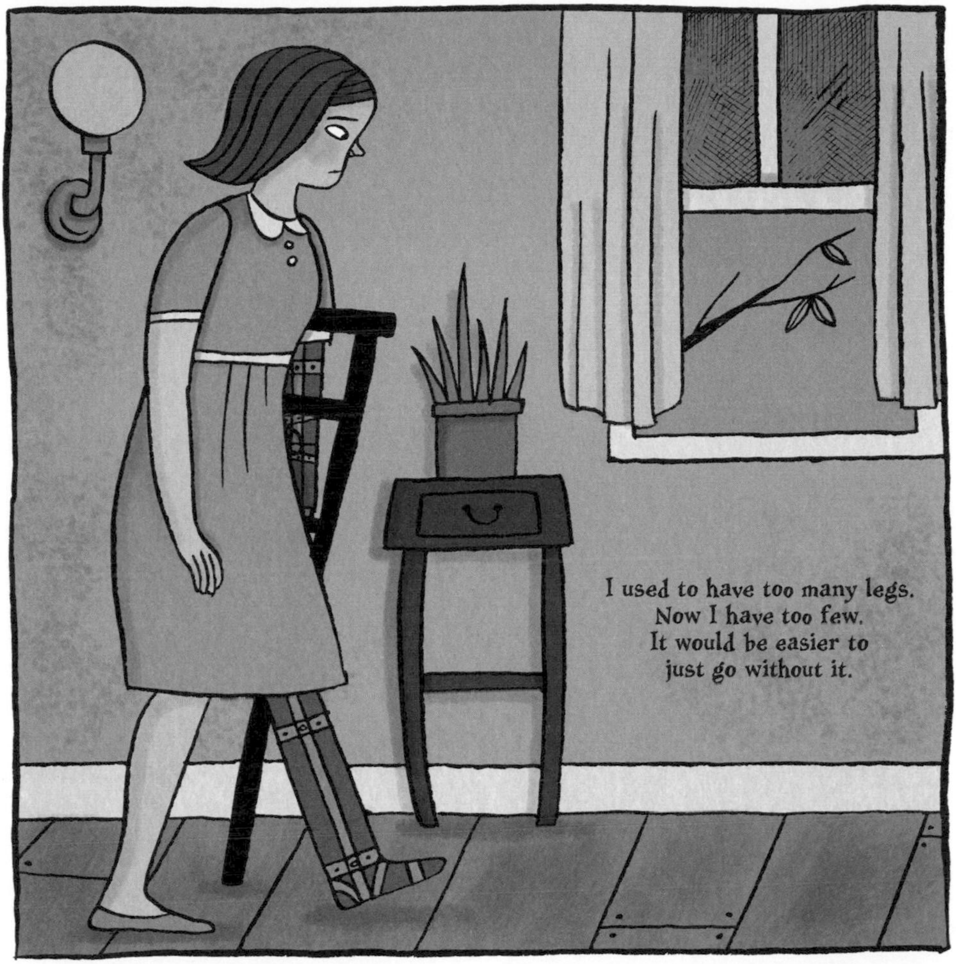
I used to have too many legs.
Now I have too few.
It would be easier to
just go without it.

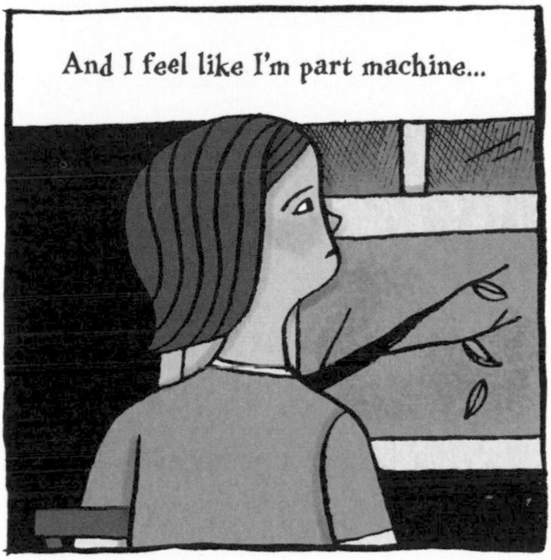
And I feel like I'm part machine...

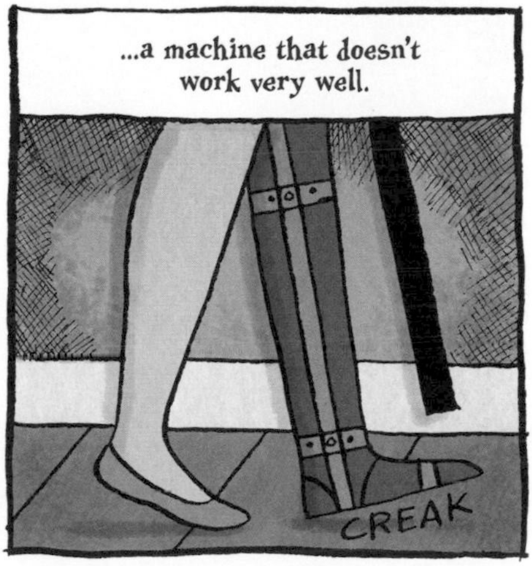
...a machine that doesn't
work very well.
CREAK

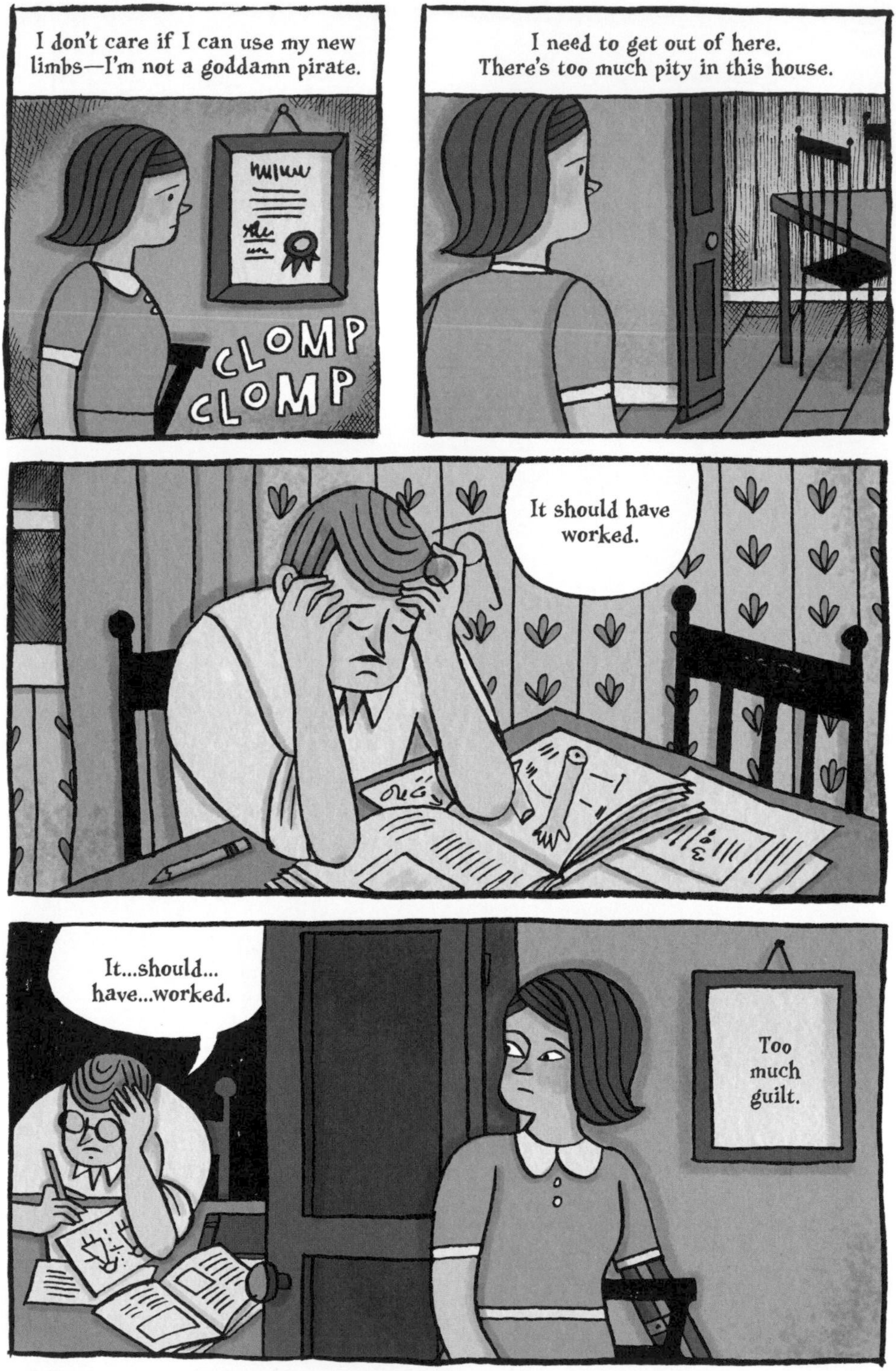
I don't care if I can use my new limbs—I'm not a goddamn pirate.
CLOMP CLOMP
I need to get out of here. There's too much pity in this house.
It should have worked.
It...should... have...worked.
Too much guilt.

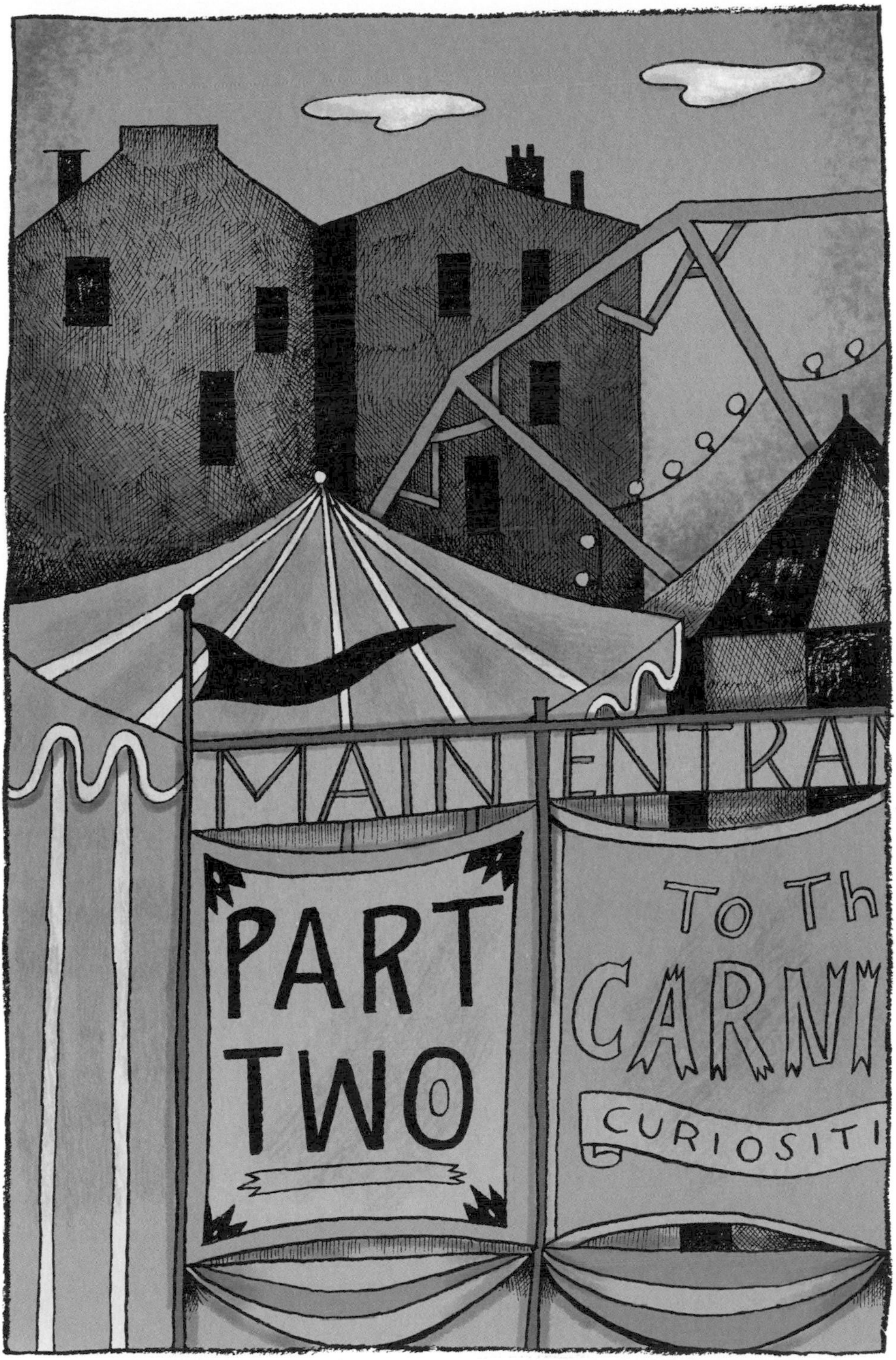
MAIN ENTRAN
PART TWO
To Th
CARNI
CURIOSITI

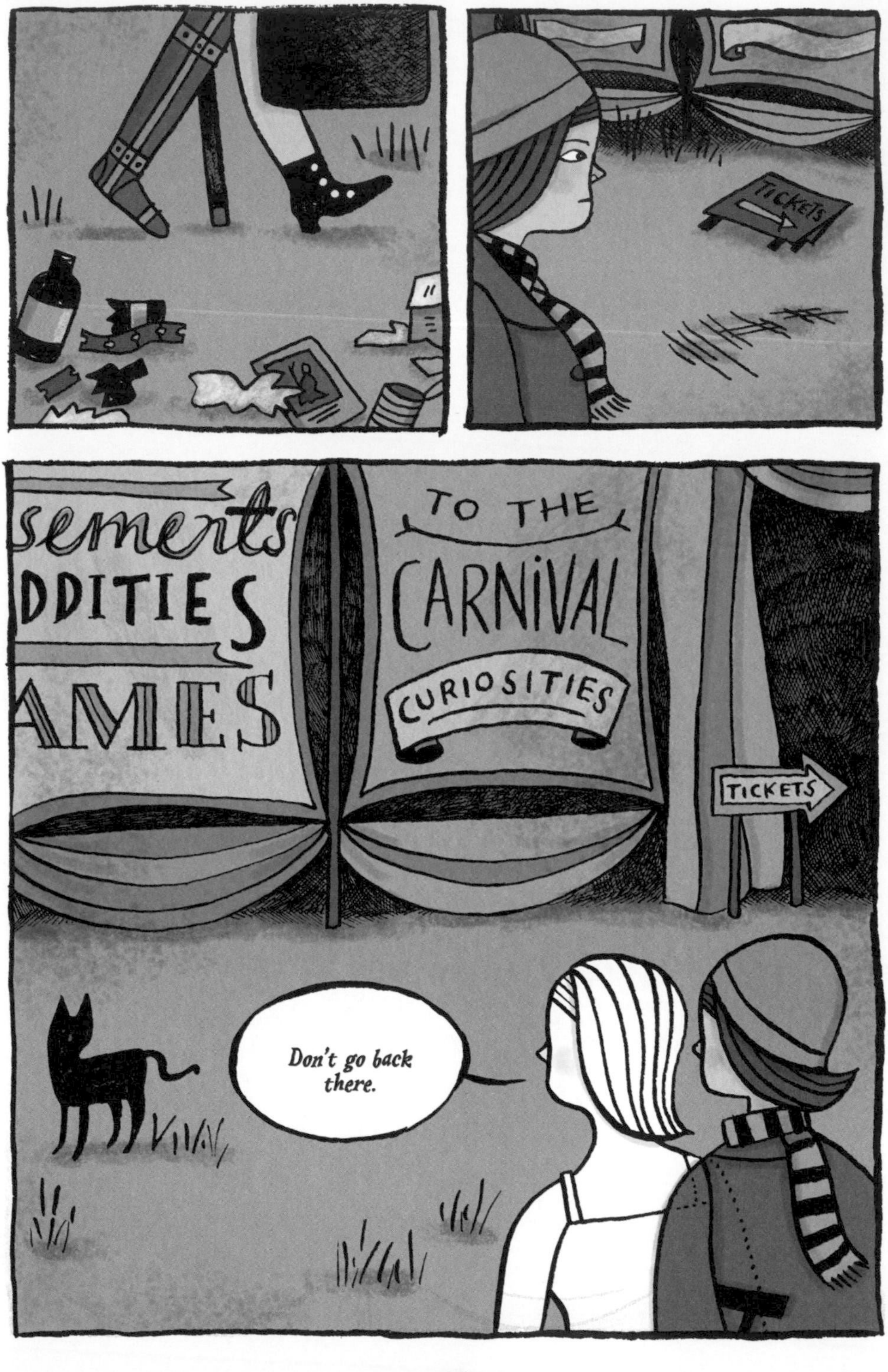
TICKETS
sements
DDITIES
AMES
TO THE
CARNIVAL
CURIOSITIES
TICKETS
Don't go back there.

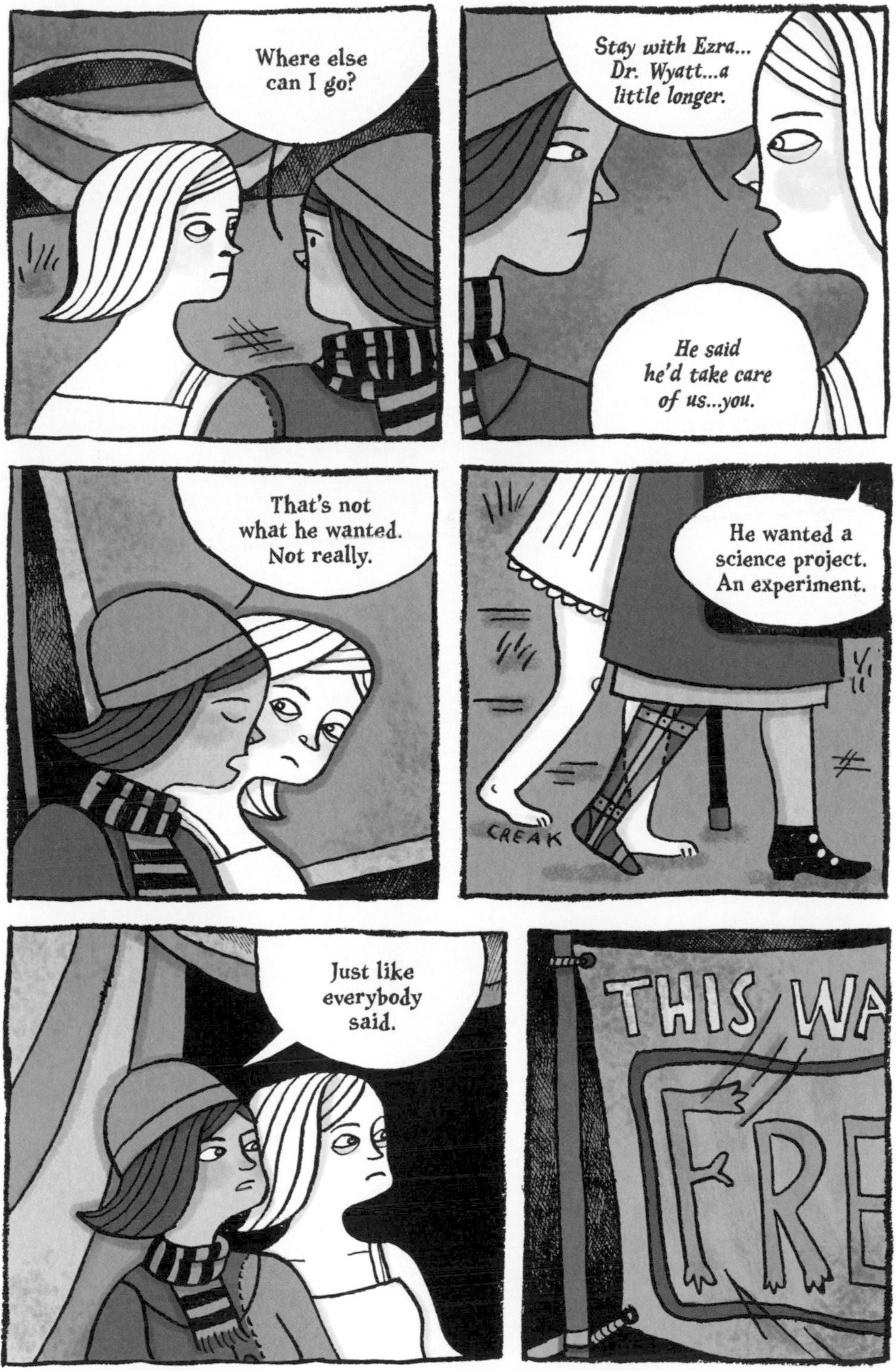
Where else can I go?
Stay with Ezra... Dr. Wyatt...a little longer.
He said he'd take care of us...you.
That's not what he wanted. Not really.
He wanted a science project. An experiment.
CREAK
Just like everybody said.
THIS WA
FRE

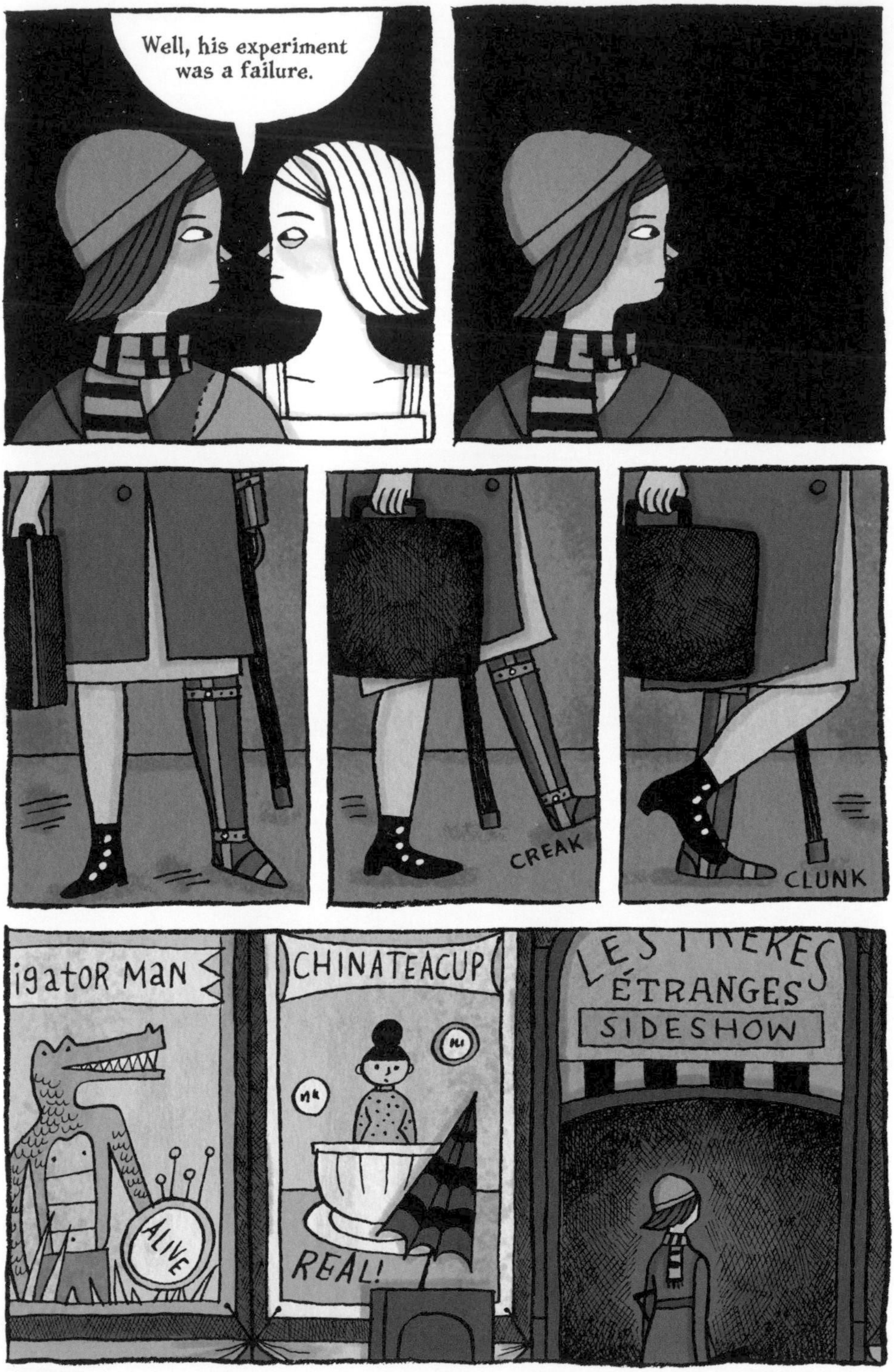
Well, his experiment was a failure.
CREAK
CLUNK
igator MAN
ALIVE
CHINATEACUP
REAL!
LES
ÉTRANGES
SIDESHOW

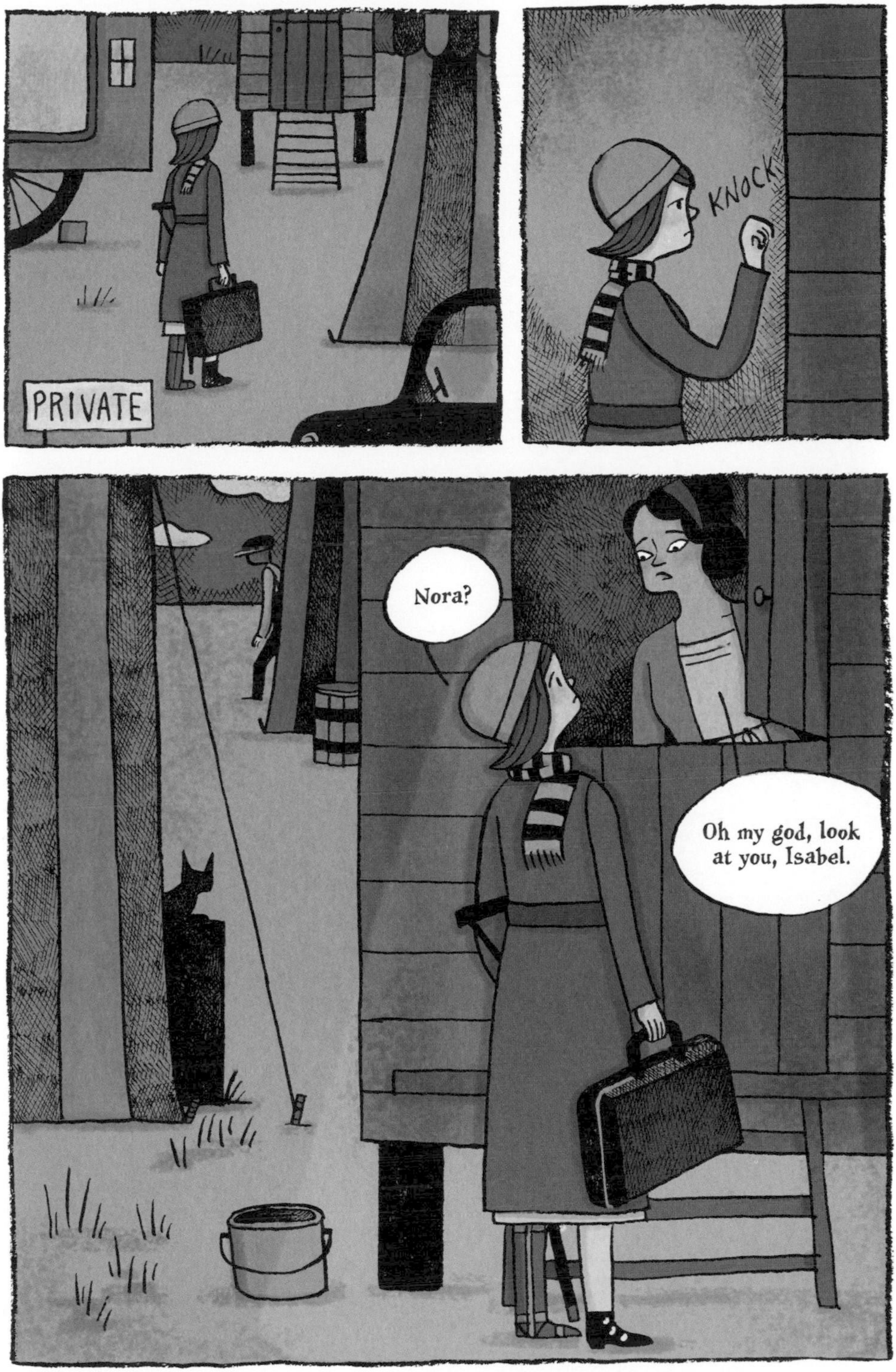
PRIVATE
KNOCK
Nora?
Oh my god, look at you, Isabel.

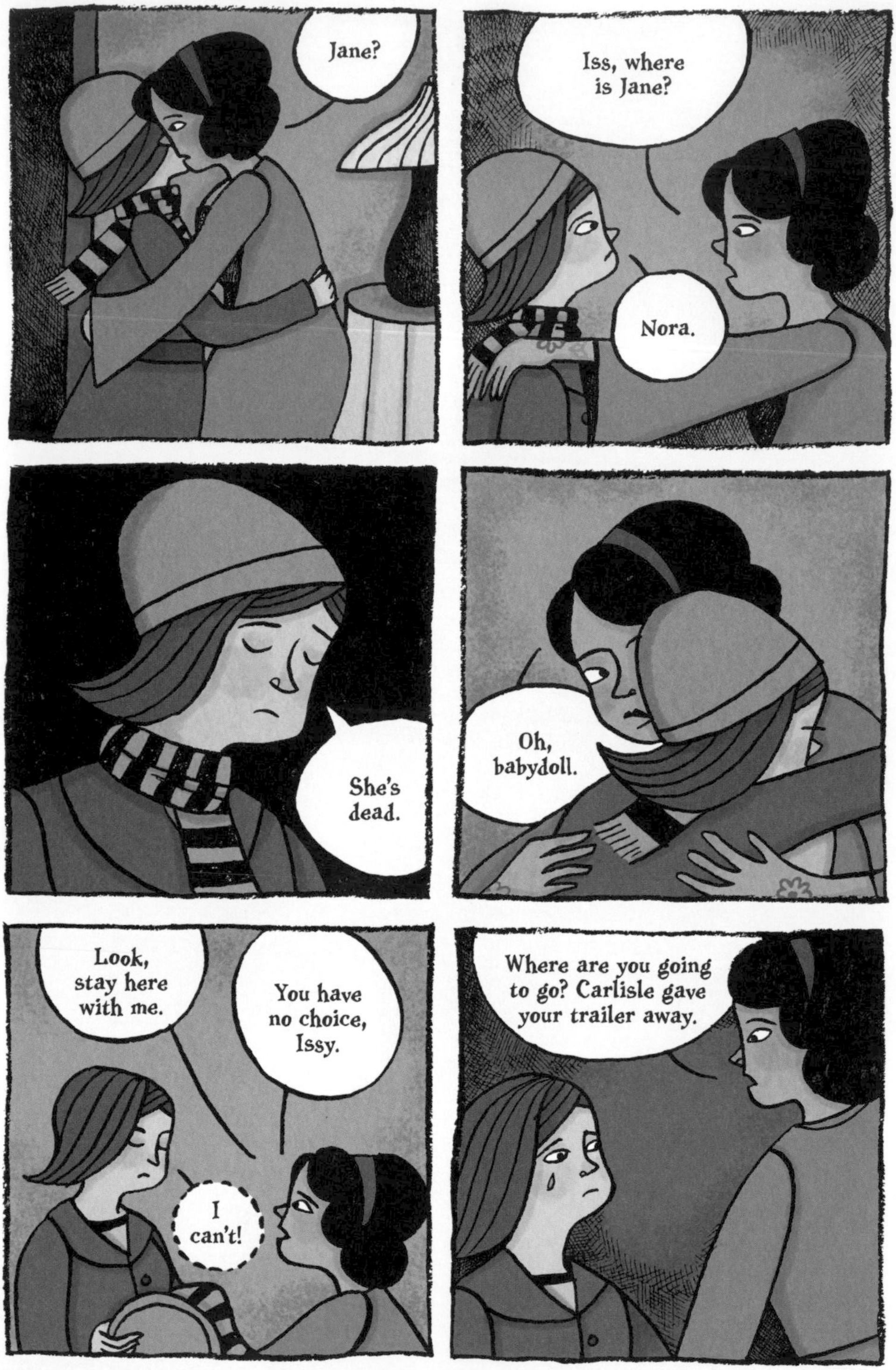
Jane?
Iss, where is Jane?
Nora.
She's dead.
Oh, babydoll.
Look, stay here with me.
You have no choice, Issy.
I can't!
Where are you going to go? Carlisle gave your trailer away.

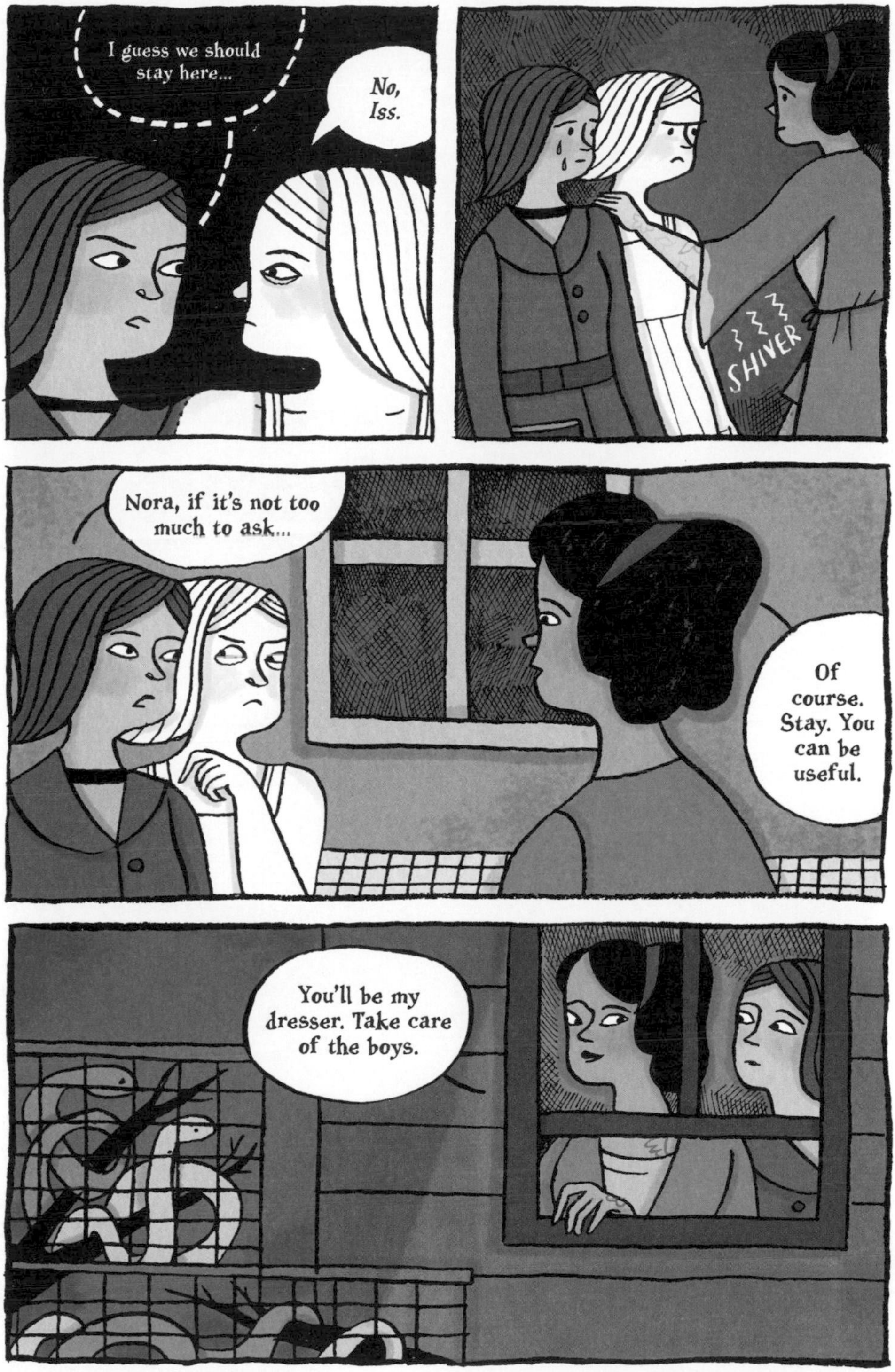

I guess we should stay here...
No, Iss.
SHIVER
Nora, if it's not too much to ask...
Of course. Stay. You can be useful.
You'll be my dresser. Take care of the boys.

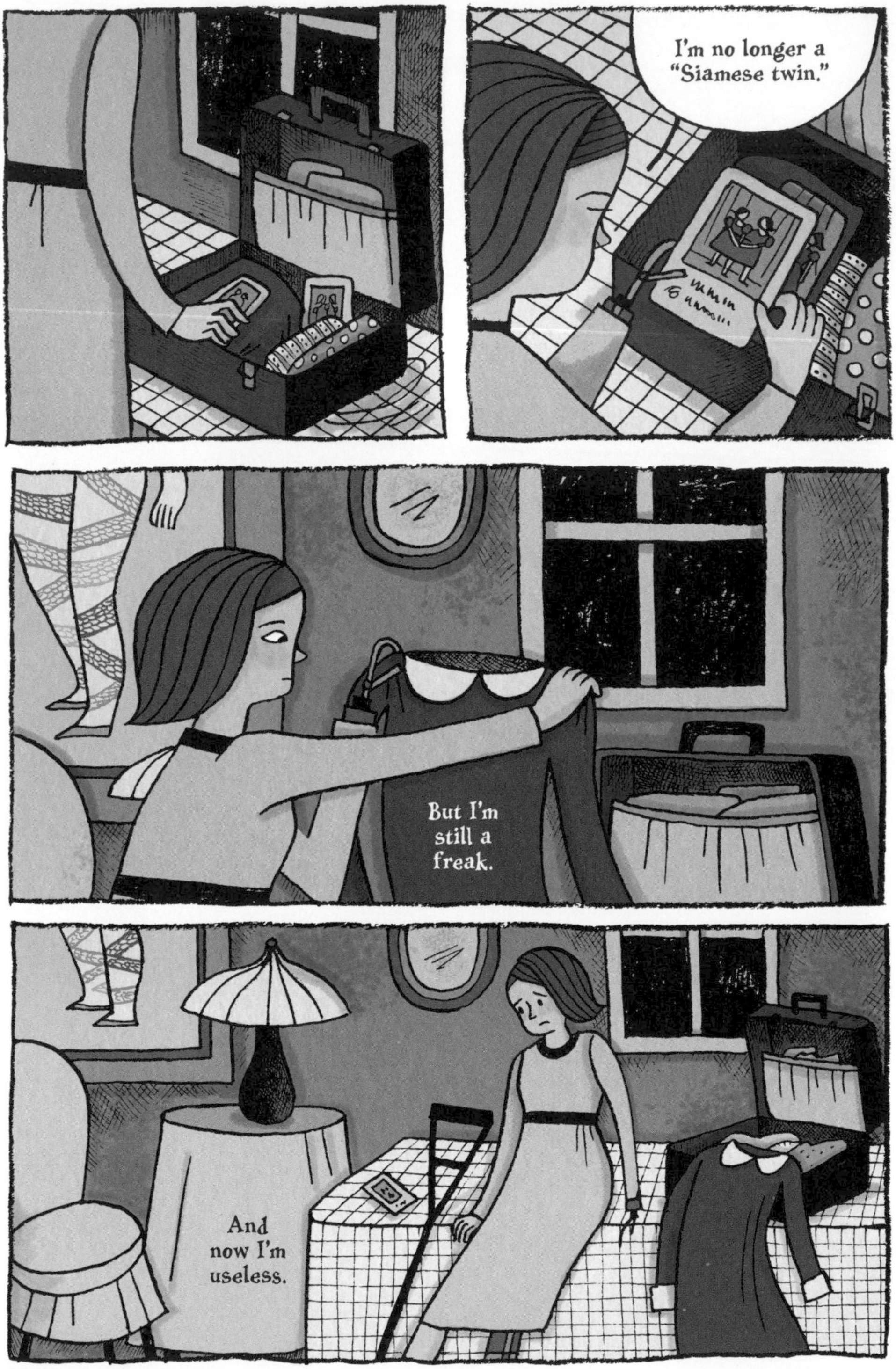
I'm no longer a "Siamese twin."
But I'm still a freak.
And now I'm useless.

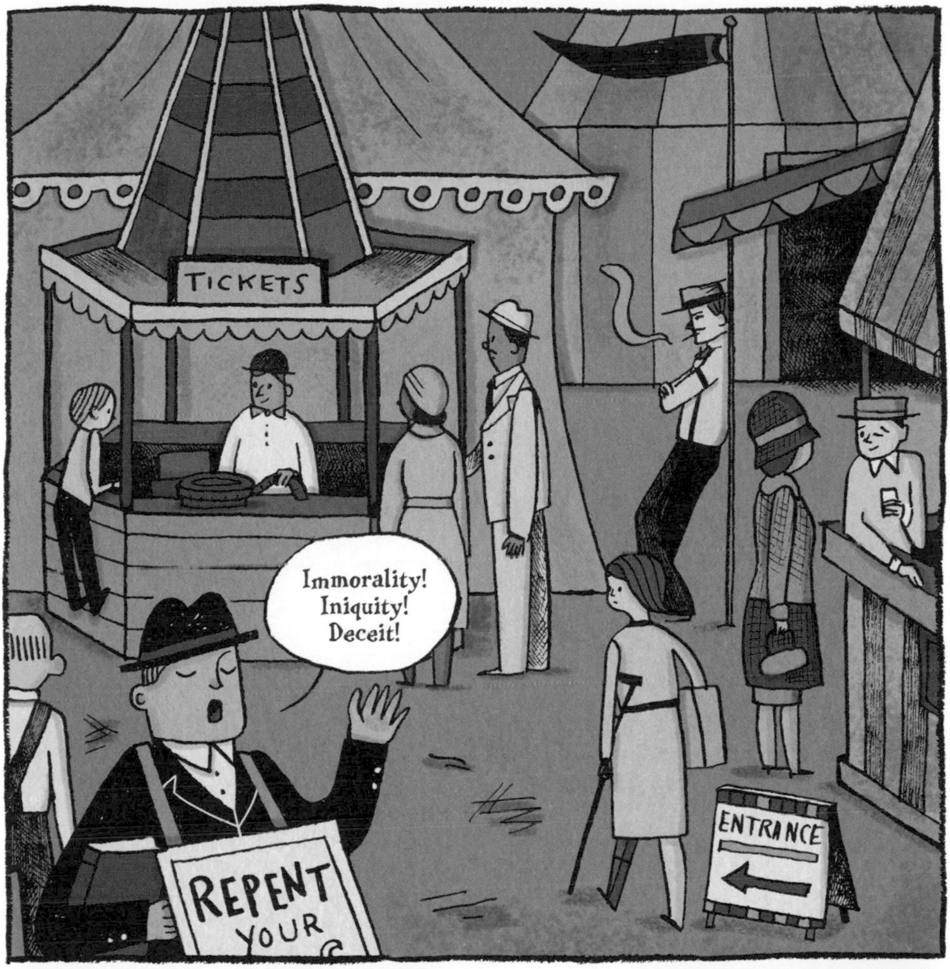
TICKETS
Immorality! Iniquity! Deceit!
ENTRANCE
REPENT YOUR

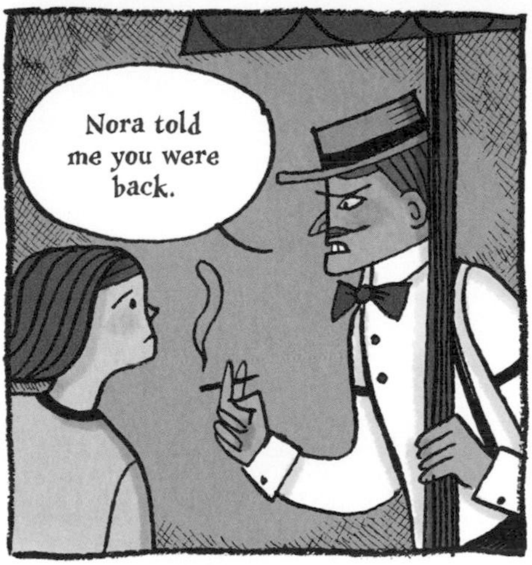
Nora told me you were back.

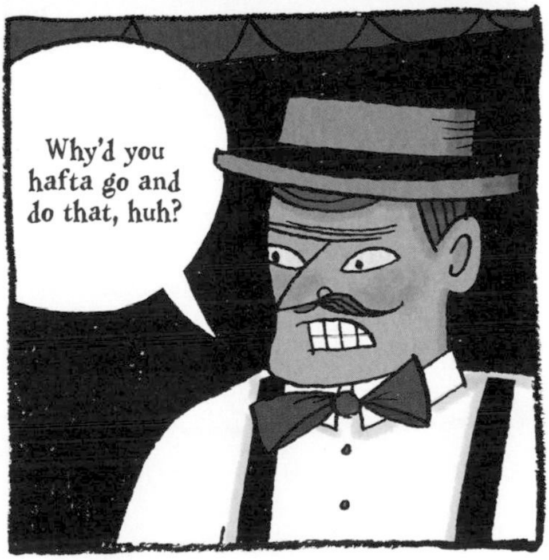
Why'd you hafta go and do that, huh?

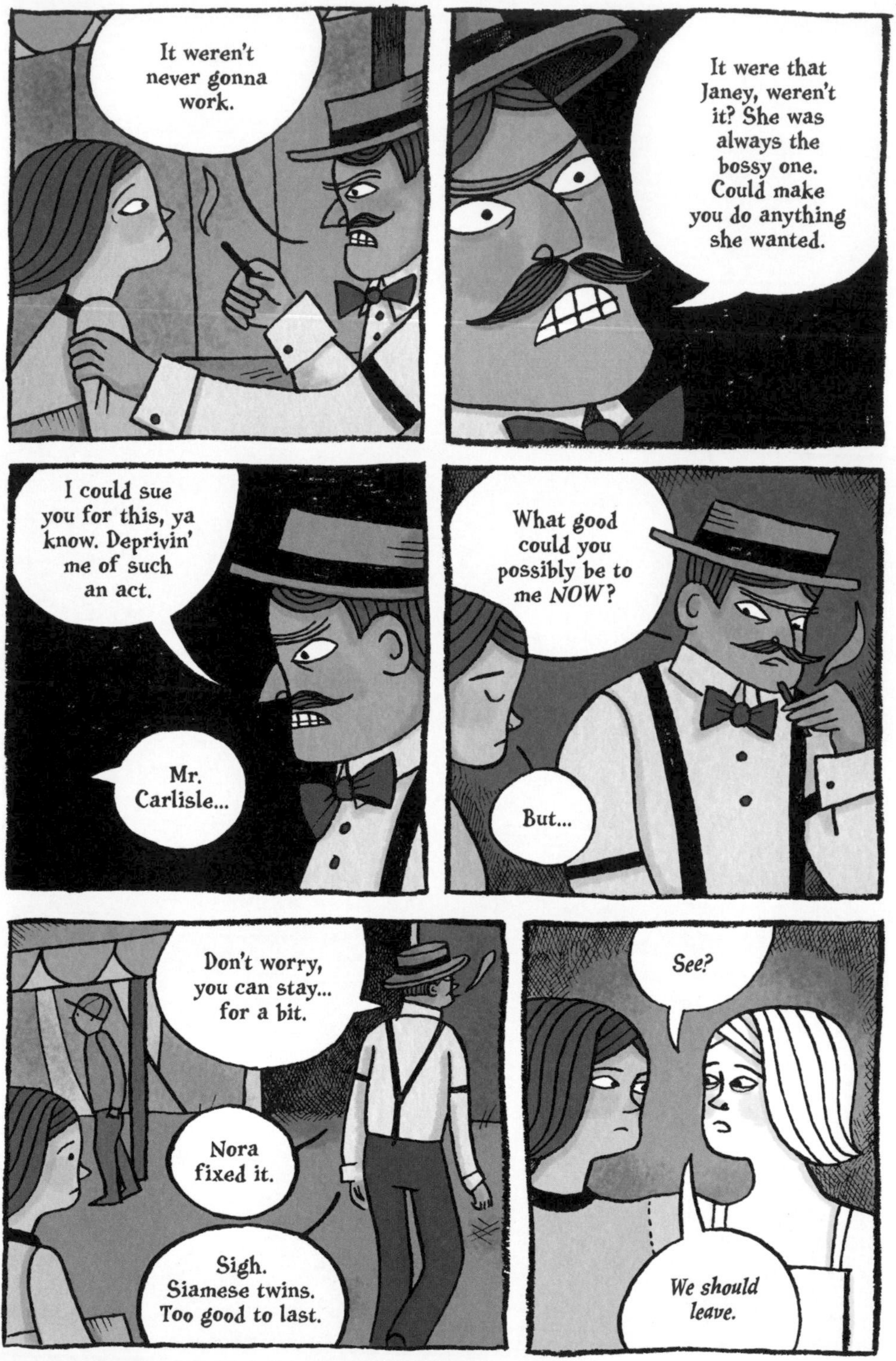
It weren't never gonna work.
It were that Janey, weren't it? She was always the bossy one. Could make you do anything she wanted.
I could sue you for this, ya know. Deprivin' me of such an act.
Mr. Carlisle...
What good could you possibly be to me *NOW*?
But...
Don't worry, you can stay... for a bit.
Nora fixed it.
Sigh. Siamese twins. Too good to last.
See?
We should leave.

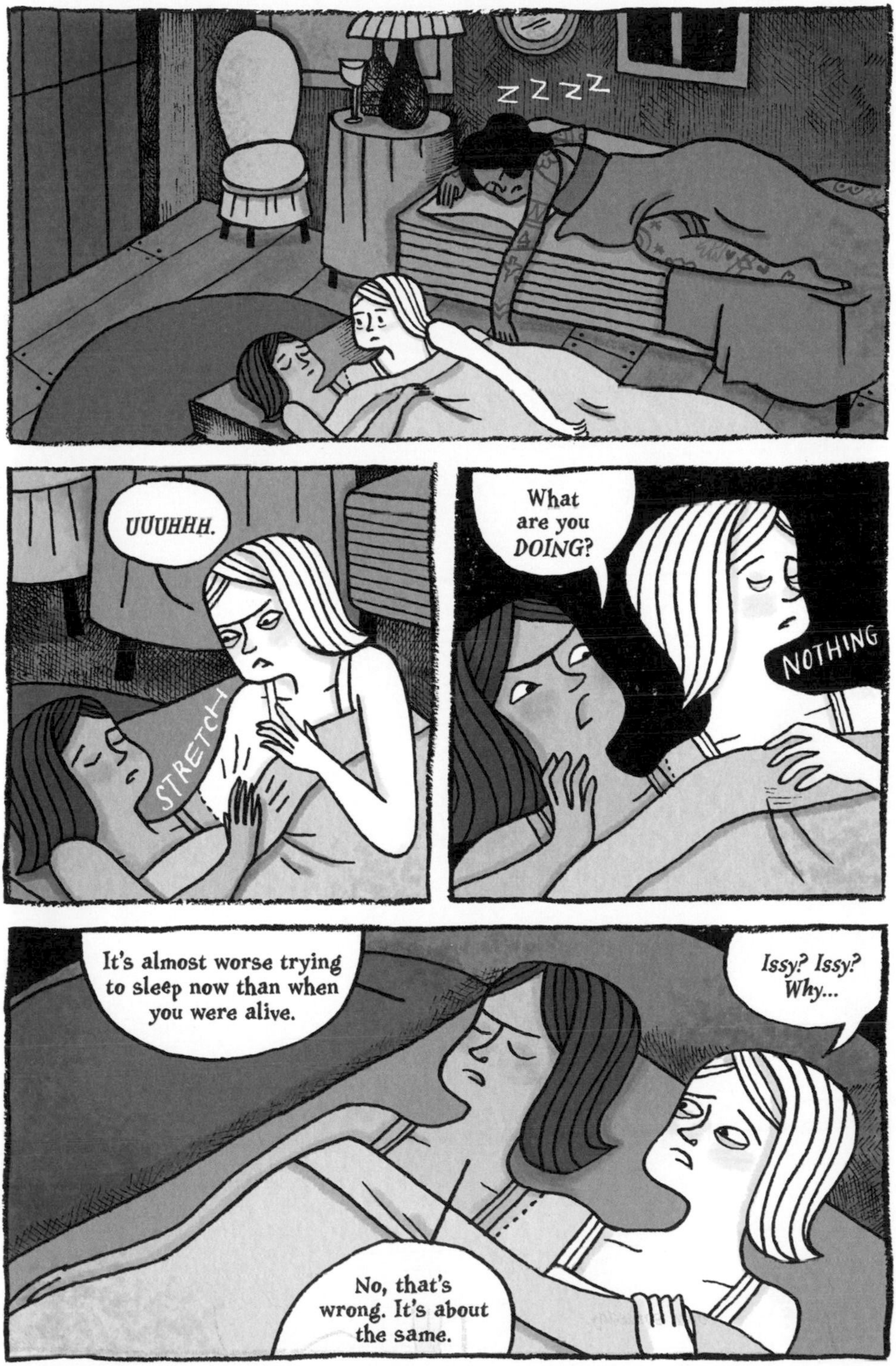
ZZZZ
UUUHHH.
STRETCH
What are you DOING?
NOTHING
It's almost worse trying to sleep now than when you were alive.
Issy? Issy? Why...
No, that's wrong. It's about the same.

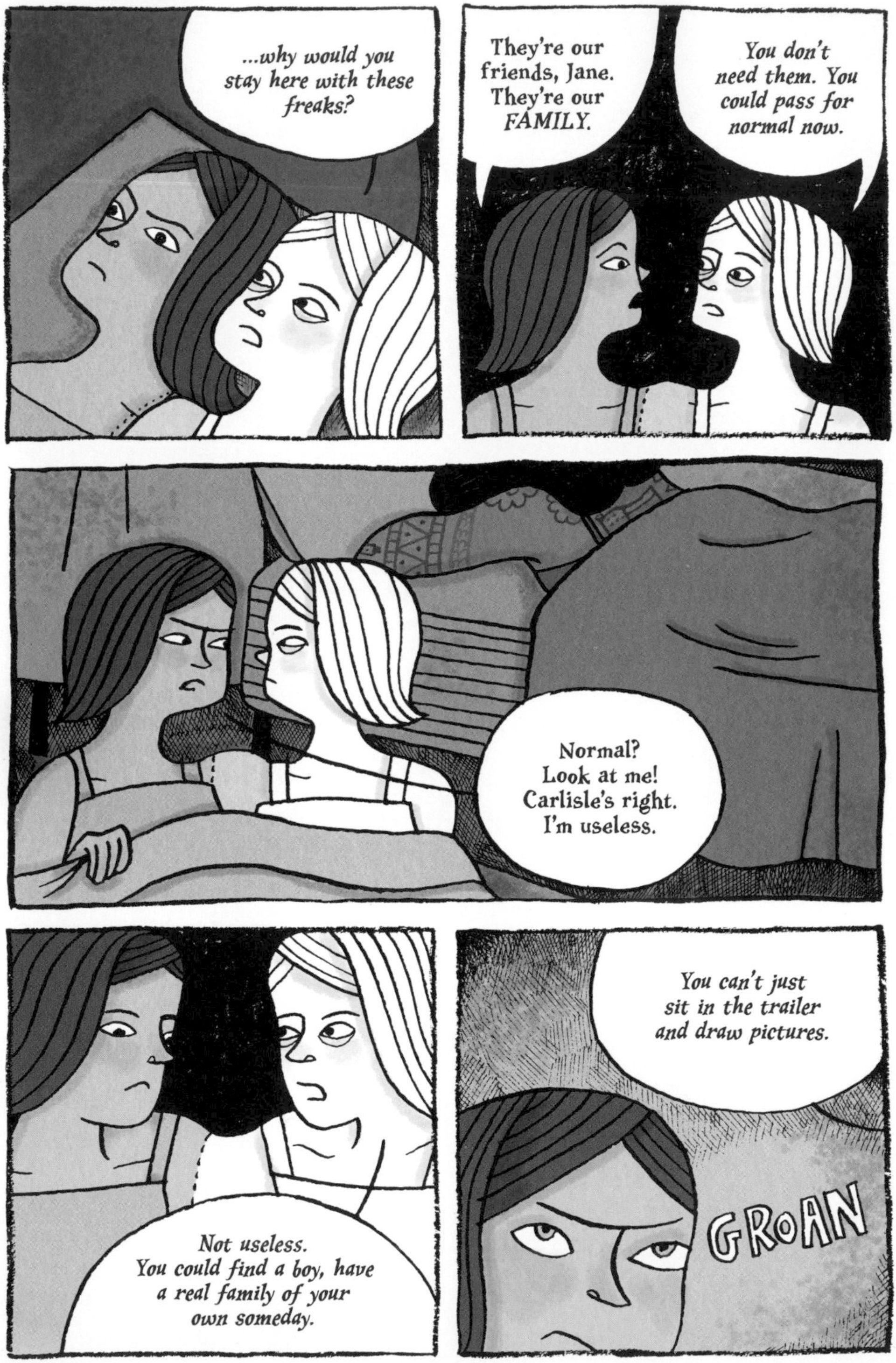
...why would you stay here with these freaks?
They're our friends, Jane. They're our FAMILY.
You don't need them. You could pass for normal now.
Normal? Look at me! Carlisle's right. I'm useless.
Not useless. You could find a boy, have a real family of your own someday.
You can't just sit in the trailer and draw pictures.
GROAN

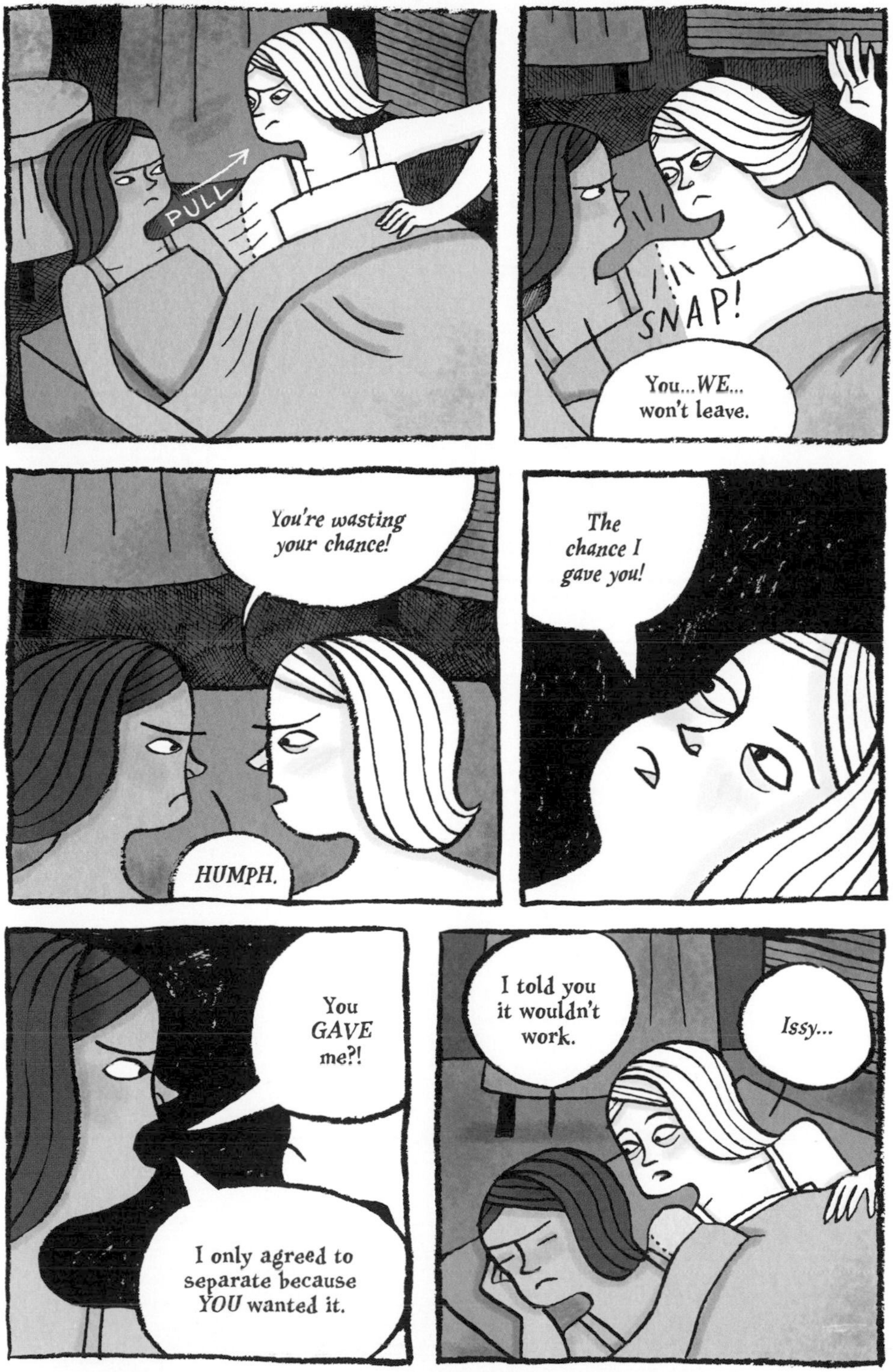
PULL
SNAP!
You...WE... won't leave.
You're wasting your chance!
HUMPH.
The chance I gave you!
You GAVE me?!
I only agreed to separate because YOU wanted it.
I told you it wouldn't work.
Issy...

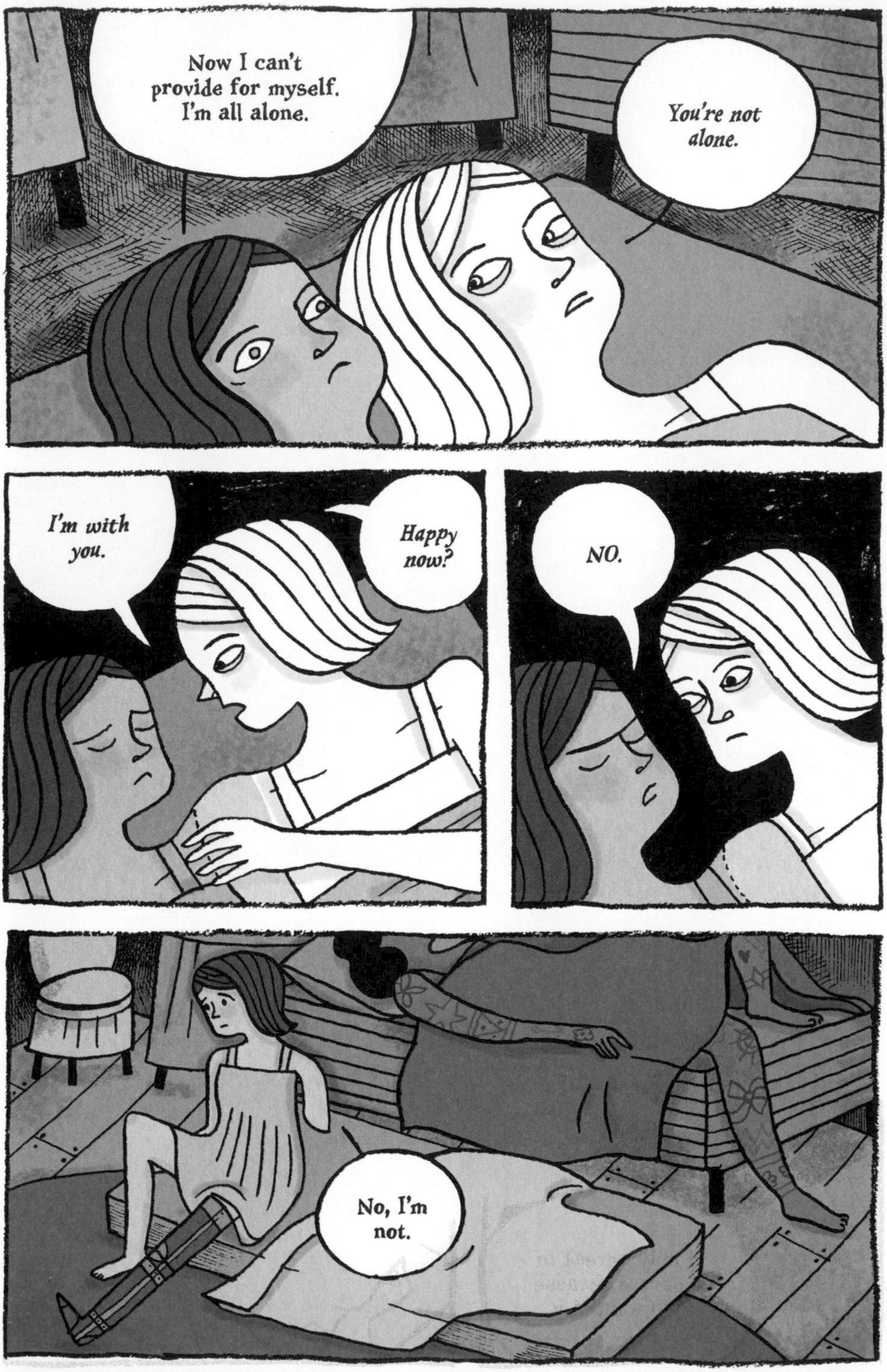
Now I can't provide for myself. I'm all alone.
You're not alone.
I'm with you.
Happy now?
NO.
No, I'm not.

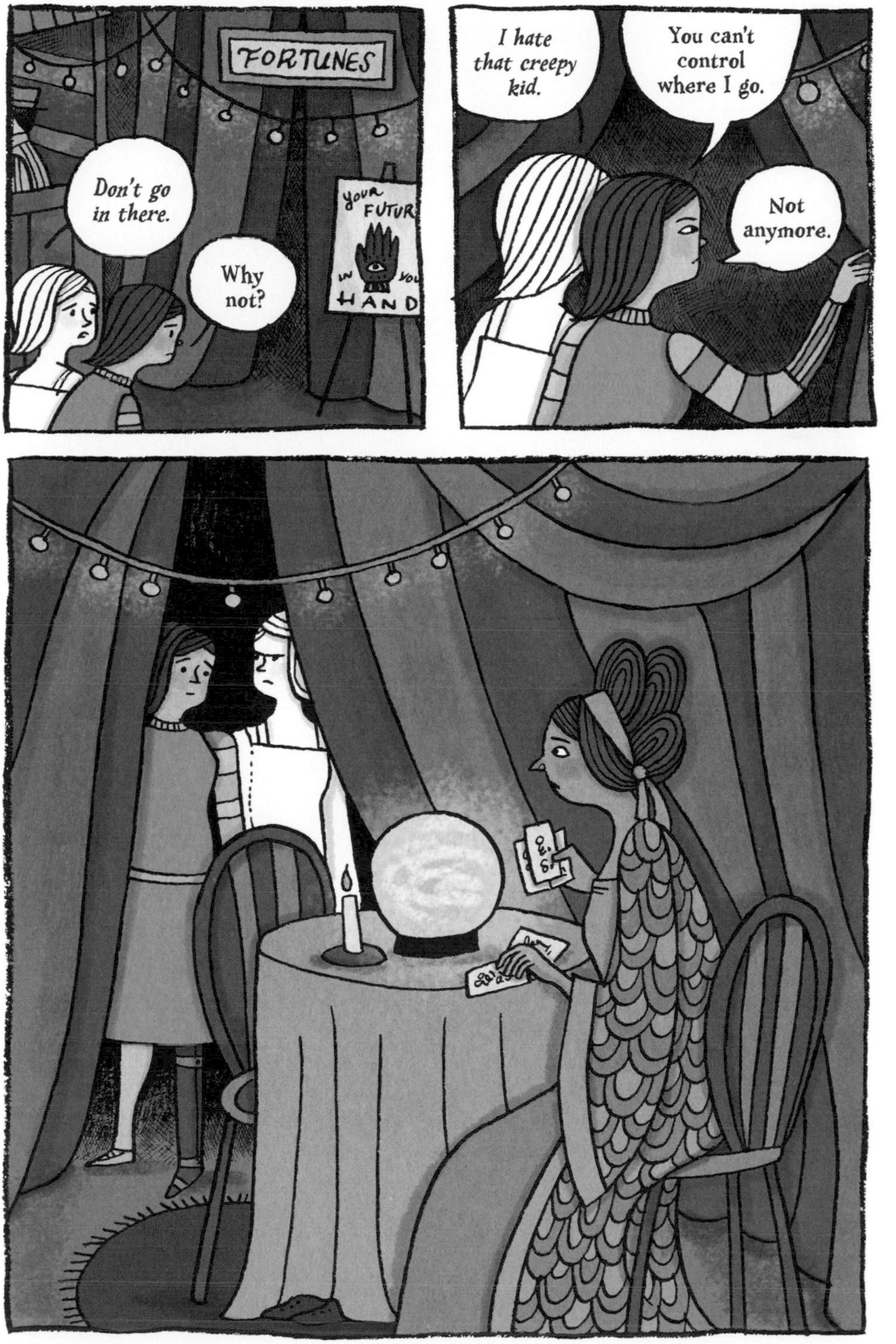
FORTUNES
Don't go in there.
Why not?
YOUR FUTUR
IN YOU
HAND
I hate that creepy kid.
You can't control where I go.
Not anymore.

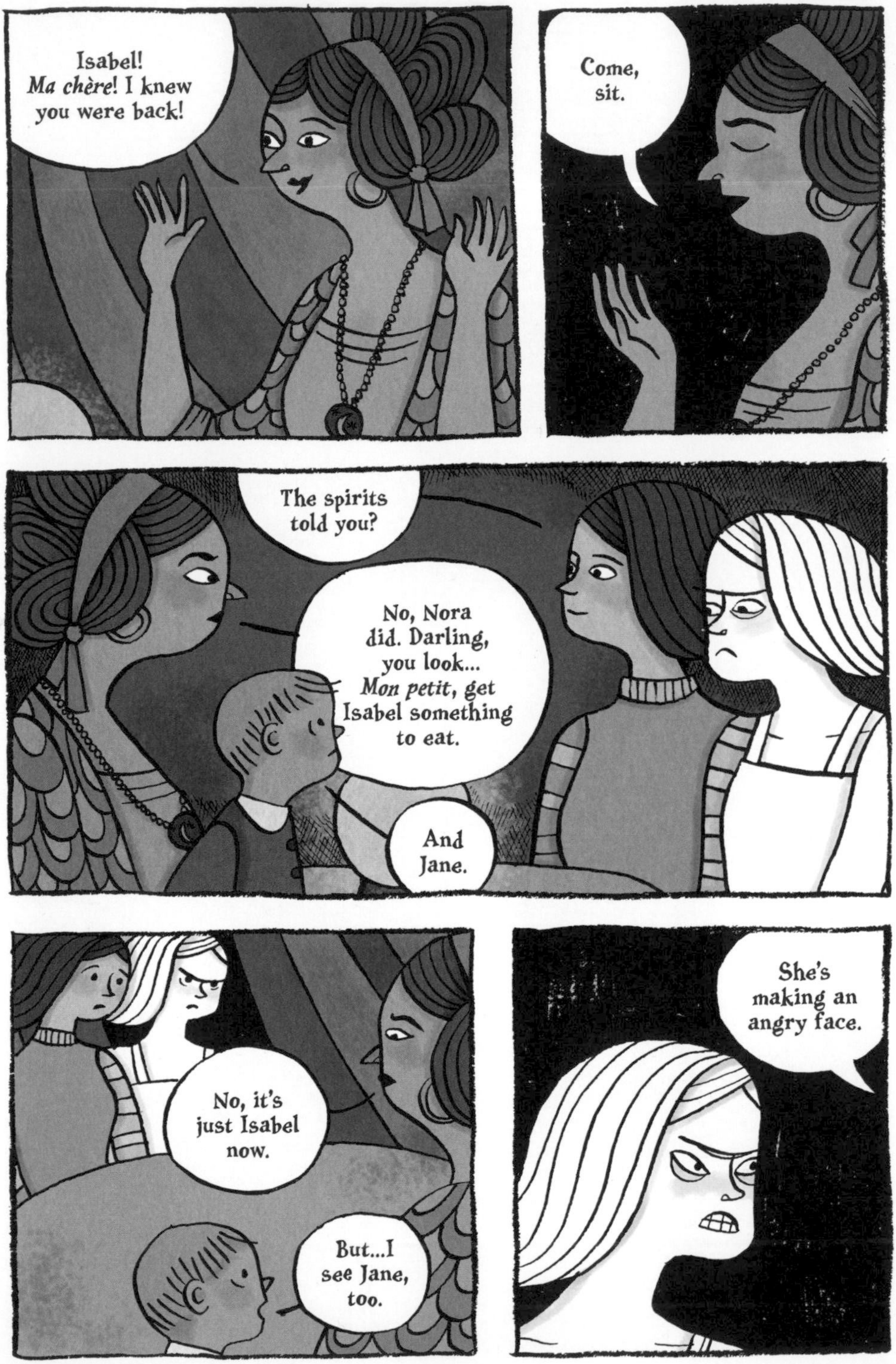
Isabel! *Ma chère*! I knew you were back!
Come, sit.
The spirits told you?
No, Nora did. Darling, you look... *Mon petit*, get Isabel something to eat.
And Jane.
No, it's just Isabel now.
But...I see Jane, too.
She's making an angry face.

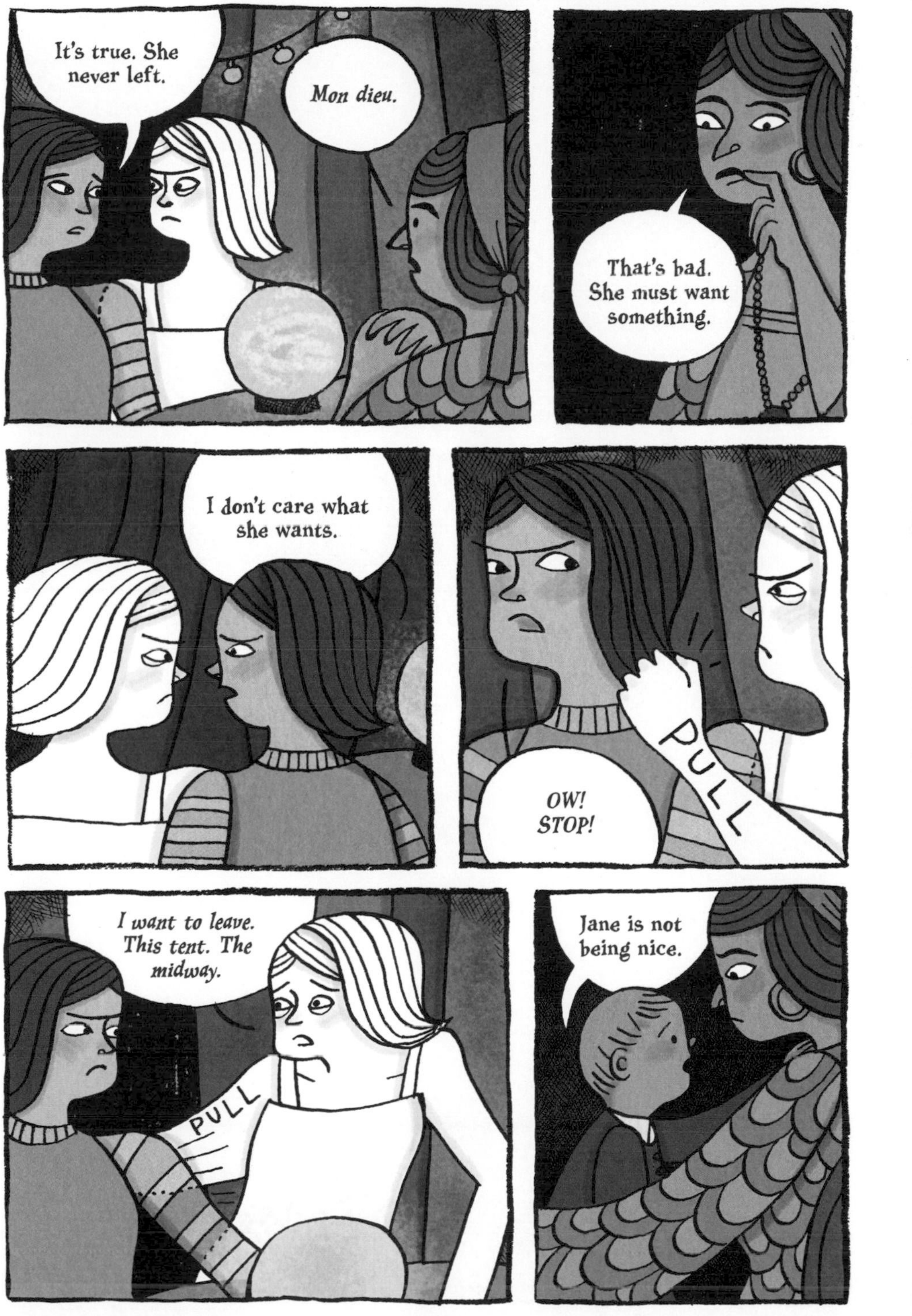
It's true. She never left.
Mon dieu.
That's bad. She must want something.
I don't care what she wants.
PULL
OW! STOP!
I want to leave. This tent. The midway.
PULL
Jane is not being nice.

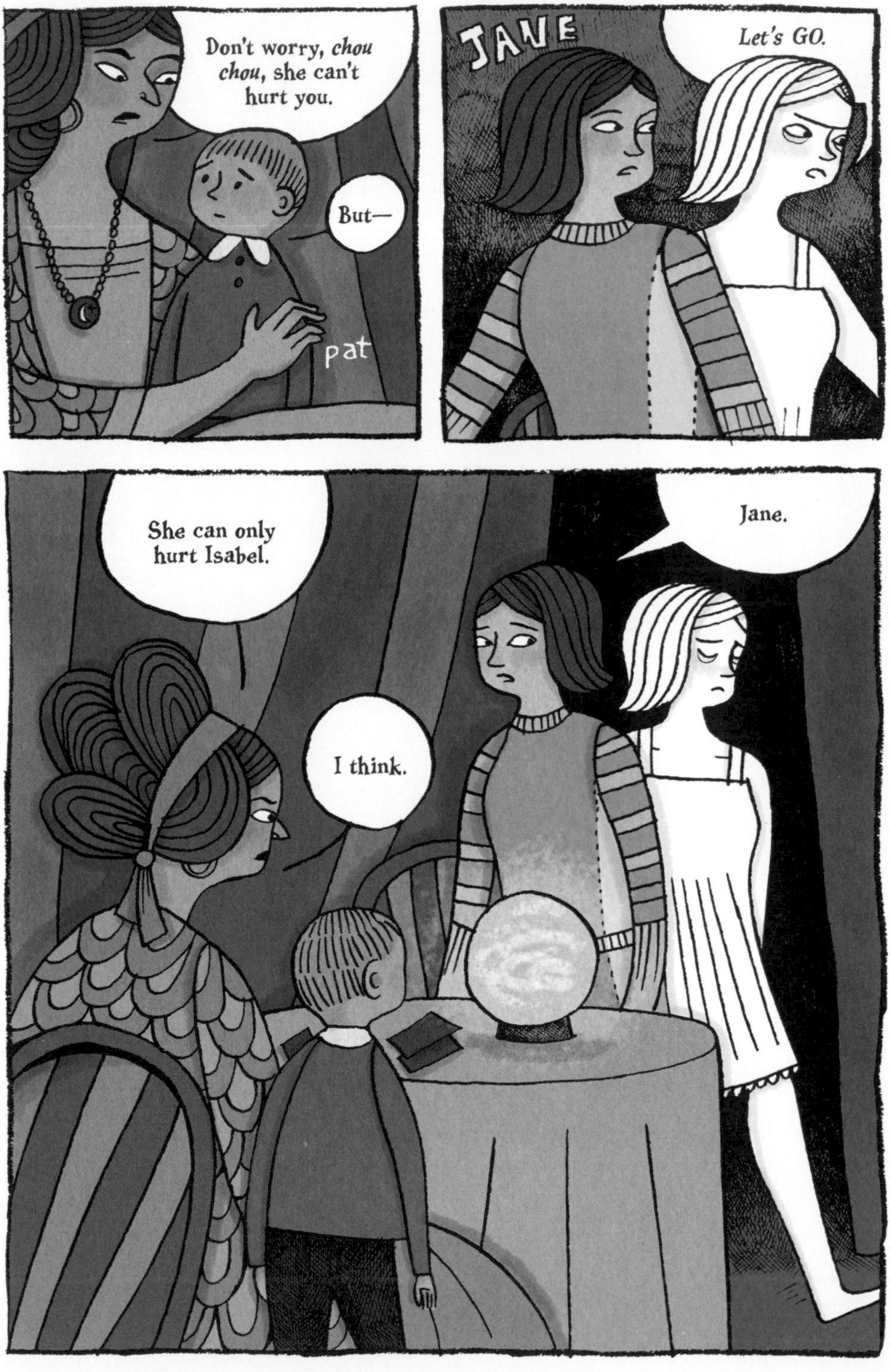
Don't worry, *chou chou*, she can't hurt you.
But—
pat
JANE
Let's GO.
She can only hurt Isabel.
I think.
Jane.

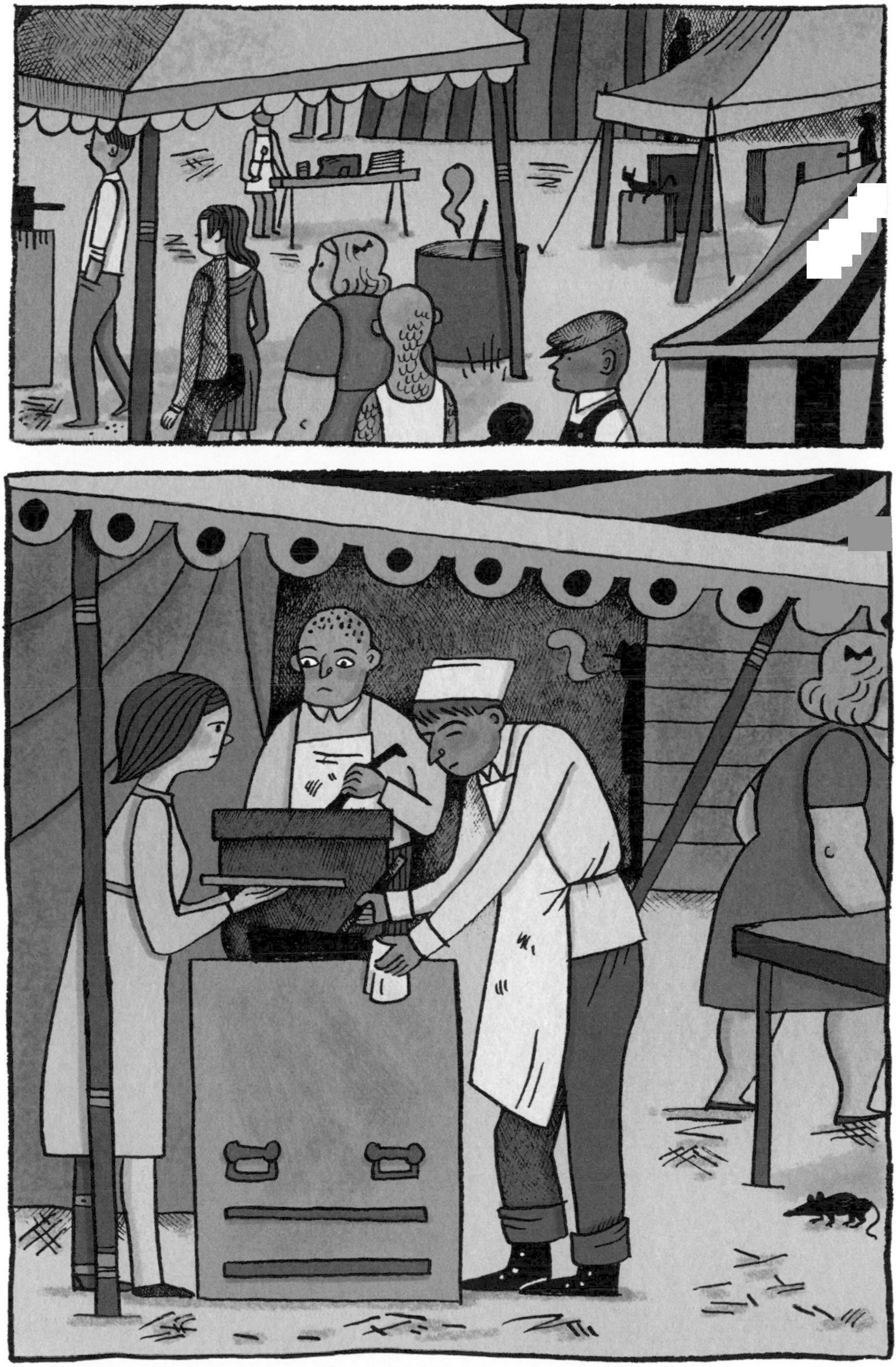

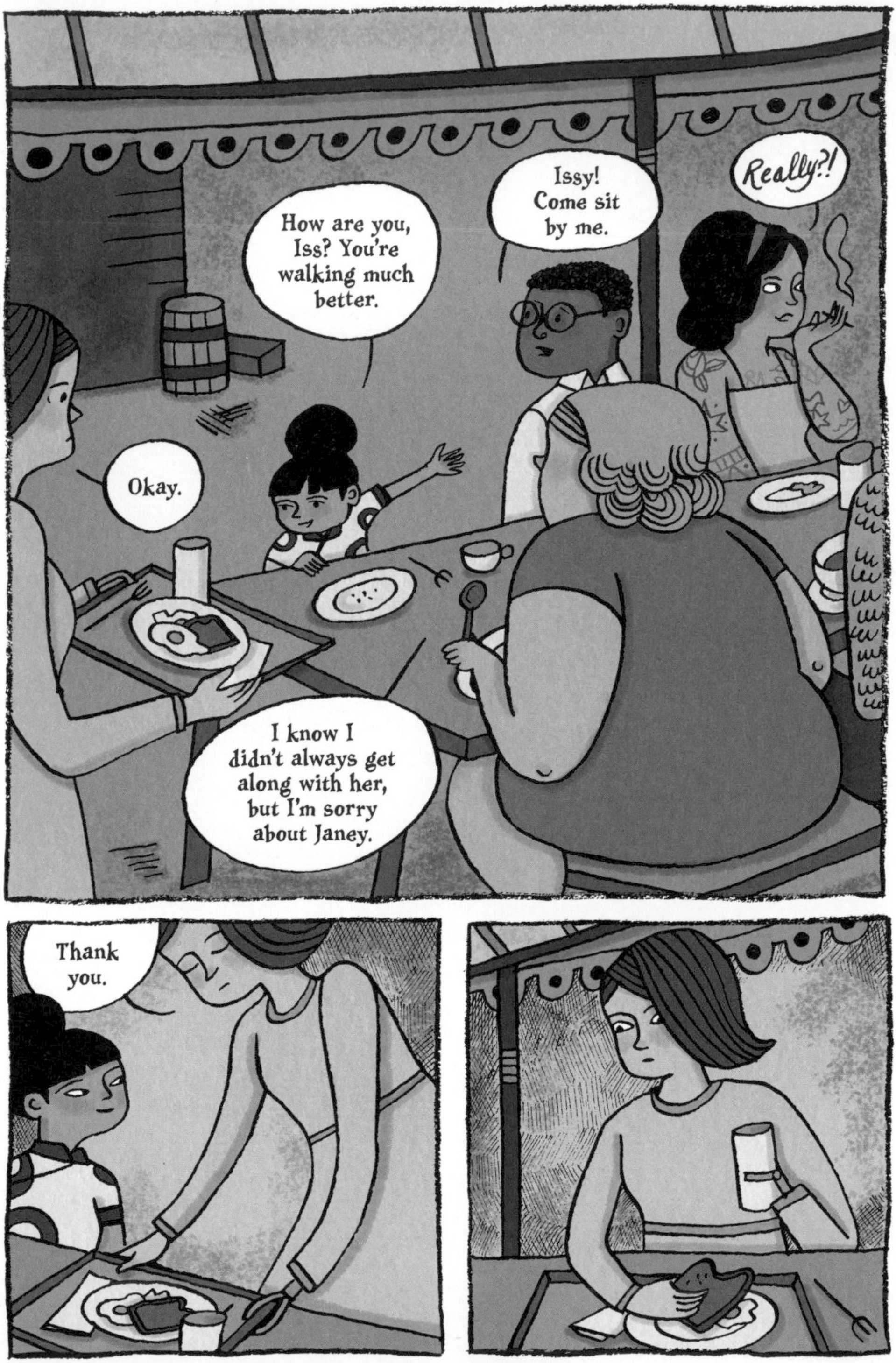
Issy! Come sit by me.
Really?!
How are you, Iss? You're walking much better.
Okay.
I know I didn't always get along with her, but I'm sorry about Janey.
Thank you.

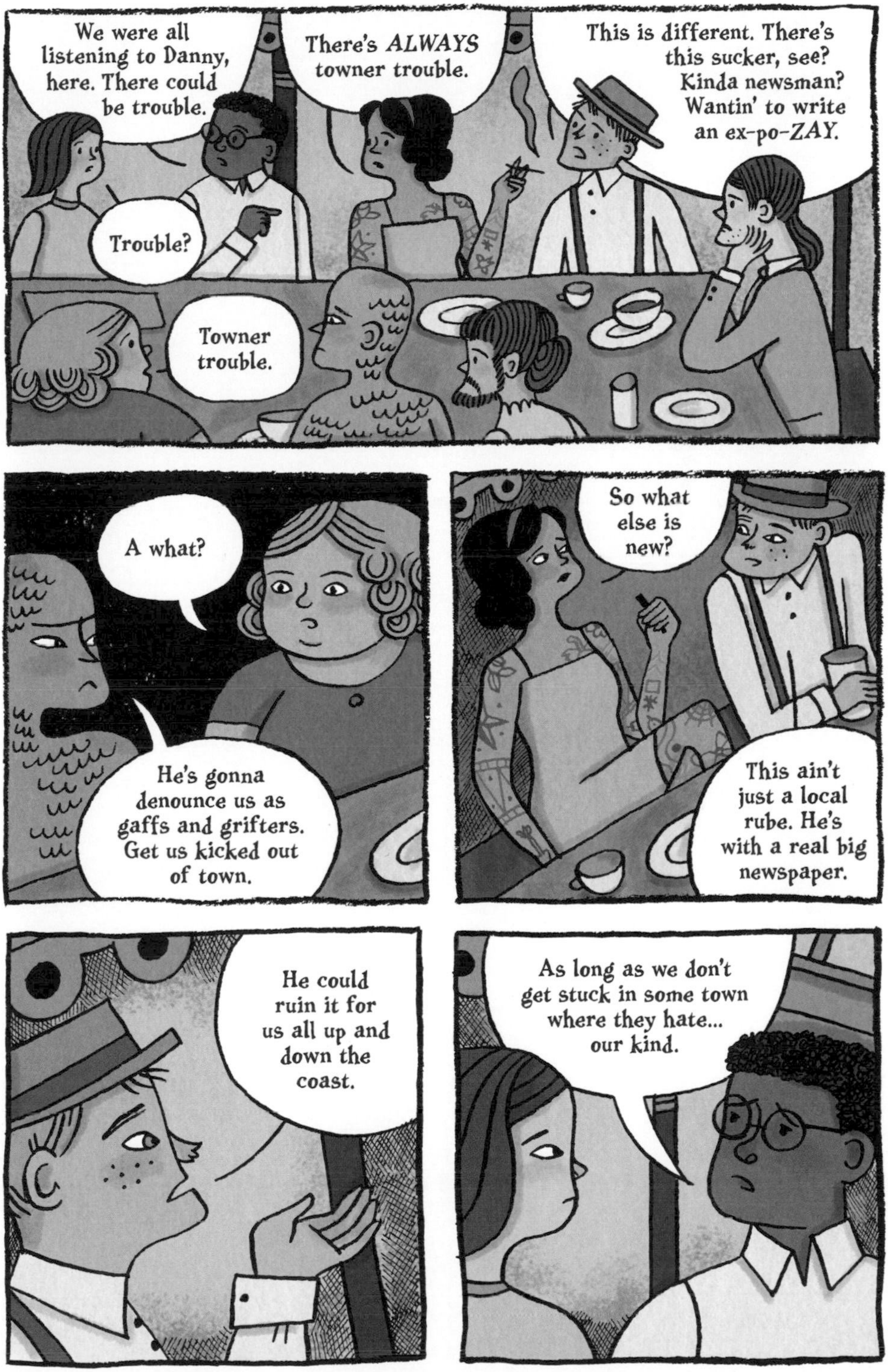

We were all listening to Danny, here. There could be trouble.
Trouble?
There's *ALWAYS* towner trouble.
Towner trouble.
This is different. There's this sucker, see? Kinda newsman? Wantin' to write an ex-po-*ZAY*.
A what?
He's gonna denounce us as gaffs and grifters. Get us kicked out of town.
So what else is new?
This ain't just a local rube. He's with a real big newspaper.
He could ruin it for us all up and down the coast.
As long as we don't get stuck in some town where they hate... our kind.

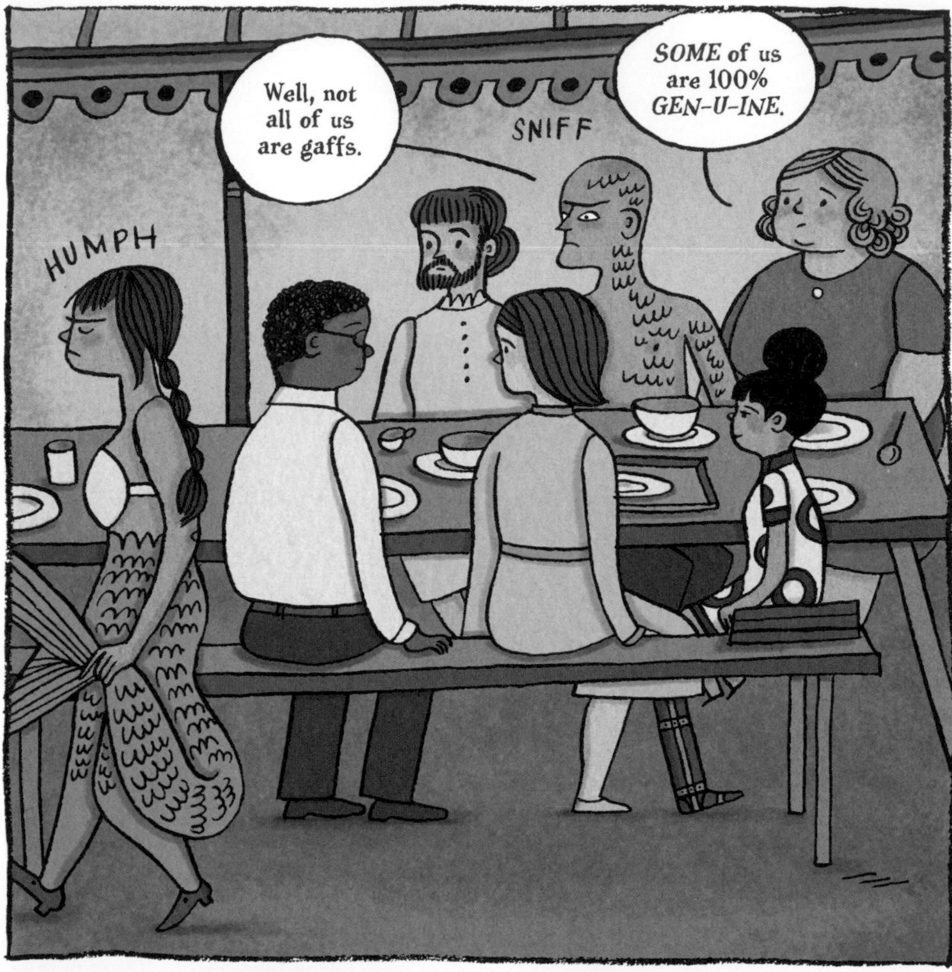
Well, not all of us are gaffs.
SNIFF
SOME of us are 100% GEN-U-INE.
HUMPH

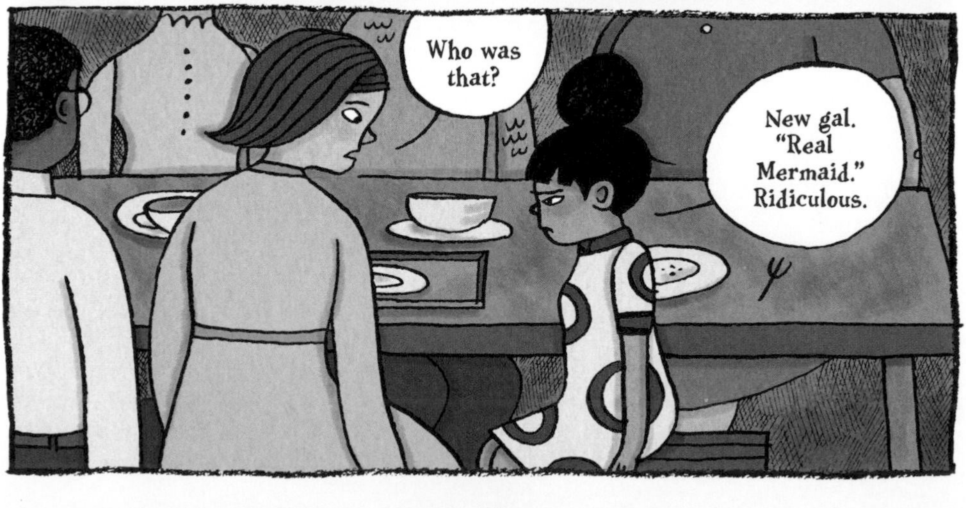
Who was that?
New gal. "Real Mermaid." Ridiculous.

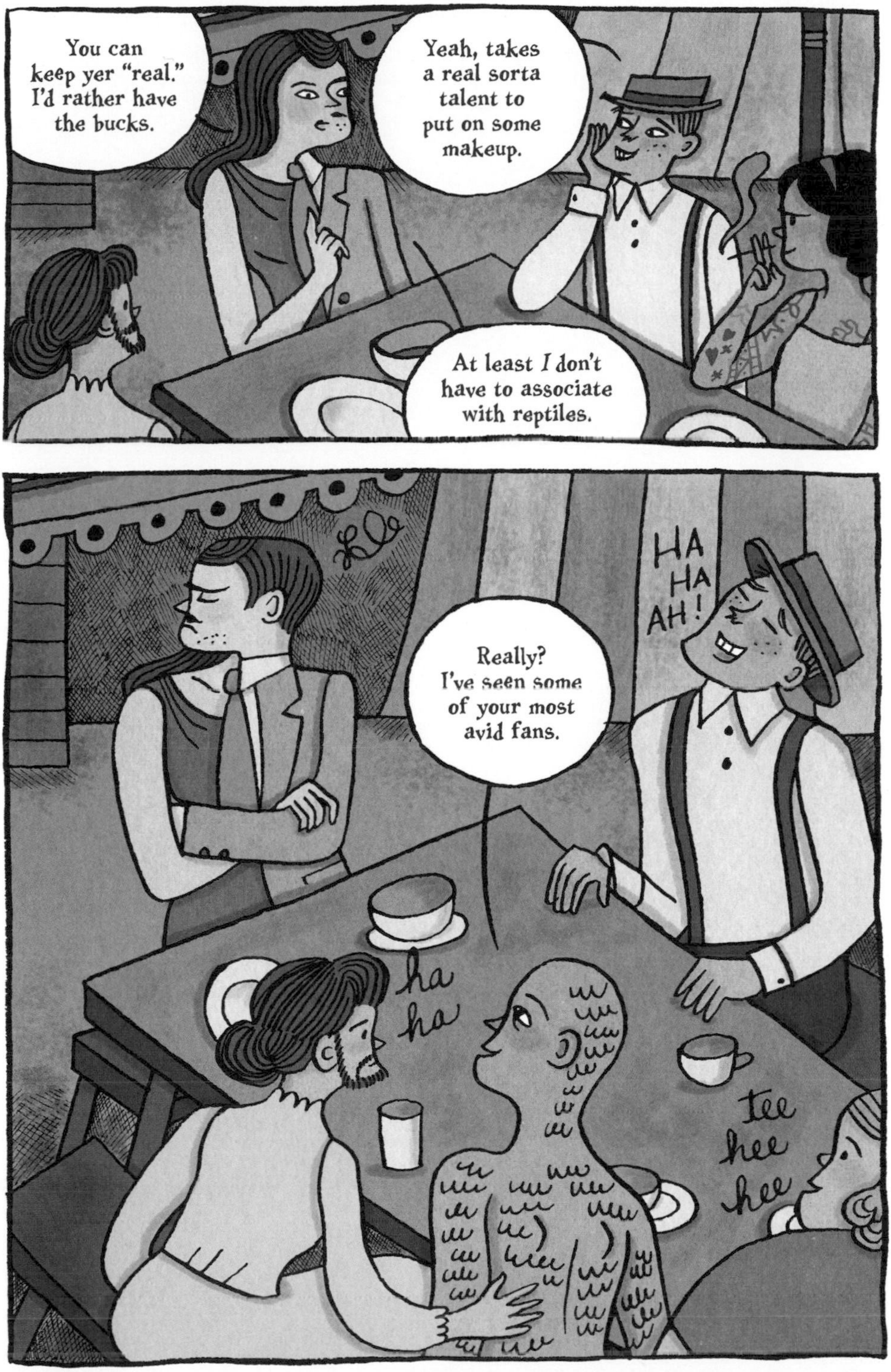
You can keep yer "real." I'd rather have the bucks.
Yeah, takes a real sorta talent to put on some makeup.
At least I don't have to associate with reptiles.
HA HA AH!
Really? I've seen some of your most avid fans.
ha ha
tee hee hee

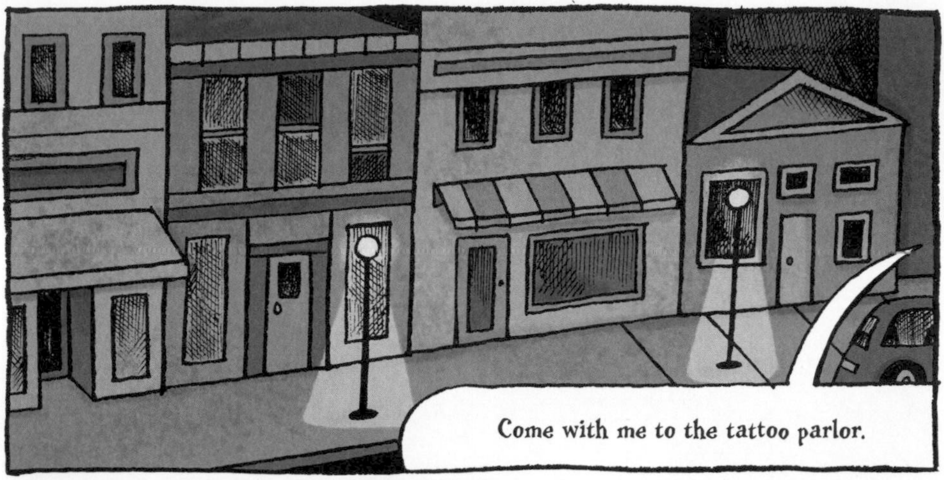
Come with me to the tattoo parlor.

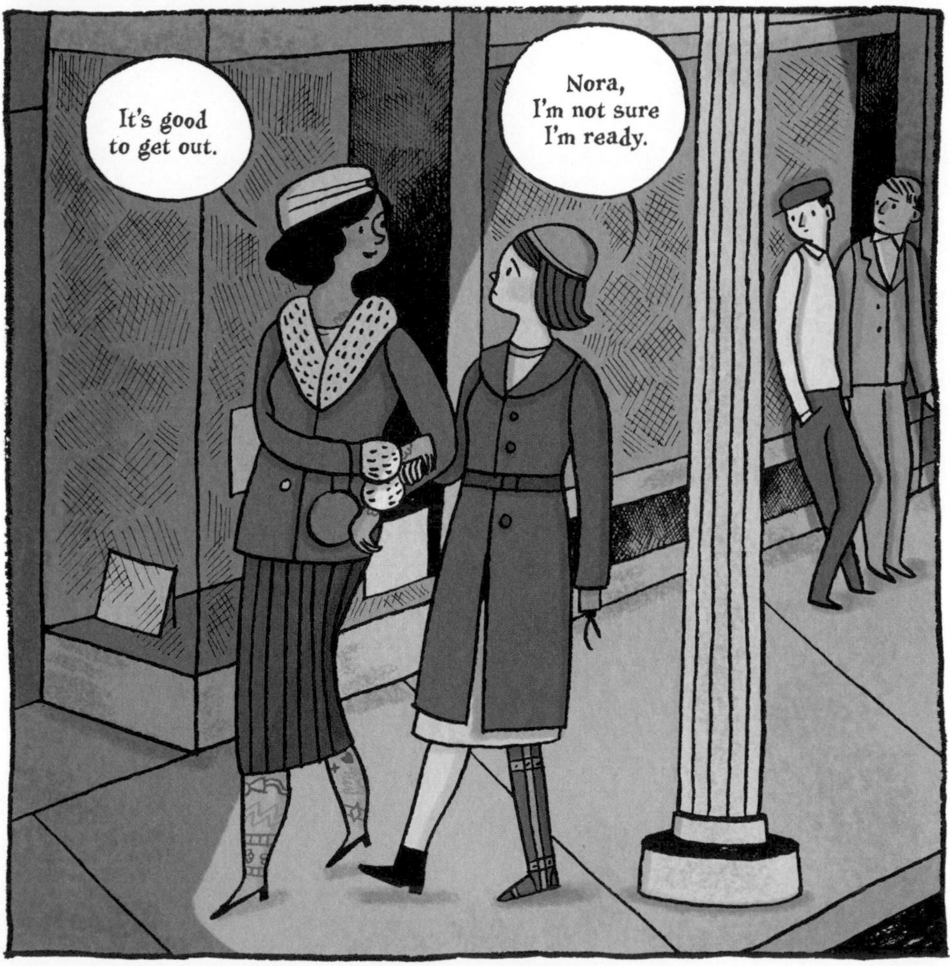
It's good to get out.
Nora, I'm not sure I'm ready.

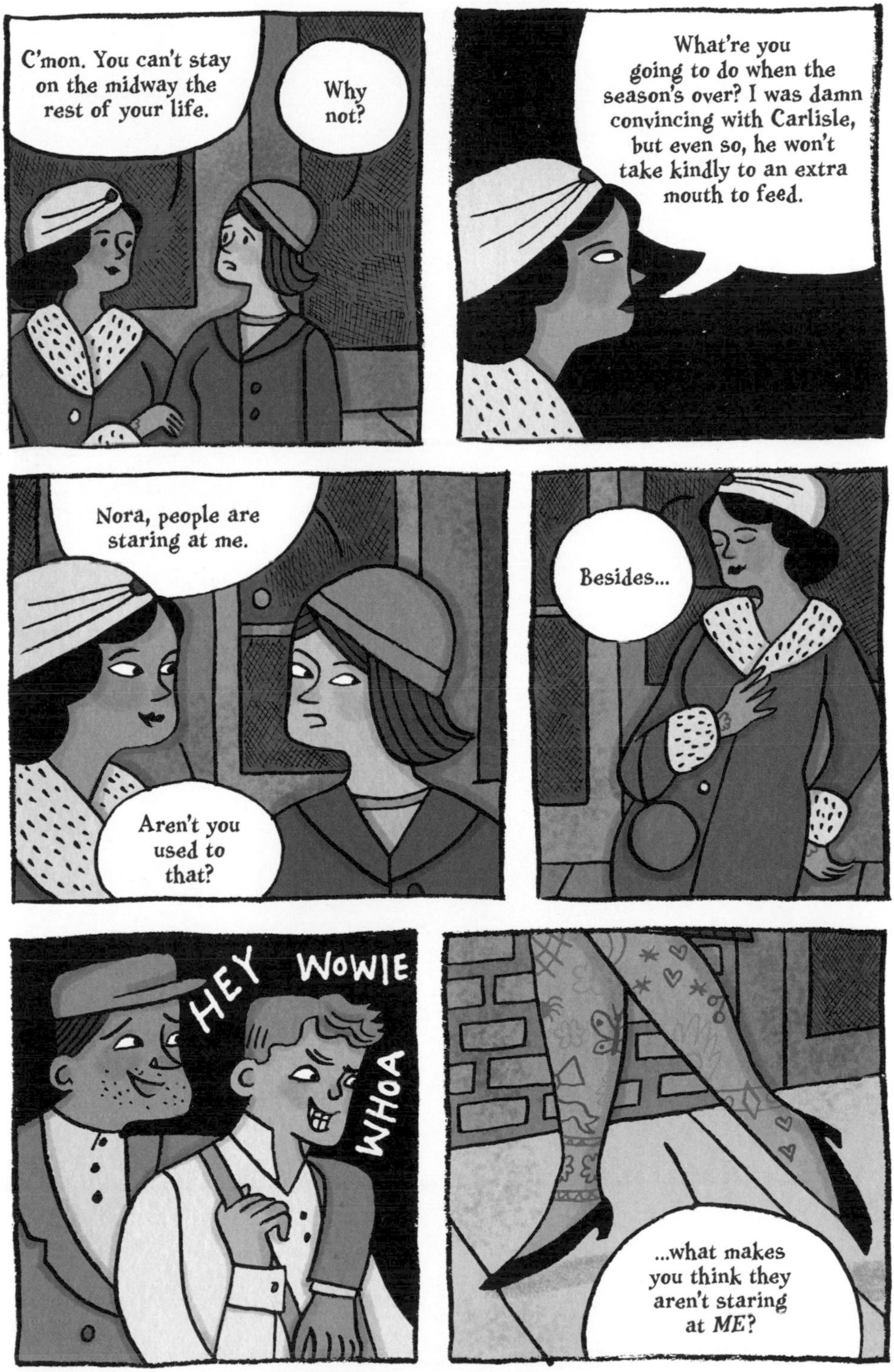
C'mon. You can't stay on the midway the rest of your life.
Why not?
What're you going to do when the season's over? I was damn convincing with Carlisle, but even so, he won't take kindly to an extra mouth to feed.
Nora, people are staring at me.
Aren't you used to that?
Besides...
HEY
WOWIE
WHOA
...what makes you think they aren't staring at *ME*?

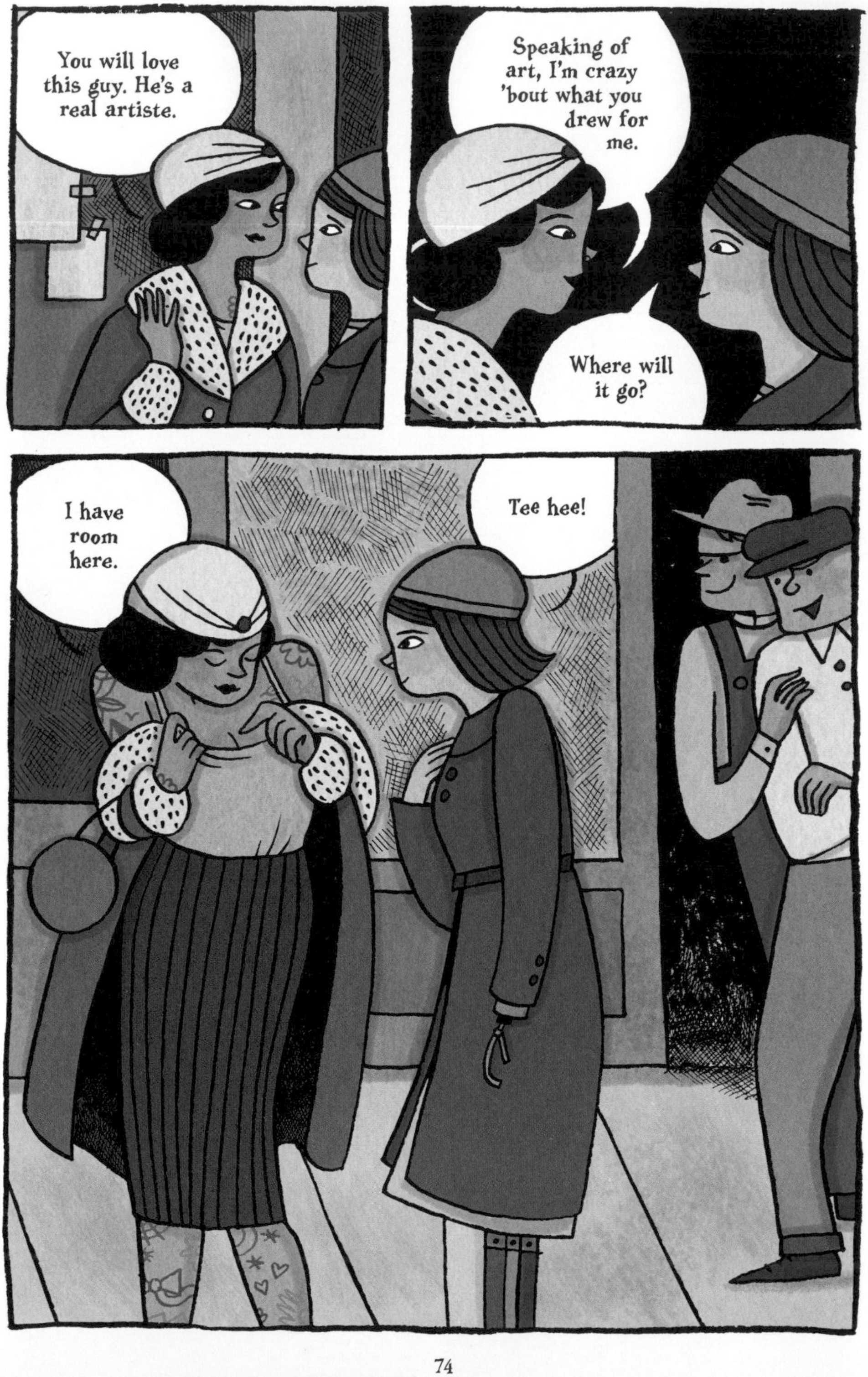
You will love this guy. He's a real artiste.
Speaking of art, I'm crazy 'bout what you drew for me.
Where will it go?
I have room here.
Tee hee!

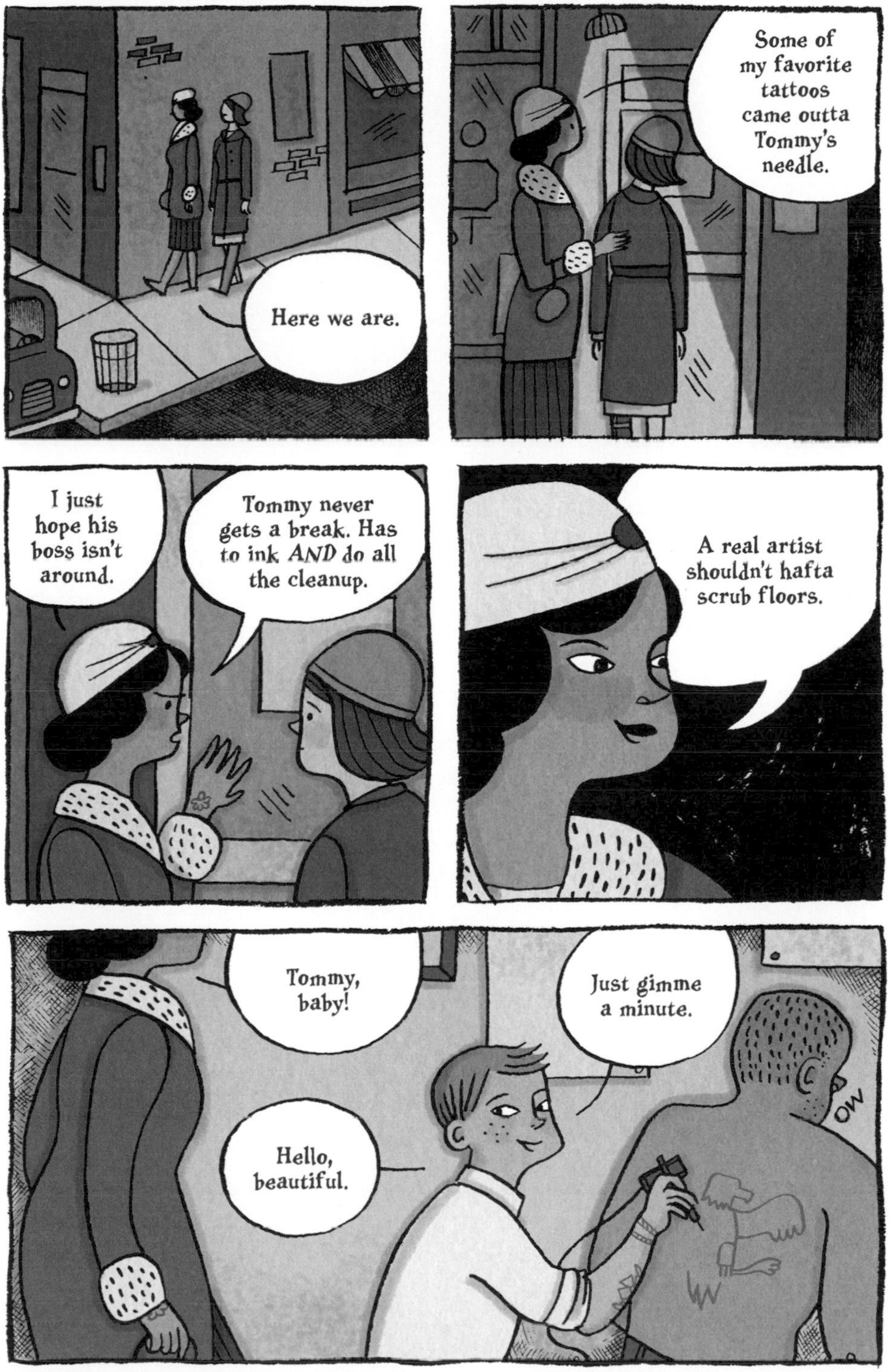
Here we are.
Some of my favorite tattoos came outta Tommy's needle.
I just hope his boss isn't around.
Tommy never gets a break. Has to ink *AND* do all the cleanup.
A real artist shouldn't hafta scrub floors.
Tommy, baby!
Just gimme a minute.
OW
Hello, beautiful.

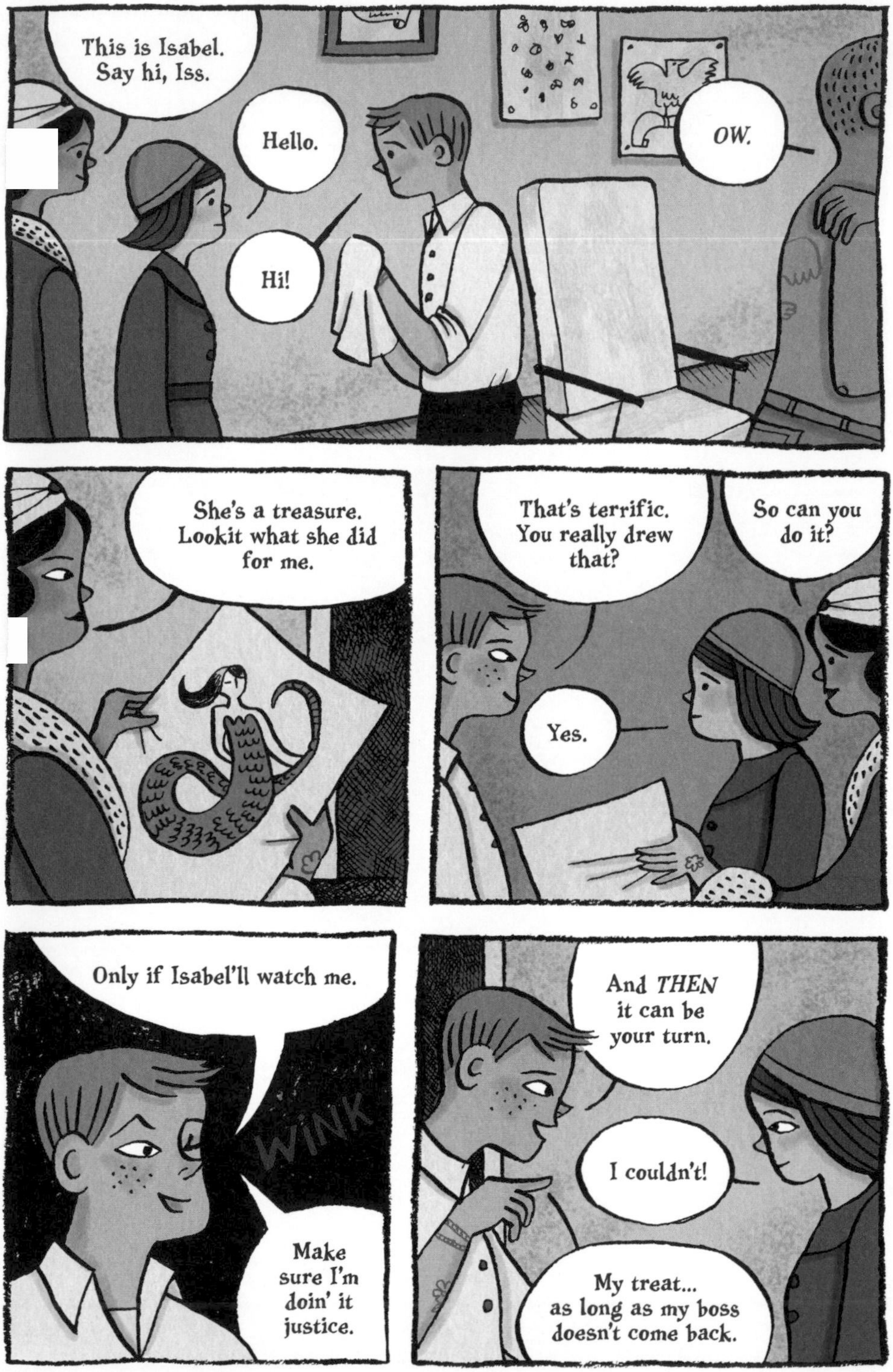
This is Isabel. Say hi, Iss.
Hello.
Hi!
OW.
She's a treasure. Lookit what she did for me.
That's terrific. You really drew that?
So can you do it?
Yes.
Only if Isabel'll watch me.
WINK
Make sure I'm doin' it justice.
And *THEN* it can be your turn.
I couldn't!
My treat... as long as my boss doesn't come back.

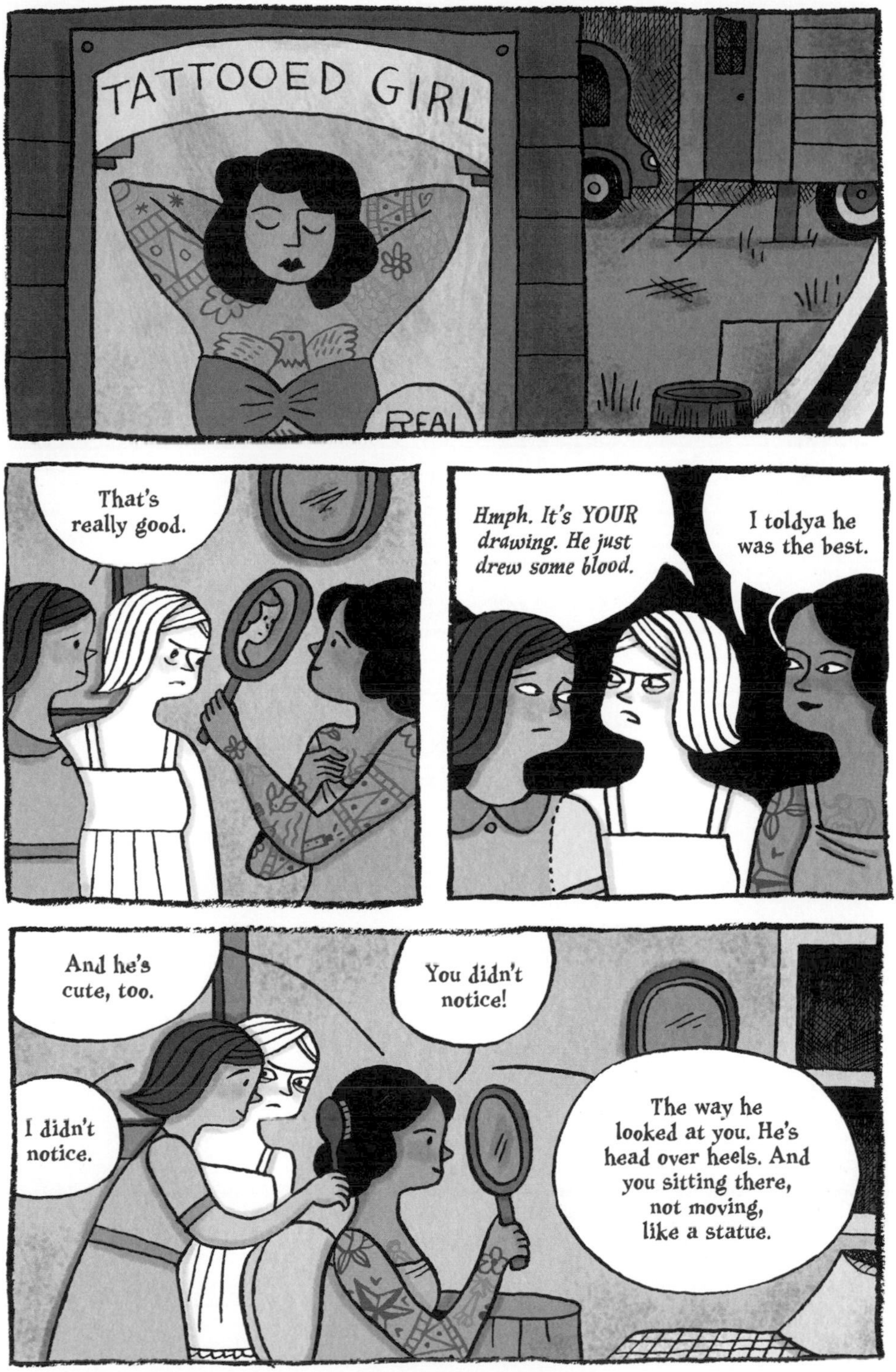
TATTOOED GIRL
REAL
That's really good.
Hmph. It's YOUR drawing. He just drew some blood.
I toldya he was the best.
And he's cute, too.
I didn't notice.
You didn't notice!
The way he looked at you. He's head over heels. And you sitting there, not moving, like a statue.

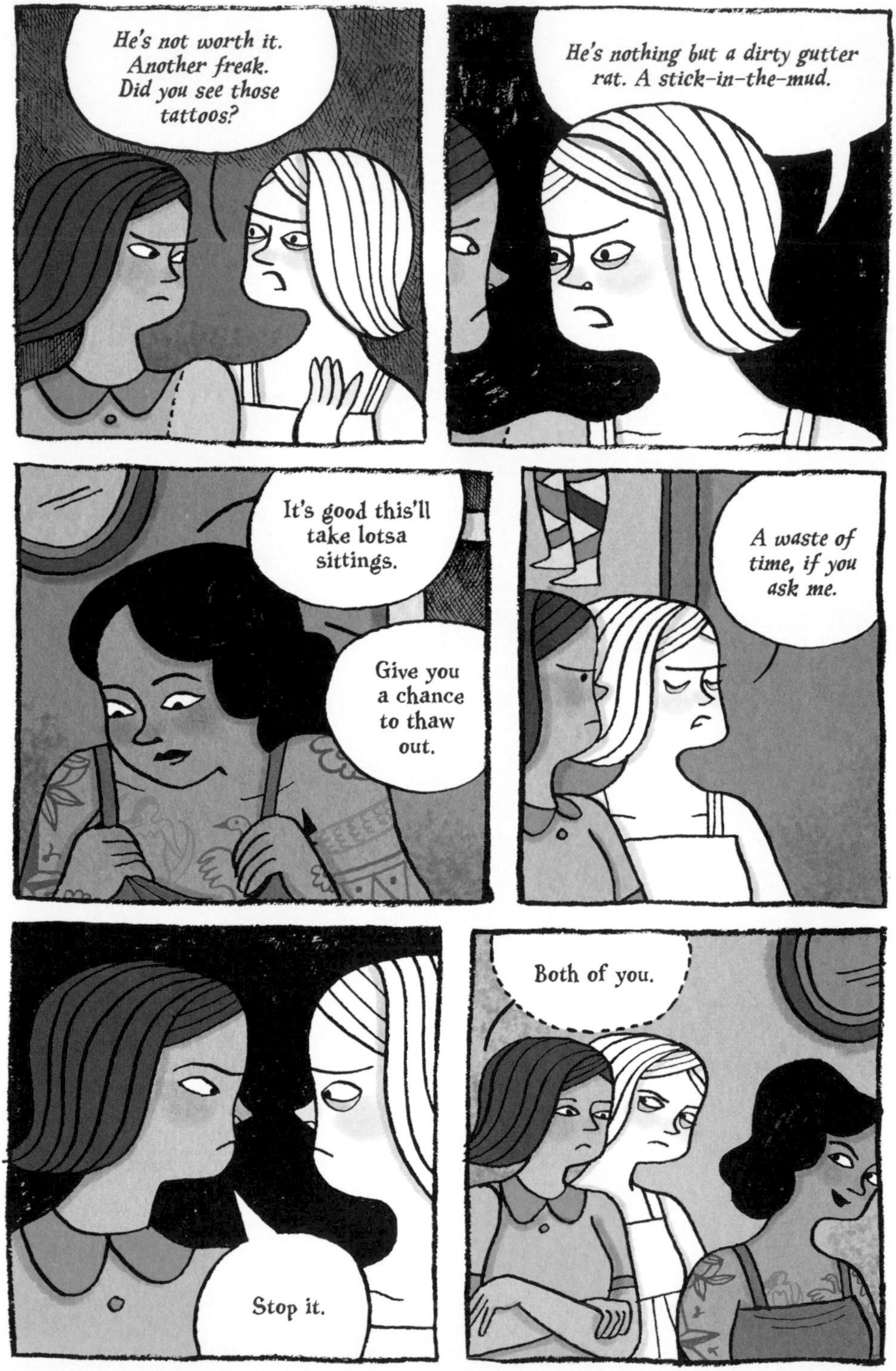
He's not worth it. Another freak. Did you see those tattoos?
He's nothing but a dirty gutter rat. A stick-in-the-mud.
It's good this'll take lotsa sittings.
Give you a chance to thaw out.
A waste of time, if you ask me.
Stop it.
Both of you.

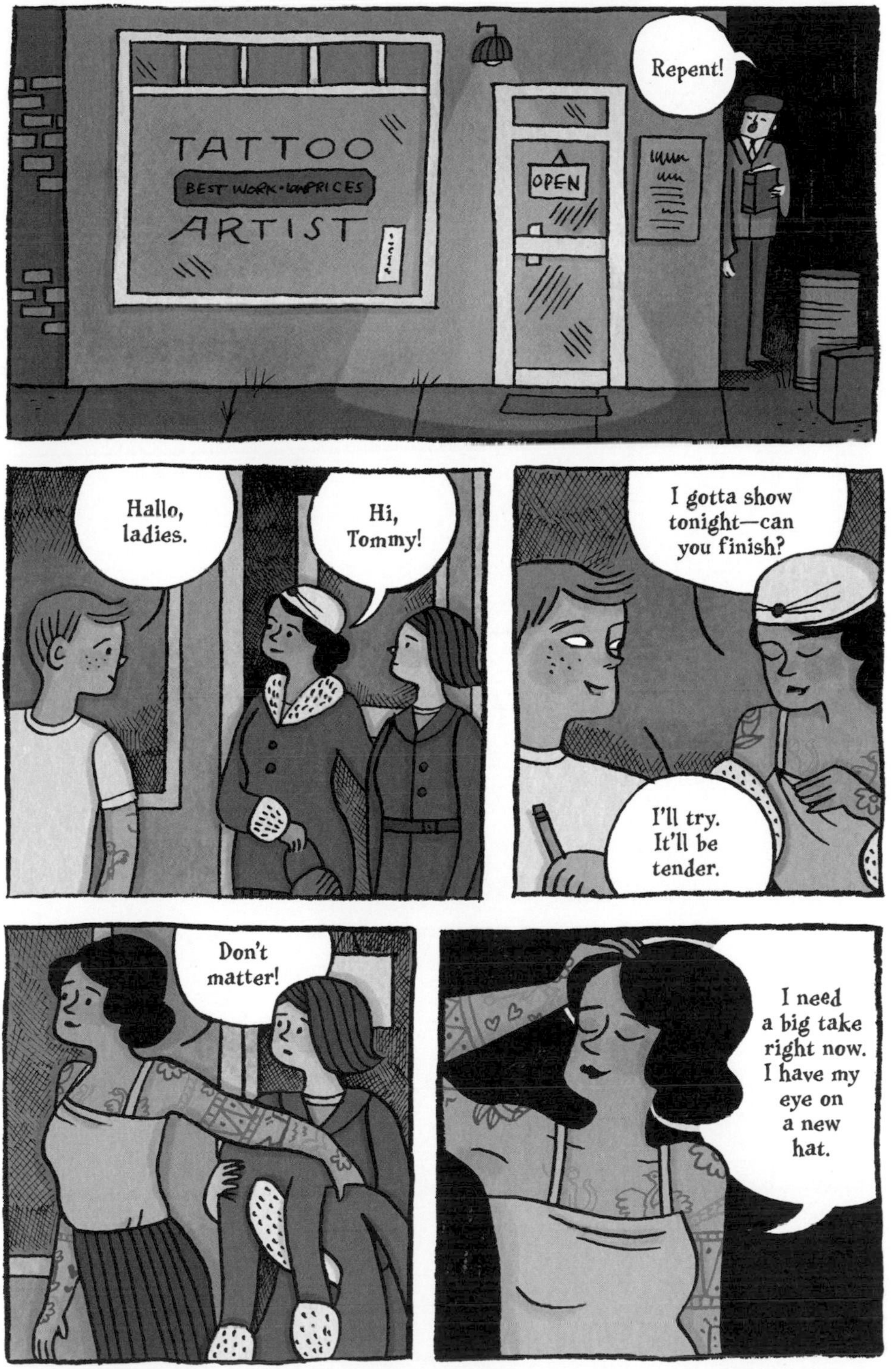
TATTOO
BEST WORK • LOW PRICES
ARTIST
OPEN
Repent!
Hallo, ladies.
Hi, Tommy!
I gotta show tonight—can you finish?
I'll try. It'll be tender.
Don't matter!
I need a big take right now. I have my eye on a new hat.

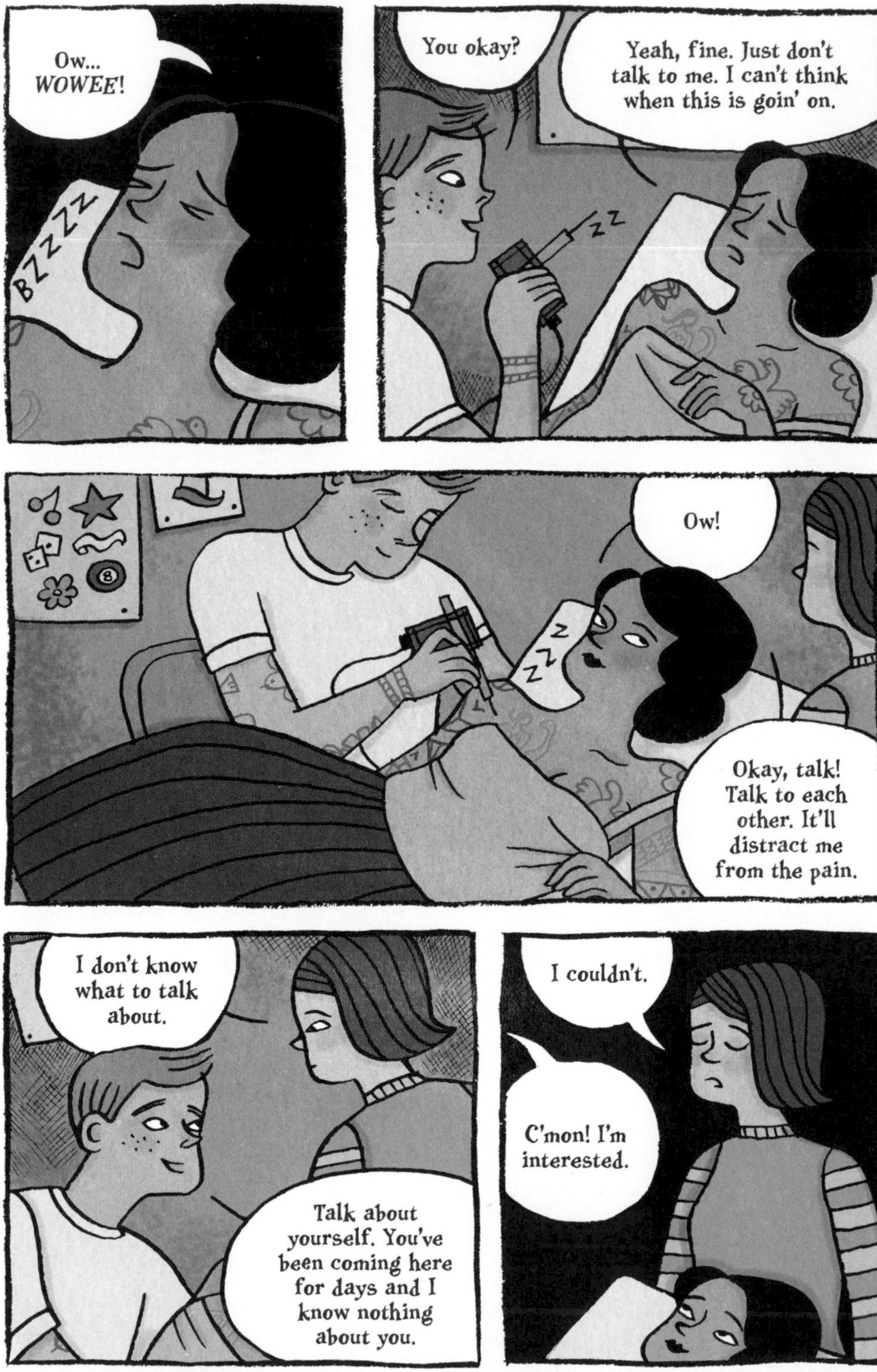
Ow...
WOWEE!
BZZZZ
You okay?
ZZZ
Yeah, fine. Just don't talk to me. I can't think when this is goin' on.
Ow!
ZZZ
Okay, talk! Talk to each other. It'll distract me from the pain.
I don't know what to talk about.
Talk about yourself. You've been coming here for days and I know nothing about you.
I couldn't.
C'mon! I'm interested.

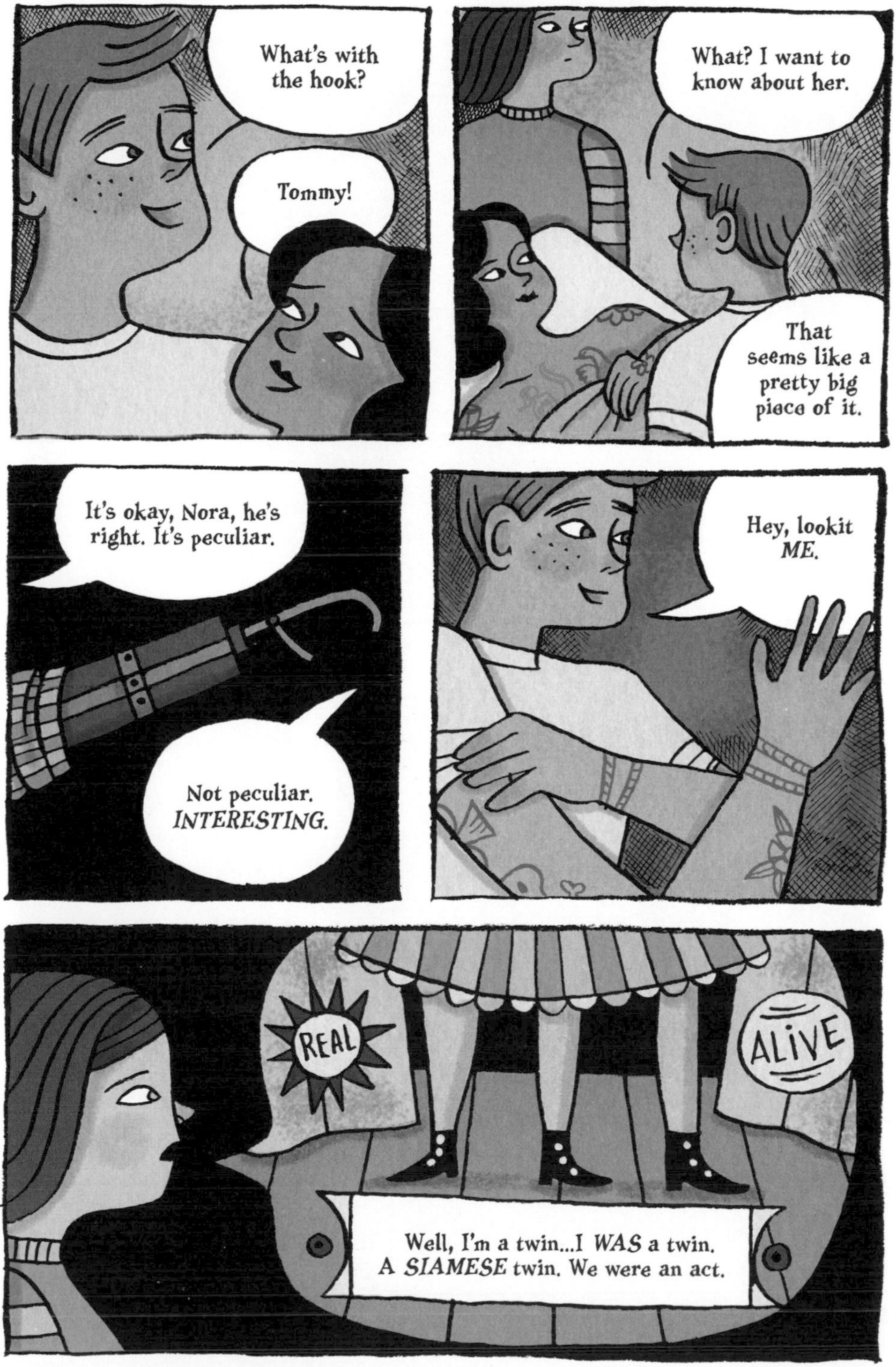
What's with the hook?
Tommy!
What? I want to know about her.
That seems like a pretty big piece of it.
It's okay, Nora, he's right. It's peculiar.
Not peculiar. INTERESTING.
Hey, lookit ME.
REAL
ALIVE
Well, I'm a twin...I WAS a twin. A SIAMESE twin. We were an act.

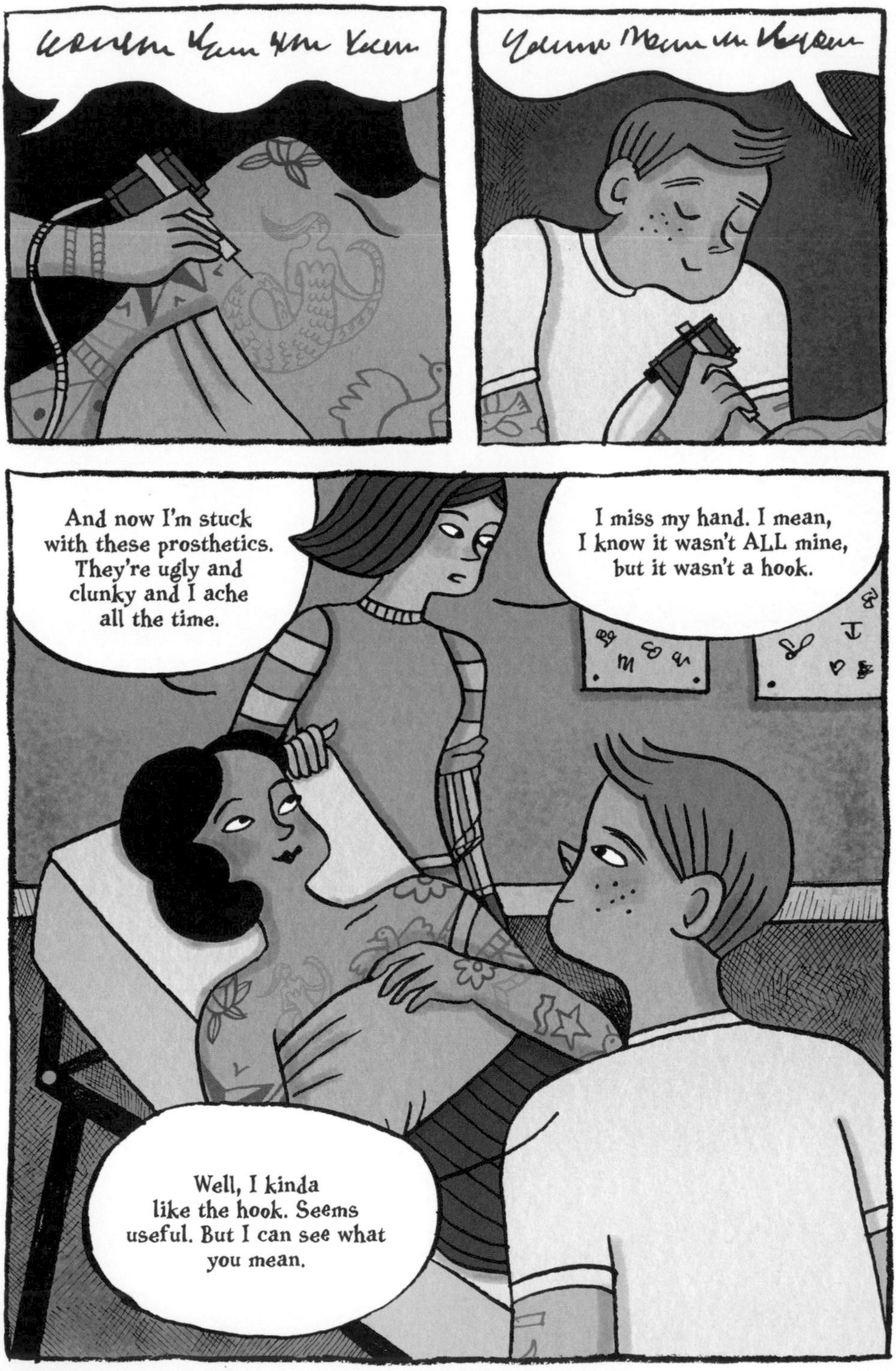
And now I'm stuck with these prosthetics. They're ugly and clunky and I ache all the time.
I miss my hand. I mean, I know it wasn't ALL mine, but it wasn't a hook.
Well, I kinda like the hook. Seems useful. But I can see what you mean.

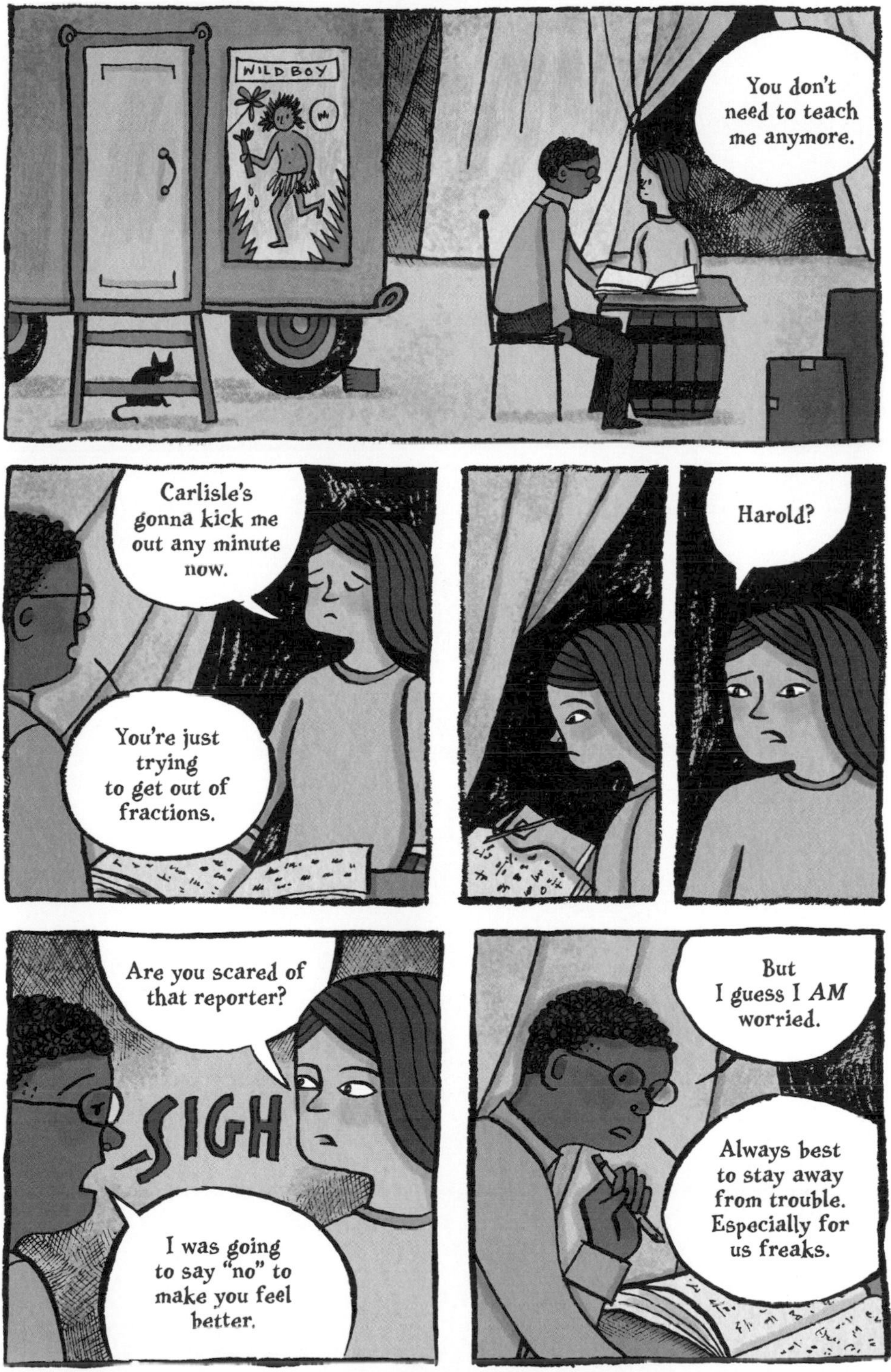
WILD BOY
You don't need to teach me anymore.
Carlisle's gonna kick me out any minute now.
You're just trying to get out of fractions.
Harold?
Are you scared of that reporter?
SIGH
I was going to say "no" to make you feel better.
But I guess I *AM* worried.
Always best to stay away from trouble. Especially for us freaks.

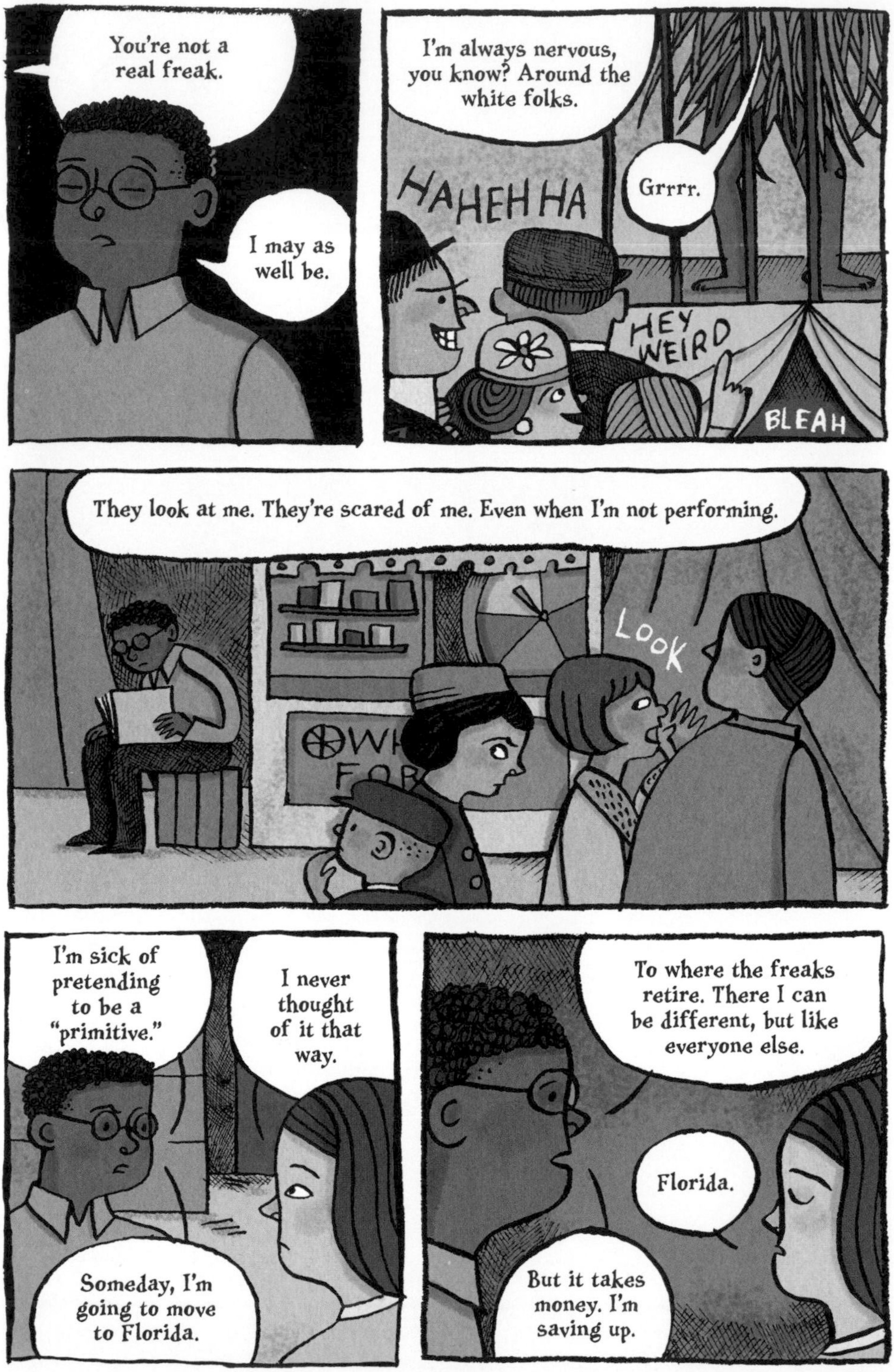
You're not a real freak.
I may as well be.
I'm always nervous, you know? Around the white folks.
HAHEHHA
Grrrr.
HEY WEIRD
BLEAH
They look at me. They're scared of me. Even when I'm not performing.
LOOK
I'm sick of pretending to be a "primitive."
I never thought of it that way.
Someday, I'm going to move to Florida.
To where the freaks retire. There I can be different, but like everyone else.
Florida.
But it takes money. I'm saving up.

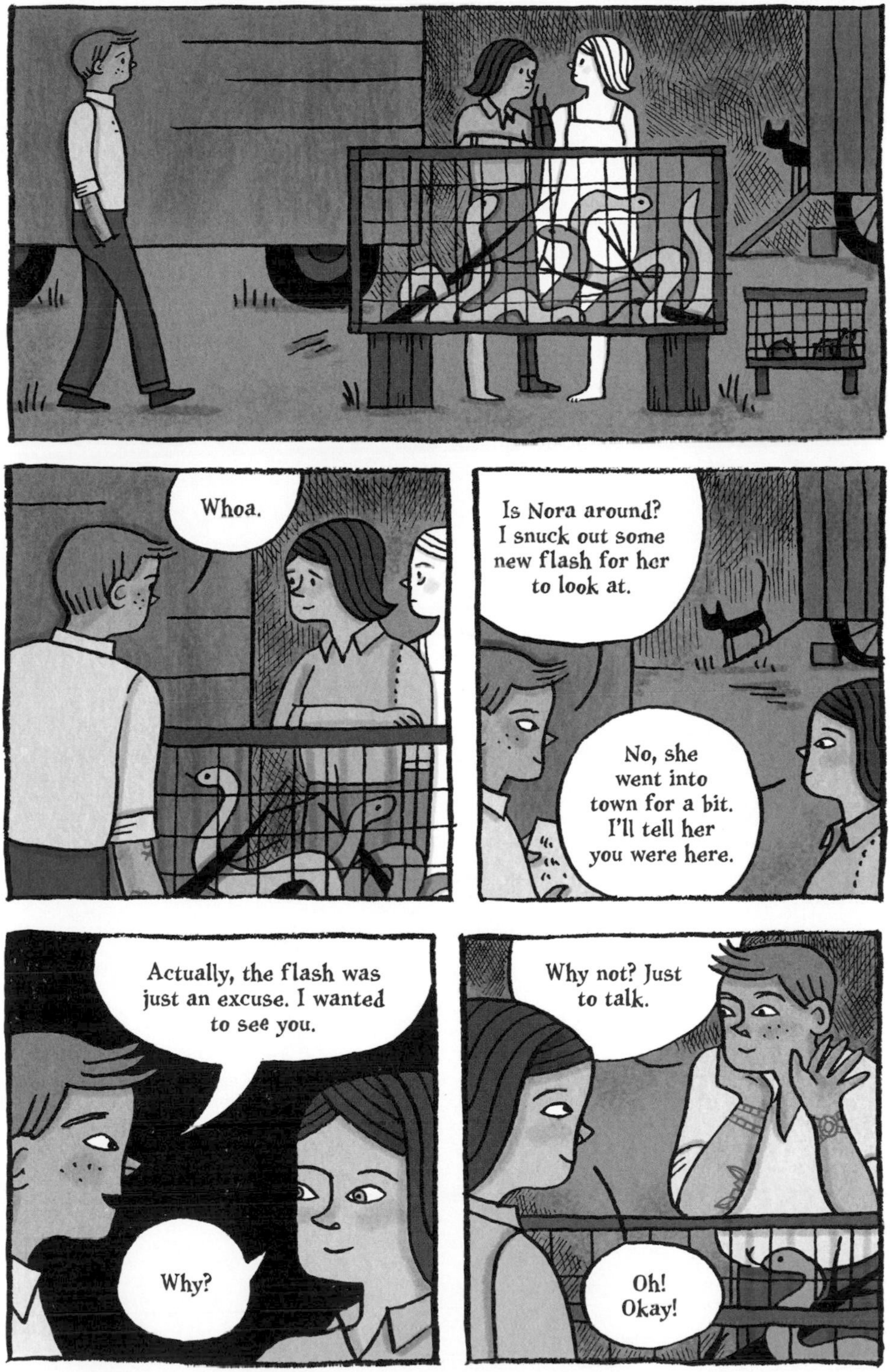
Whoa.
Is Nora around? I snuck out some new flash for her to look at.
No, she went into town for a bit. I'll tell her you were here.
Actually, the flash was just an excuse. I wanted to see you.
Why?
Why not? Just to talk.
Oh! Okay!

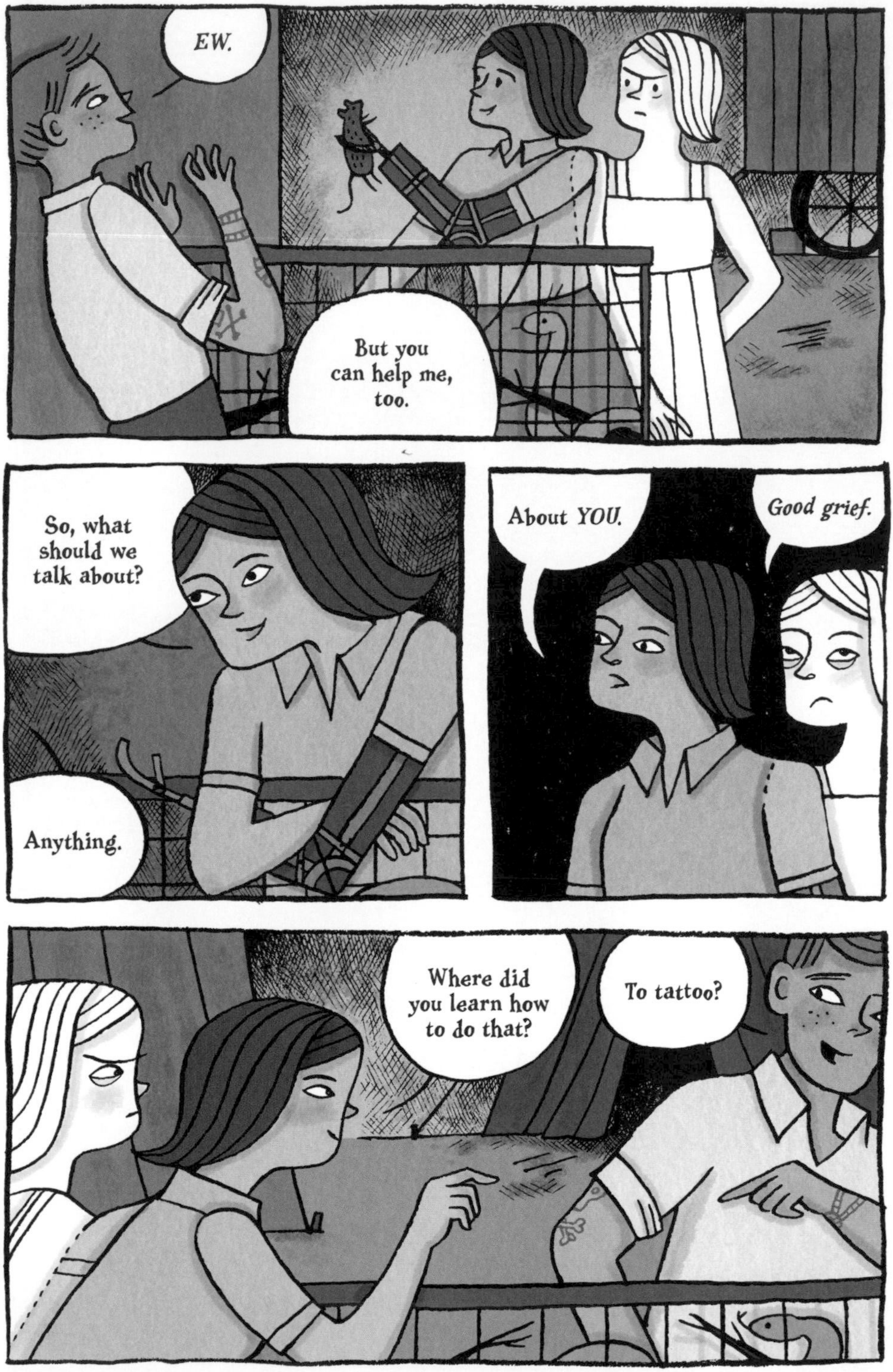
EW.
But you can help me, too.
So, what should we talk about?
Anything.
About YOU.
Good grief.
Where did you learn how to do that?
To tattoo?

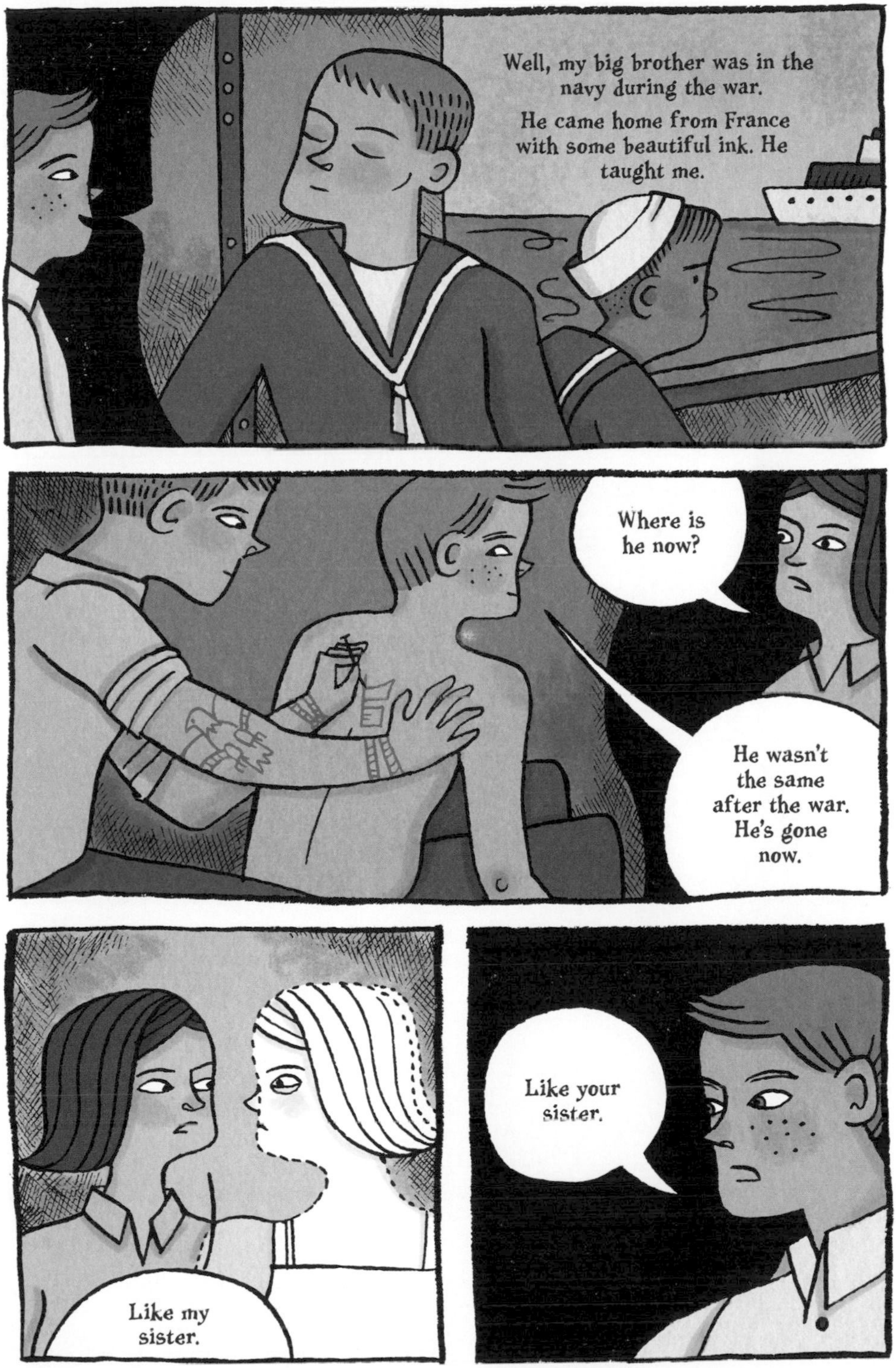
Well, my big brother was in the navy during the war.
He came home from France with some beautiful ink. He taught me.
Where is he now?
He wasn't the same after the war. He's gone now.
Like my sister.
Like your sister.

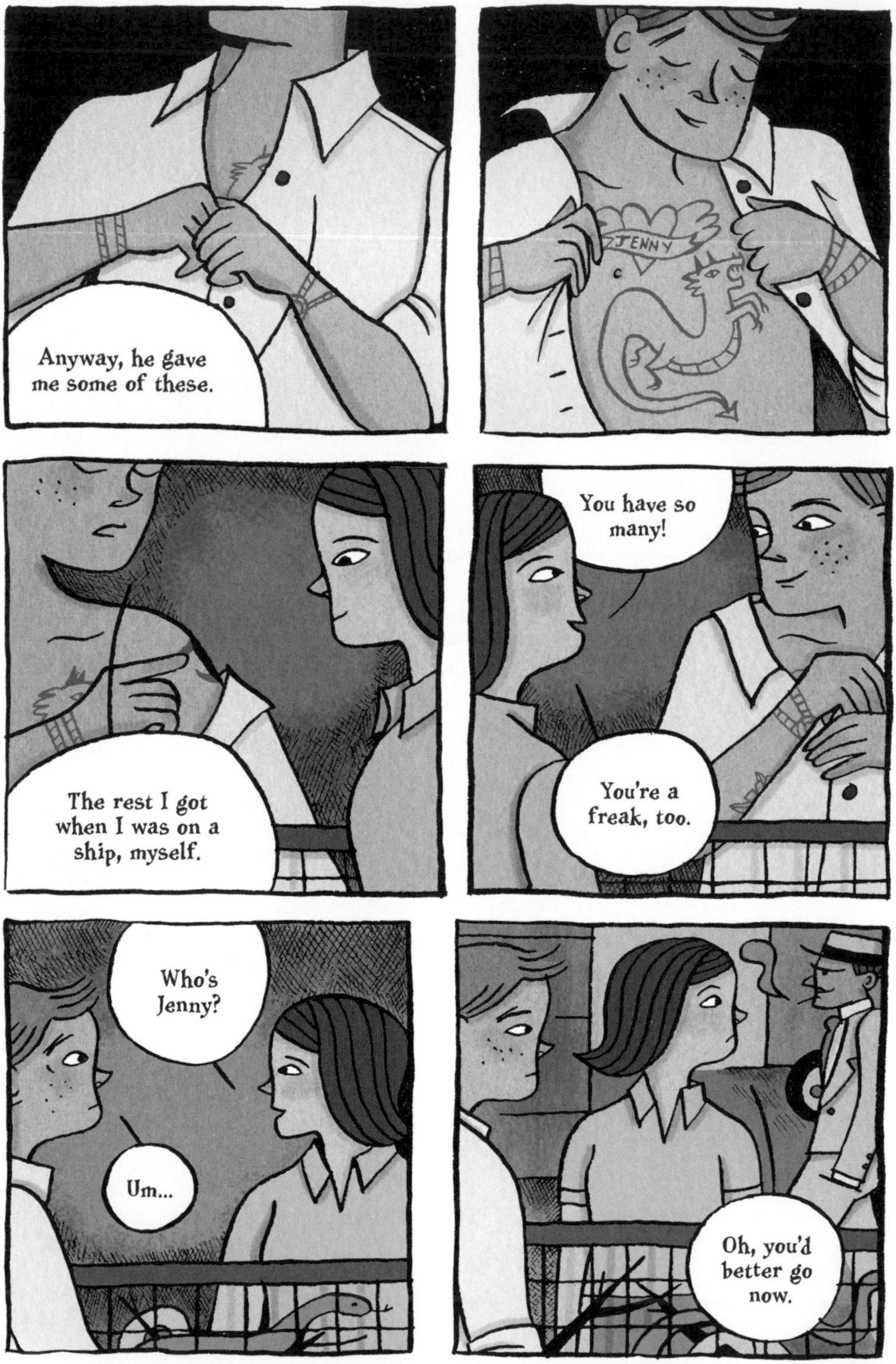
Anyway, he gave me some of these.
JENNY
The rest I got when I was on a ship, myself.
You have so many!
You're a freak, too.
Who's Jenny?
Um...
Oh, you'd better go now.

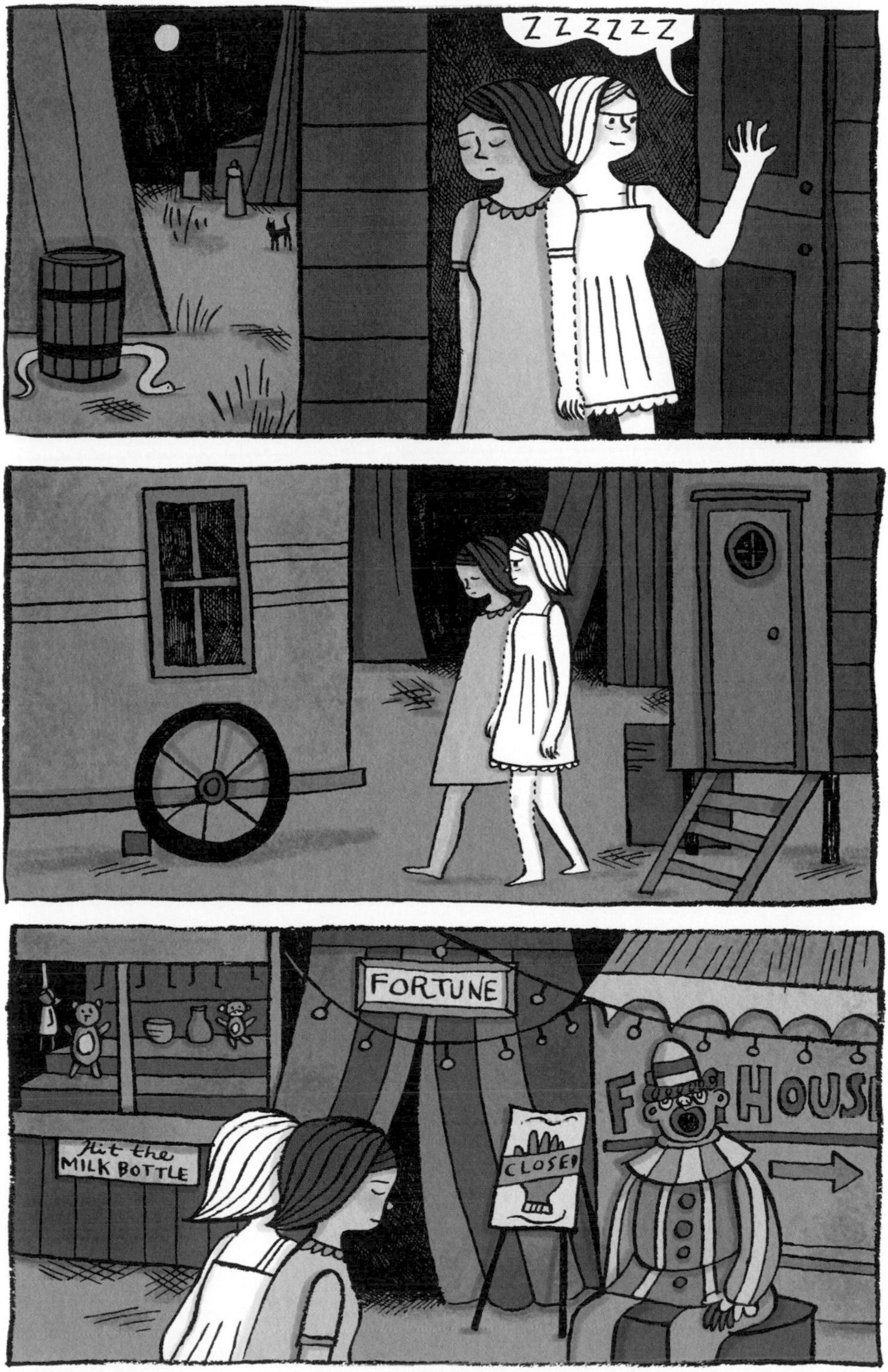
ZZZZZZ
FORTUNE
Hit the MILK BOTTLE
CLOSED

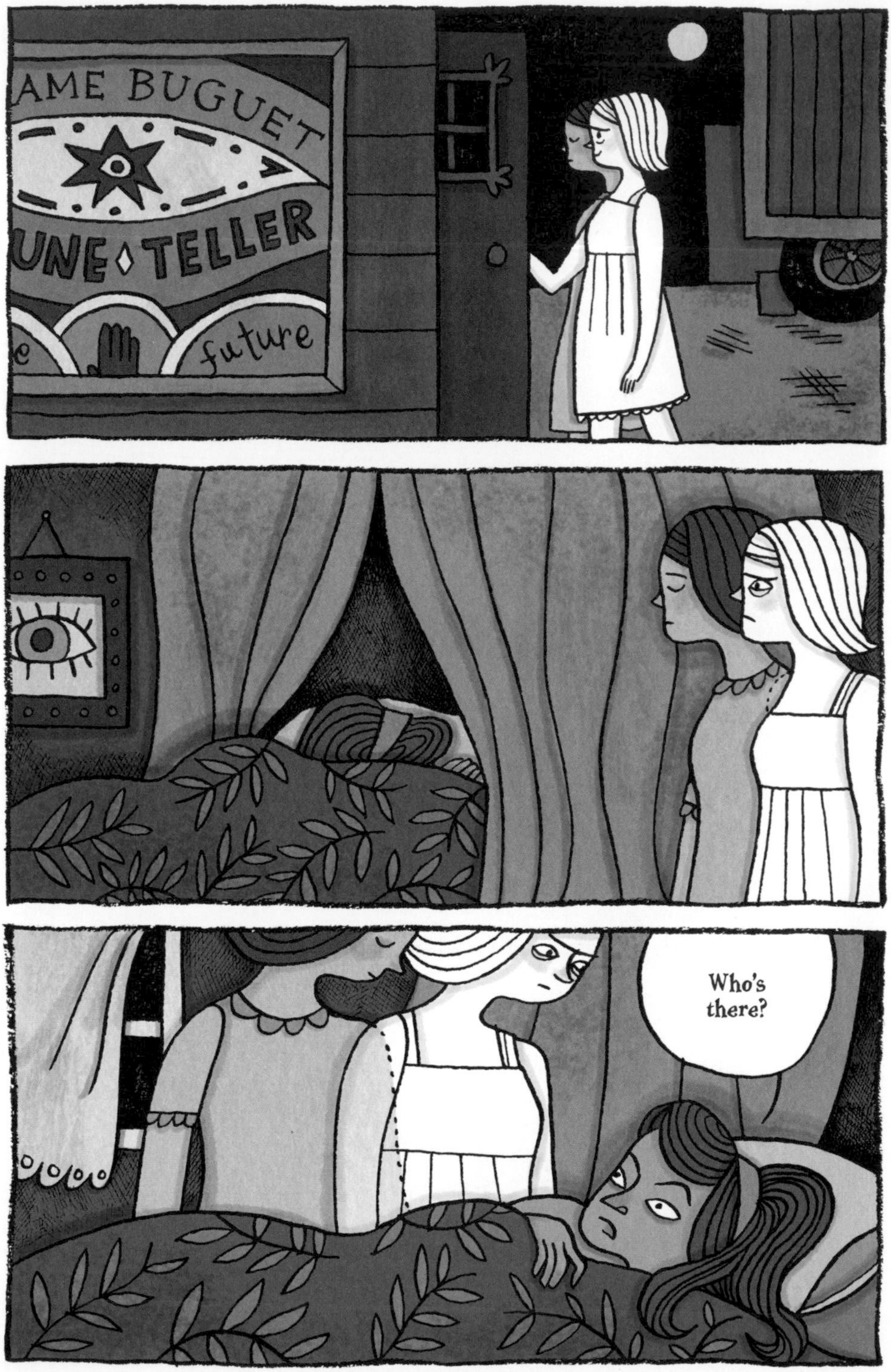
AME BUGUET
UNE TELLER
future
Who's there?

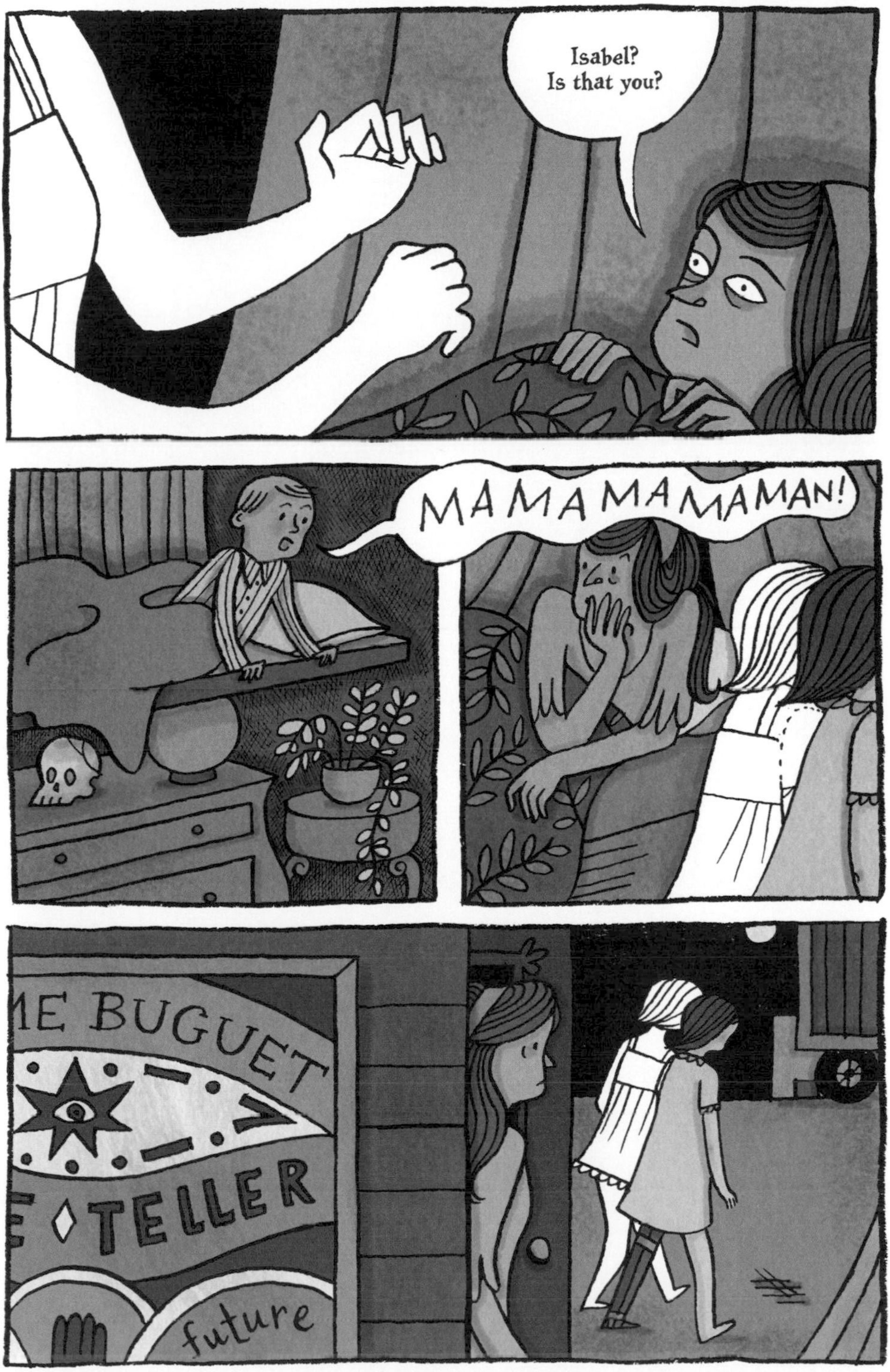
Isabel?
Is that you?
MAMAMAMAMAN!
ME BUGUET
E TELLER
future

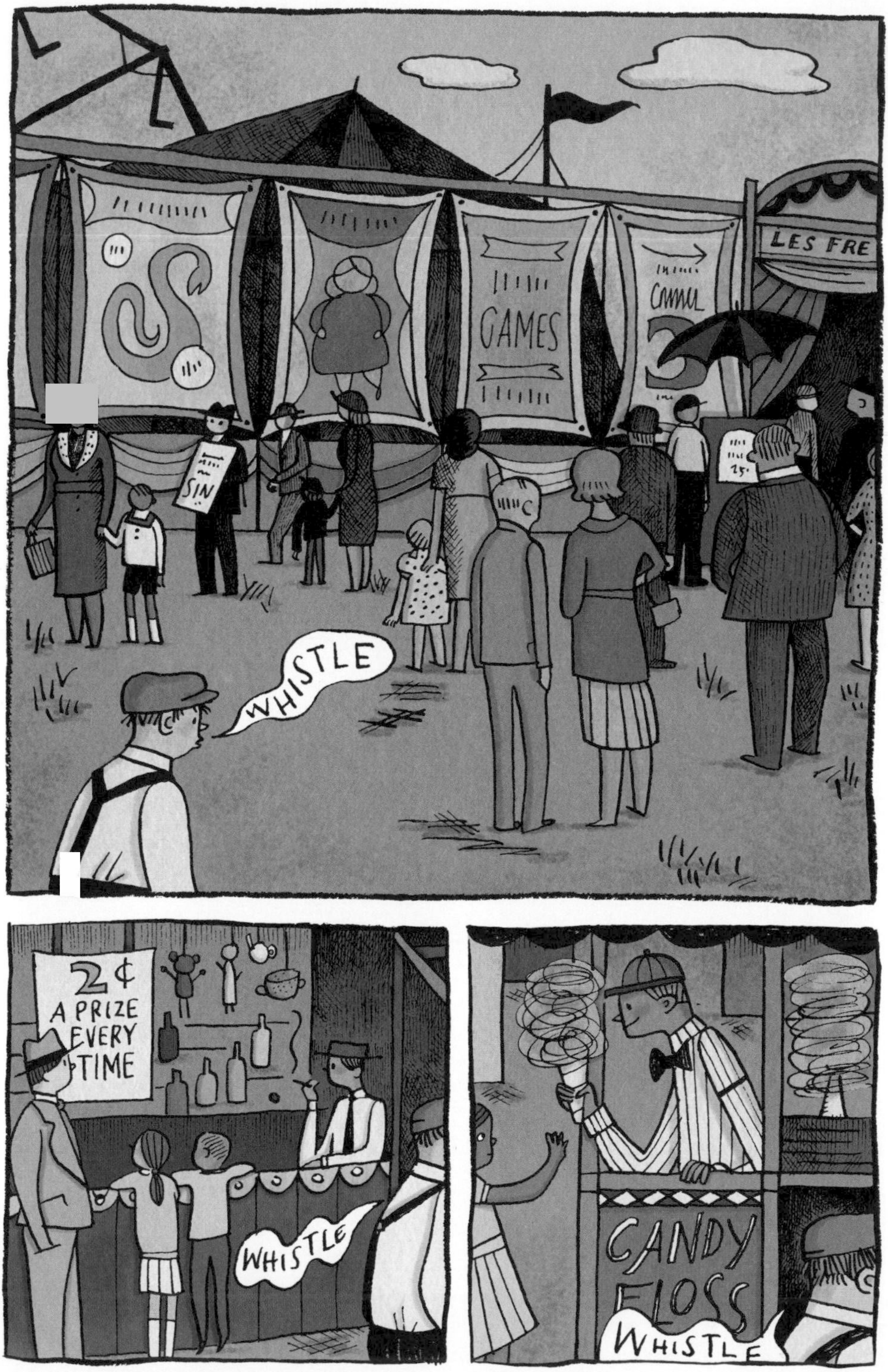
LES FRE
GAMES
SIN
WHISTLE
2¢
A PRIZE
EVERY
TIME
WHISTLE
CANDY
FLOSS
WHISTLE

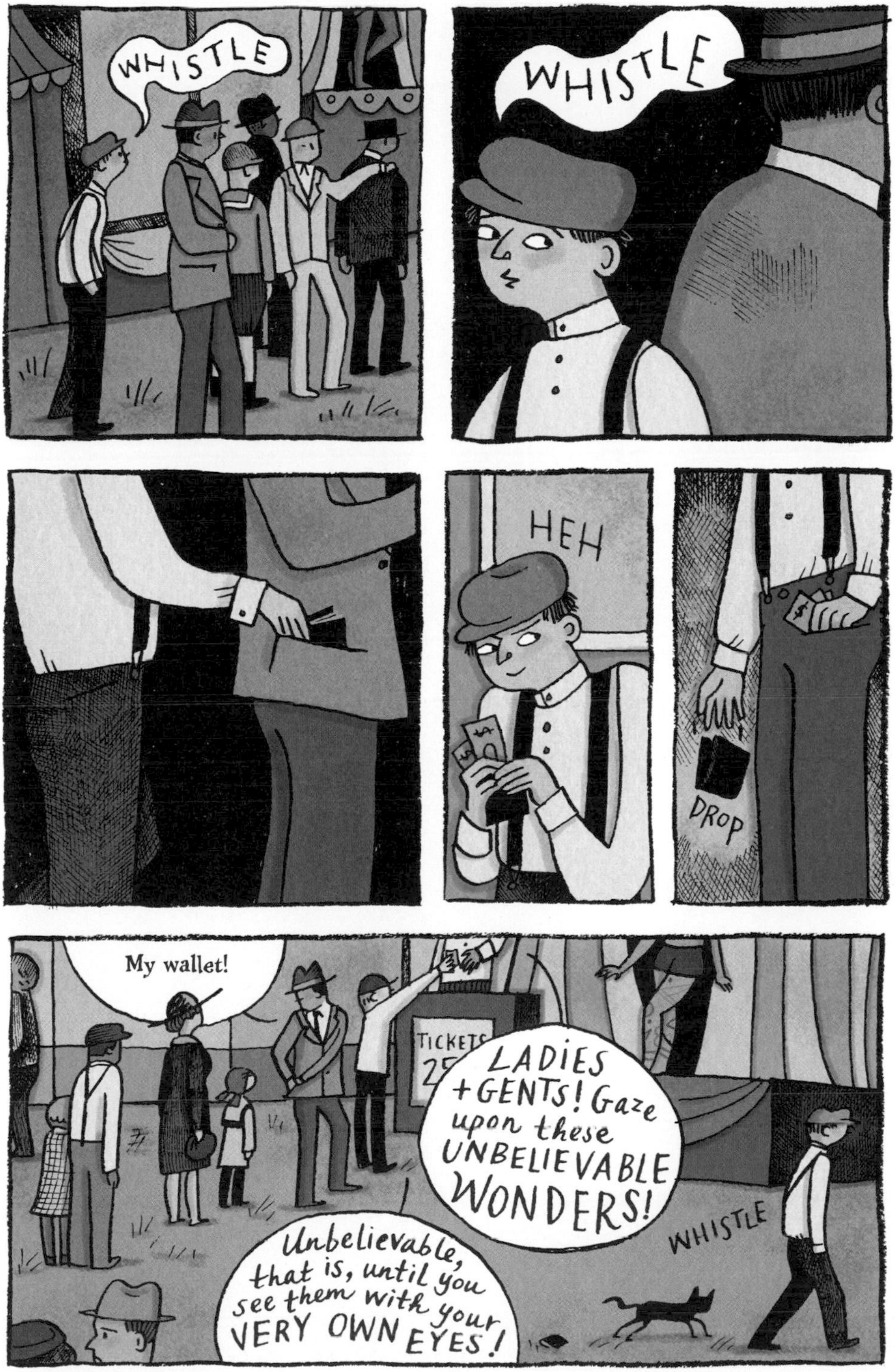
WHISTLE
WHISTLE
HEH
DROP
My wallet!
TICKETS 25
LADIES + GENTS! Gaze upon these UNBELIEVABLE WONDERS!
Unbelievable, that is, until you see them with your VERY OWN EYES!
WHISTLE

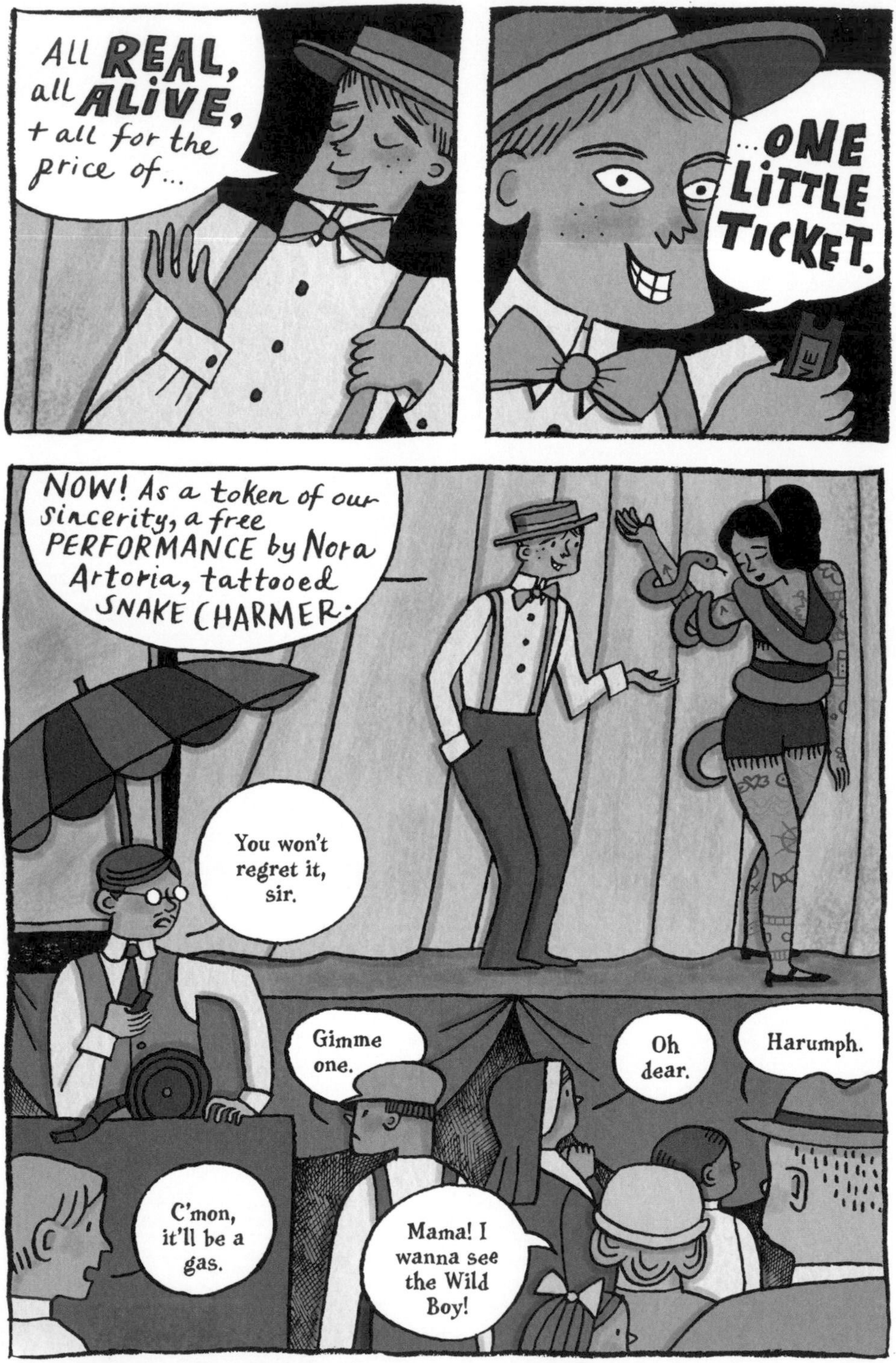
All REAL, all ALIVE, + all for the price of...
...ONE LITTLE TICKET.
NOW! As a token of our sincerity, a free PERFORMANCE by Nora Artoria, tattooed SNAKE CHARMER.
You won't regret it, sir.
Gimme one.
Oh dear.
Harumph.
C'mon, it'll be a gas.
Mama! I wanna see the Wild Boy!

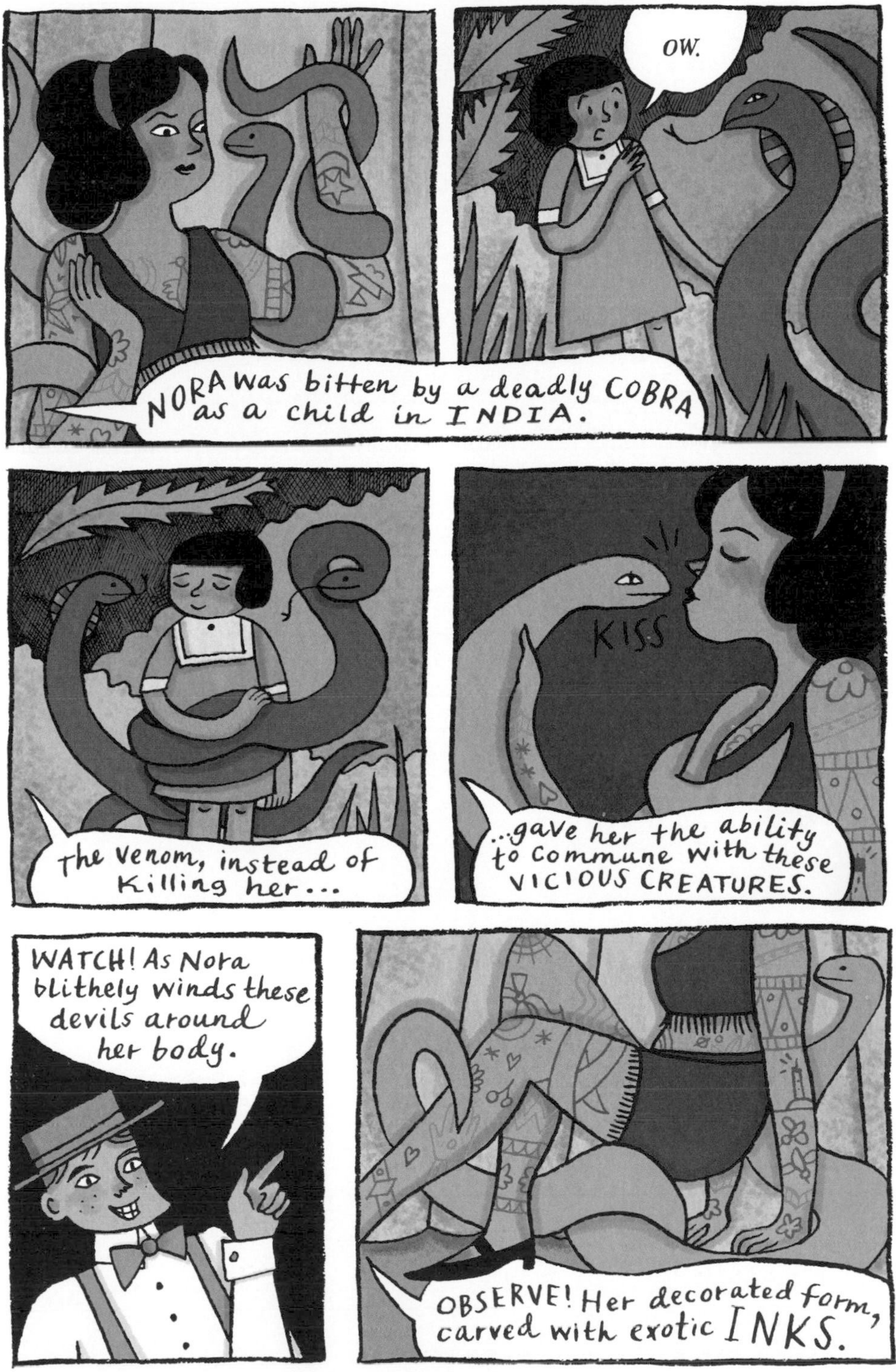
OW.
NORA was bitten by a deadly COBRA as a child in INDIA.
The venom, instead of Killing her...
KISS
...gave her the ability to commune with these VICIOUS CREATURES.
WATCH! As Nora blithely winds these devils around her body.
OBSERVE! Her decorated form, carved with exotic INKS.

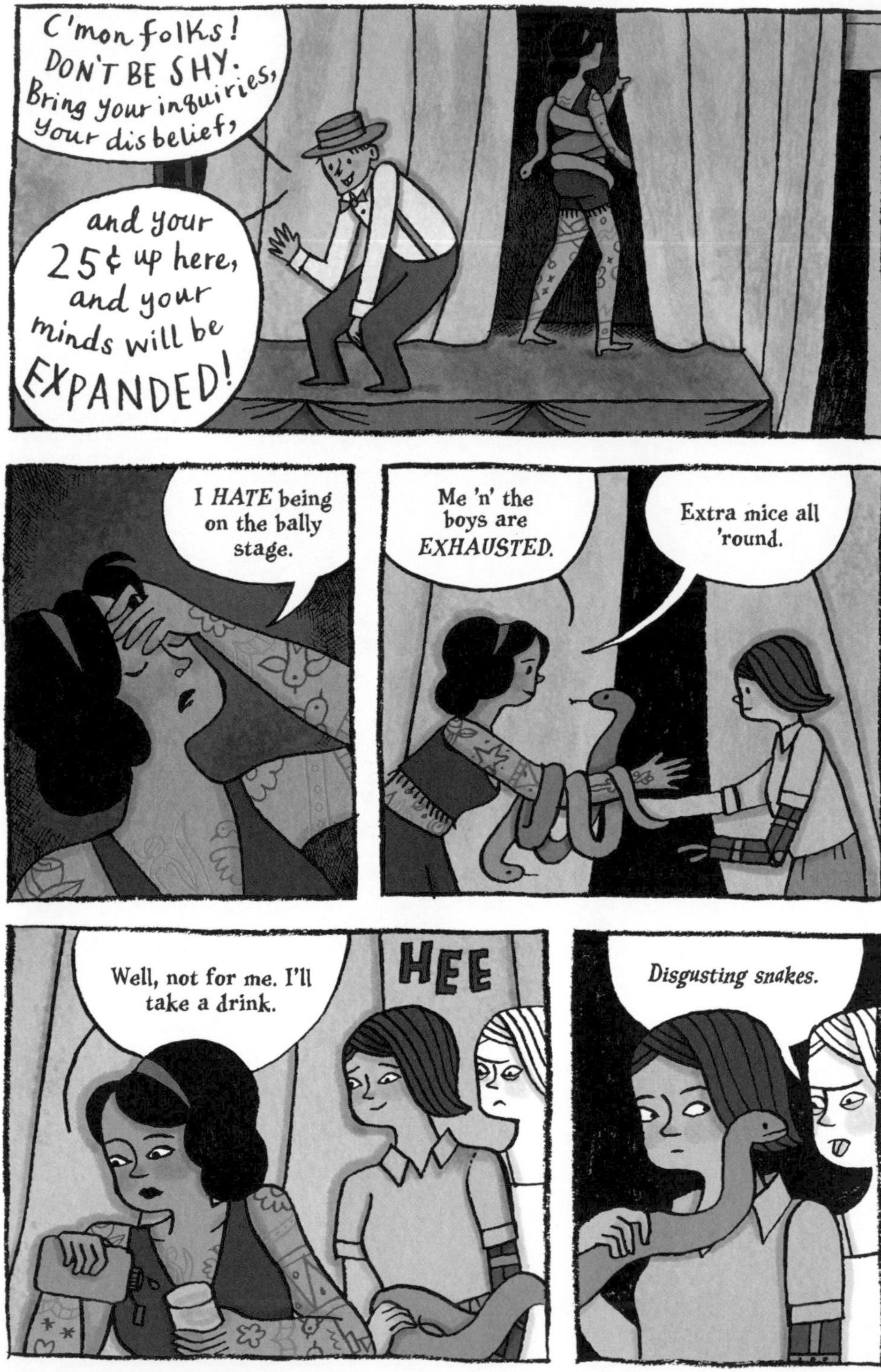
C'mon folks! DON'T BE SHY. Bring your inquiries, your disbelief,
and your 25¢ up here, and your minds will be EXPANDED!
I *HATE* being on the bally stage.
Me 'n' the boys are *EXHAUSTED.*
Extra mice all 'round.
Well, not for me. I'll take a drink.
HEE
Disgusting snakes.

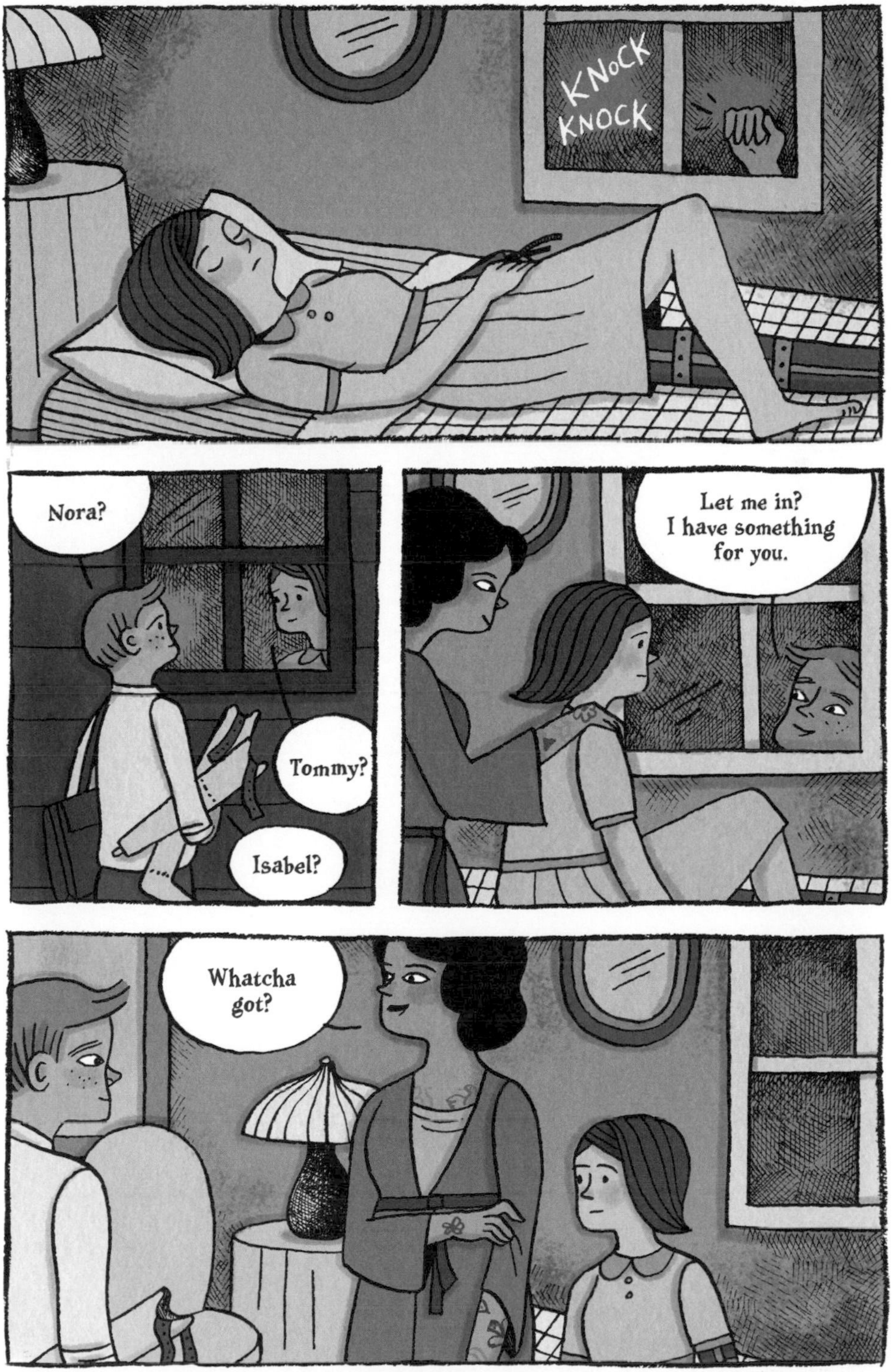
KNOCK
KNOCK
Nora?
Tommy?
Isabel?
Let me in? I have something for you.
Whatcha got?

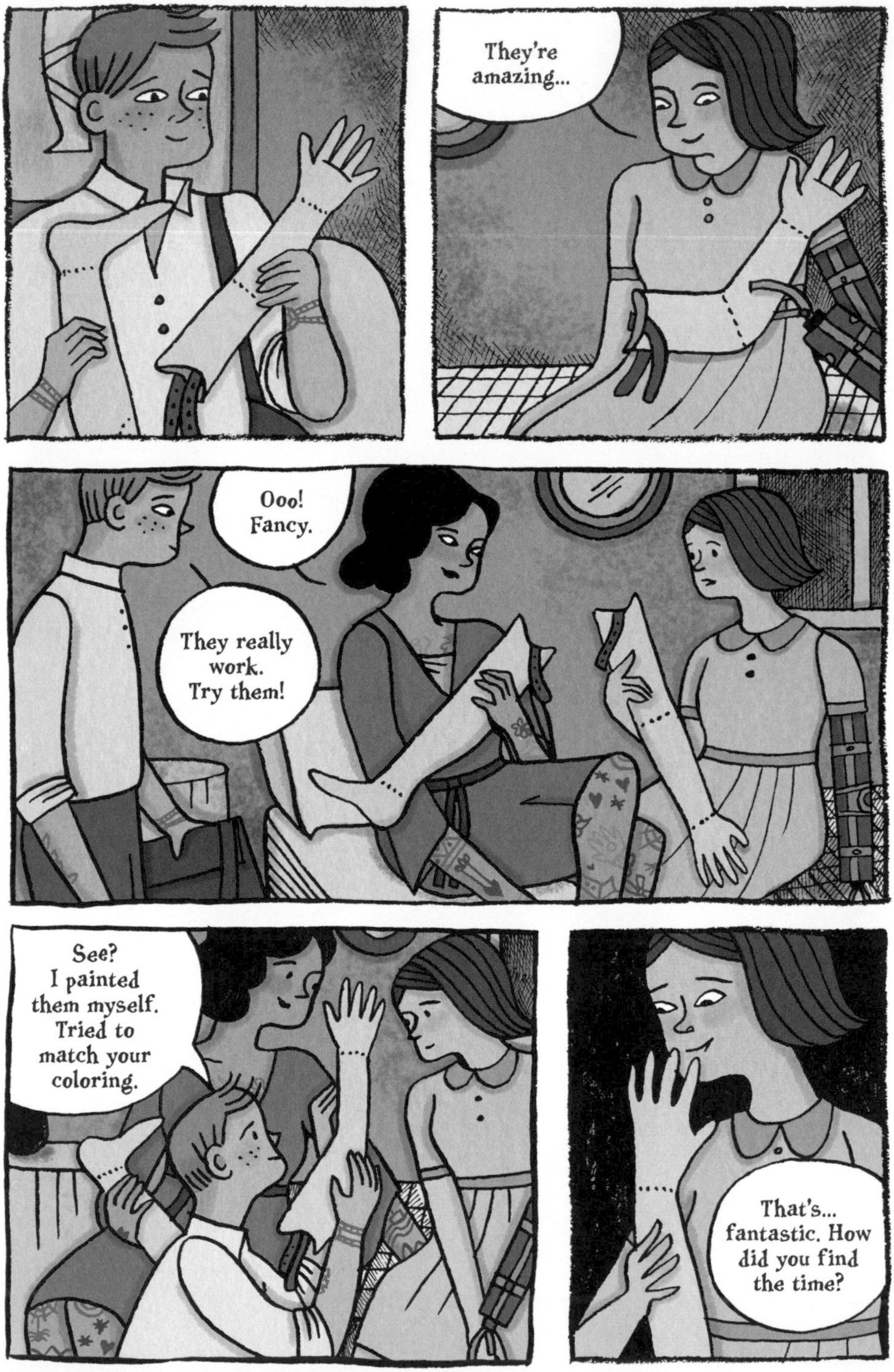
They're amazing...
Ooo! Fancy.
They really work. Try them!
See? I painted them myself. Tried to match your coloring.
That's... fantastic. How did you find the time?

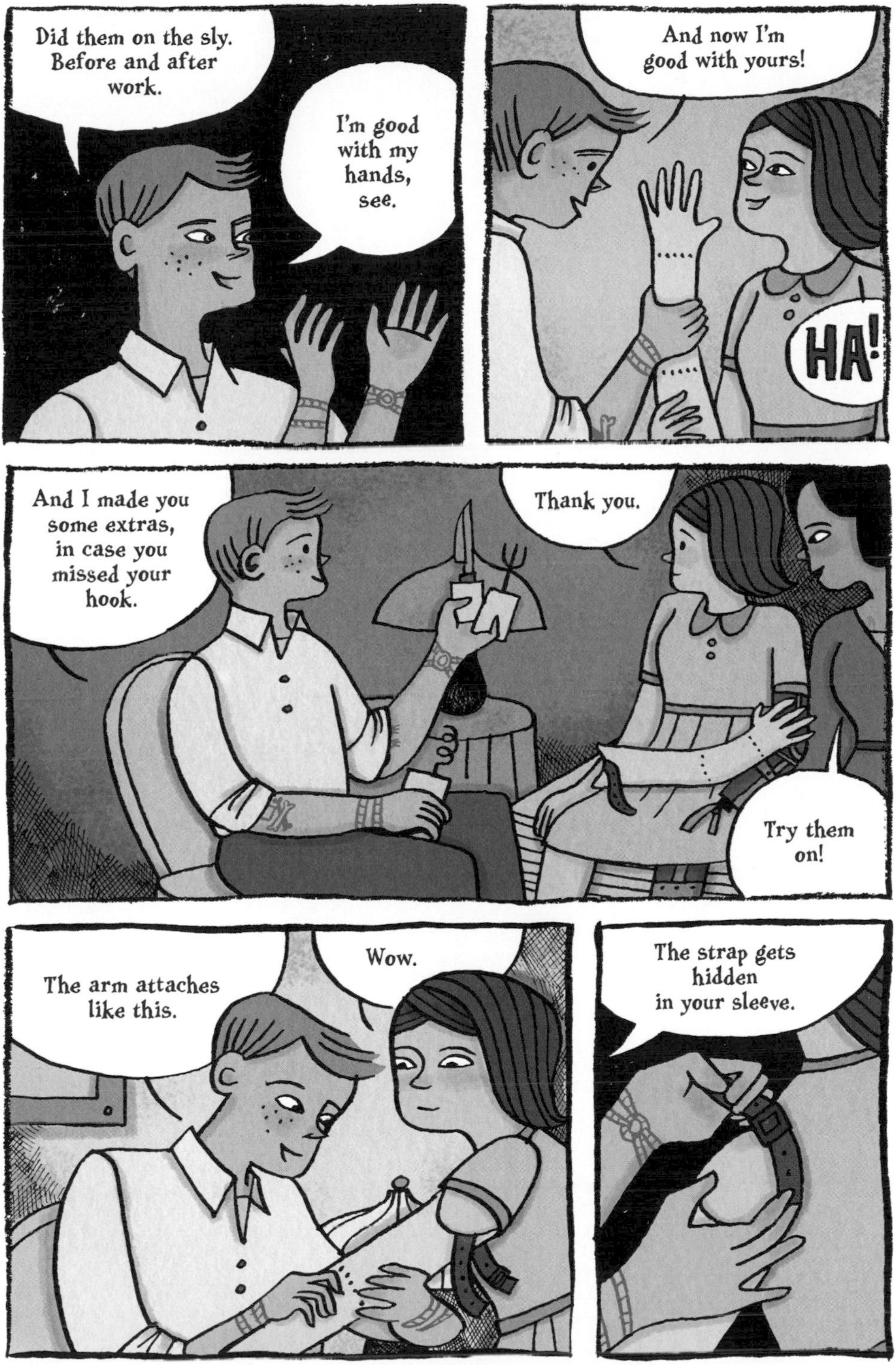
Did them on the sly. Before and after work.
I'm good with my hands, see.
And now I'm good with yours!
HA!
And I made you some extras, in case you missed your hook.
Thank you.
Try them on!
The arm attaches like this.
Wow.
The strap gets hidden in your sleeve.

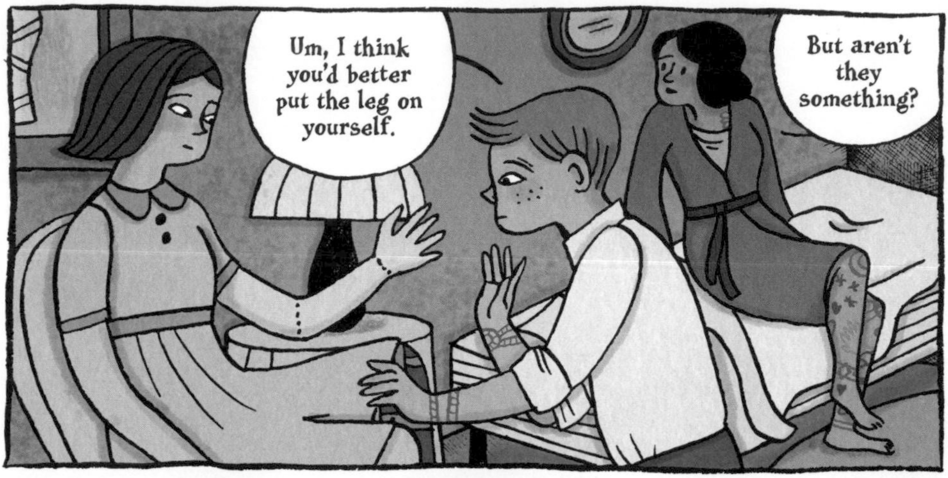
Um, I think you'd better put the leg on yourself.
But aren't they something?

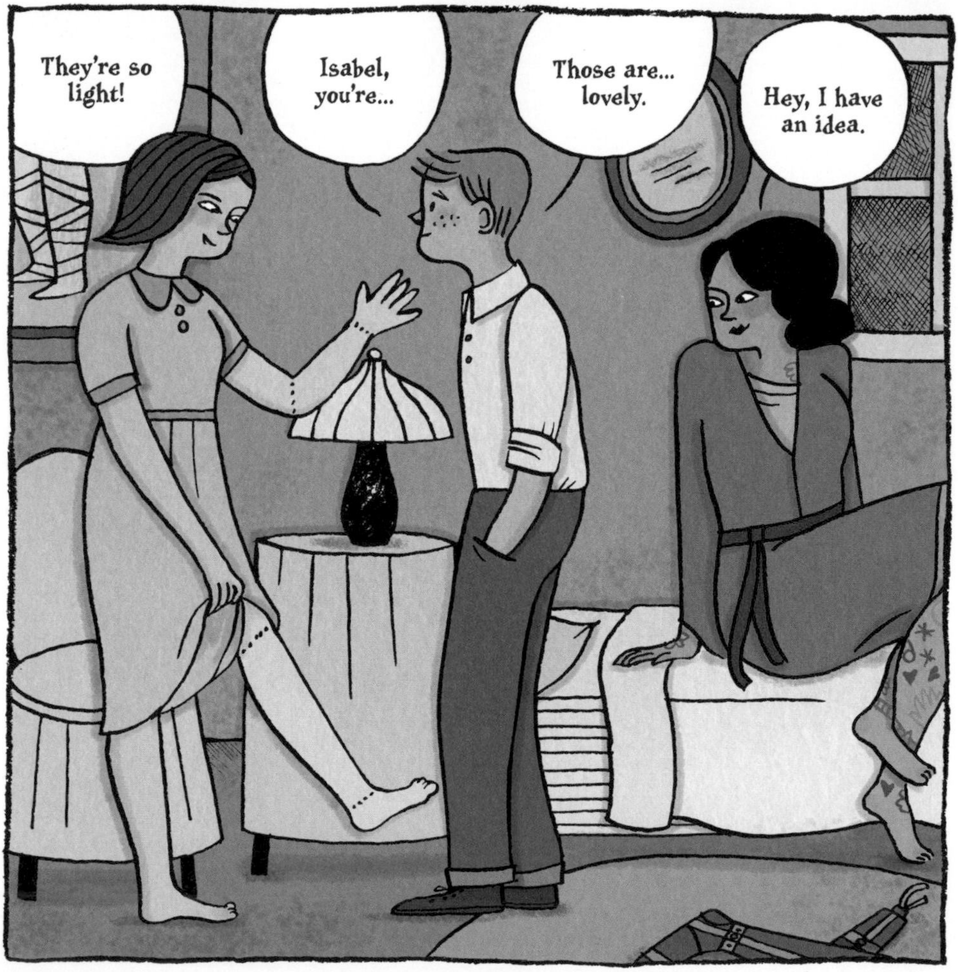
They're so light!
Isabel, you're...
Those are... lovely.
Hey, I have an idea.

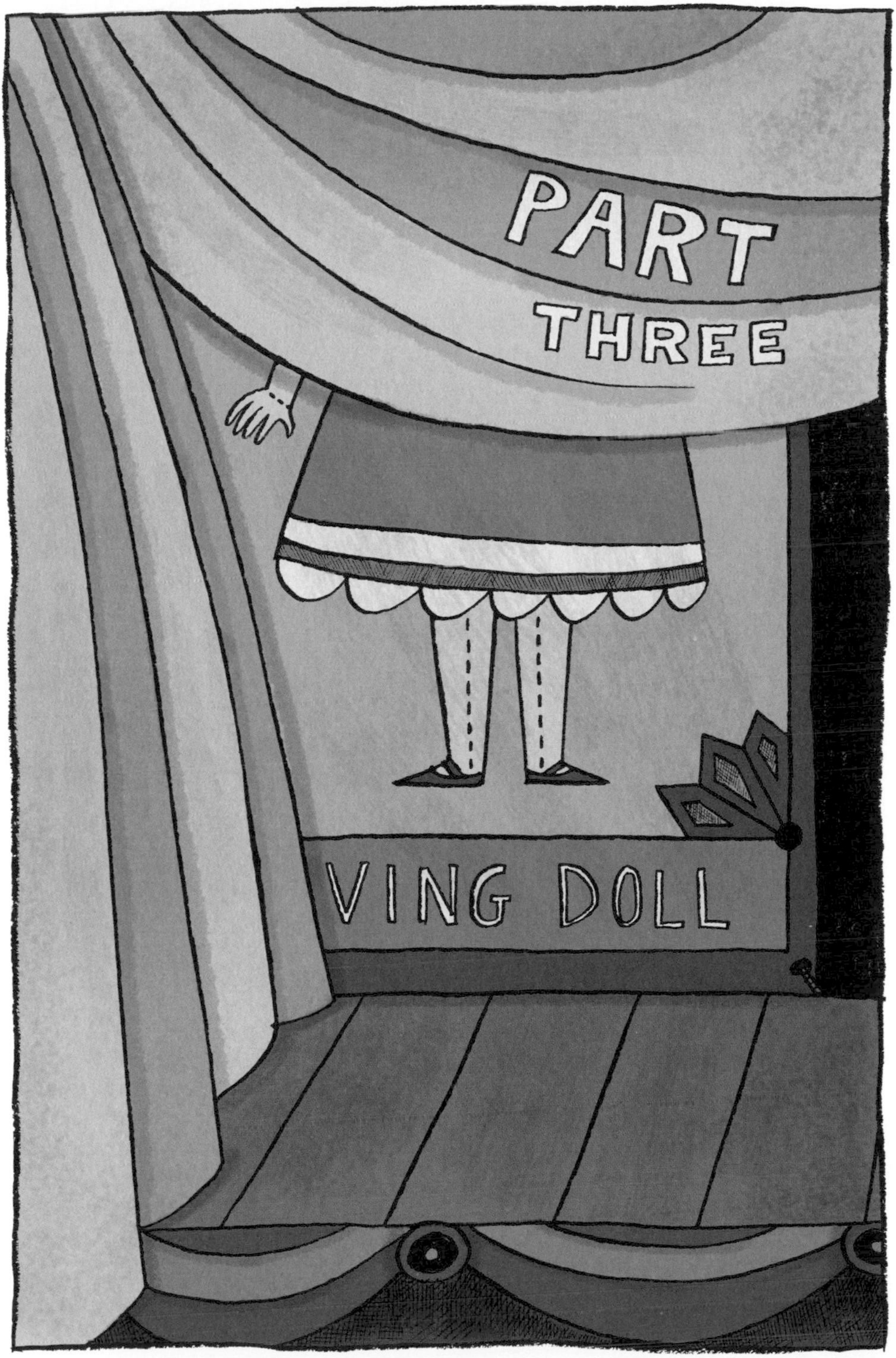
PART
THREE
VING DOLL

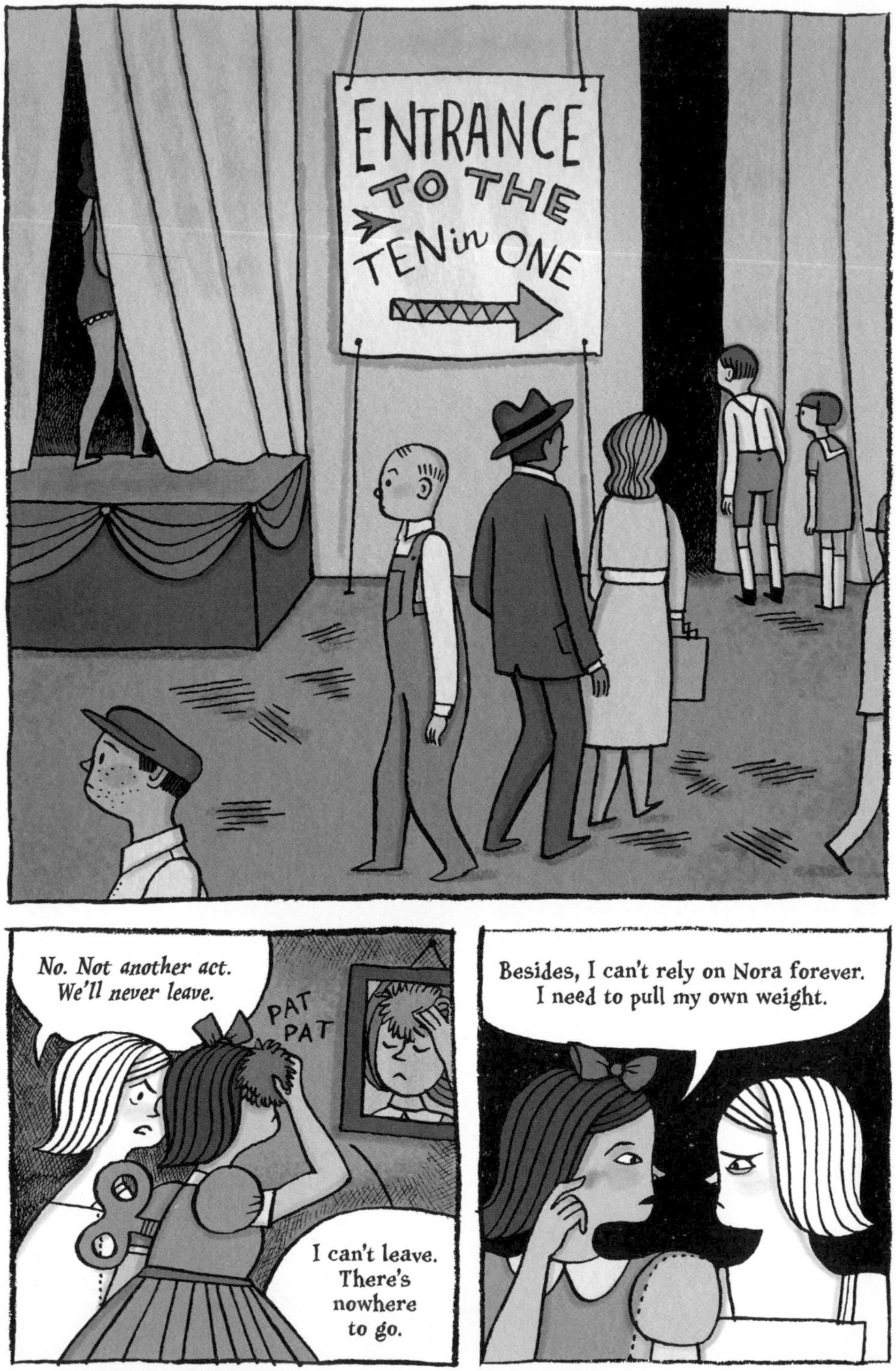
ENTRANCE TO THE TEN in ONE
No. Not another act. We'll never leave.
PAT PAT
I can't leave. There's nowhere to go.
Besides, I can't rely on Nora forever. I need to pull my own weight.

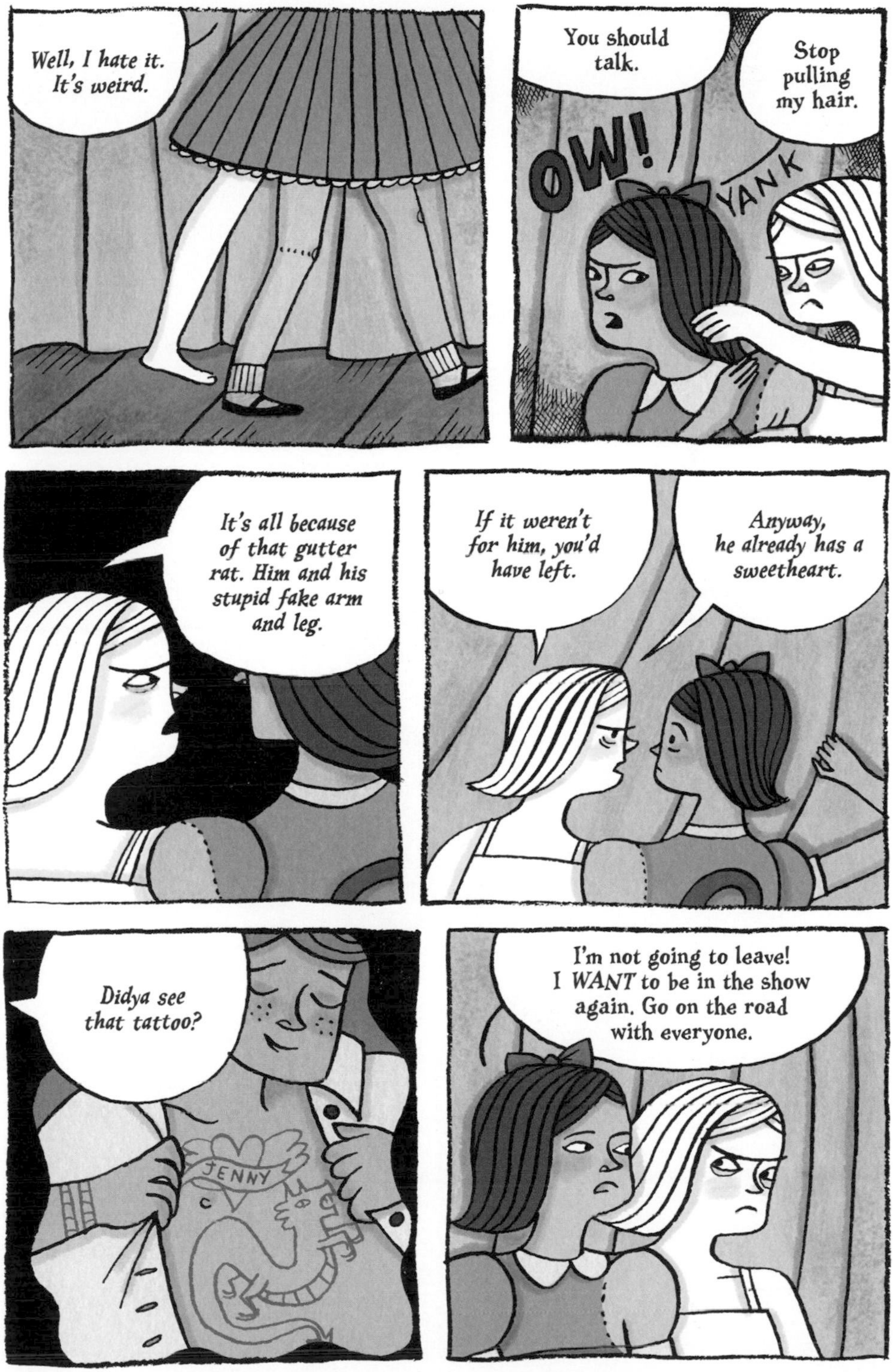
Well, I hate it. It's weird.
You should talk.
Stop pulling my hair.
OW!
YANK
It's all because of that gutter rat. Him and his stupid fake arm and leg.
If it weren't for him, you'd have left.
Anyway, he already has a sweetheart.
Didya see that tattoo?
JENNY
I'm not going to leave! I WANT to be in the show again. Go on the road with everyone.

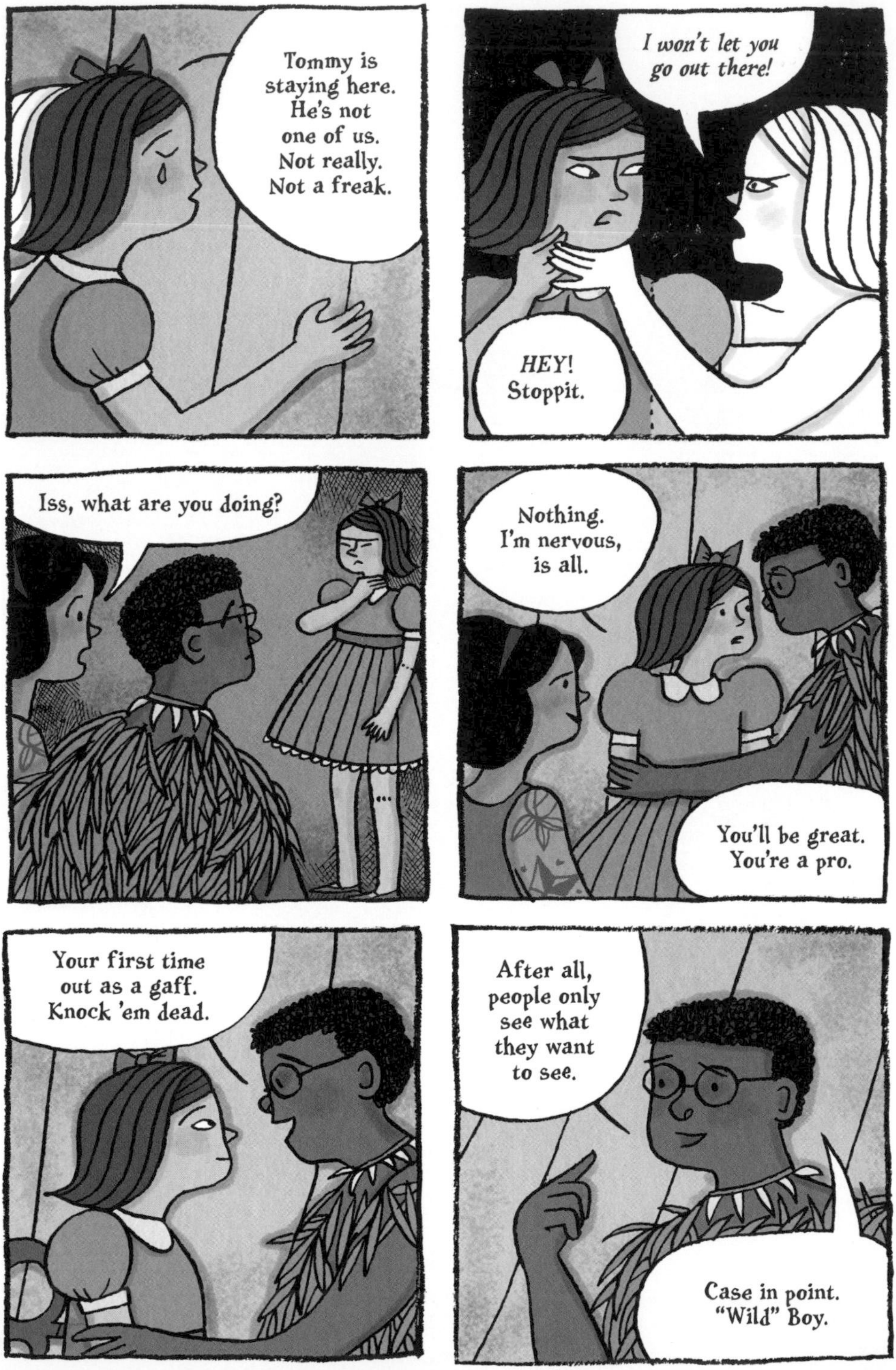
Tommy is staying here. He's not one of us. Not really. Not a freak.
I won't let you go out there!
HEY! Stoppit.
Iss, what are you doing?
Nothing. I'm nervous, is all.
You'll be great. You're a pro.
Your first time out as a gaff. Knock 'em dead.
After all, people only see what they want to see.
Case in point. "Wild" Boy.

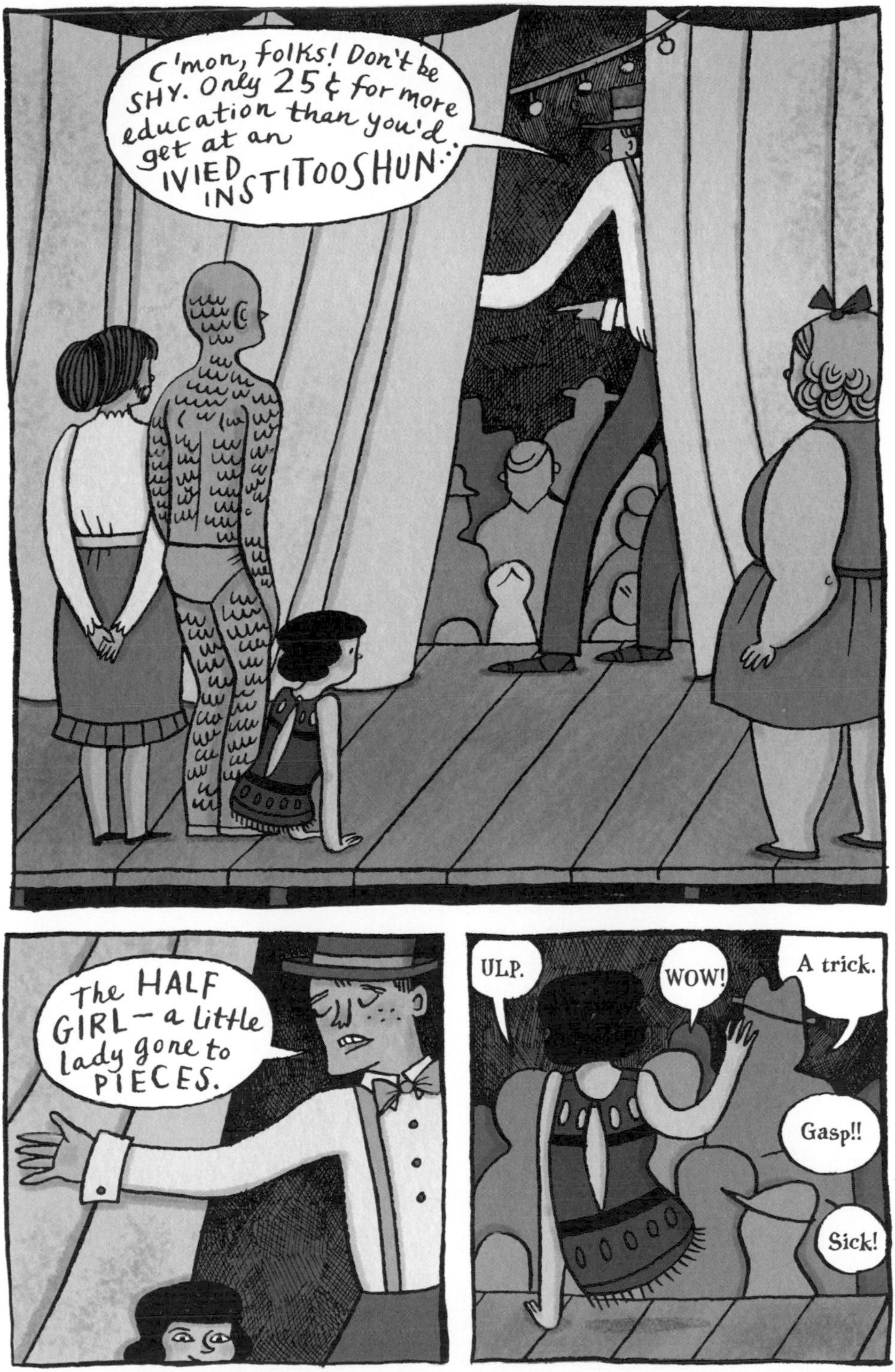
C'mon, folks! Don't be SHY. Only 25¢ for more education than you'd get at an IVIED INSTITOOSHUN...
The HALF GIRL—a little lady gone to PIECES.
ULP.
WOW!
A trick.
Gasp!!
Sick!

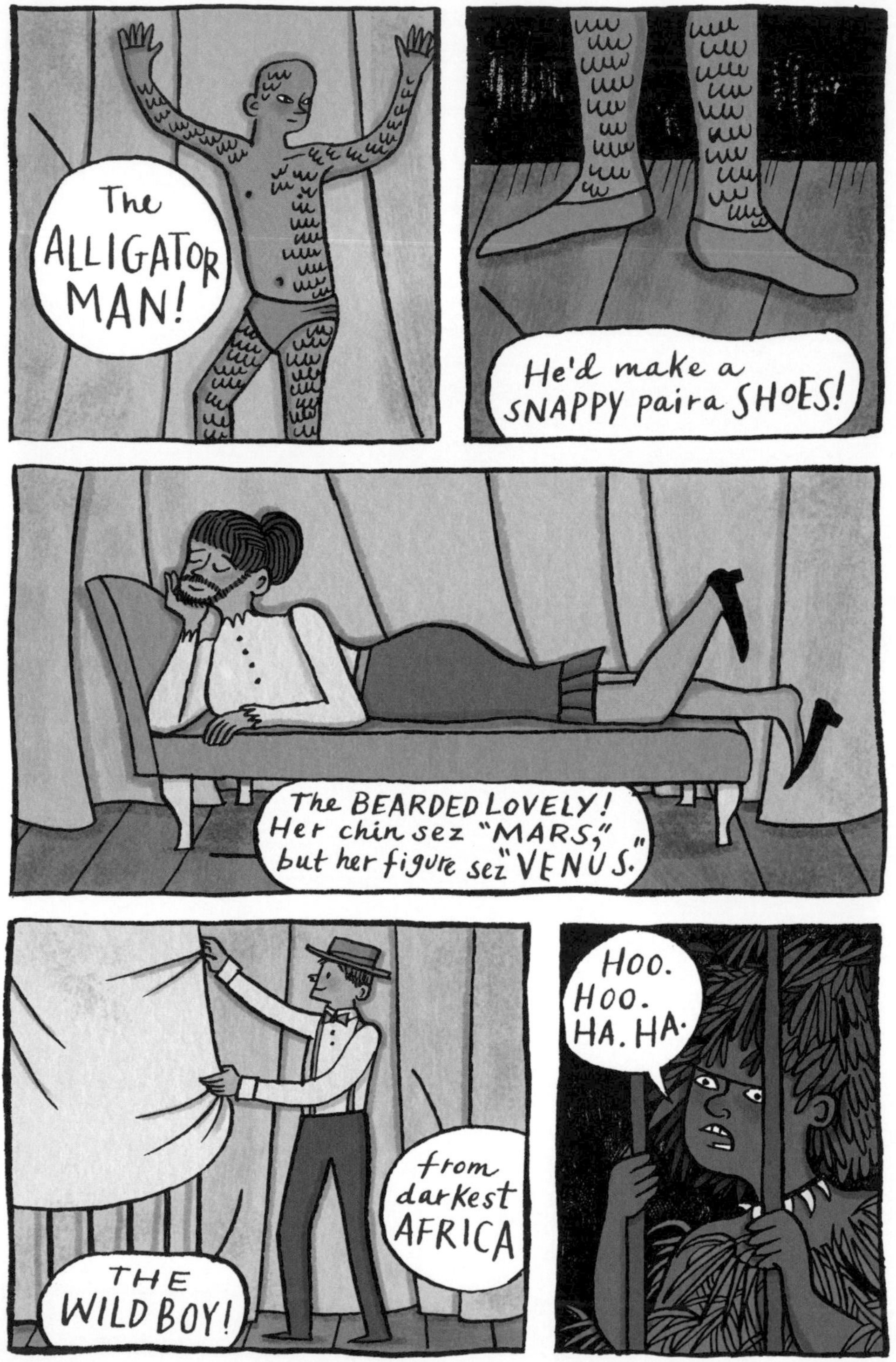
The ALLIGATOR MAN!
He'd make a SNAPPY paira SHOES!
The BEARDED LOVELY! Her chin sez "MARS," but her figure sez "VENUS."
THE WILD BOY!
from darkest AFRICA
HOO. HOO. HA. HA.

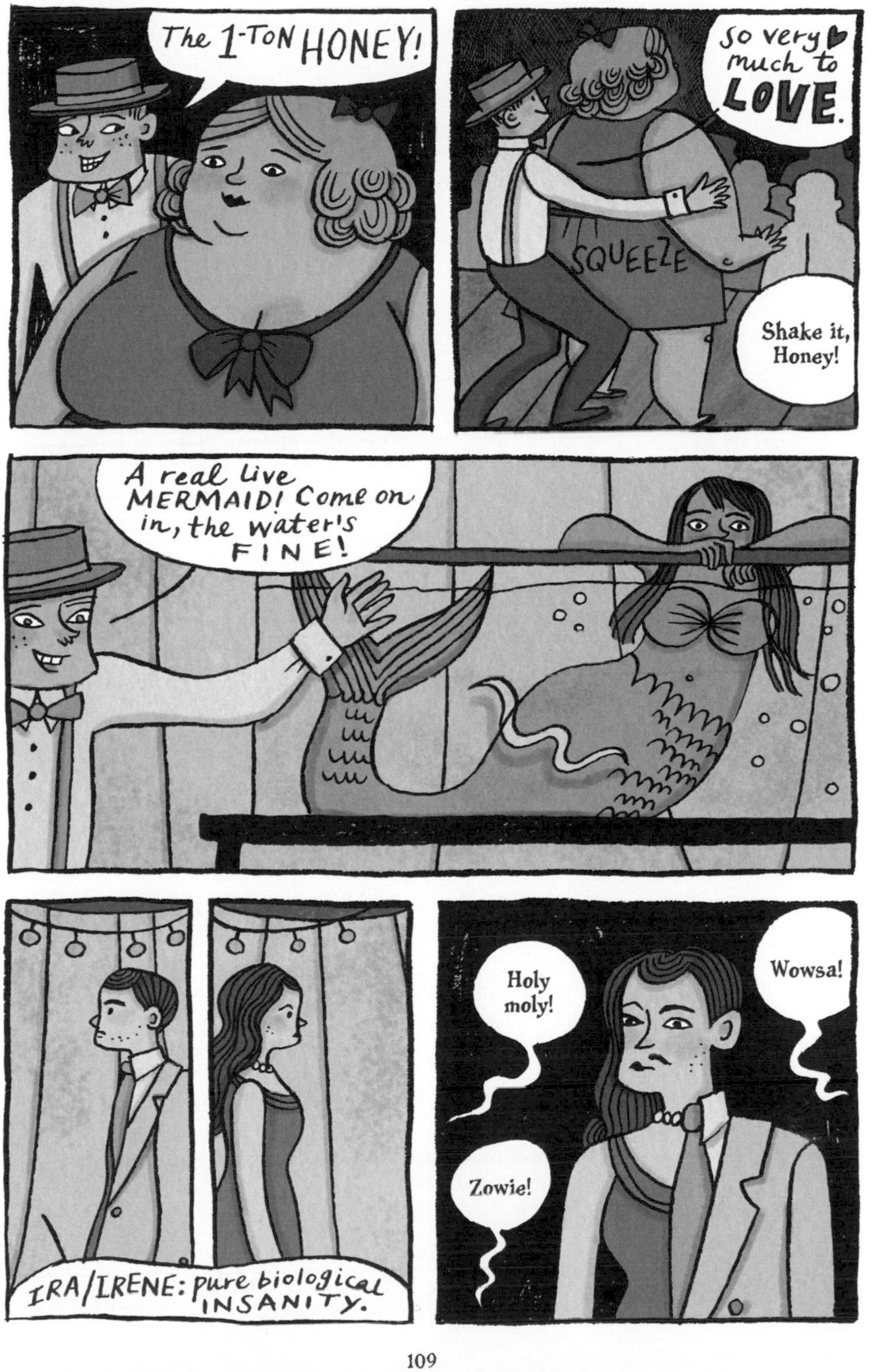
The 1-TON HONEY!
So very much to LOVE.
SQUEEZE
Shake it, Honey!
A real live MERMAID! Come on in, the water's FINE!
IRA/IRENE: pure biological INSANITY.
Holy moly!
Wowsa!
Zowie!

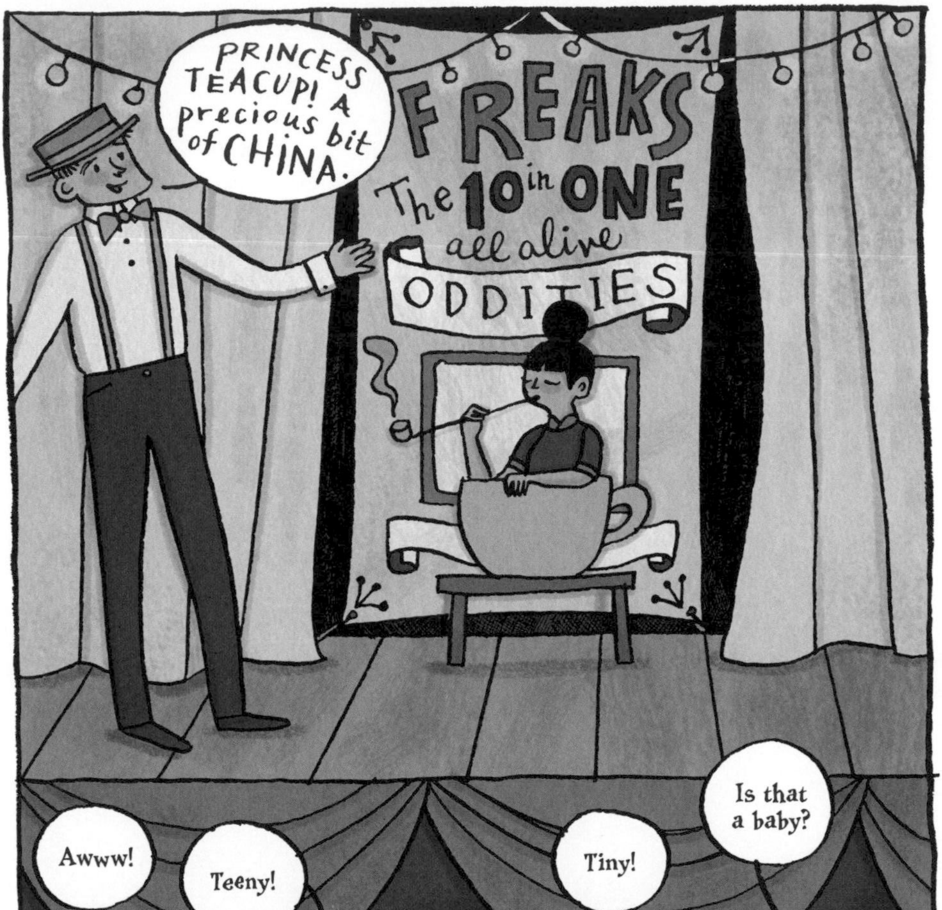
PRINCESS TEACUP! A precious bit of CHINA.
FREAKS
The 10 in ONE
all alive
ODDITIES
Awww!
Teeny!
Tiny!
Is that a baby?

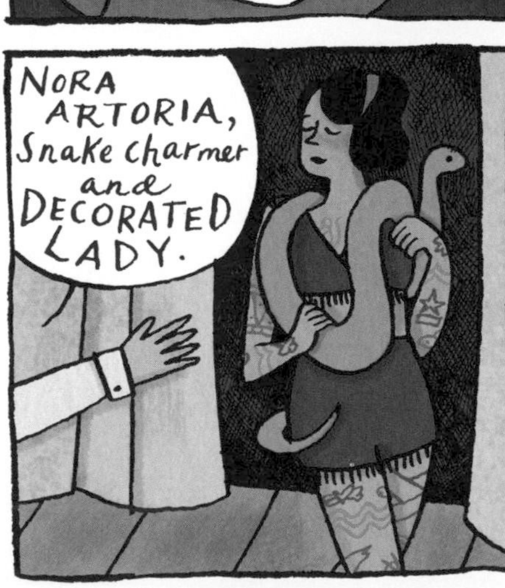
NORA ARTORIA, Snake charmer and DECORATED LADY.

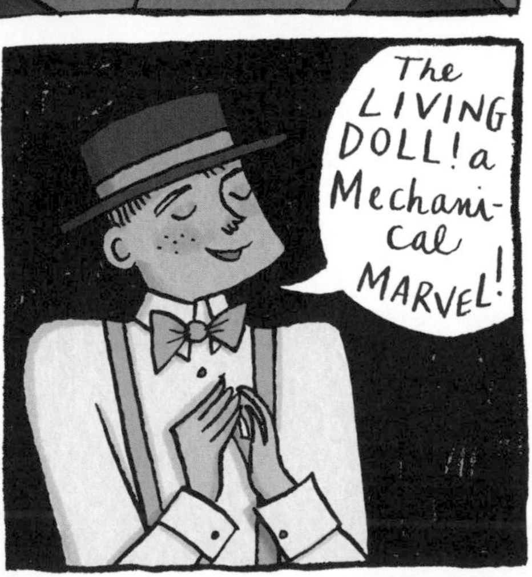
The LIVING DOLL! a Mechanical MARVEL!

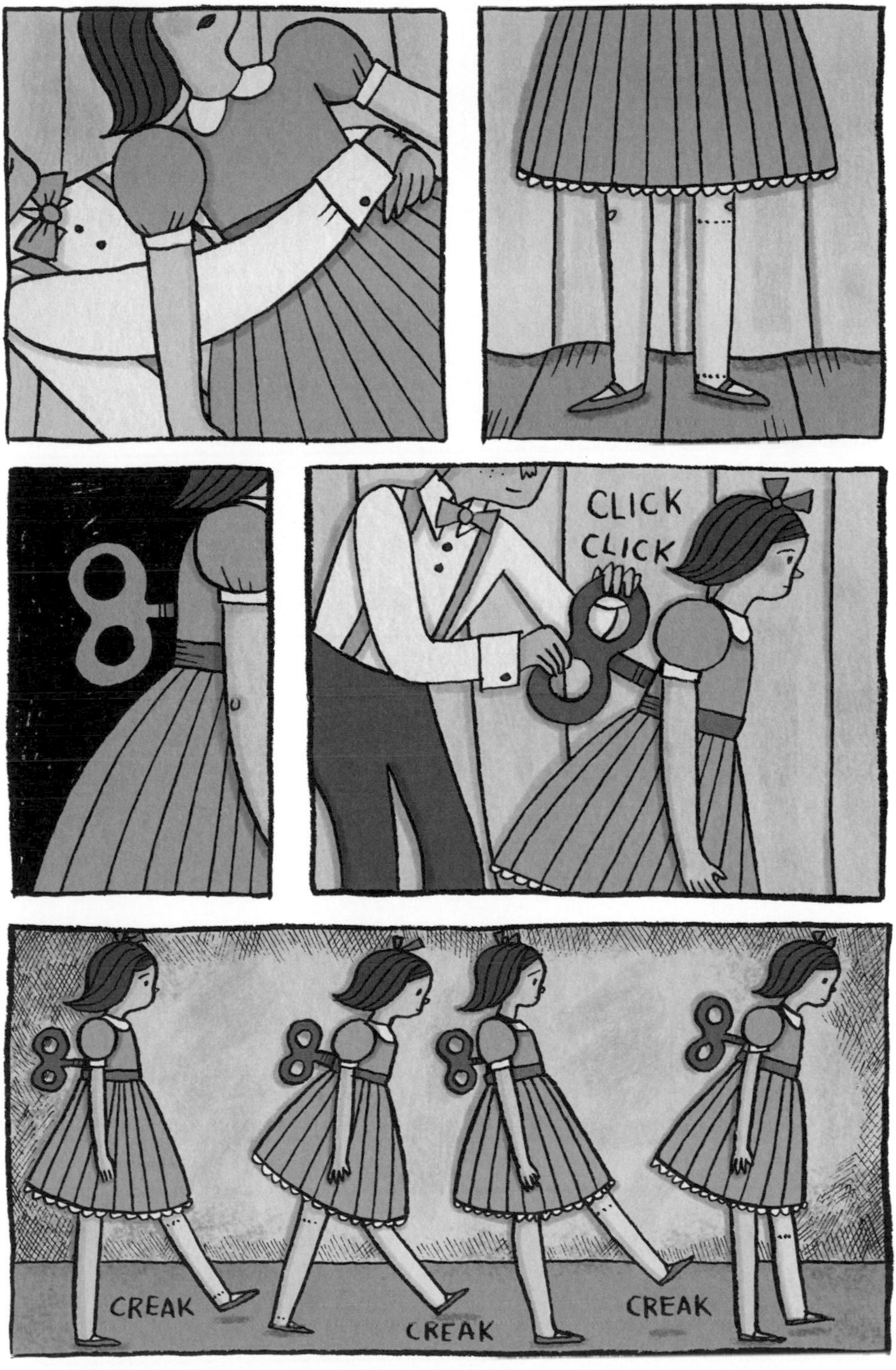
CLICK
CLICK
CREAK
CREAK
CREAK

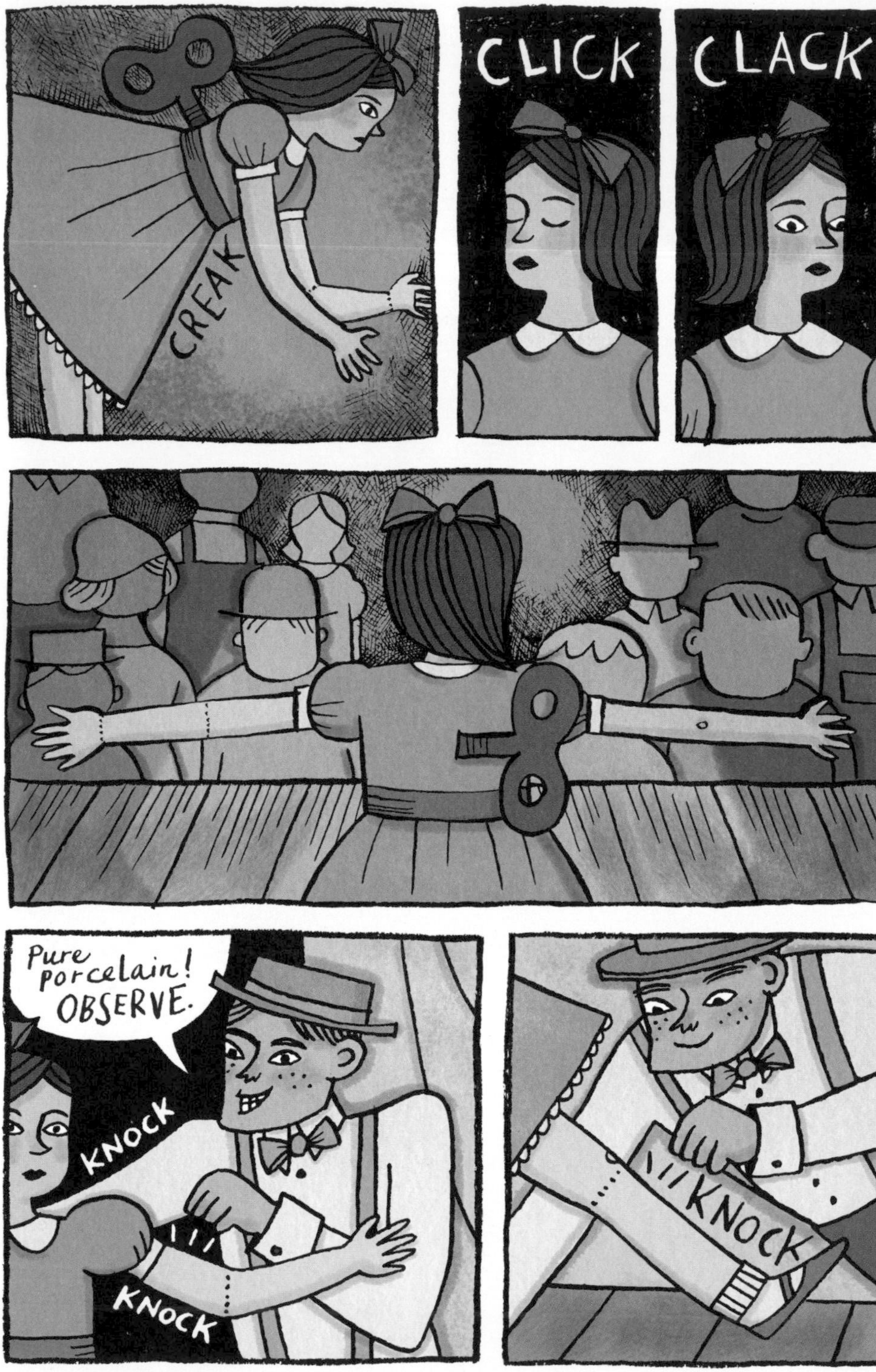
CREAK
CLICK
CLACK
Pure porcelain! OBSERVE.
KNOCK
KNOCK
KNOCK

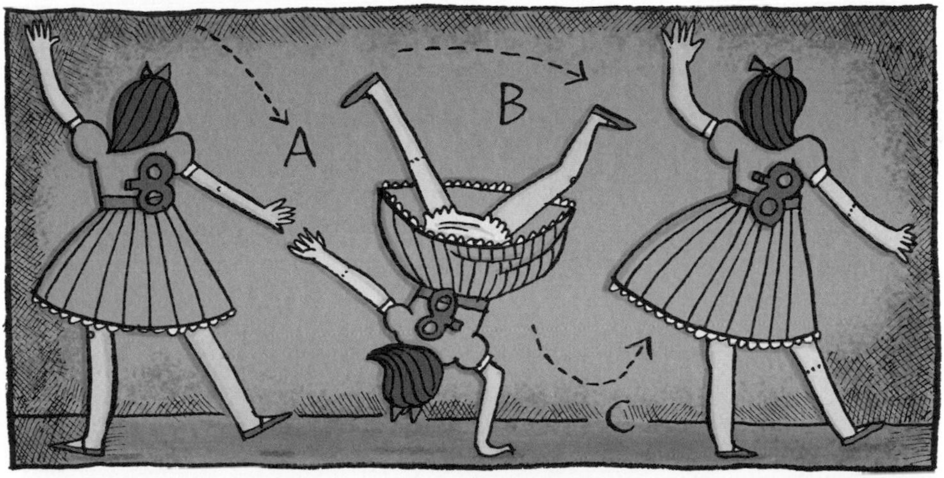
A
B
C

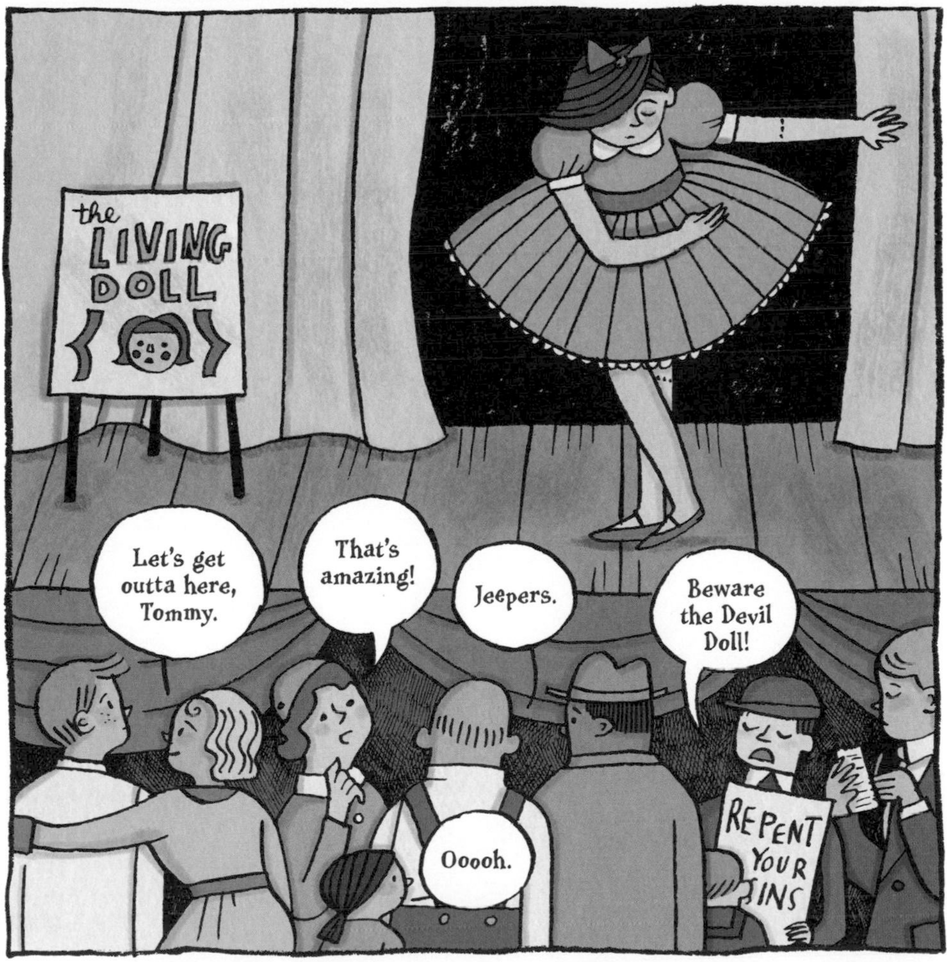
the LIVING DOLL
Let's get outta here, Tommy.
That's amazing!
Jeepers.
Beware the Devil Doll!
Ooooh.
REPENT YOUR SINS

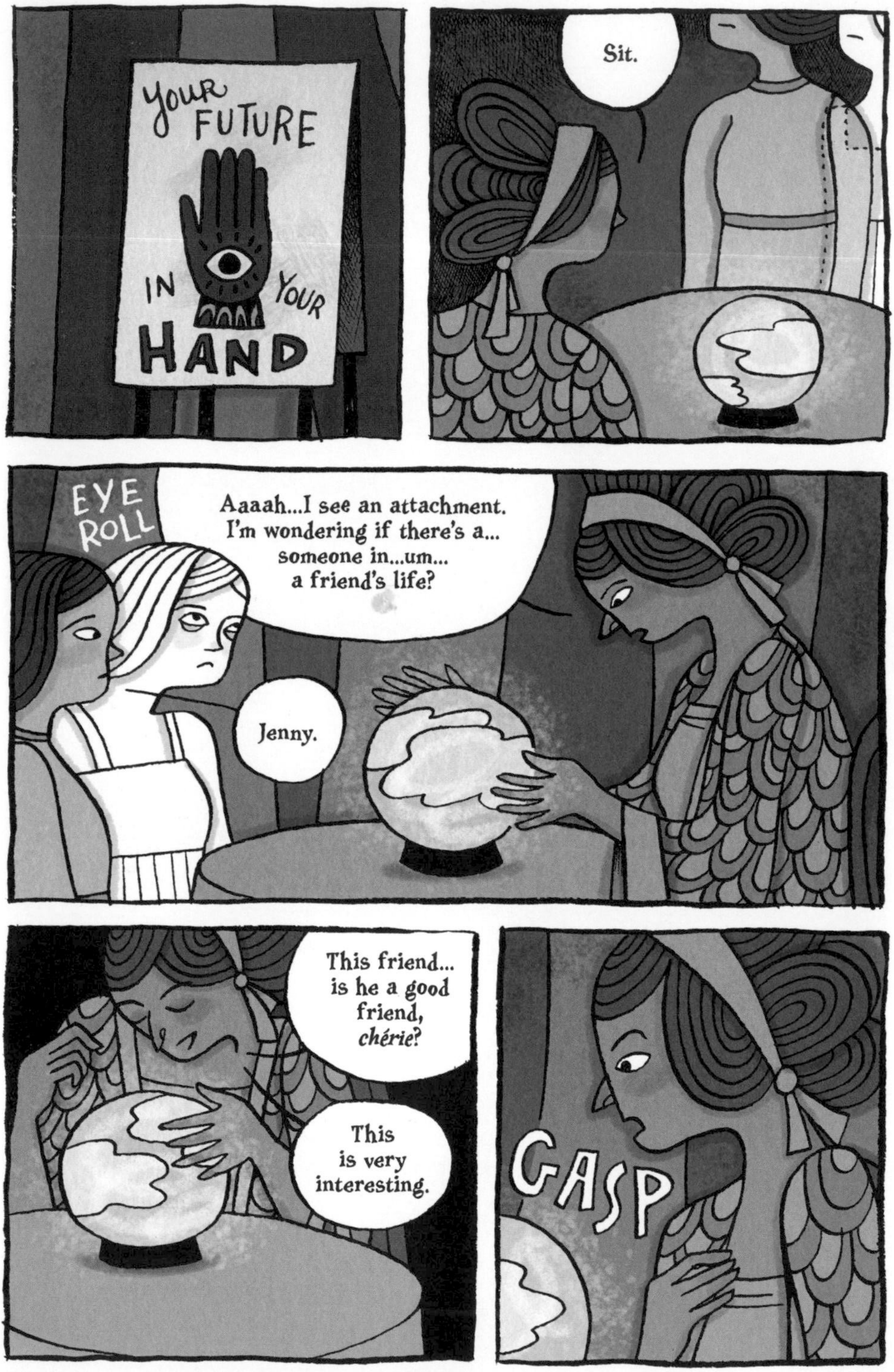

YOUR FUTURE IN YOUR HAND
Sit.
EYE ROLL
Aaaah...I see an attachment. I'm wondering if there's a... someone in...um... a friend's life?
Jenny.
This friend... is he a good friend, *chérie*?
This is very interesting.
GASP

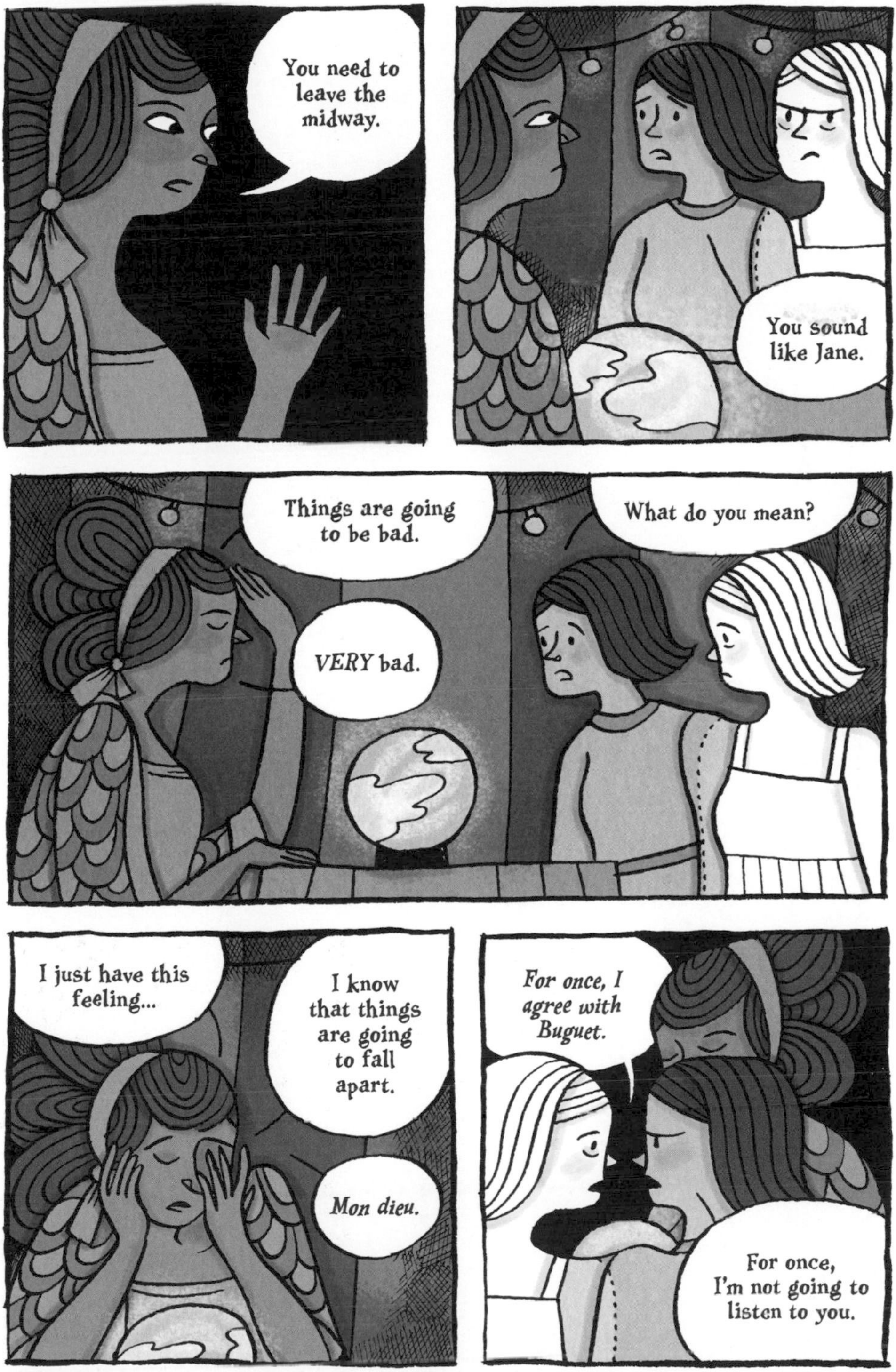
You need to leave the midway.
You sound like Jane.
Things are going to be bad.
What do you mean?
VERY bad.
I just have this feeling...
I know that things are going to fall apart.
Mon dieu.
For once, I agree with Buguet.
For once, I'm not going to listen to you.

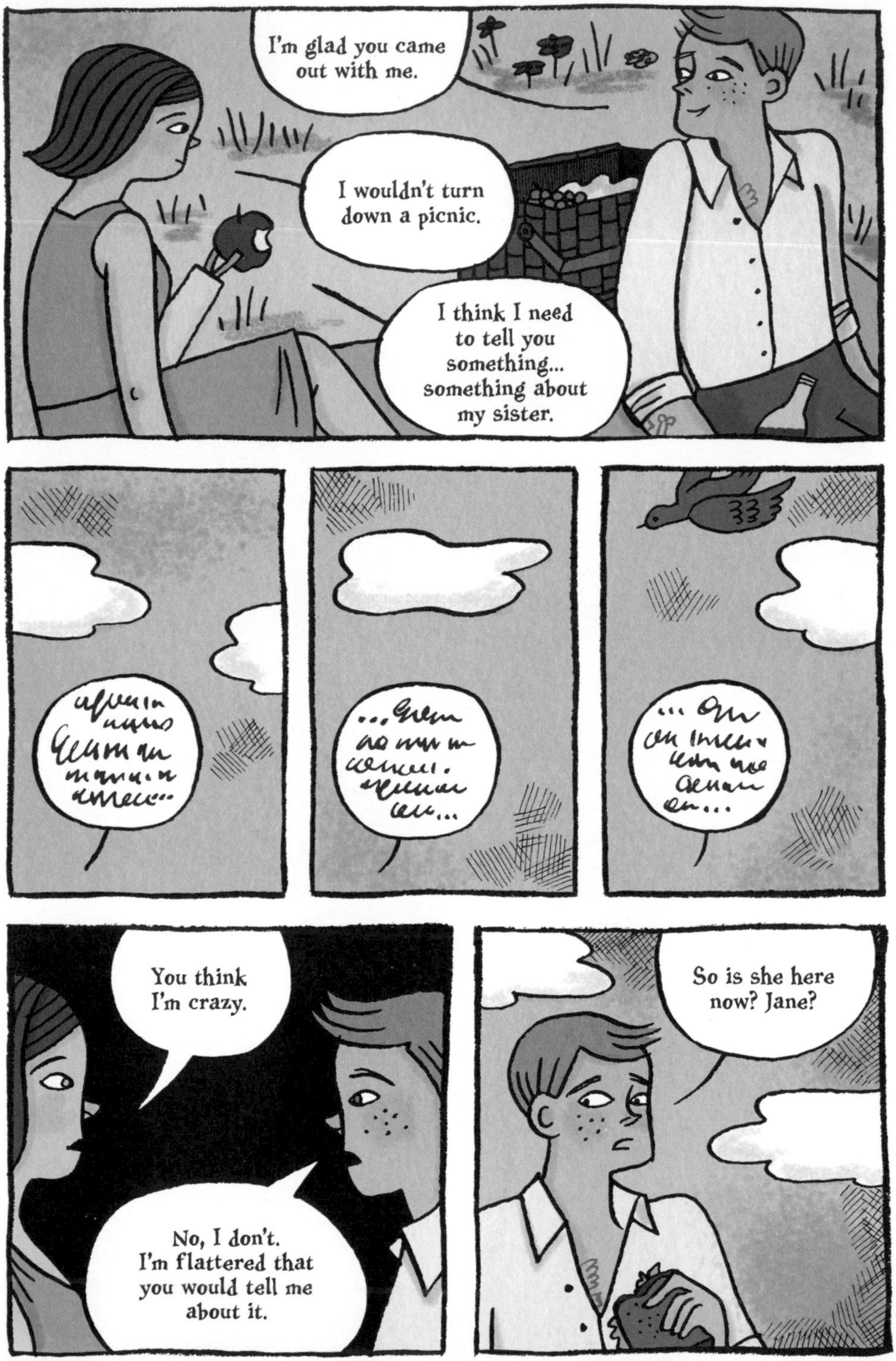
I'm glad you came out with me.
I wouldn't turn down a picnic.
I think I need to tell you something... something about my sister.
You think I'm crazy.
No, I don't. I'm flattered that you would tell me about it.
So is she here now? Jane?

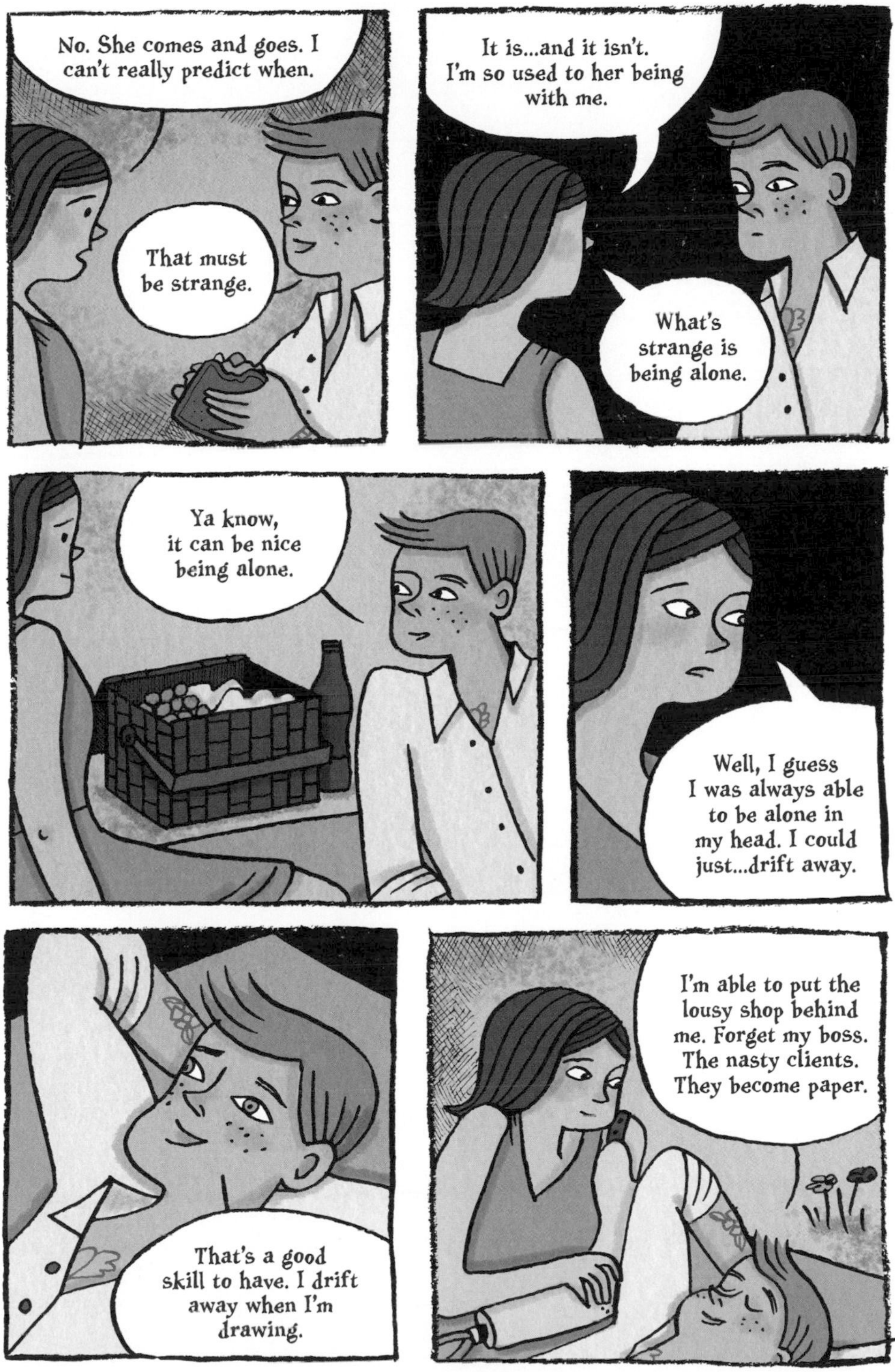
No. She comes and goes. I can't really predict when.
That must be strange.
It is...and it isn't. I'm so used to her being with me.
What's strange is being alone.
Ya know, it can be nice being alone.
Well, I guess I was always able to be alone in my head. I could just...drift away.
That's a good skill to have. I drift away when I'm drawing.
I'm able to put the lousy shop behind me. Forget my boss. The nasty clients. They become paper.

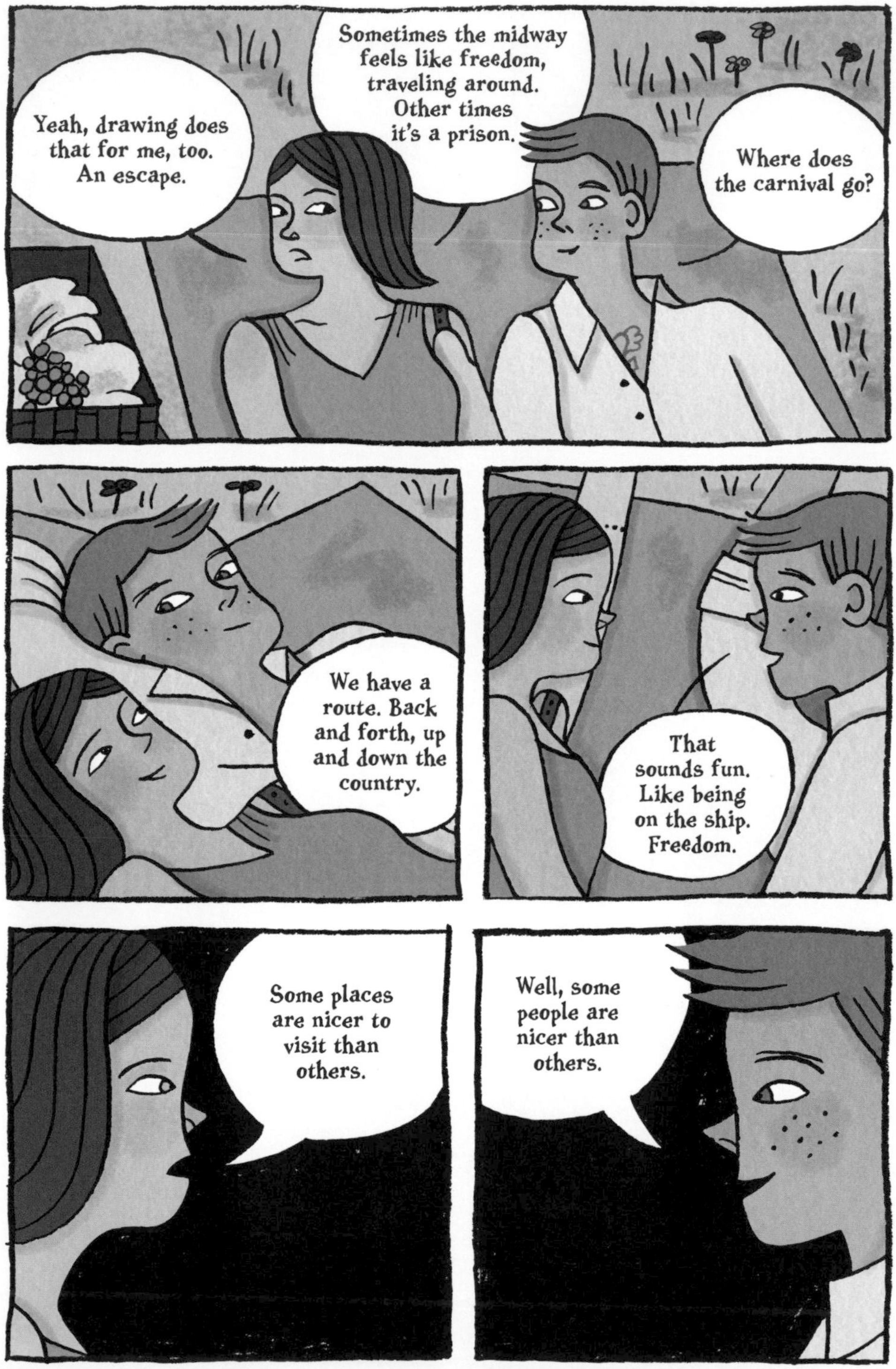
Sometimes the midway feels like freedom, traveling around. Other times it's a prison.
Yeah, drawing does that for me, too. An escape.
Where does the carnival go?
We have a route. Back and forth, up and down the country.
That sounds fun. Like being on the ship. Freedom.
Some places are nicer to visit than others.
Well, some people are nicer than others.

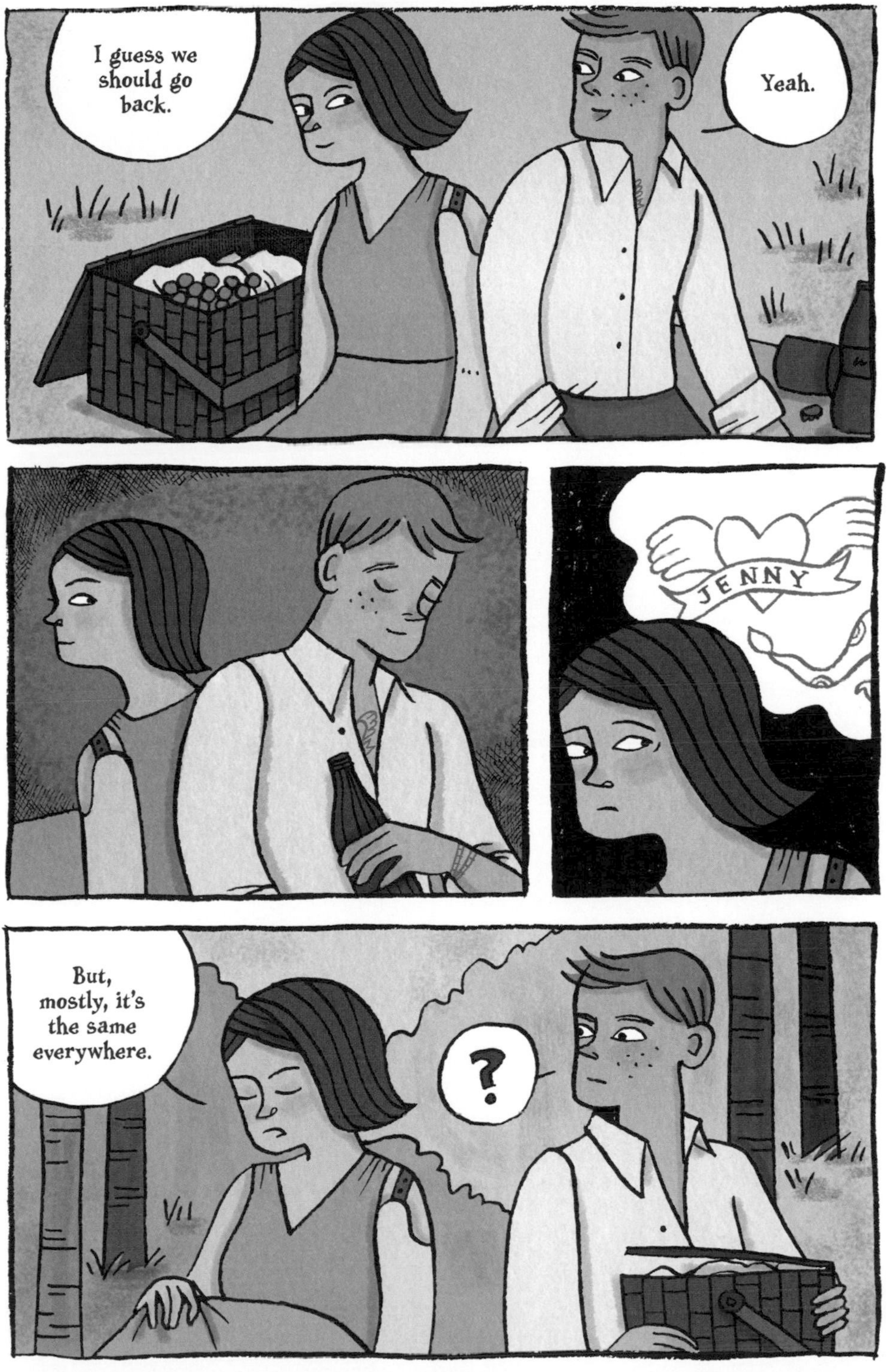
I guess we should go back.
Yeah.
JENNY
But, mostly, it's the same everywhere.
?

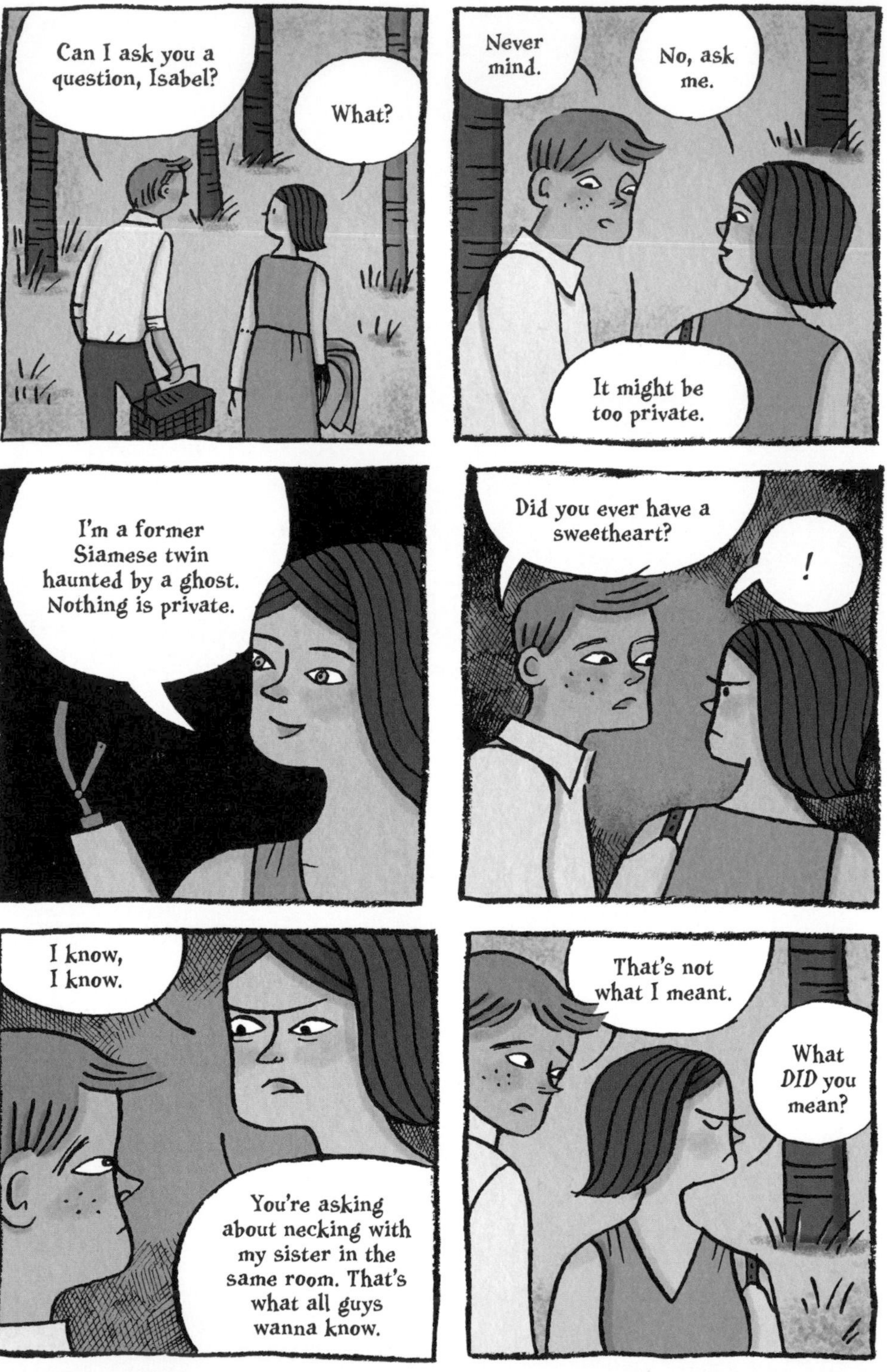
Can I ask you a question, Isabel?
What?
Never mind.
No, ask me.
It might be too private.
I'm a former Siamese twin haunted by a ghost. Nothing is private.
Did you ever have a sweetheart?
!
I know, I know.
You're asking about necking with my sister in the same room. That's what all guys wanna know.
That's not what I meant.
What *DID* you mean?

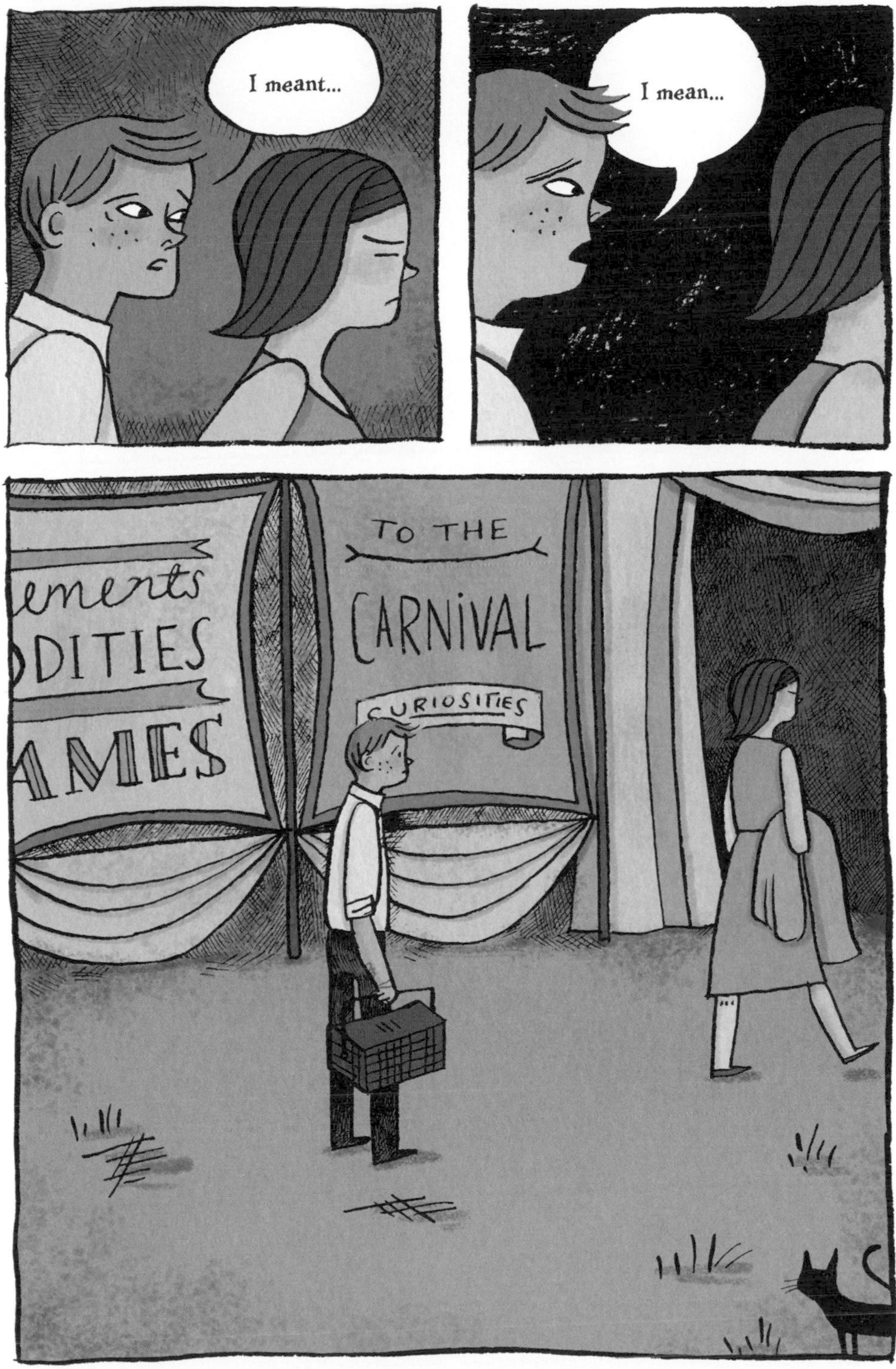
I meant...
I mean...
ements
DITIES
AMES
TO THE
CARNIVAL
CURIOSITIES

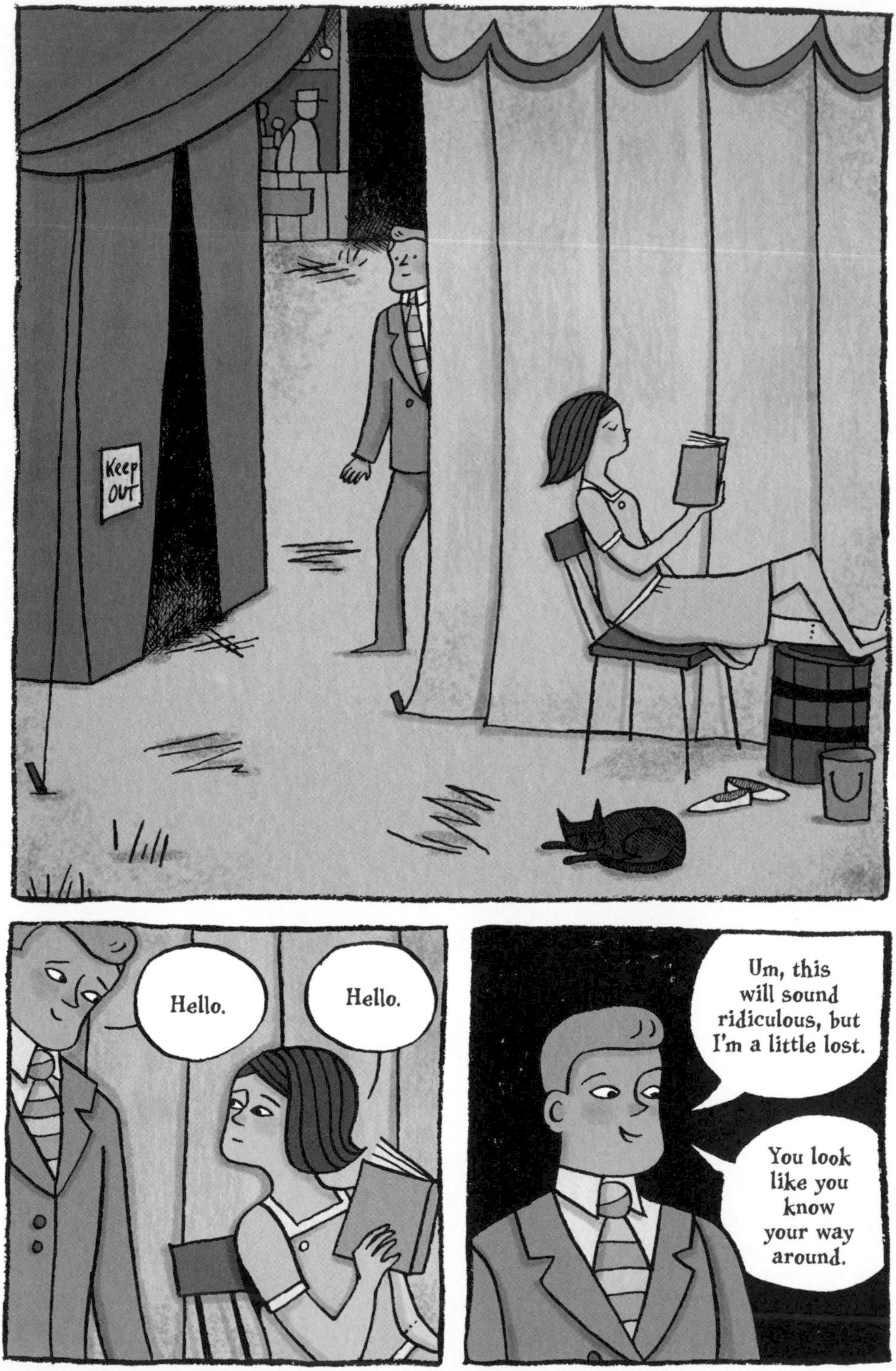
Keep OUT
Hello.
Hello.
Um, this will sound ridiculous, but I'm a little lost.
You look like you know your way around.

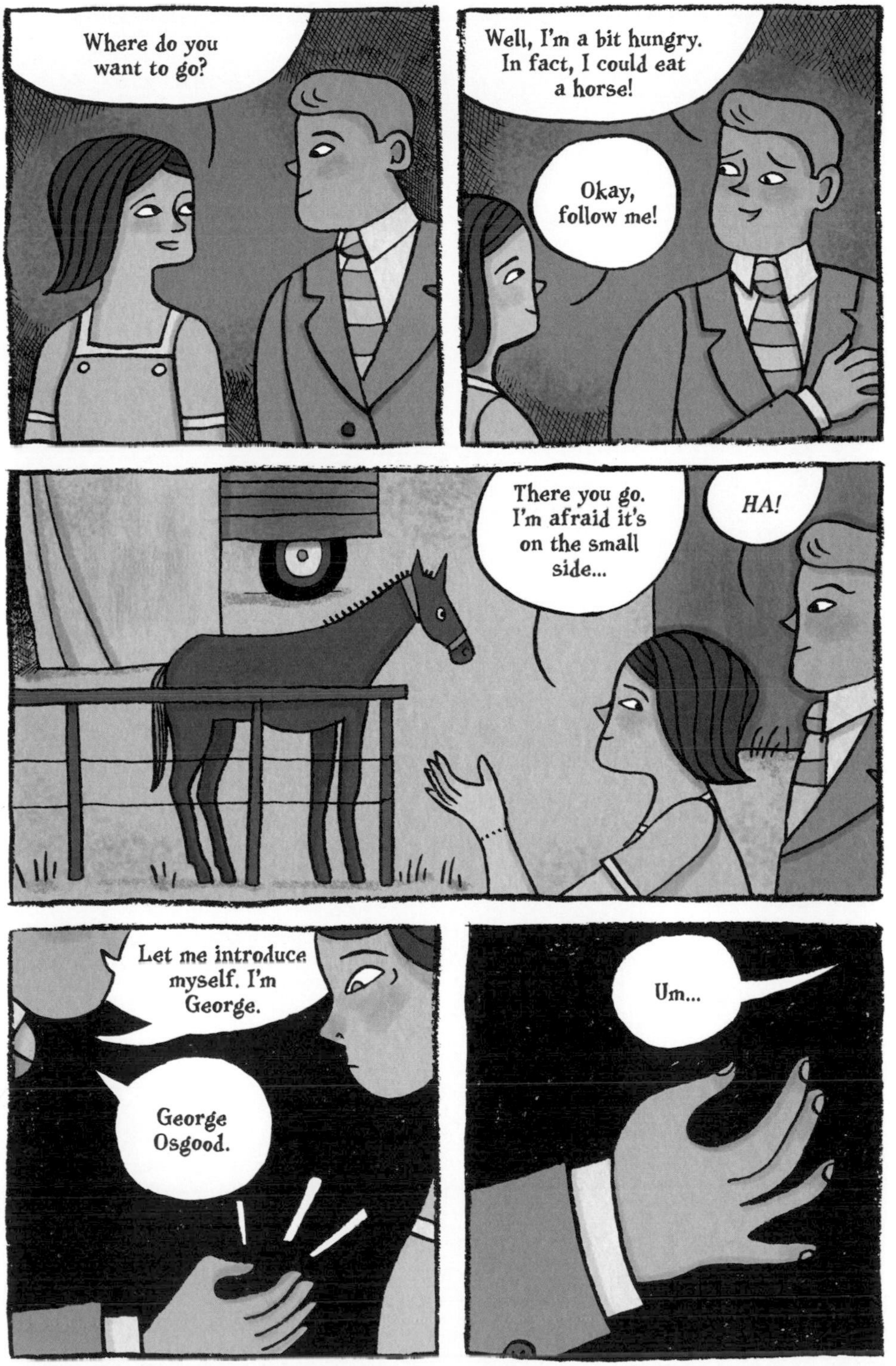
Where do you want to go?
Well, I'm a bit hungry. In fact, I could eat a horse!
Okay, follow me!
There you go. I'm afraid it's on the small side...
HA!
Let me introduce myself. I'm George.
George Osgood.
Um...

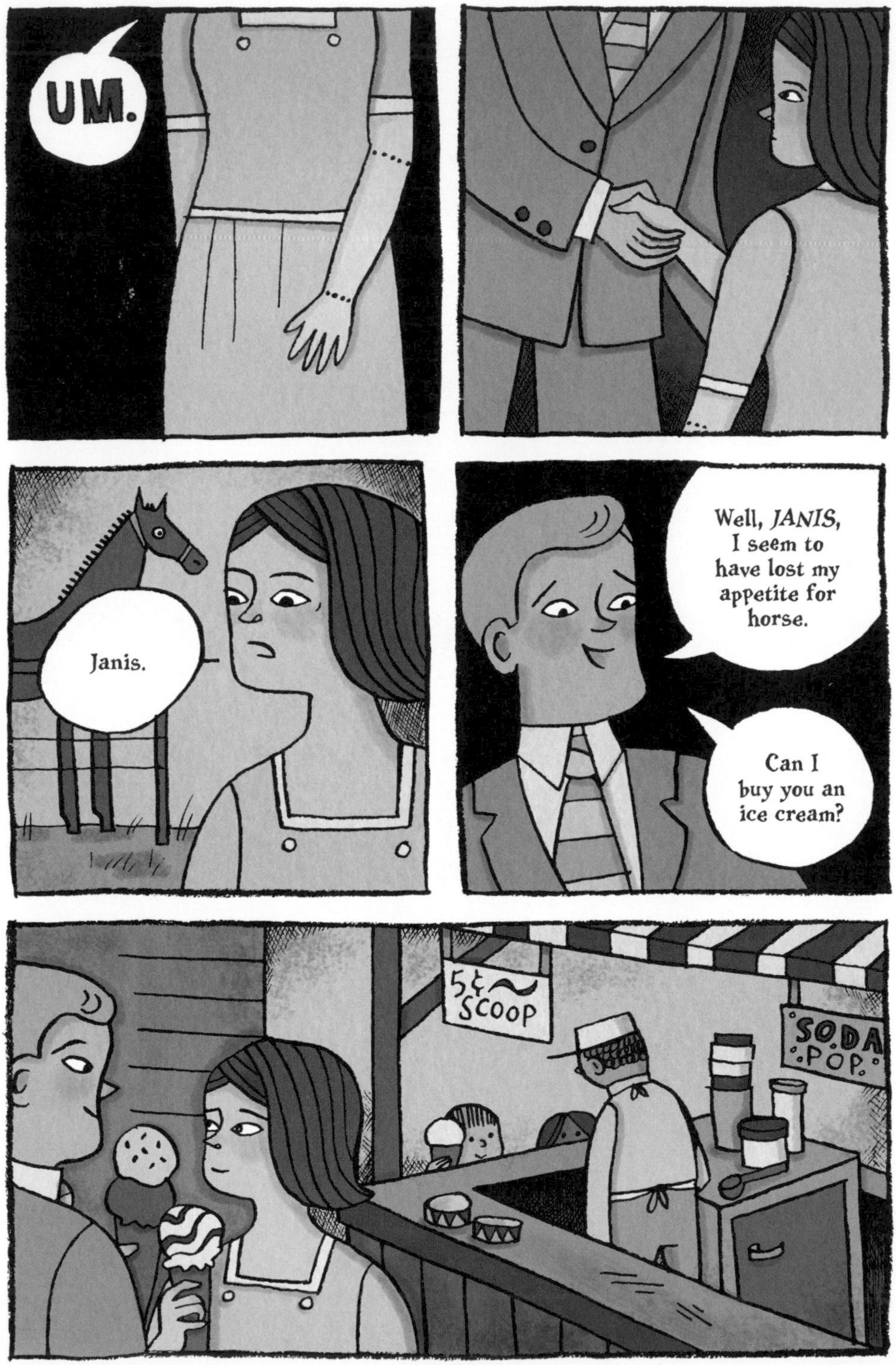
UM.
Janis.
Well, *JANIS*, I seem to have lost my appetite for horse.
Can I buy you an ice cream?
5¢ SCOOP
SODA POP

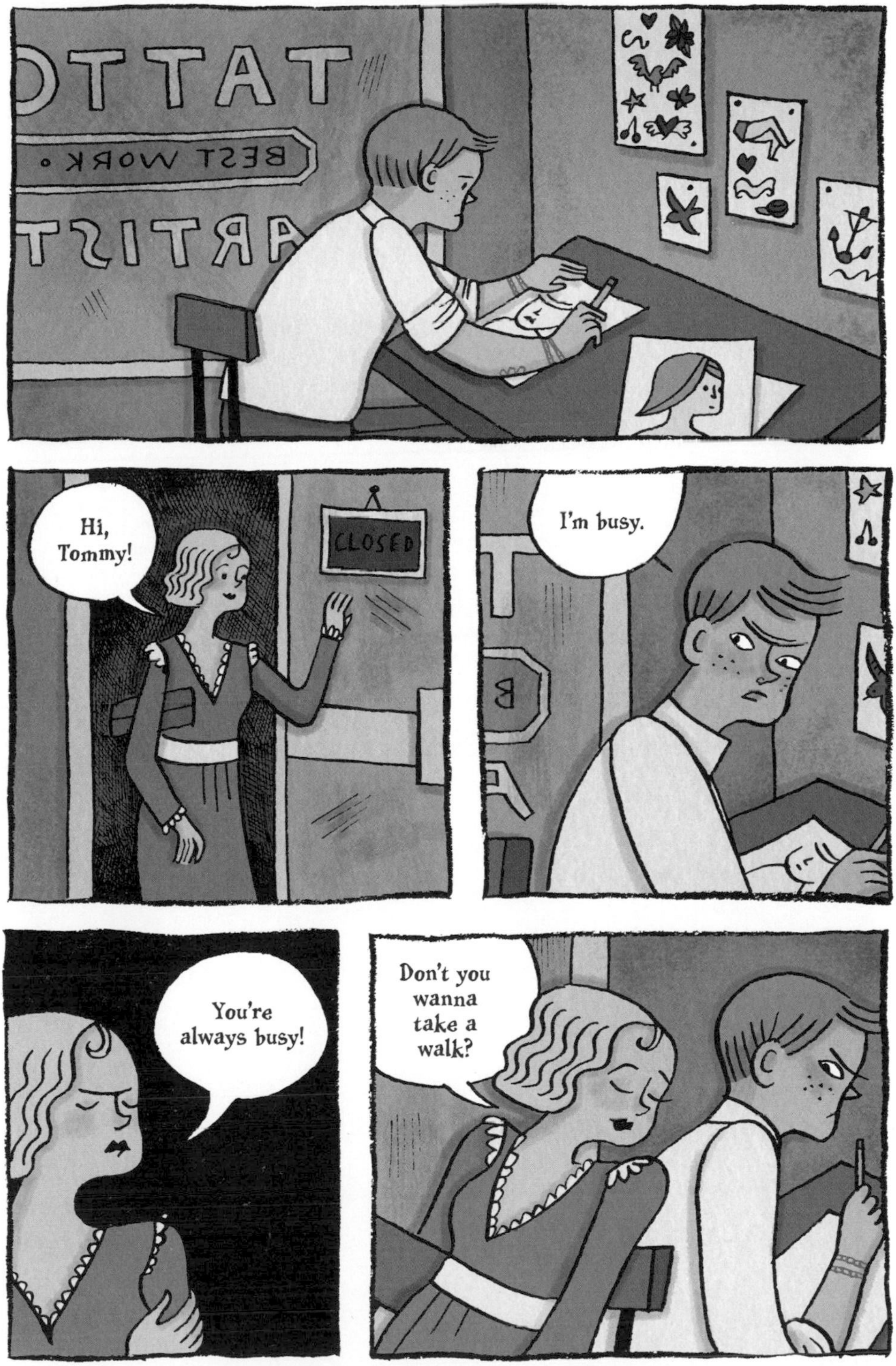
Hi, Tommy!
CLOSED
I'm busy.
You're always busy!
Don't you wanna take a walk?

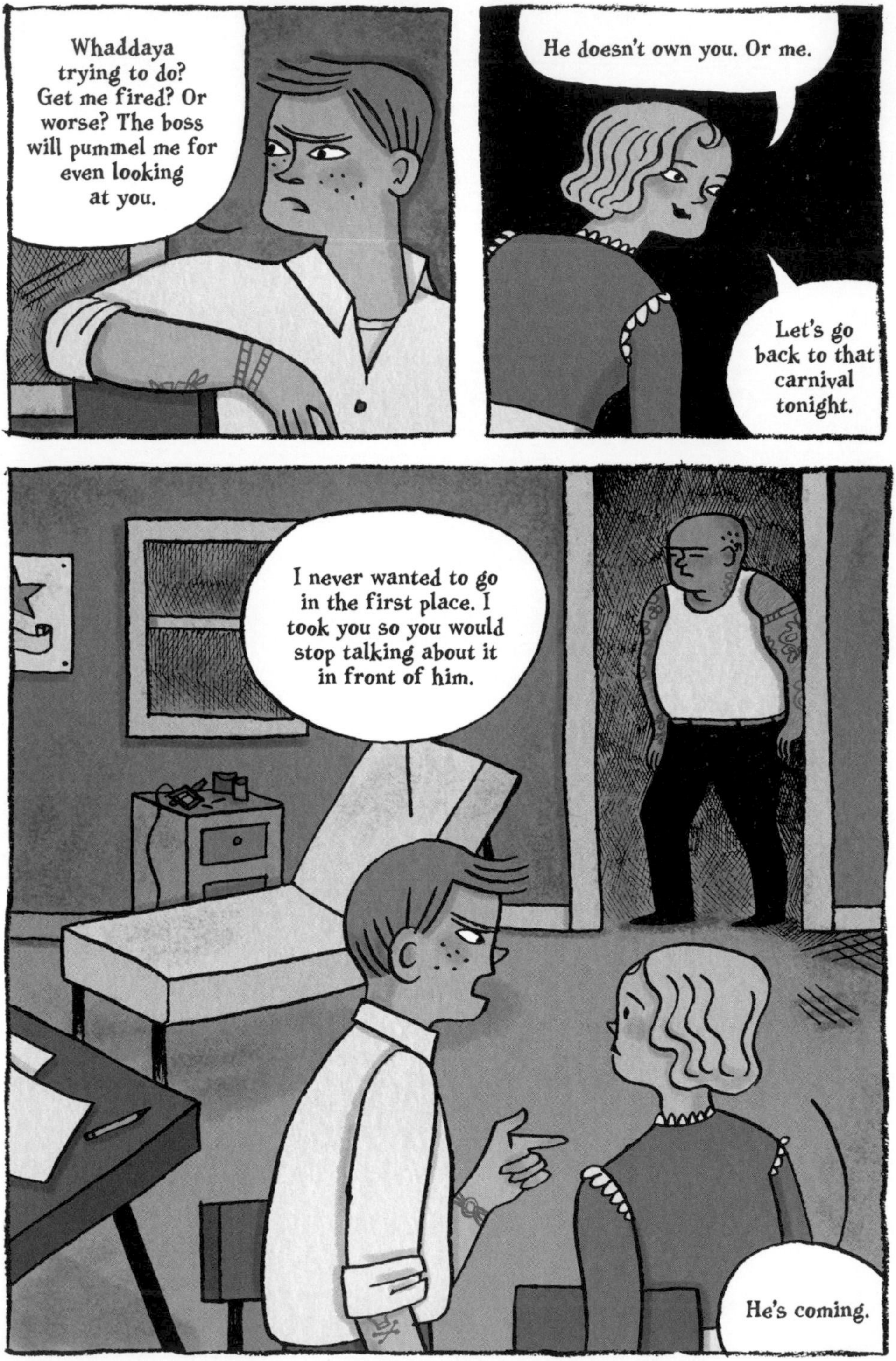
Whaddaya trying to do? Get me fired? Or worse? The boss will pummel me for even looking at you.
He doesn't own you. Or me.
Let's go back to that carnival tonight.
I never wanted to go in the first place. I took you so you would stop talking about it in front of him.
He's coming.

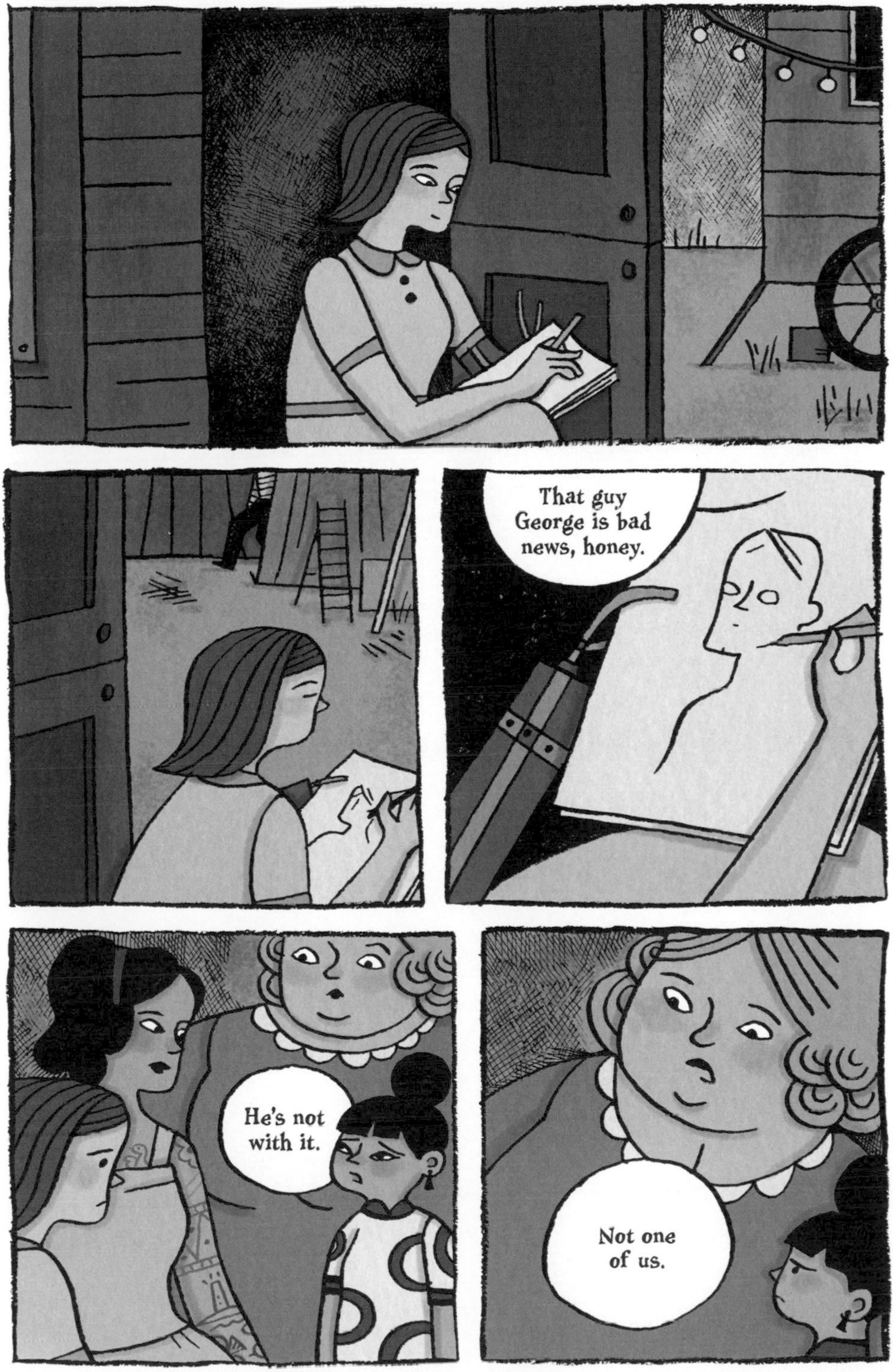
That guy George is bad news, honey.
He's not with it.
Not one of us.

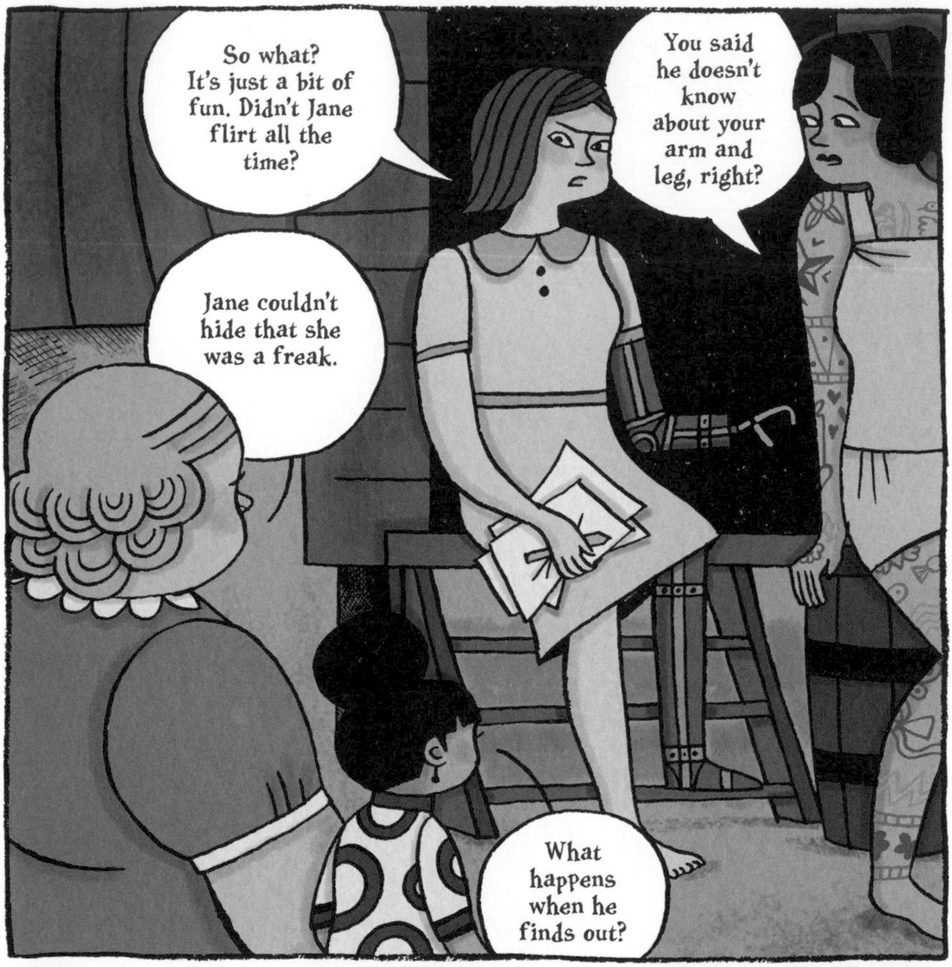
So what? It's just a bit of fun. Didn't Jane flirt all the time?
You said he doesn't know about your arm and leg, right?
Jane couldn't hide that she was a freak.
What happens when he finds out?

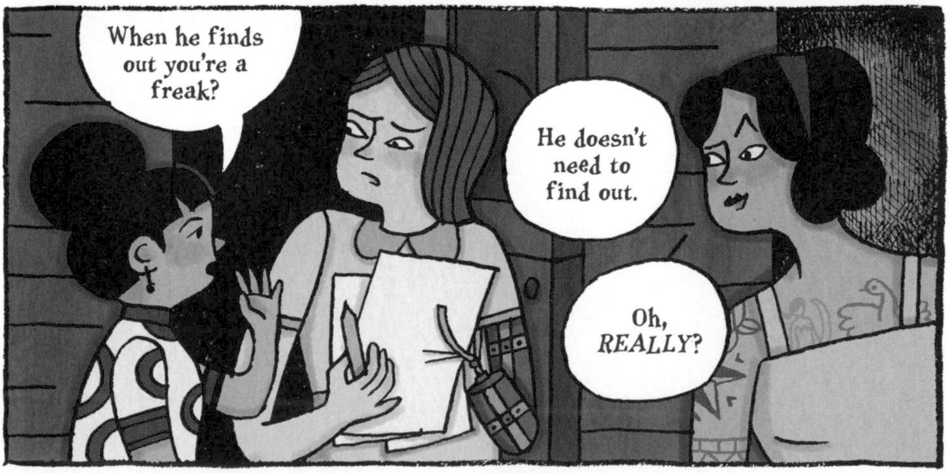
When he finds out you're a freak?
He doesn't need to find out.
Oh, *REALLY*?

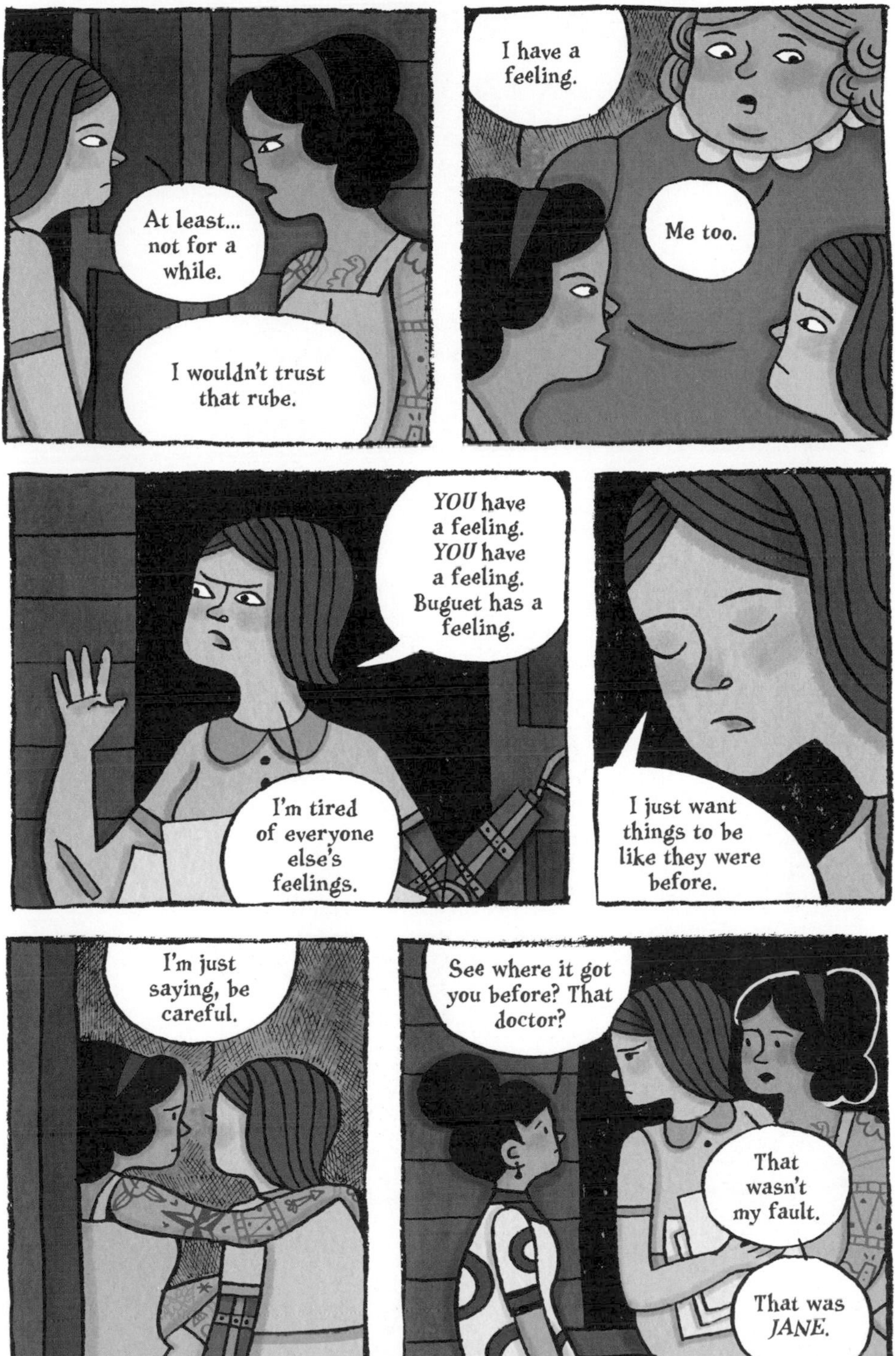
At least... not for a while.
I wouldn't trust that rube.
I have a feeling.
Me too.
YOU have a feeling. YOU have a feeling. Buguet has a feeling.
I'm tired of everyone else's feelings.
I just want things to be like they were before.
I'm just saying, be careful.
See where it got you before? That doctor?
That wasn't my fault.
That was JANE.

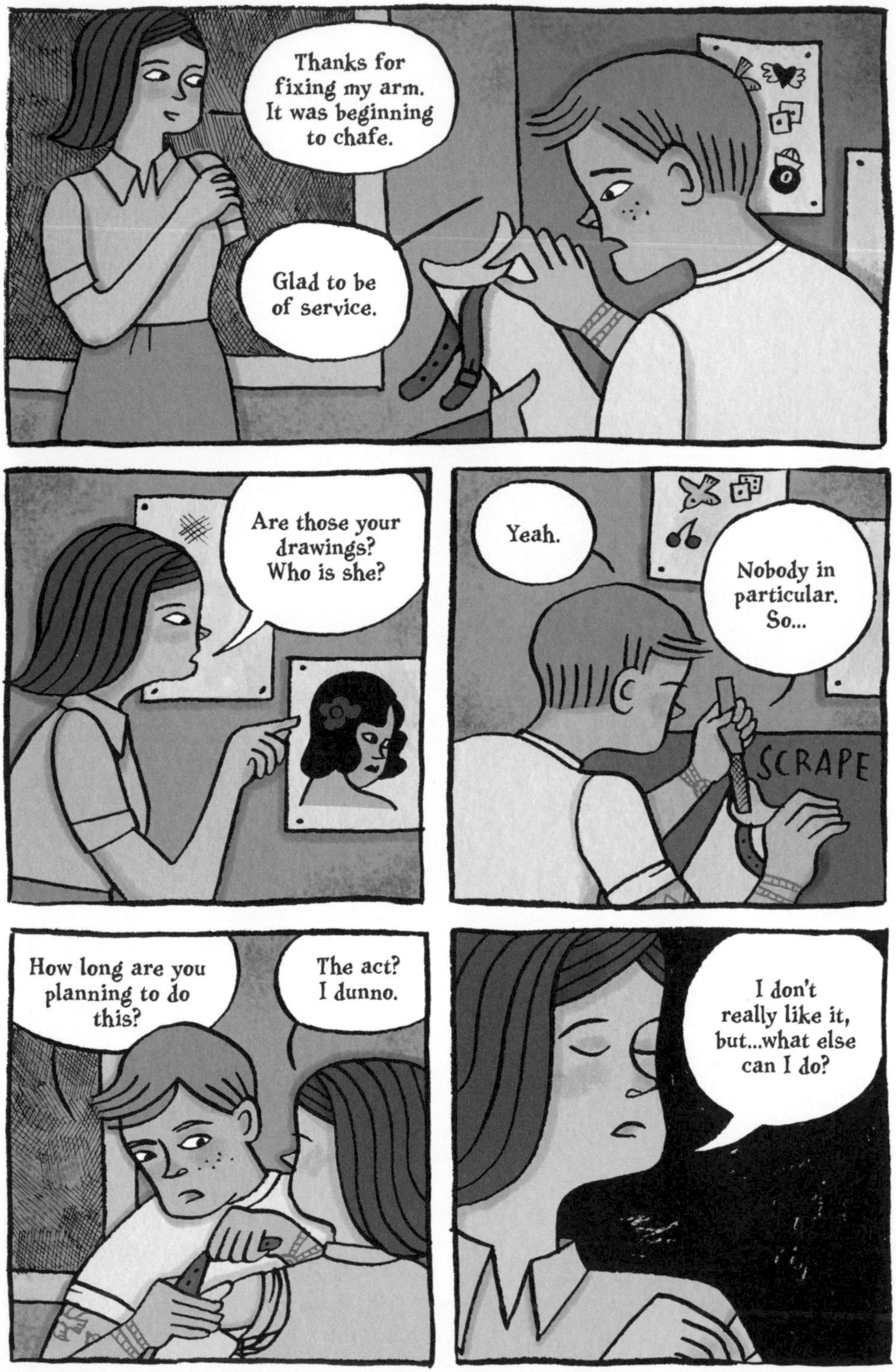
Thanks for fixing my arm. It was beginning to chafe.
Glad to be of service.
Are those your drawings? Who is she?
Yeah.
Nobody in particular. So...
SCRAPE
How long are you planning to do this?
The act? I dunno.
I don't really like it, but...what else can I do?

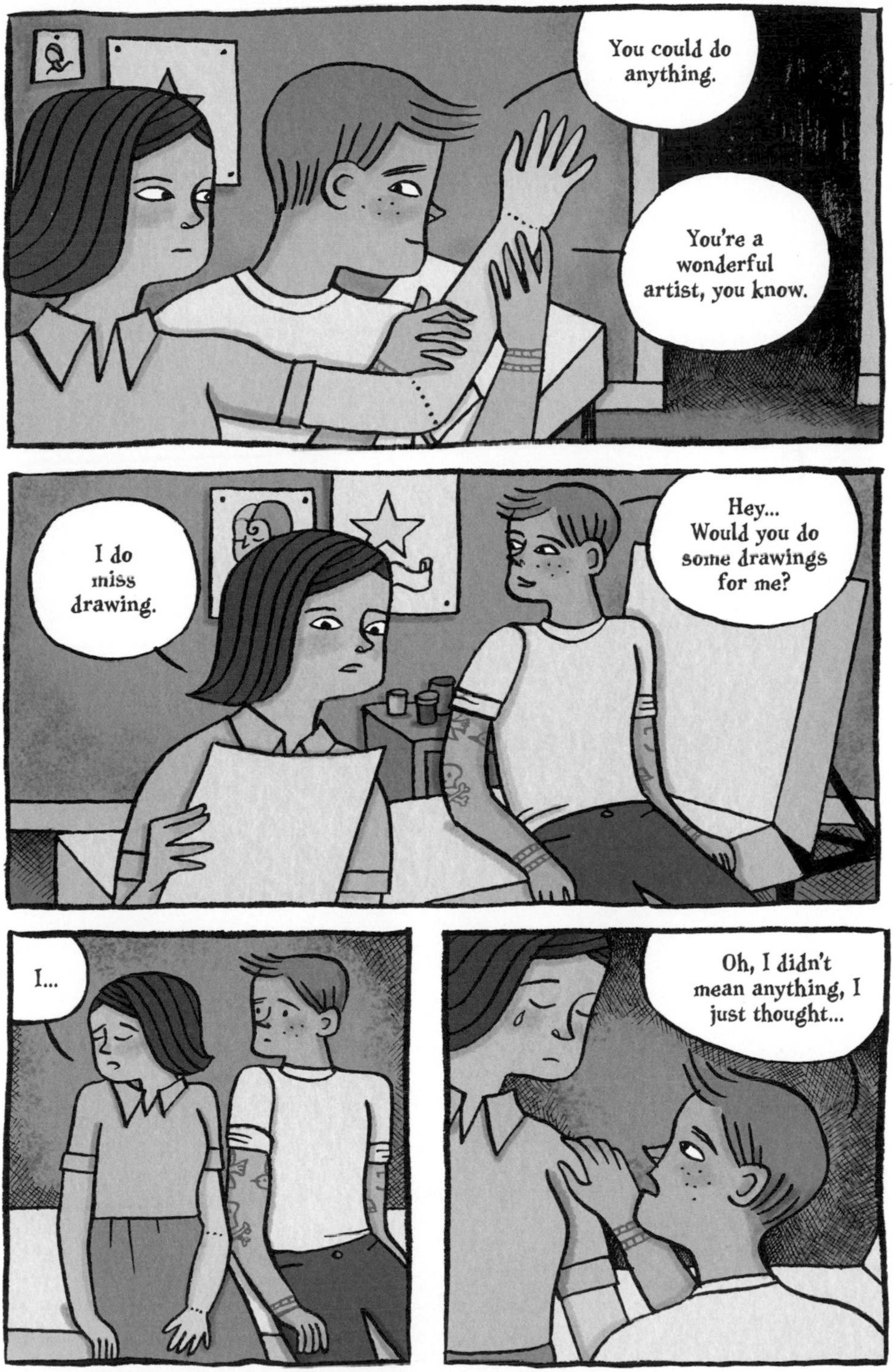
You could do anything.
You're a wonderful artist, you know.
I do miss drawing.
Hey... Would you do some drawings for me?
I...
Oh, I didn't mean anything, I just thought...

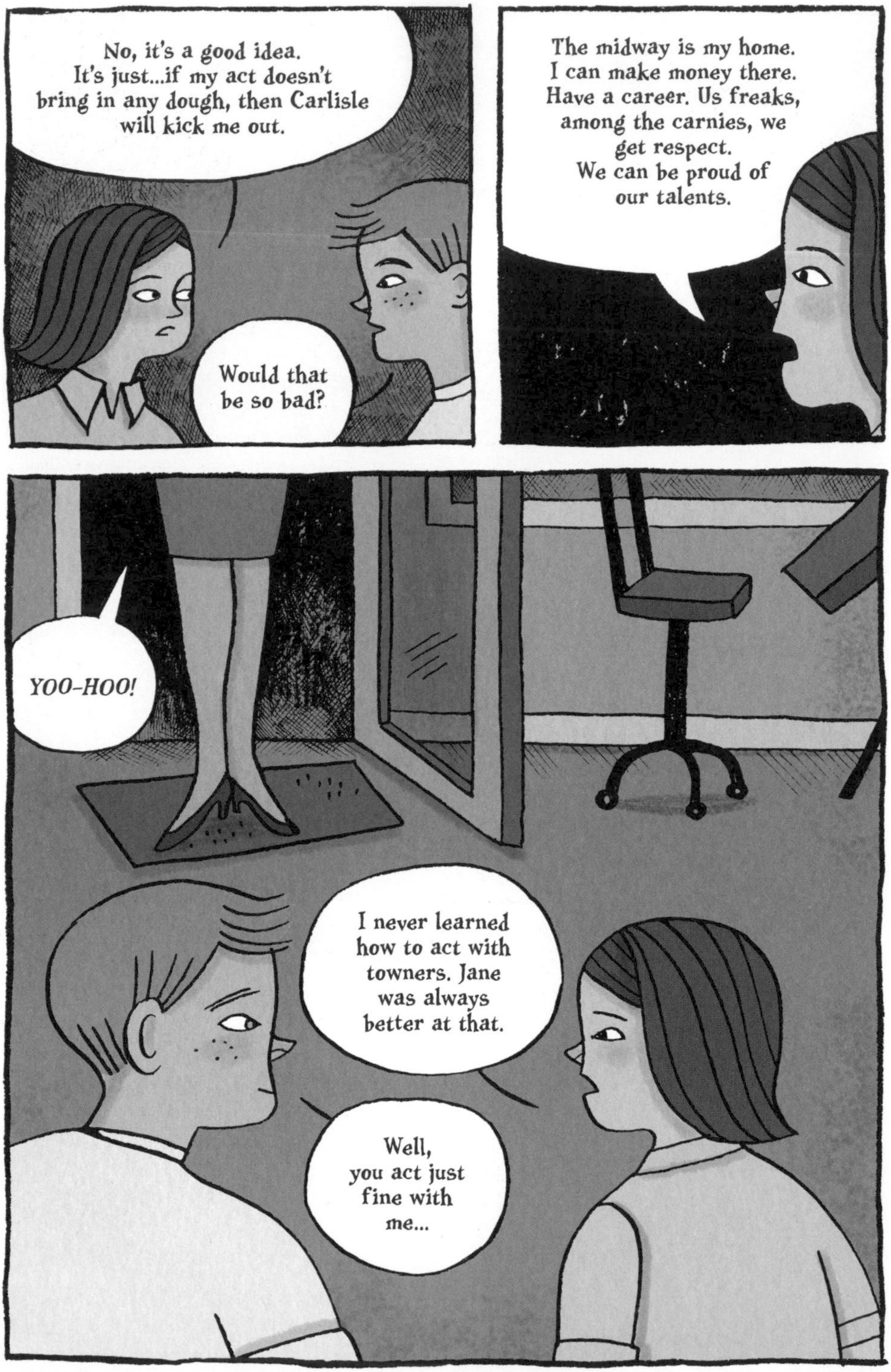
No, it's a good idea. It's just...if my act doesn't bring in any dough, then Carlisle will kick me out.
Would that be so bad?
The midway is my home. I can make money there. Have a career. Us freaks, among the carnies, we get respect. We can be proud of our talents.
YOO-HOO!
I never learned how to act with towners. Jane was always better at that.
Well, you act just fine with me...

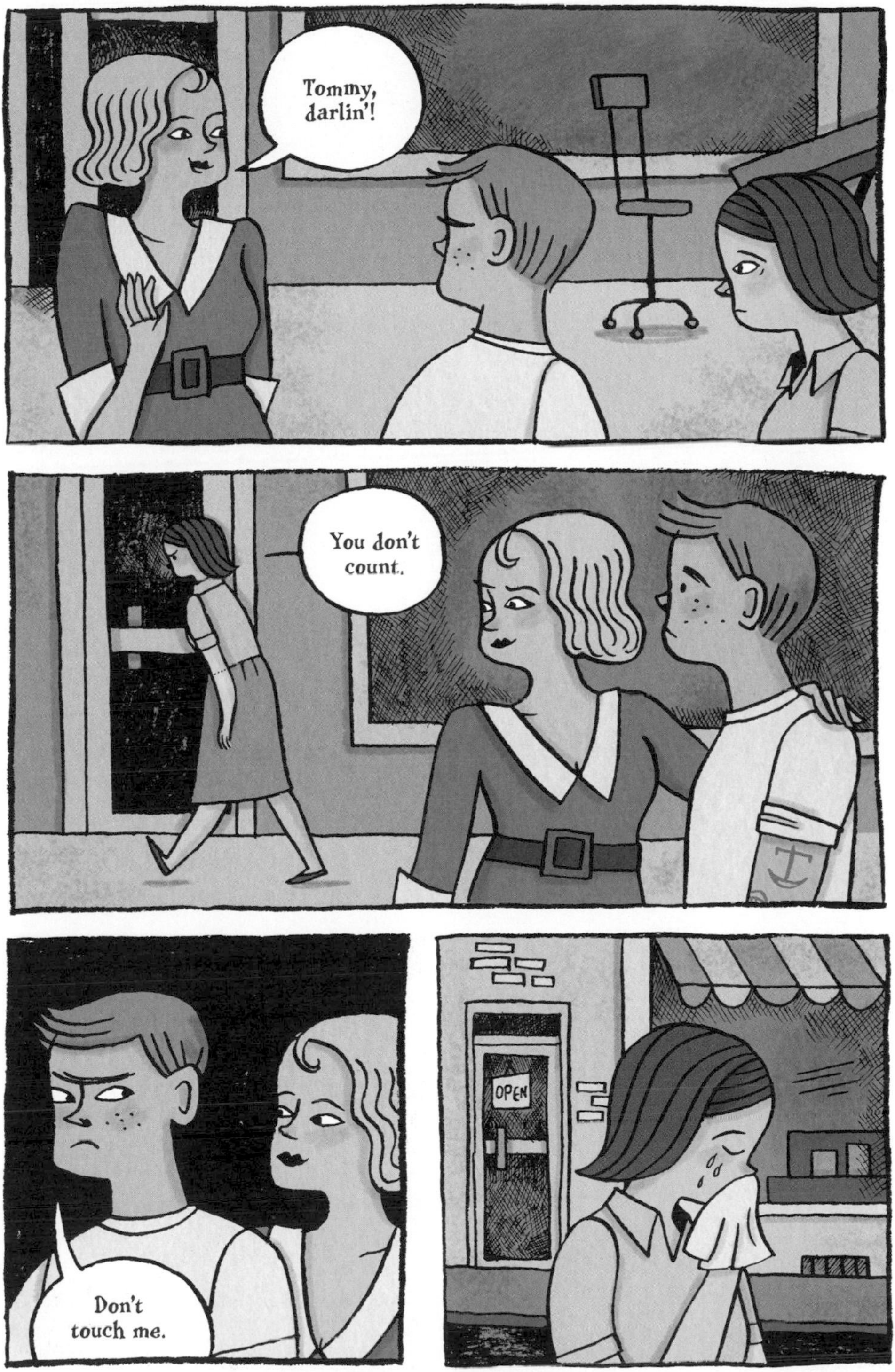
Tommy, darlin'!
You don't count.
Don't touch me.
OPEN

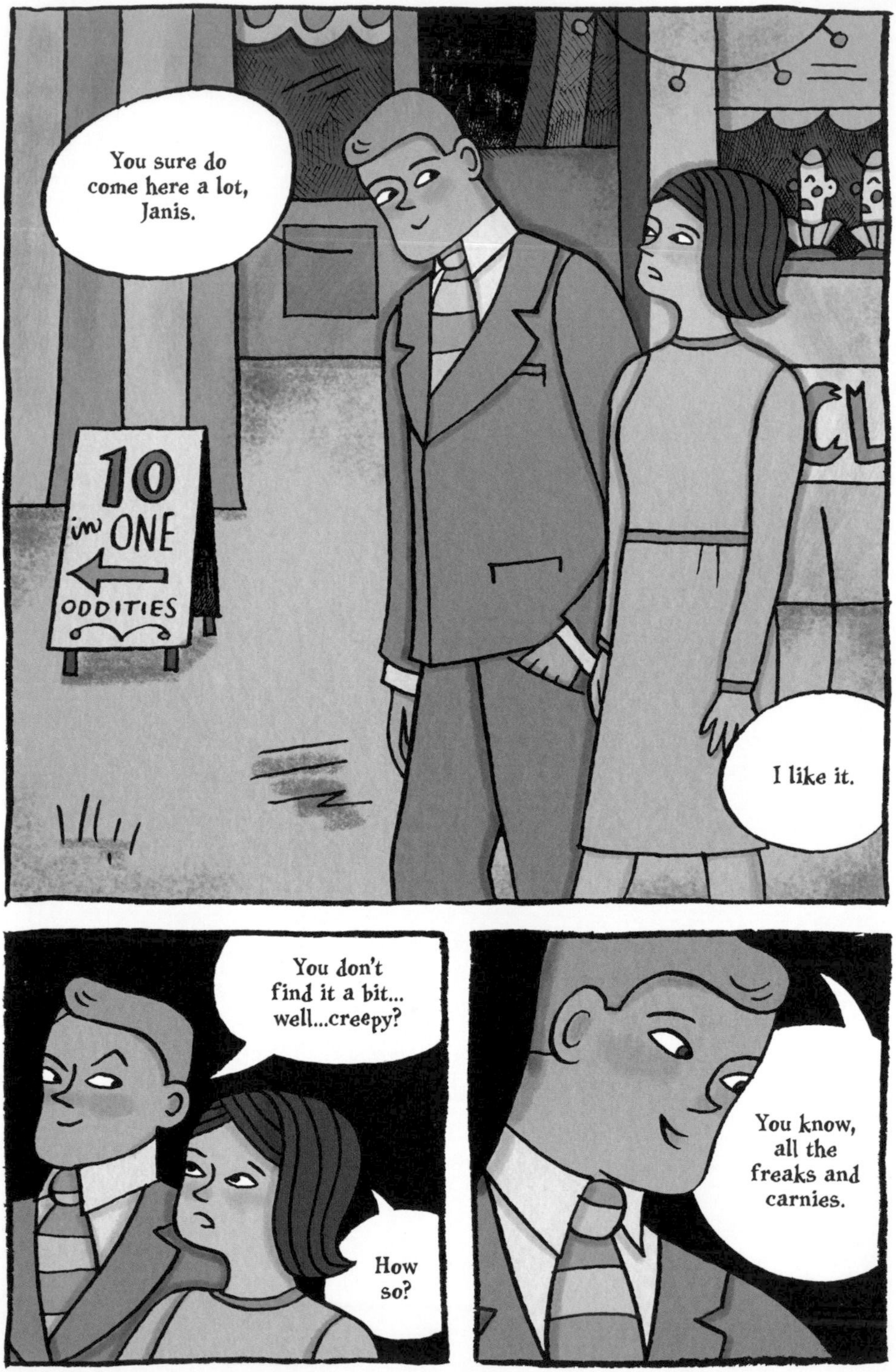
You sure do come here a lot, Janis.
10 in ONE
ODDITIES
CL
I like it.
You don't find it a bit... well...creepy?
How so?
You know, all the freaks and carnies.

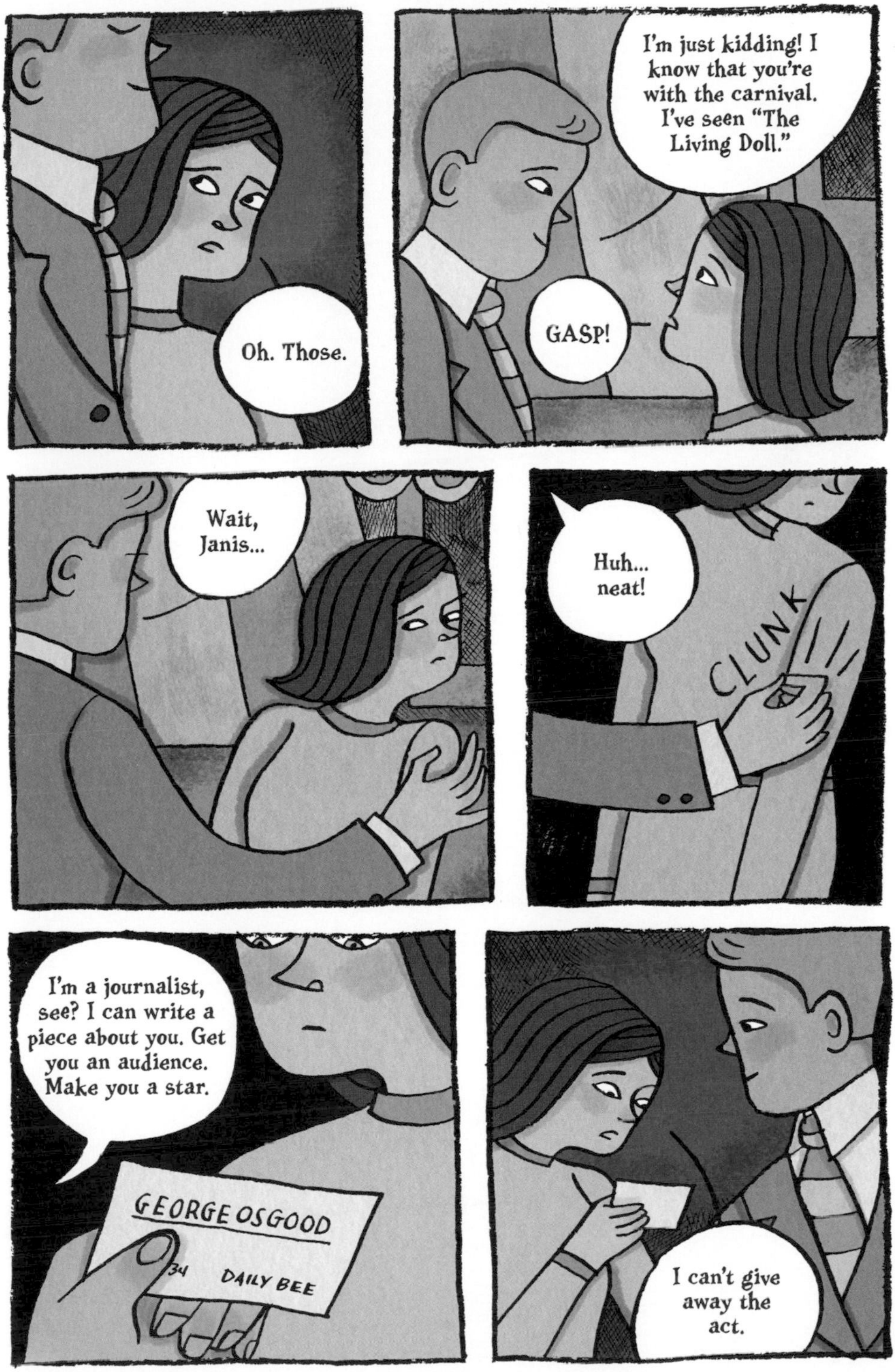
Oh. Those.
I'm just kidding! I know that you're with the carnival. I've seen "The Living Doll."
GASP!
Wait, Janis...
Huh... neat!
CLUNK
I'm a journalist, see? I can write a piece about you. Get you an audience. Make you a star.
GEORGE OSGOOD
34
DAILY BEE
I can't give away the act.

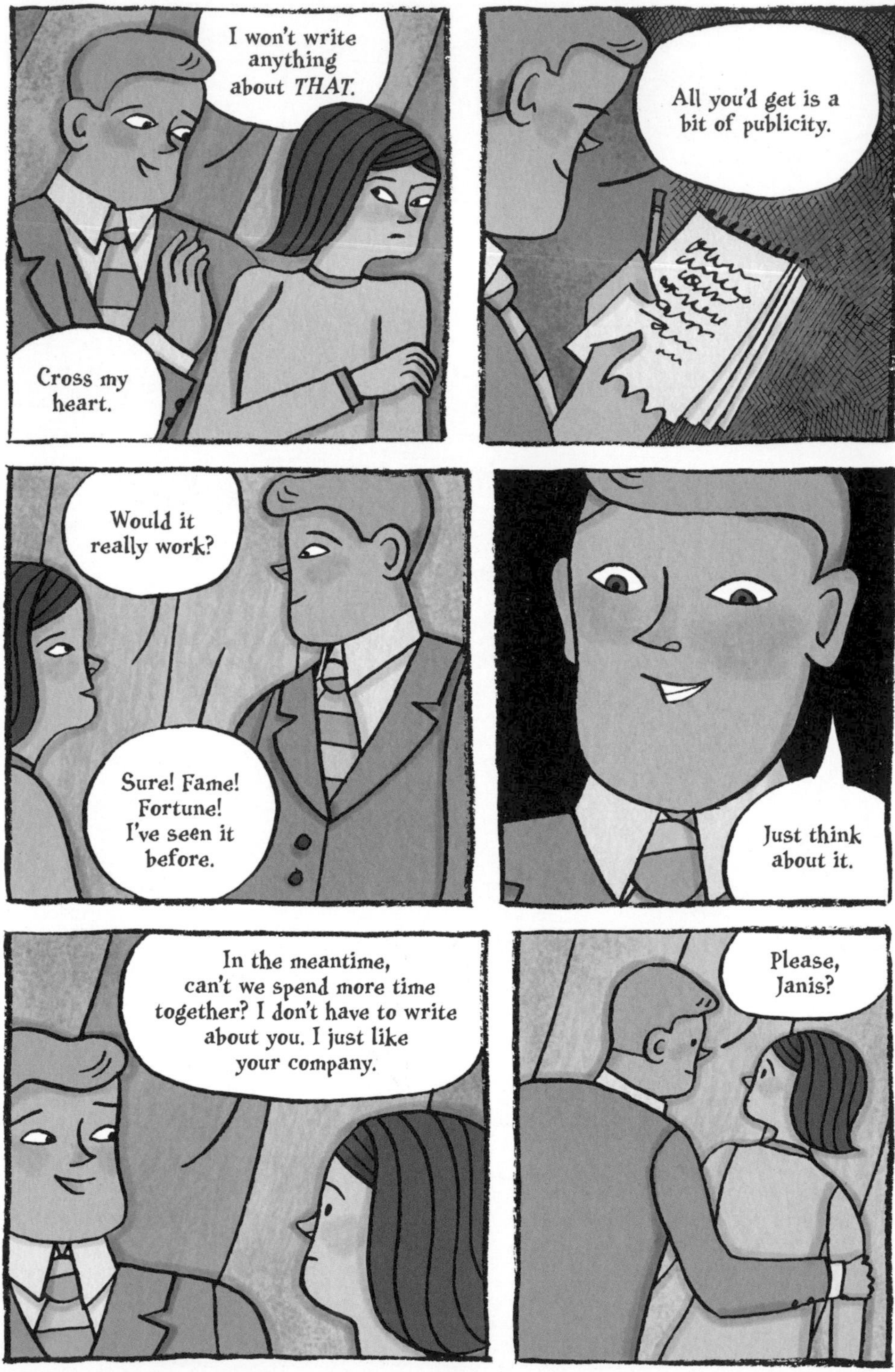
I won't write anything about THAT.
Cross my heart.
All you'd get is a bit of publicity.
Would it really work?
Sure! Fame! Fortune! I've seen it before.
Just think about it.
In the meantime, can't we spend more time together? I don't have to write about you. I just like your company.
Please, Janis?

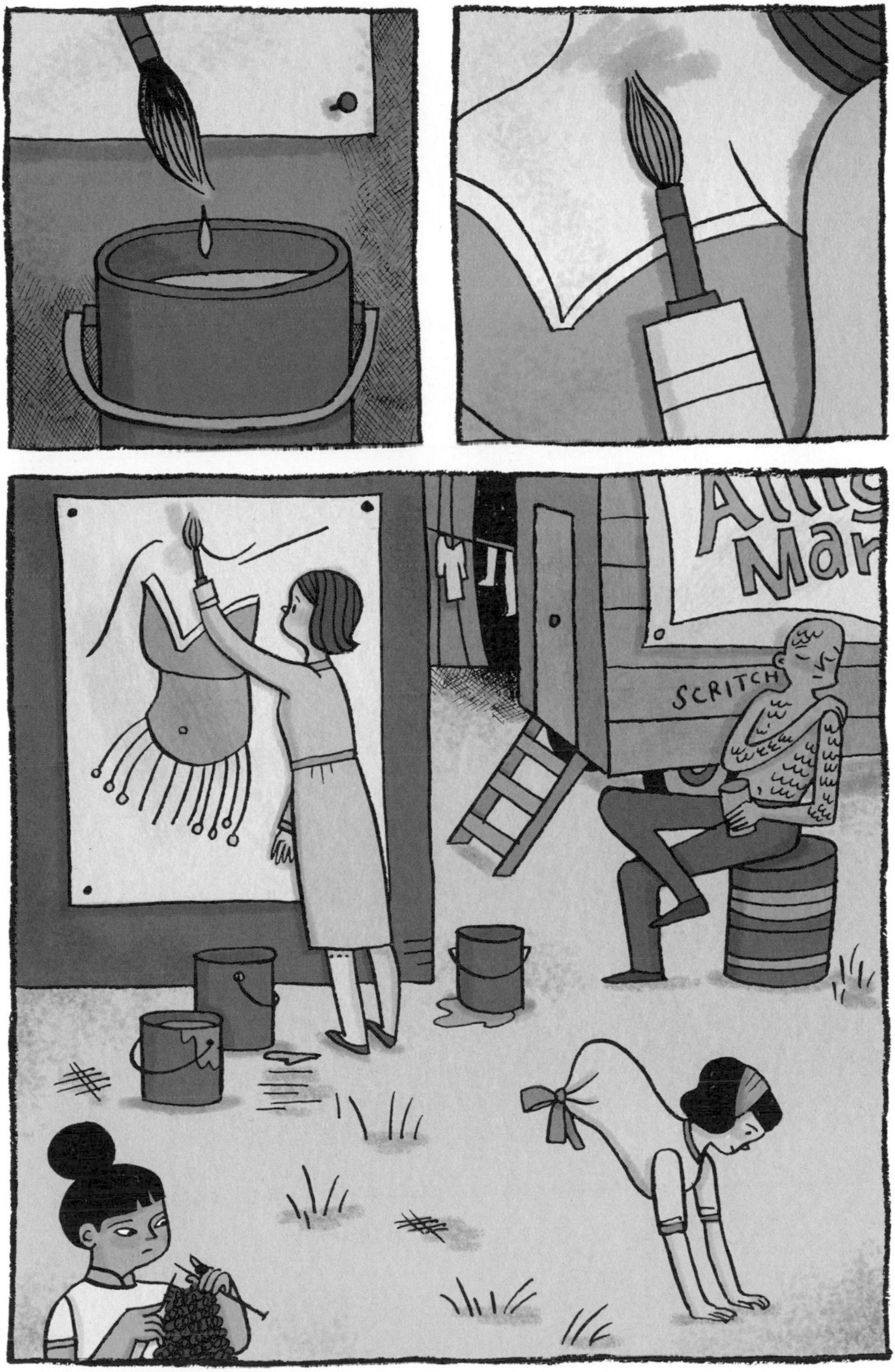
SCRITCH

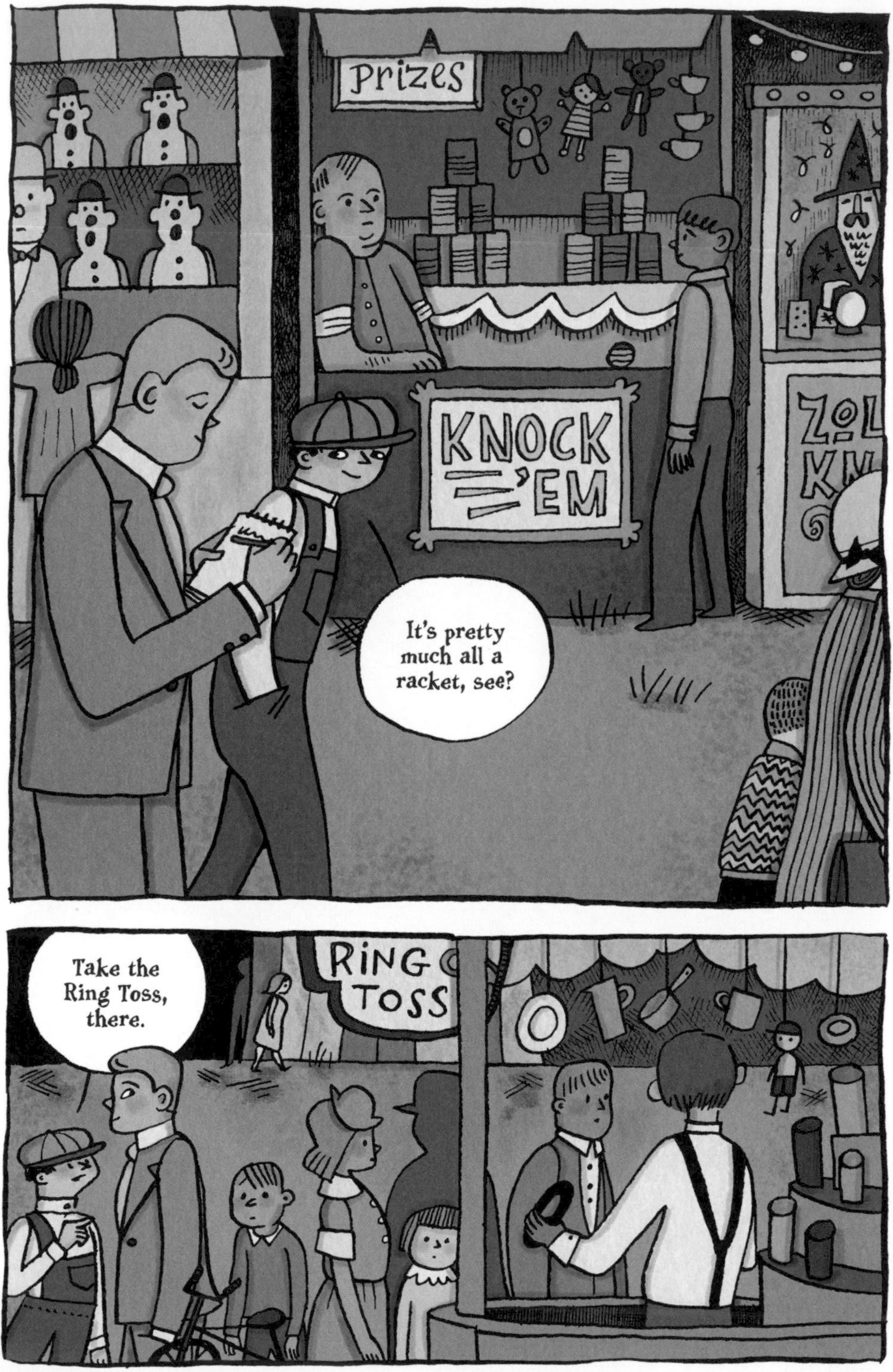
Prizes
KNOCK 'EM
It's pretty much all a racket, see?
Take the Ring Toss, there.
RING TOSS

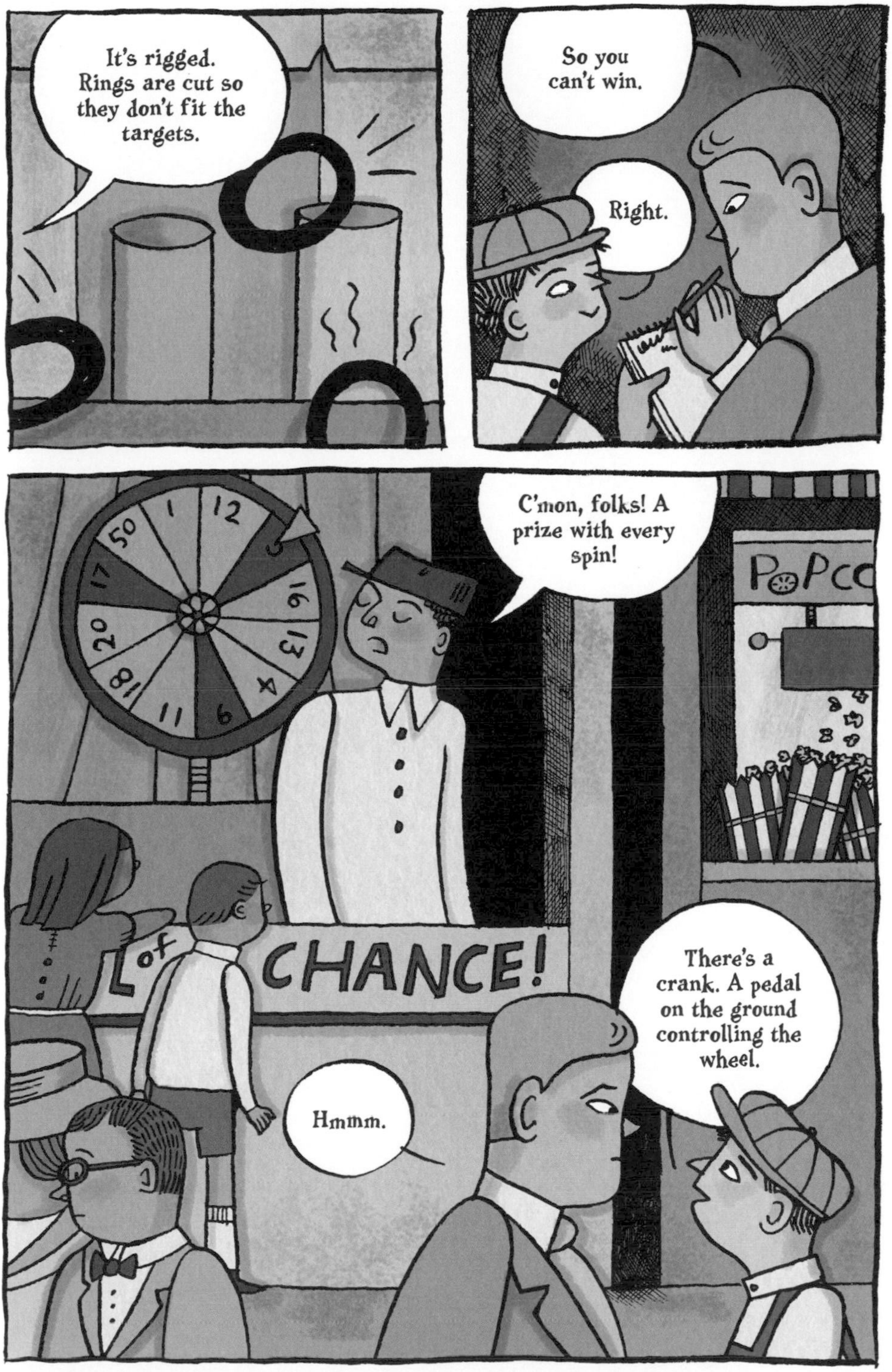
It's rigged. Rings are cut so they don't fit the targets.
So you can't win.
Right.
C'mon, folks! A prize with every spin!
L of CHANCE!
There's a crank. A pedal on the ground controlling the wheel.
Hmmm.

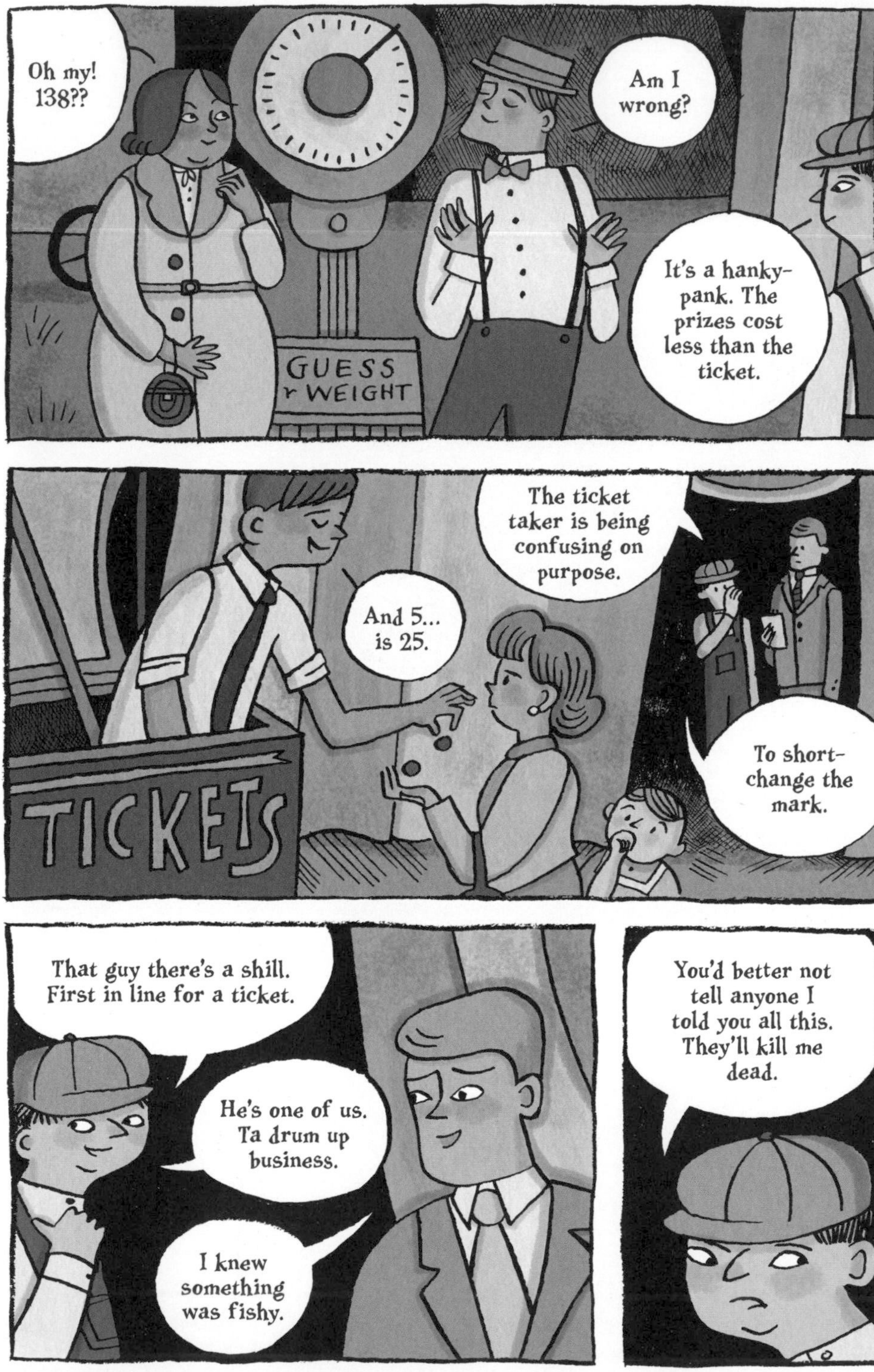
Oh my! 138??
GUESS r WEIGHT
Am I wrong?
It's a hanky-pank. The prizes cost less than the ticket.
The ticket taker is being confusing on purpose.
And 5... is 25.
TICKETS
To short-change the mark.
That guy there's a shill. First in line for a ticket.
He's one of us. Ta drum up business.
I knew something was fishy.
You'd better not tell anyone I told you all this. They'll kill me dead.

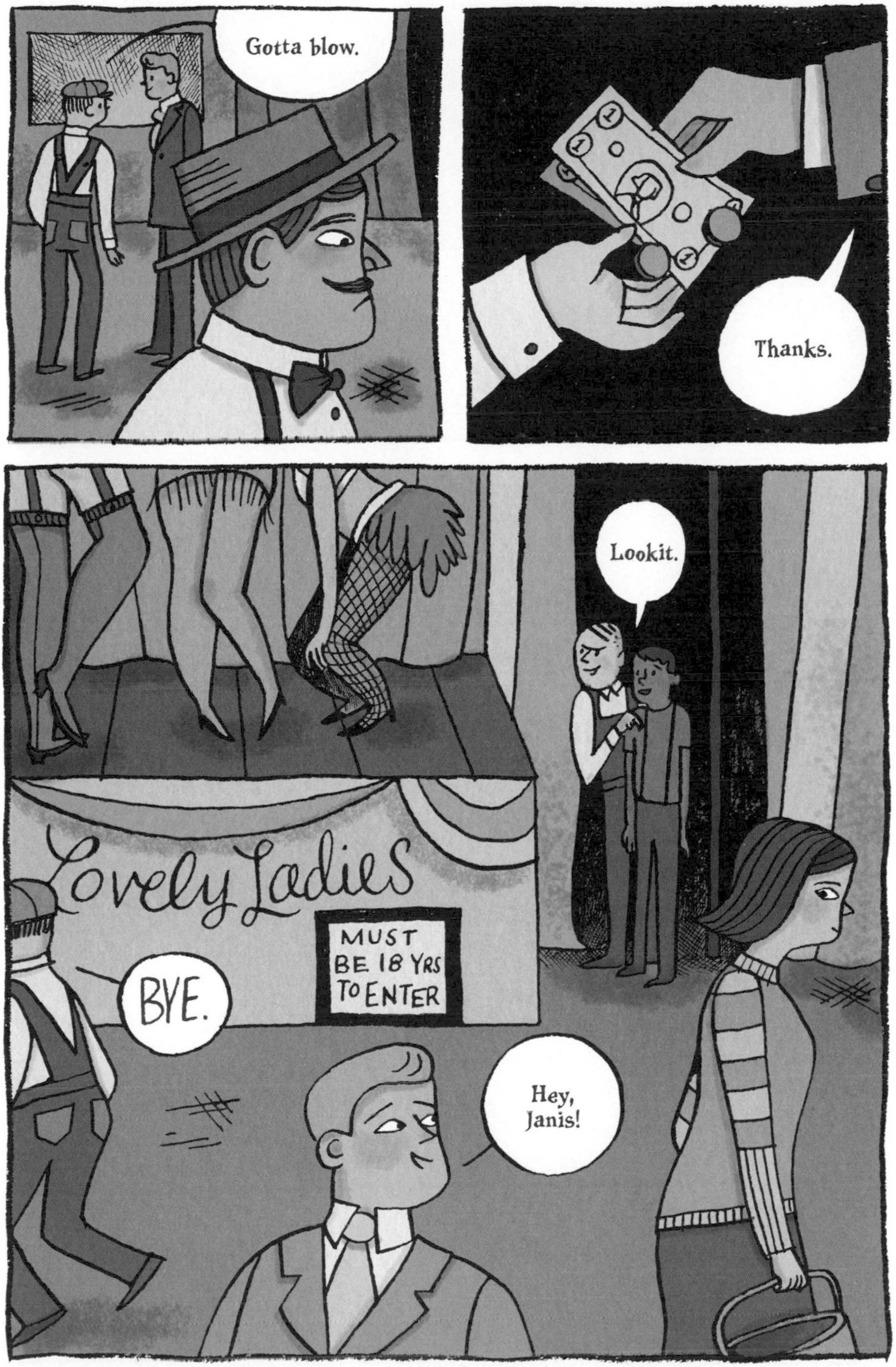
Gotta blow.
Thanks.
Lookit.
Lovely Ladies
MUST BE 18 YRS TO ENTER
BYE.
Hey, Janis!

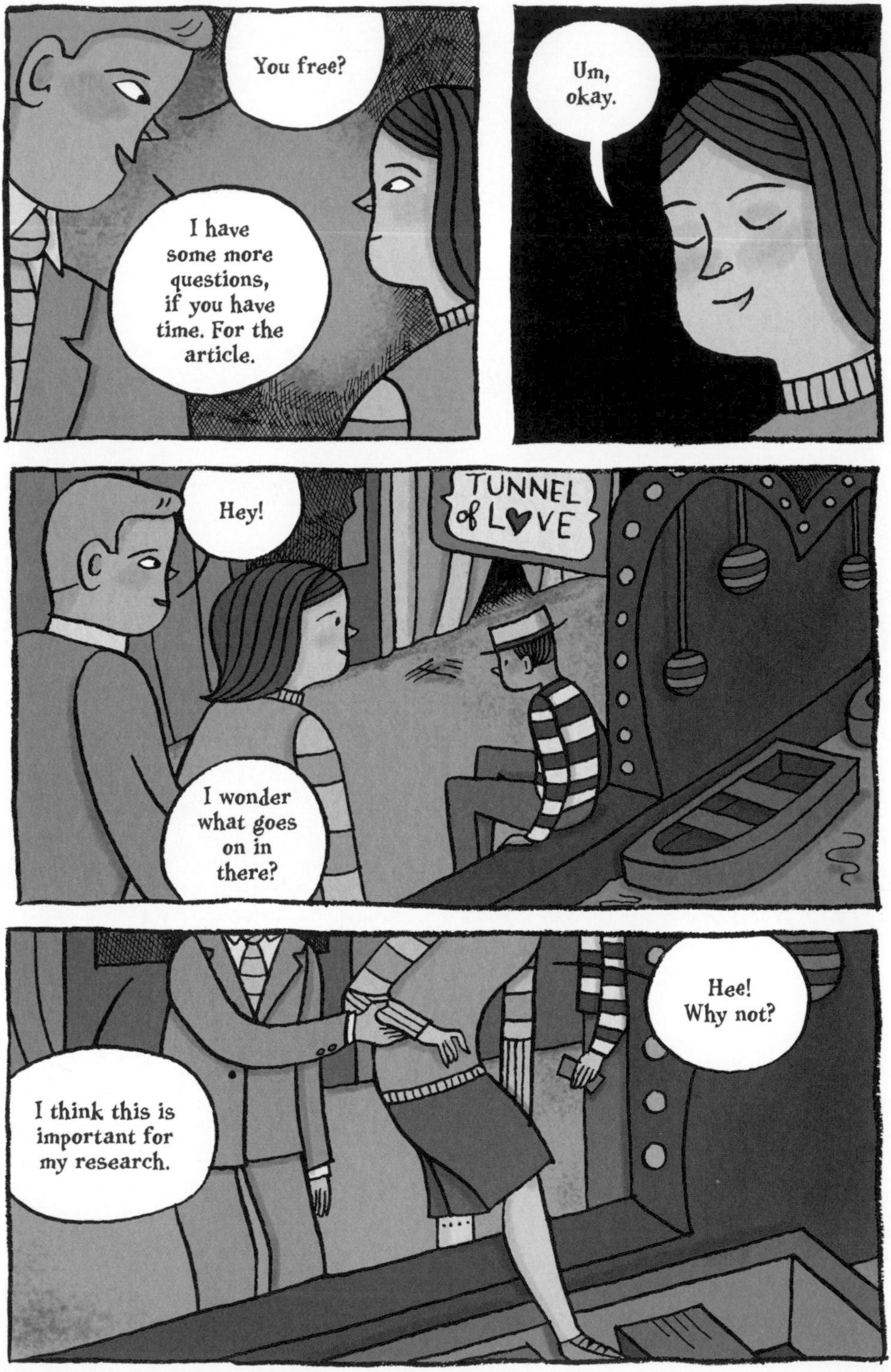
You free?
I have some more questions, if you have time. For the article.
Um, okay.
Hey!
TUNNEL of LOVE
I wonder what goes on in there?
Hee! Why not?
I think this is important for my research.

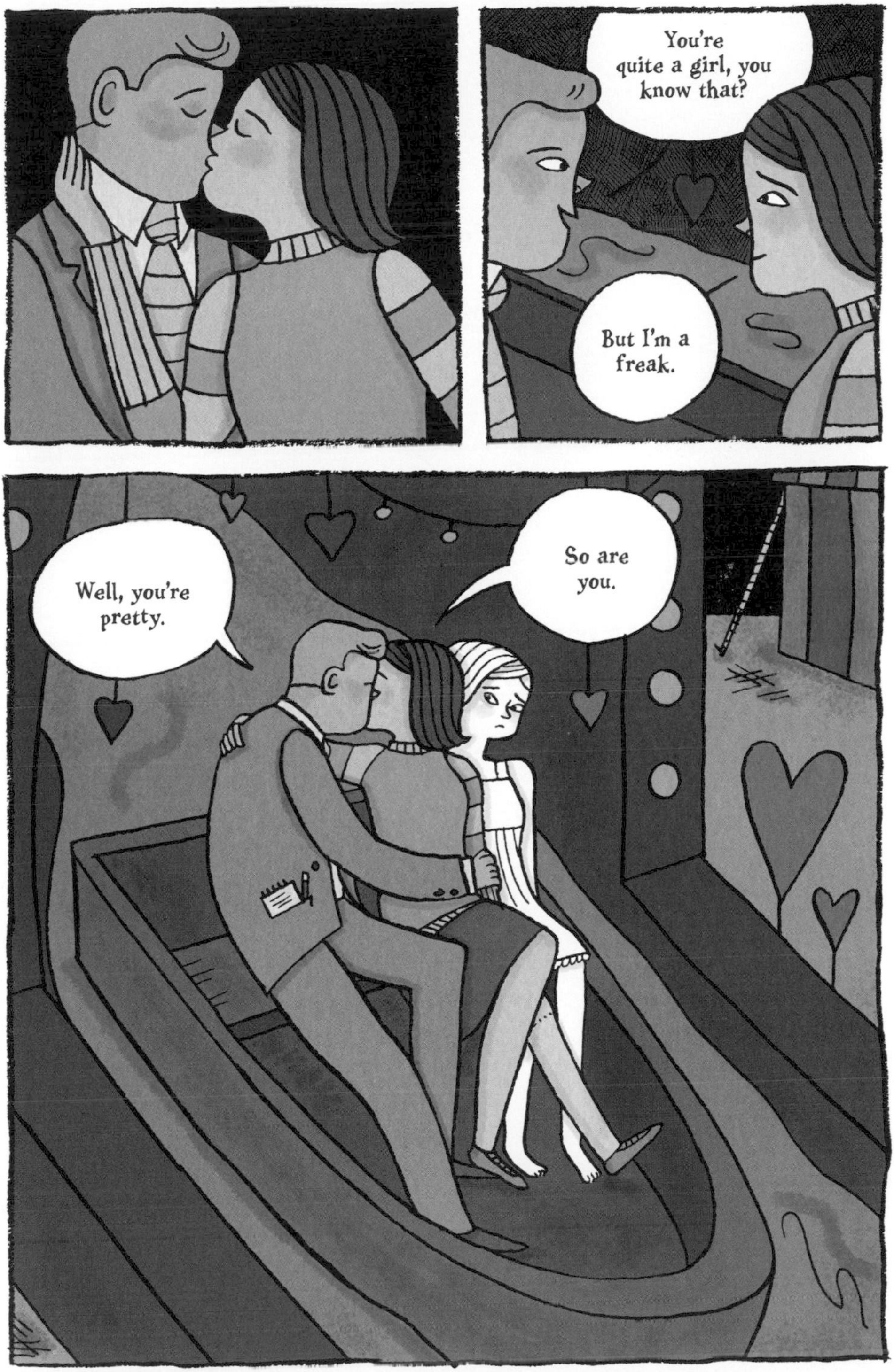
You're quite a girl, you know that?
But I'm a freak.
Well, you're pretty.
So are you.

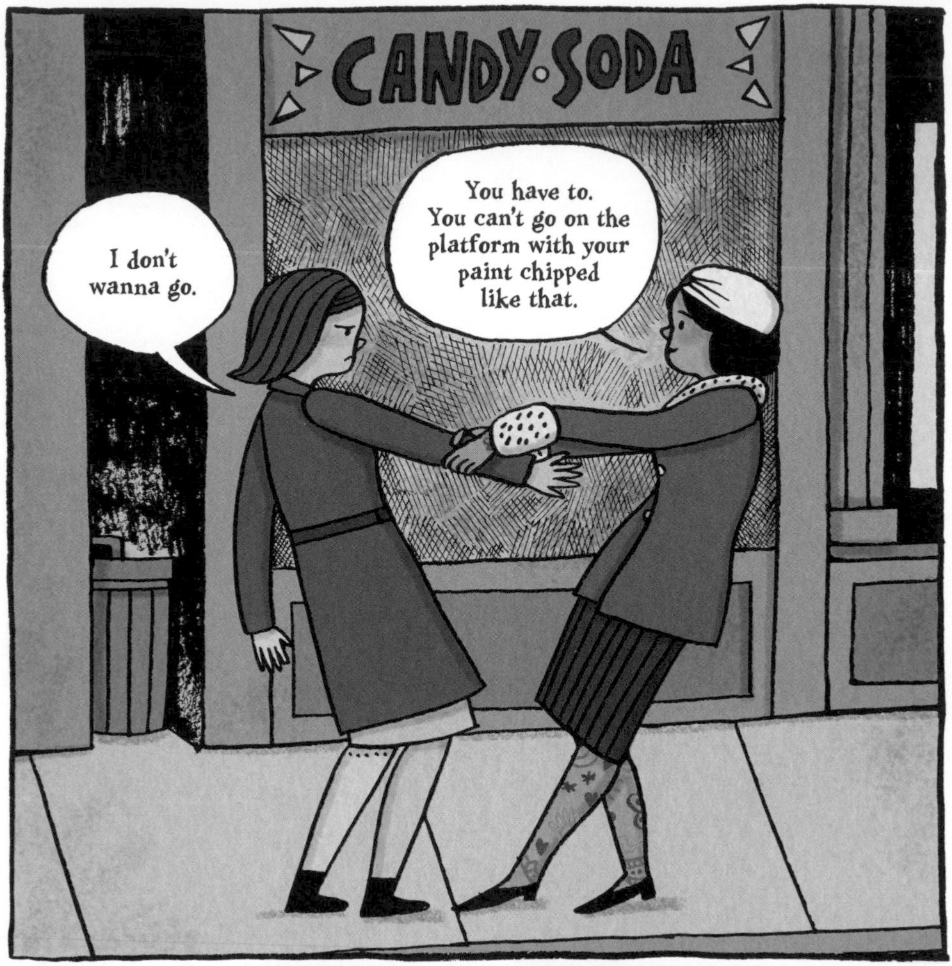
CANDY·SODA
I don't wanna go.
You have to. You can't go on the platform with your paint chipped like that.

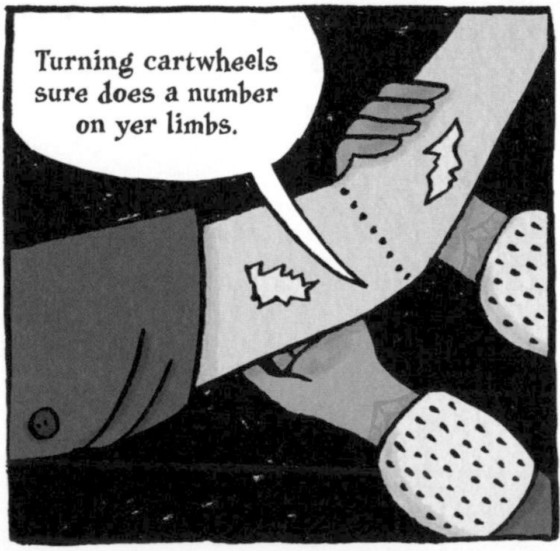
Turning cartwheels sure does a number on yer limbs.

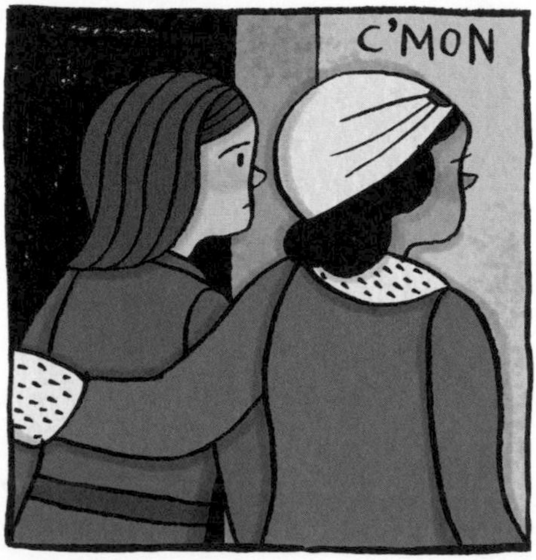
C'MON

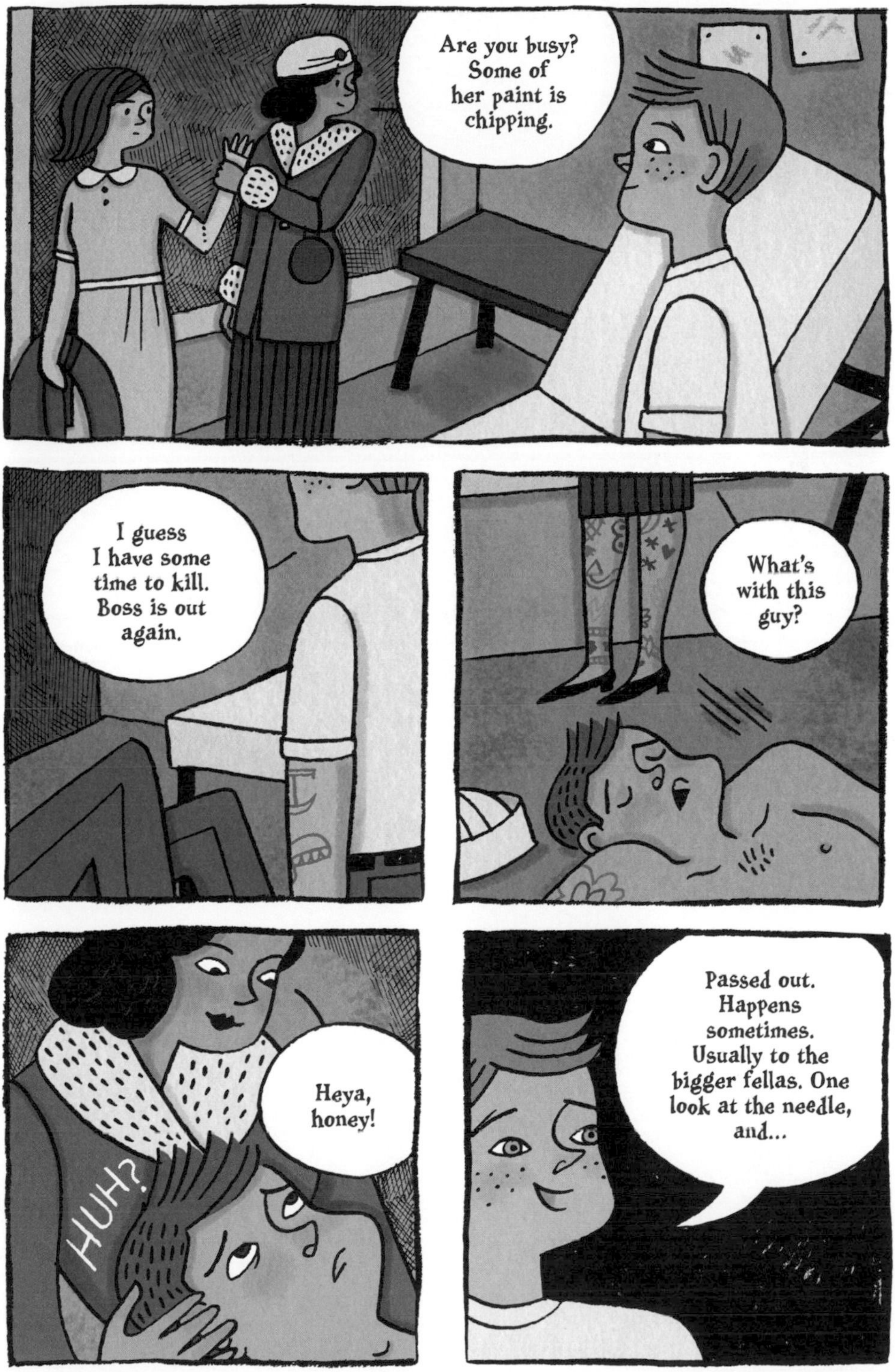
Are you busy? Some of her paint is chipping.
I guess I have some time to kill. Boss is out again.
What's with this guy?
HUH?
Heya, honey!
Passed out. Happens sometimes. Usually to the bigger fellas. One look at the needle, and...

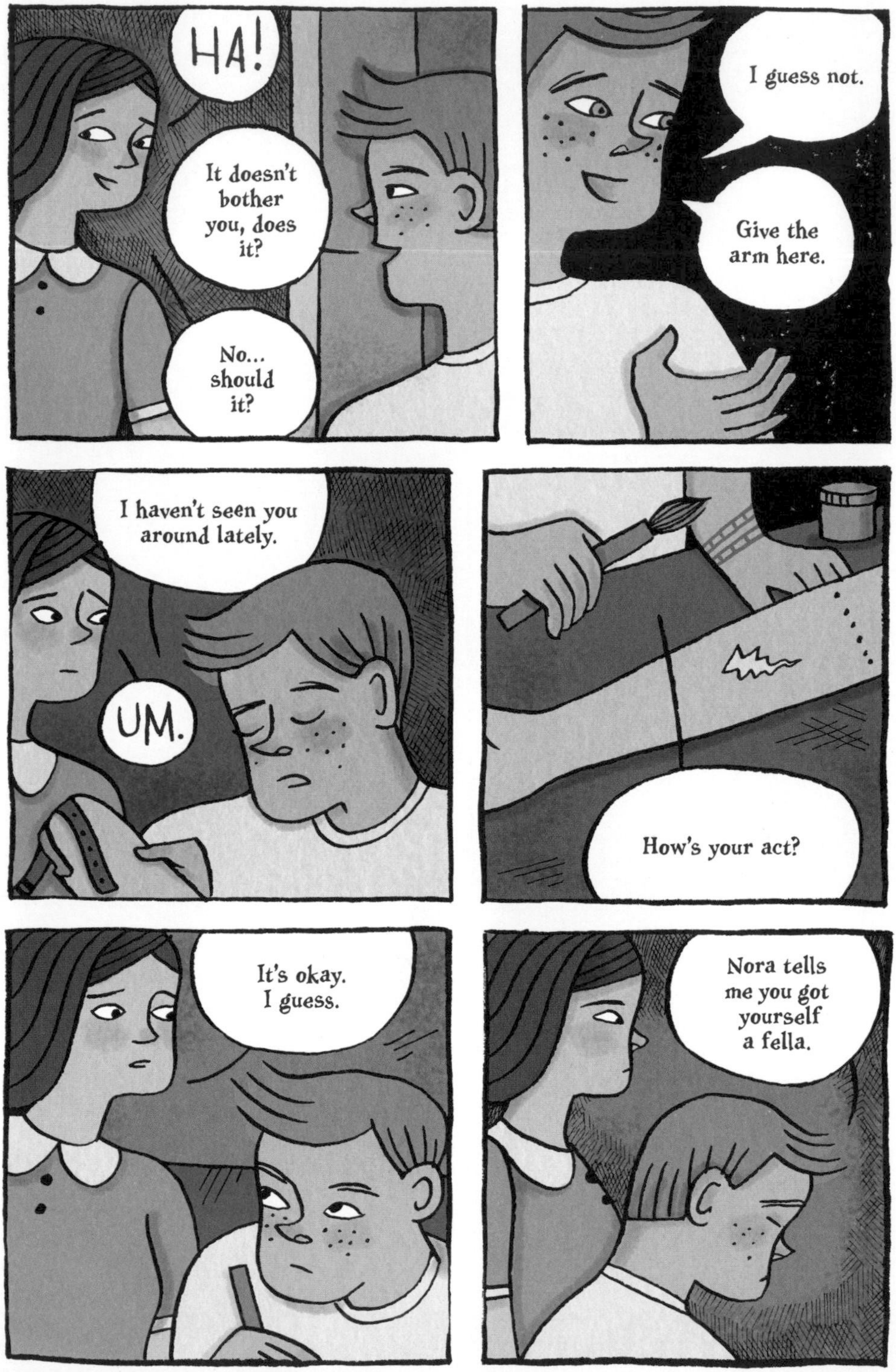
HA!
It doesn't bother you, does it?
No... should it?
I guess not.
Give the arm here.
I haven't seen you around lately.
UM.
How's your act?
It's okay. I guess.
Nora tells me you got yourself a fella.

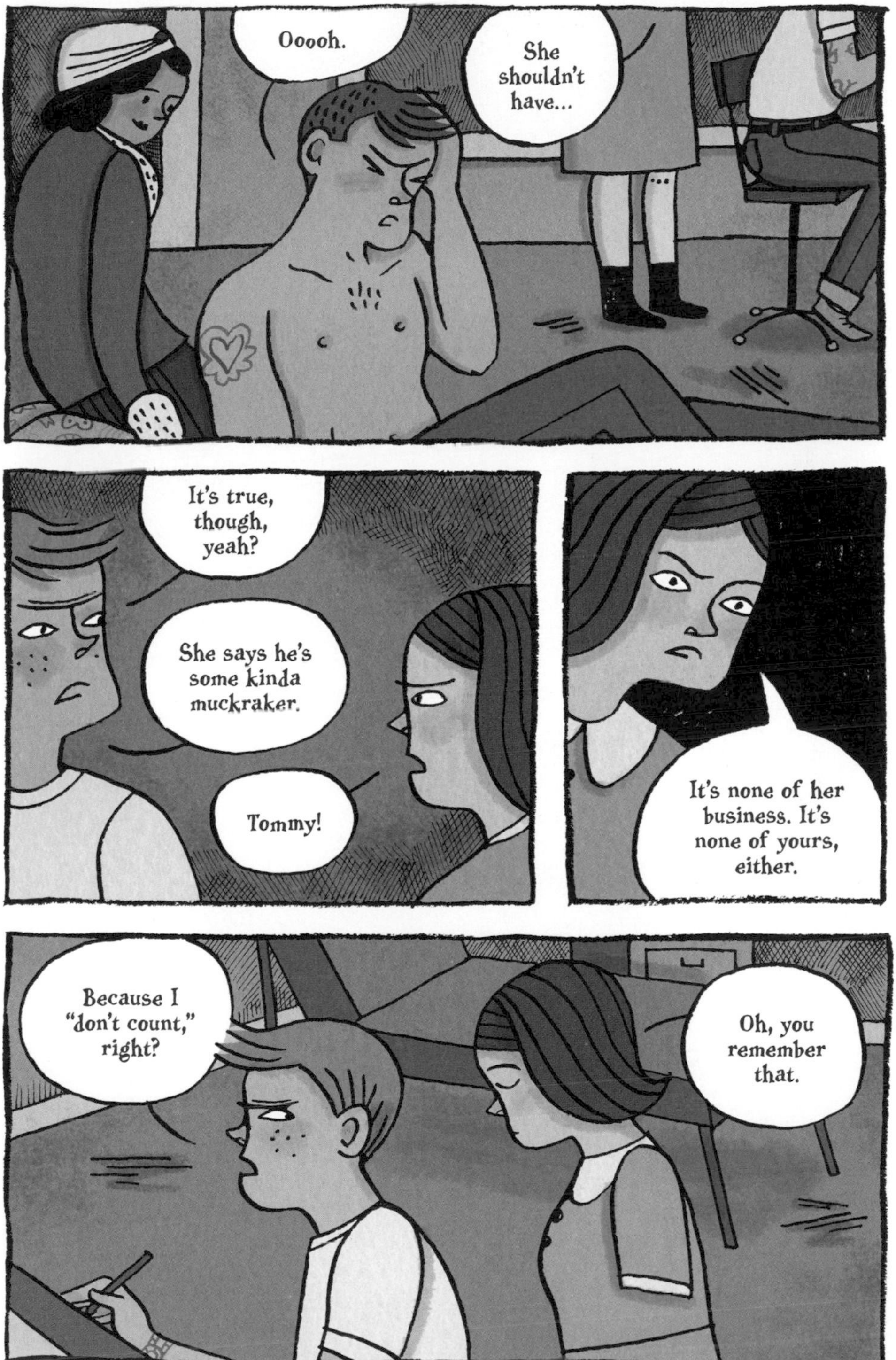
Ooooh.
She shouldn't have...
It's true, though, yeah?
She says he's some kinda muckraker.
Tommy!
It's none of her business. It's none of yours, either.
Because I "don't count," right?
Oh, you remember that.

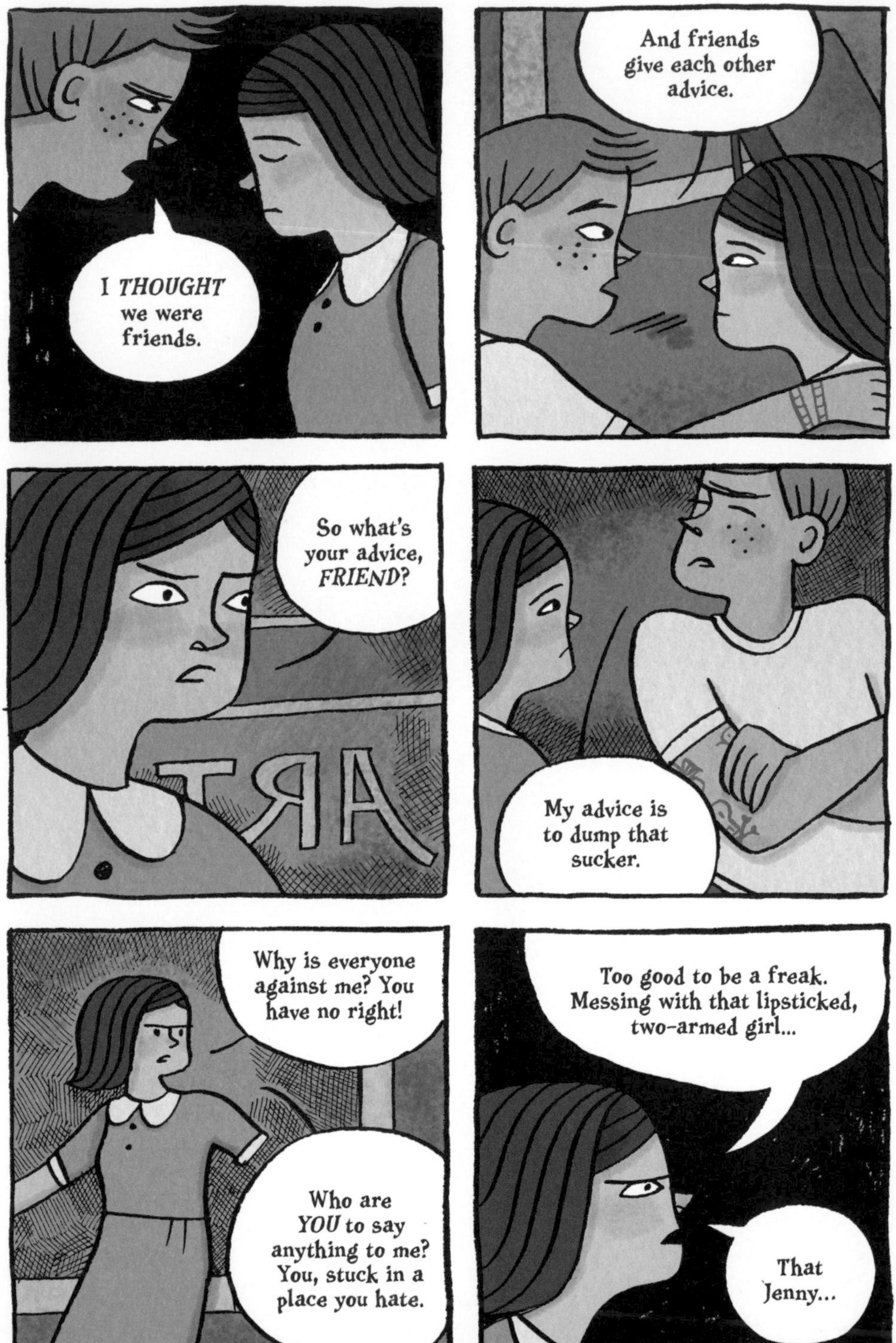
I THOUGHT we were friends.
And friends give each other advice.
So what's your advice, FRIEND?
My advice is to dump that sucker.
Why is everyone against me? You have no right!
Who are YOU to say anything to me? You, stuck in a place you hate.
Too good to be a freak. Messing with that lipsticked, two-armed girl...
That Jenny...

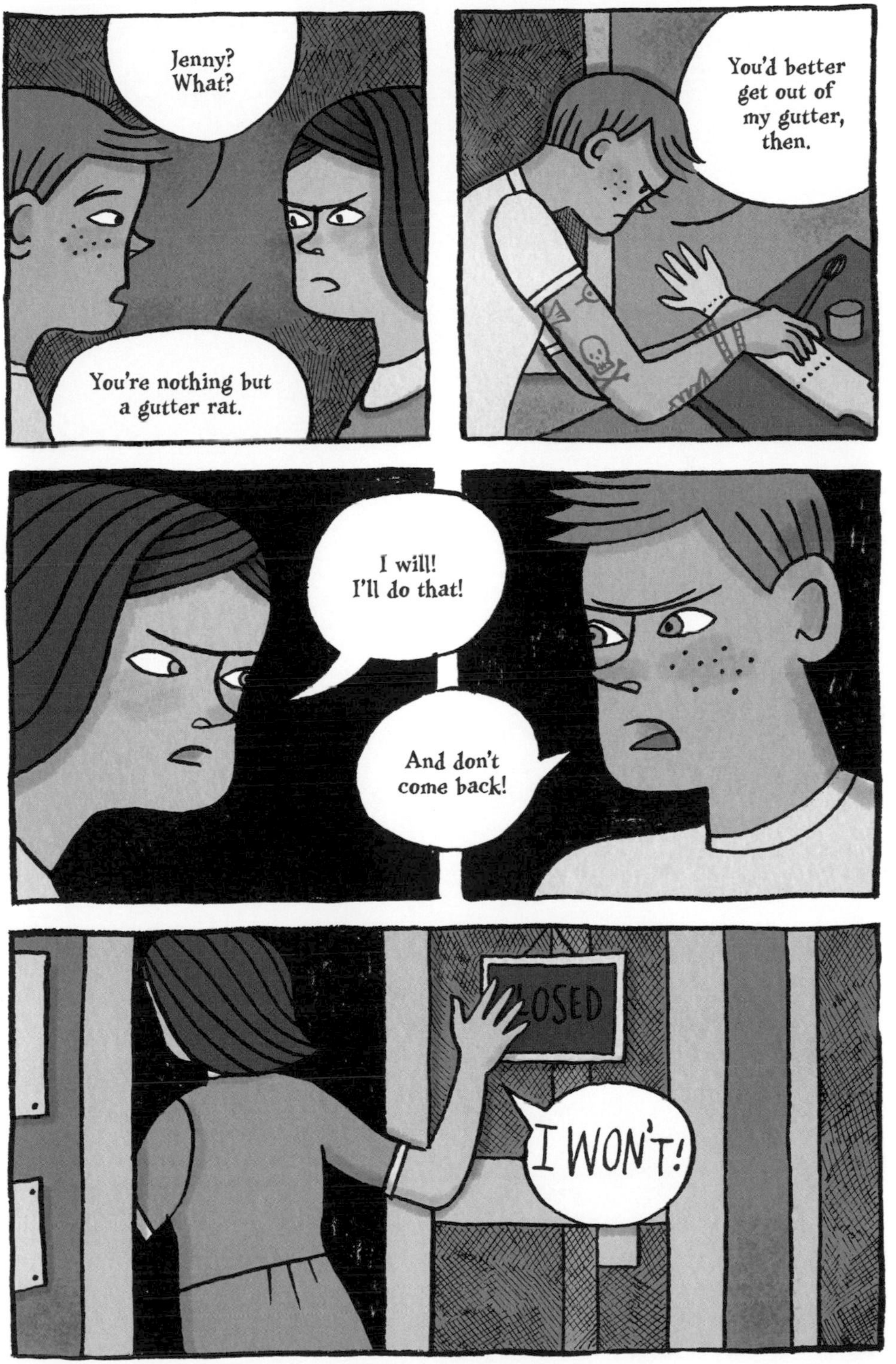
Jenny? What?
You're nothing but a gutter rat.
You'd better get out of my gutter, then.
I will! I'll do that!
And don't come back!
LOSED
I WON'T!

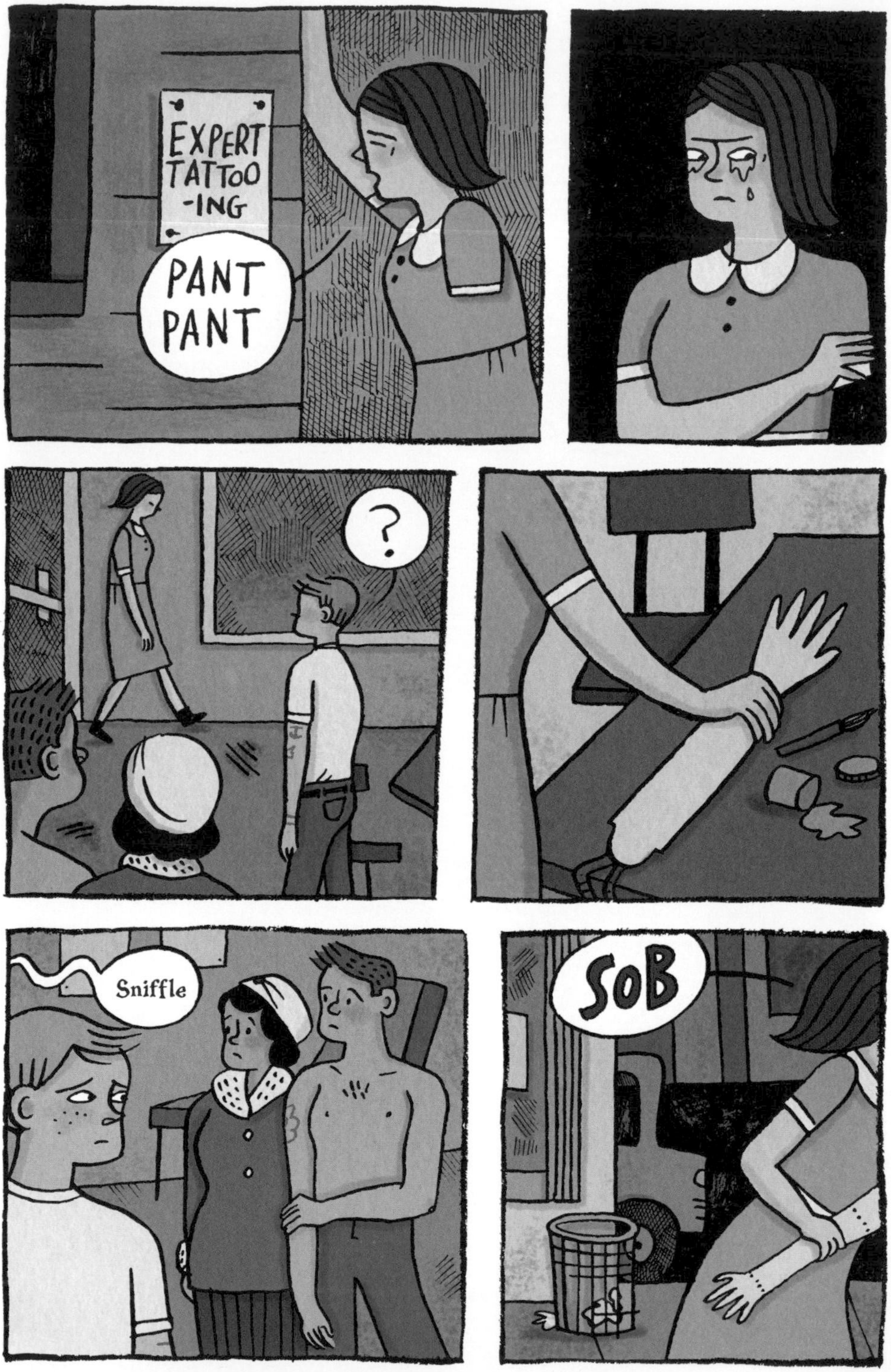
EXPERT TATTOO -ING
PANT PANT
?
Sniffle
SOB

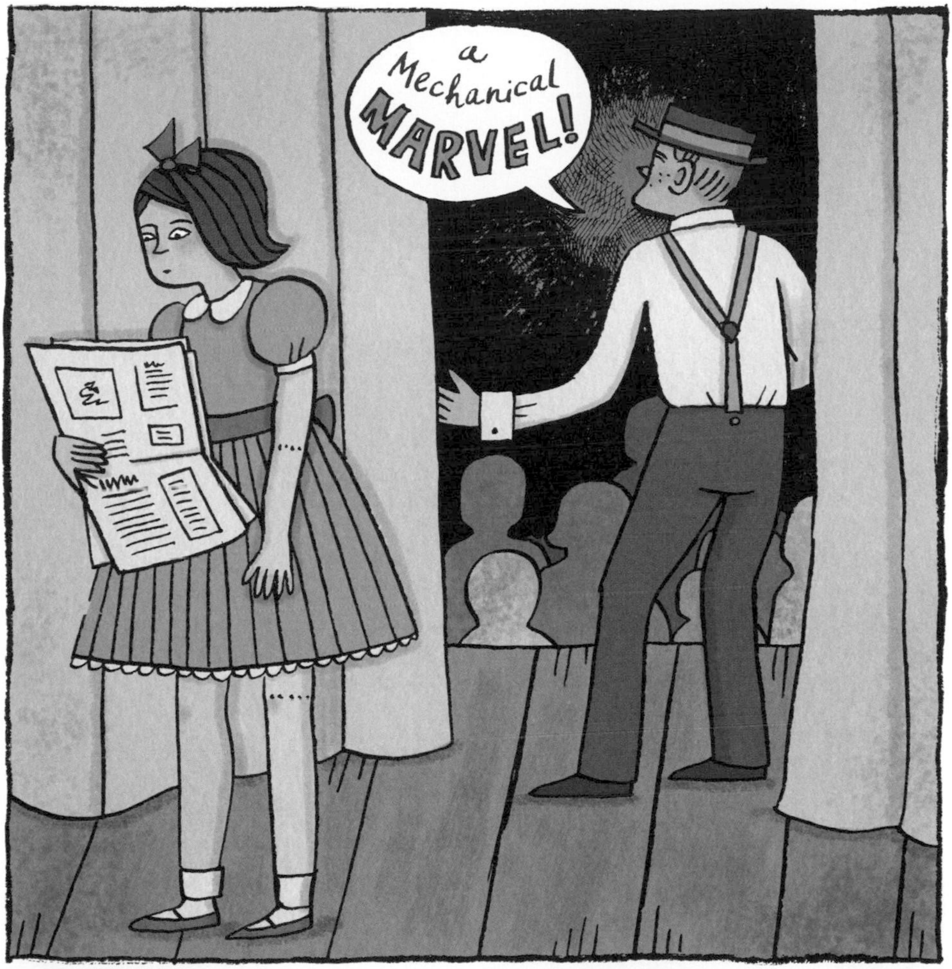
a Mechanical MARVEL!

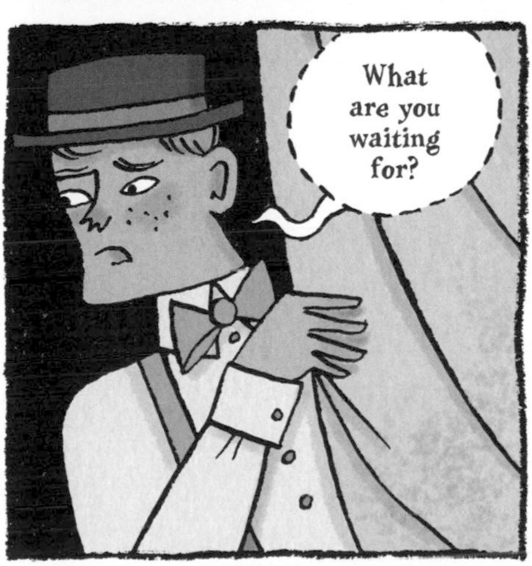
What are you waiting for?

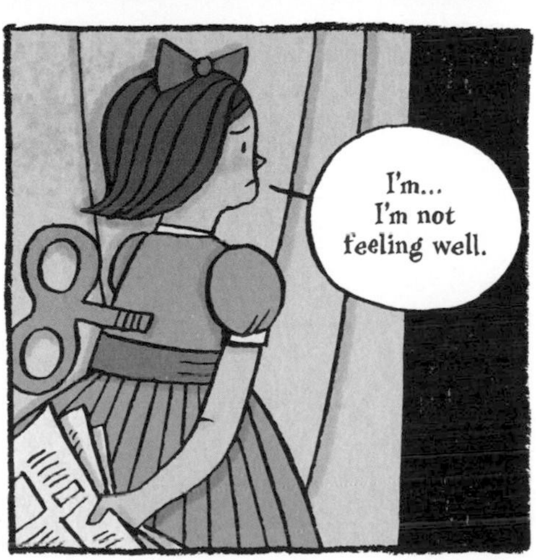
I'm... I'm not feeling well.

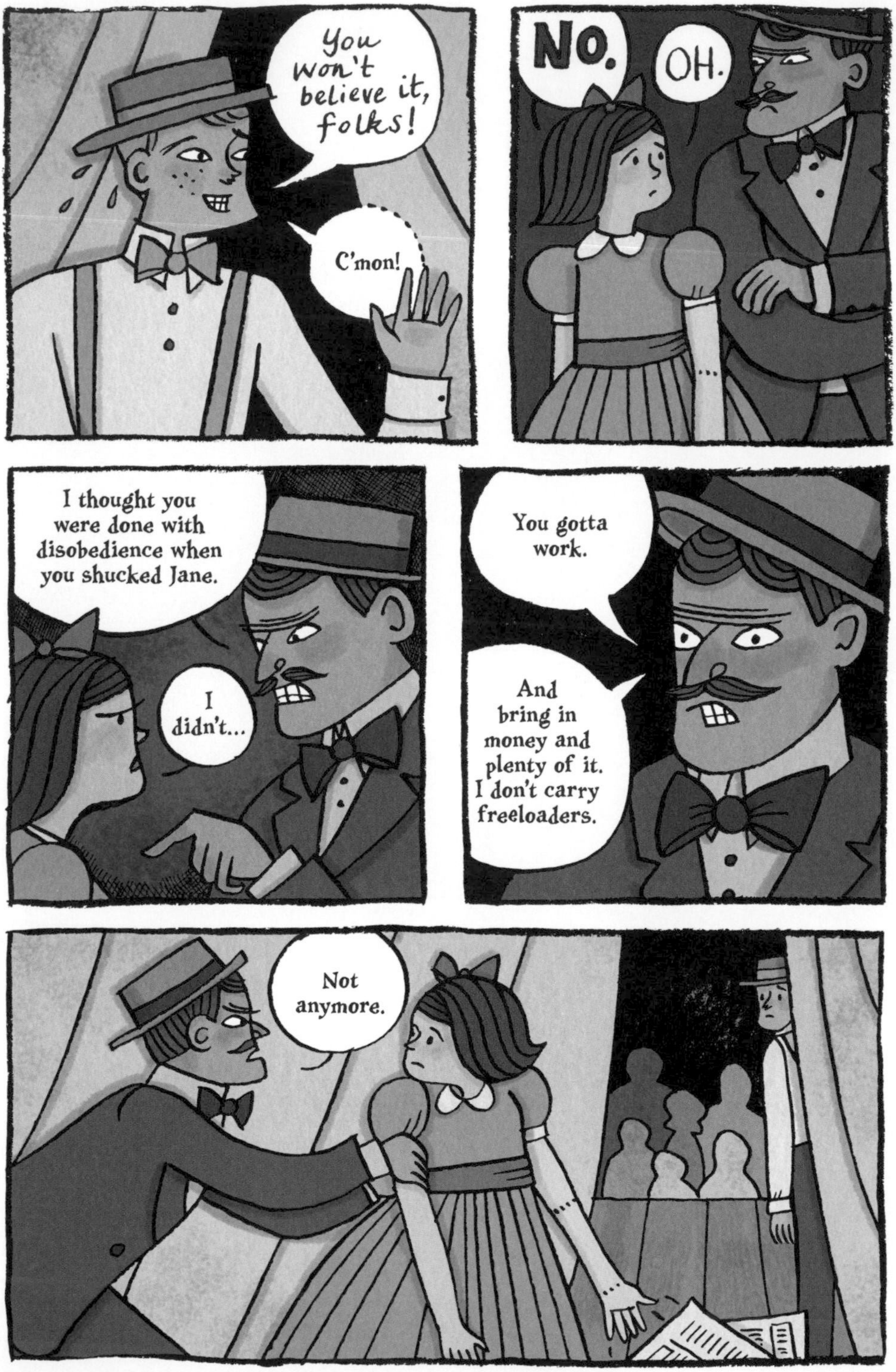
You won't believe it, folks!
C'mon!
NO.
OH.
I thought you were done with disobedience when you shucked Jane.
I didn't...
You gotta work.
And bring in money and plenty of it. I don't carry freeloaders.
Not anymore.

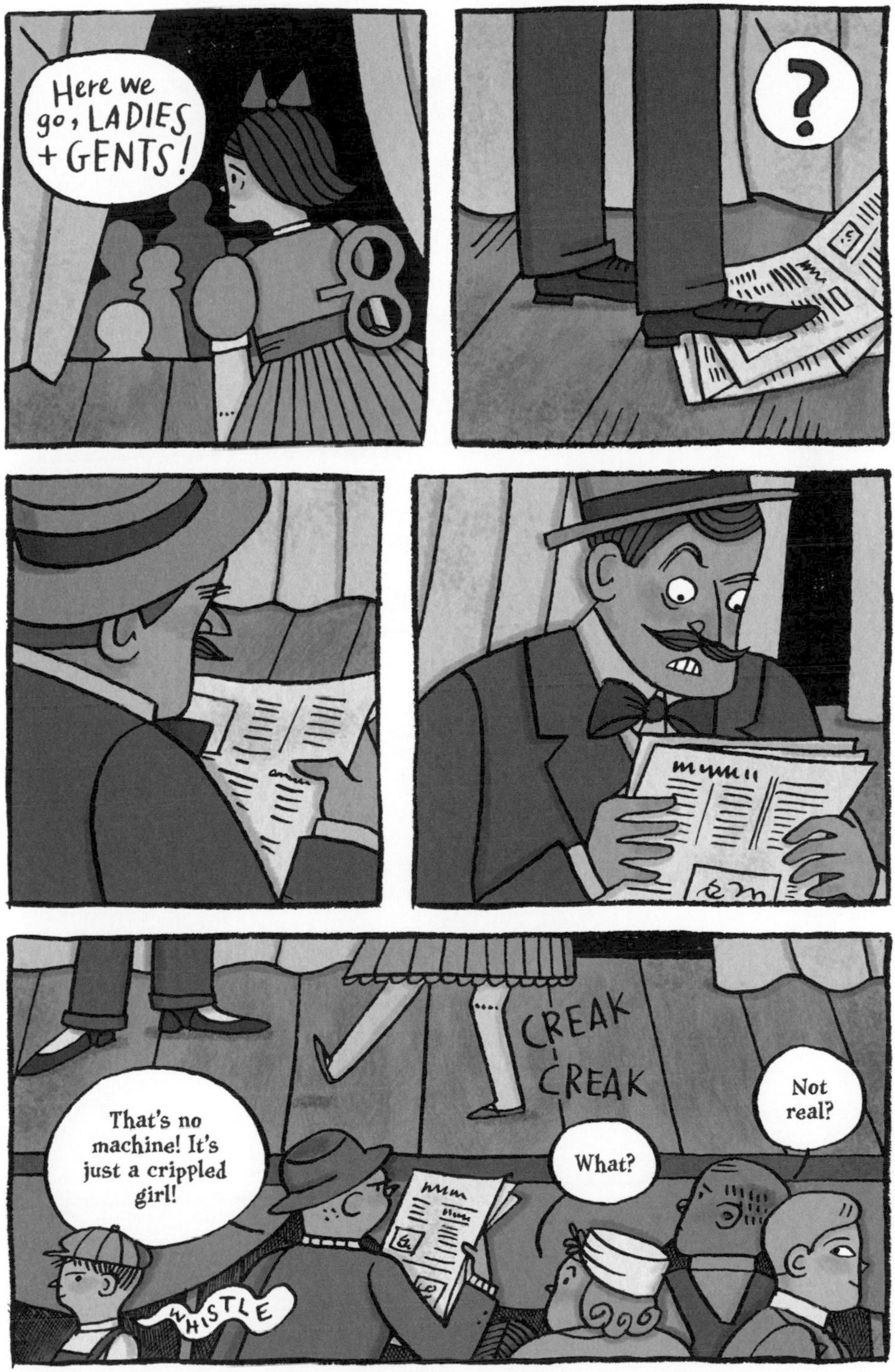
Here we go, LADIES + GENTS!
?
CREAK
CREAK
That's no machine! It's just a crippled girl!
WHISTLE
What?
Not real?

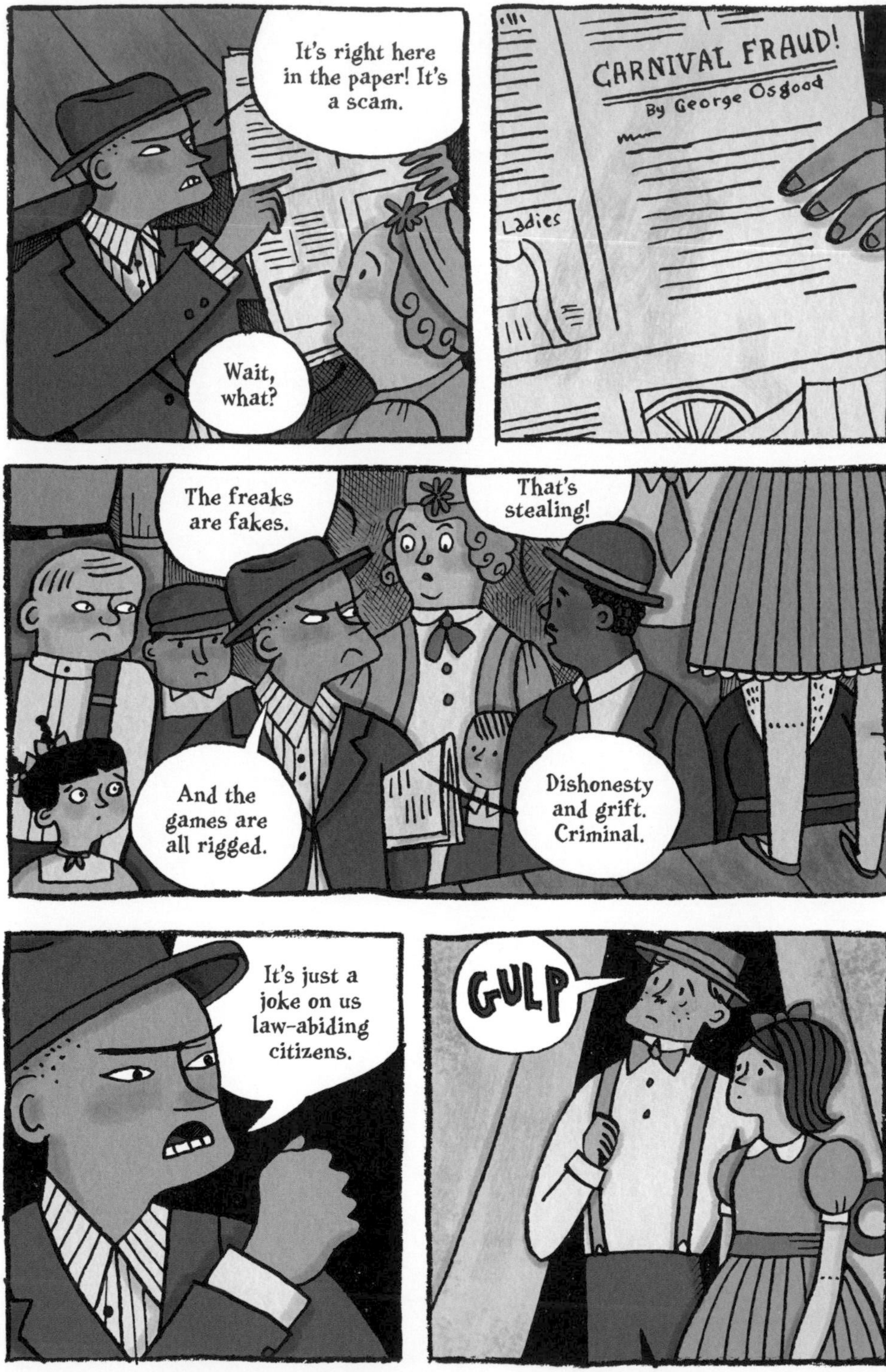
It's right here in the paper! It's a scam.
Wait, what?
CARNIVAL FRAUD!
By George Osgood
Ladies
The freaks are fakes.
That's stealing!
And the games are all rigged.
Dishonesty and grift. Criminal.
It's just a joke on us law-abiding citizens.
GULP

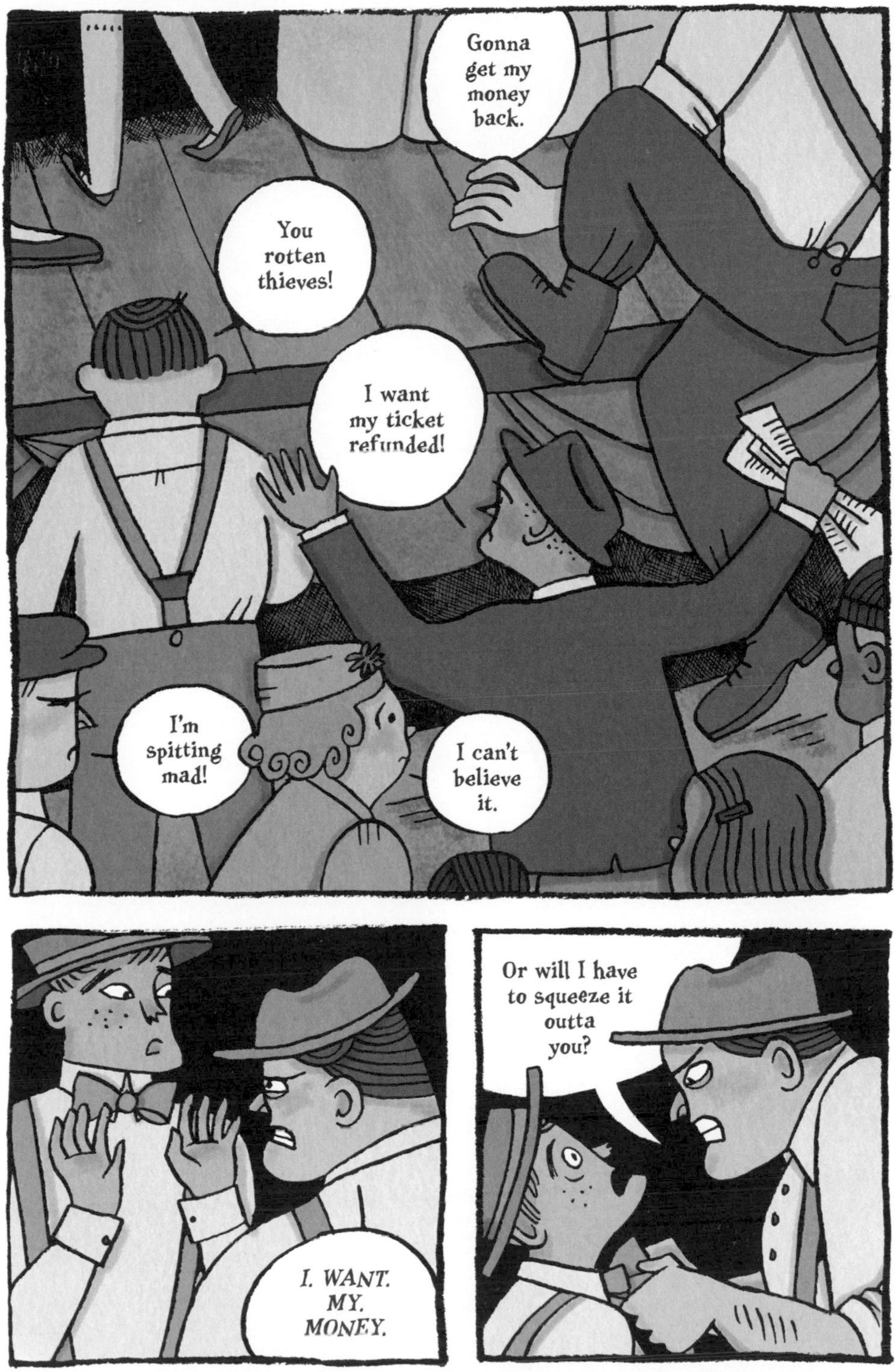
Gonna get my money back.
You rotten thieves!
I want my ticket refunded!
I'm spitting mad!
I can't believe it.
I. WANT. MY. MONEY.
Or will I have to squeeze it outta you?

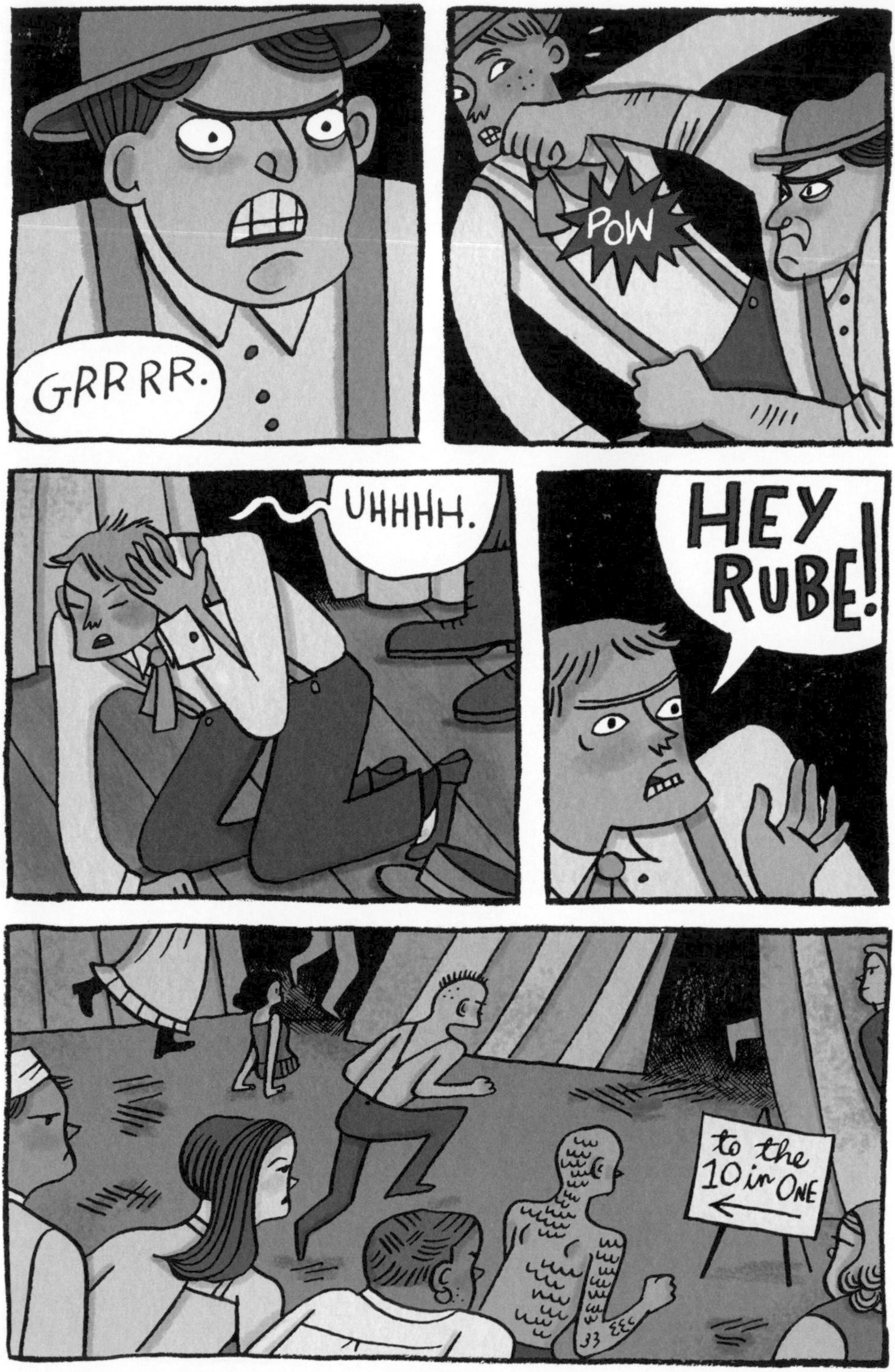
GRRRR.
POW
UHHHH.
HEY RUBE!
to the 10 in ONE

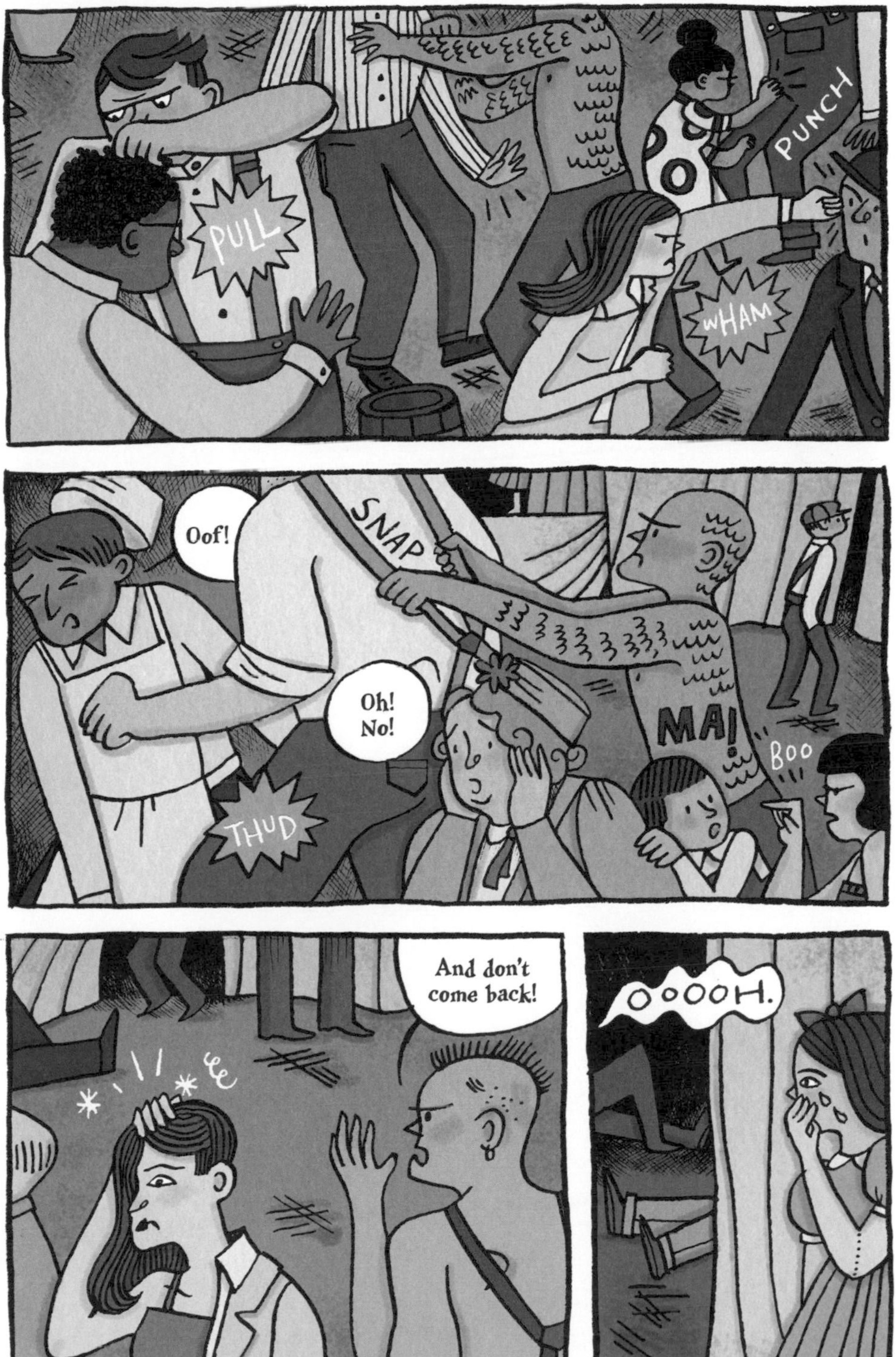
PULL
PUNCH
WHAM
Oof!
SNAP
Oh! No!
THUD
MAI
BOO
And don't come back!
OOOOH.

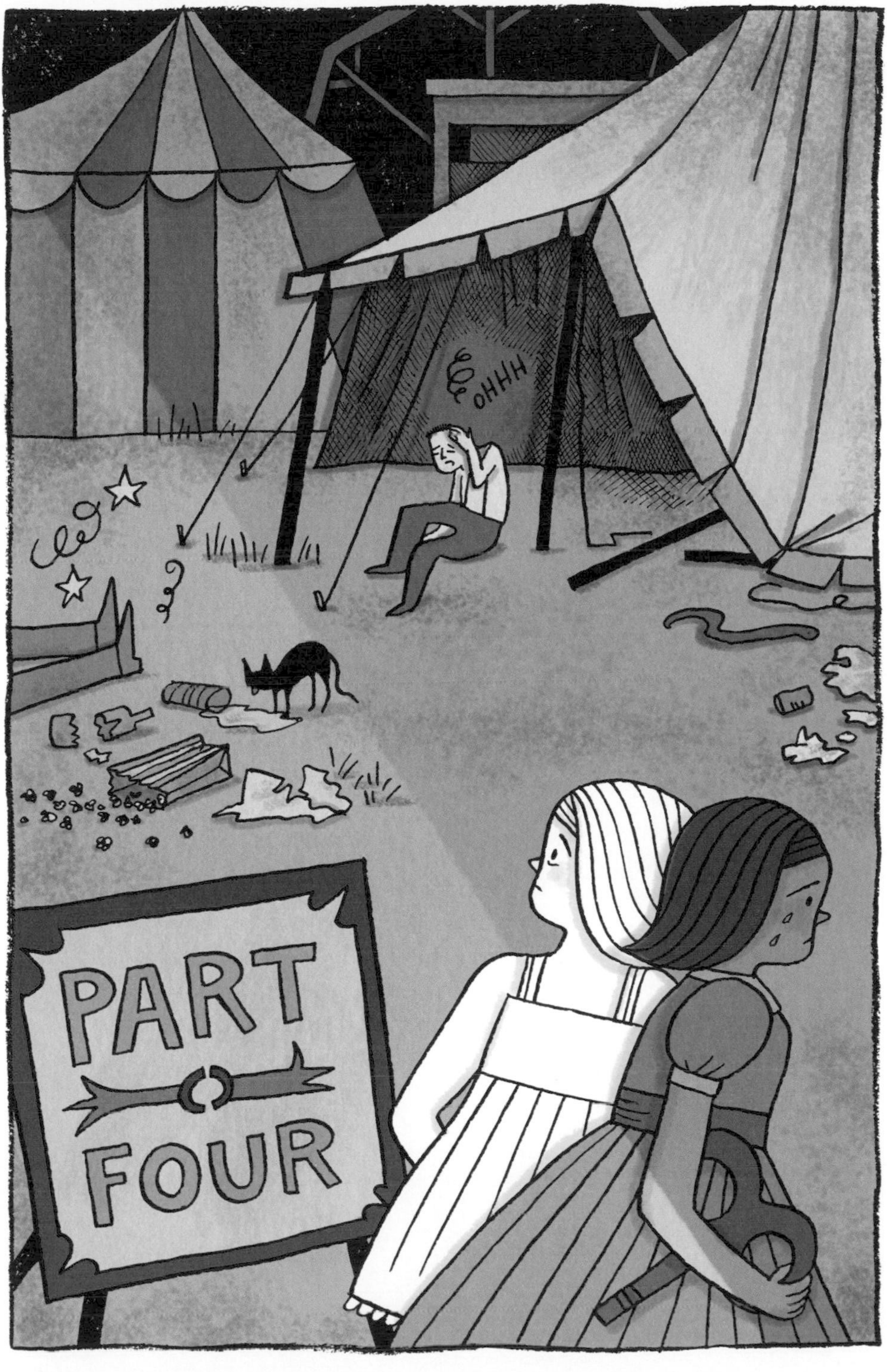
OHHH
PART
FOUR

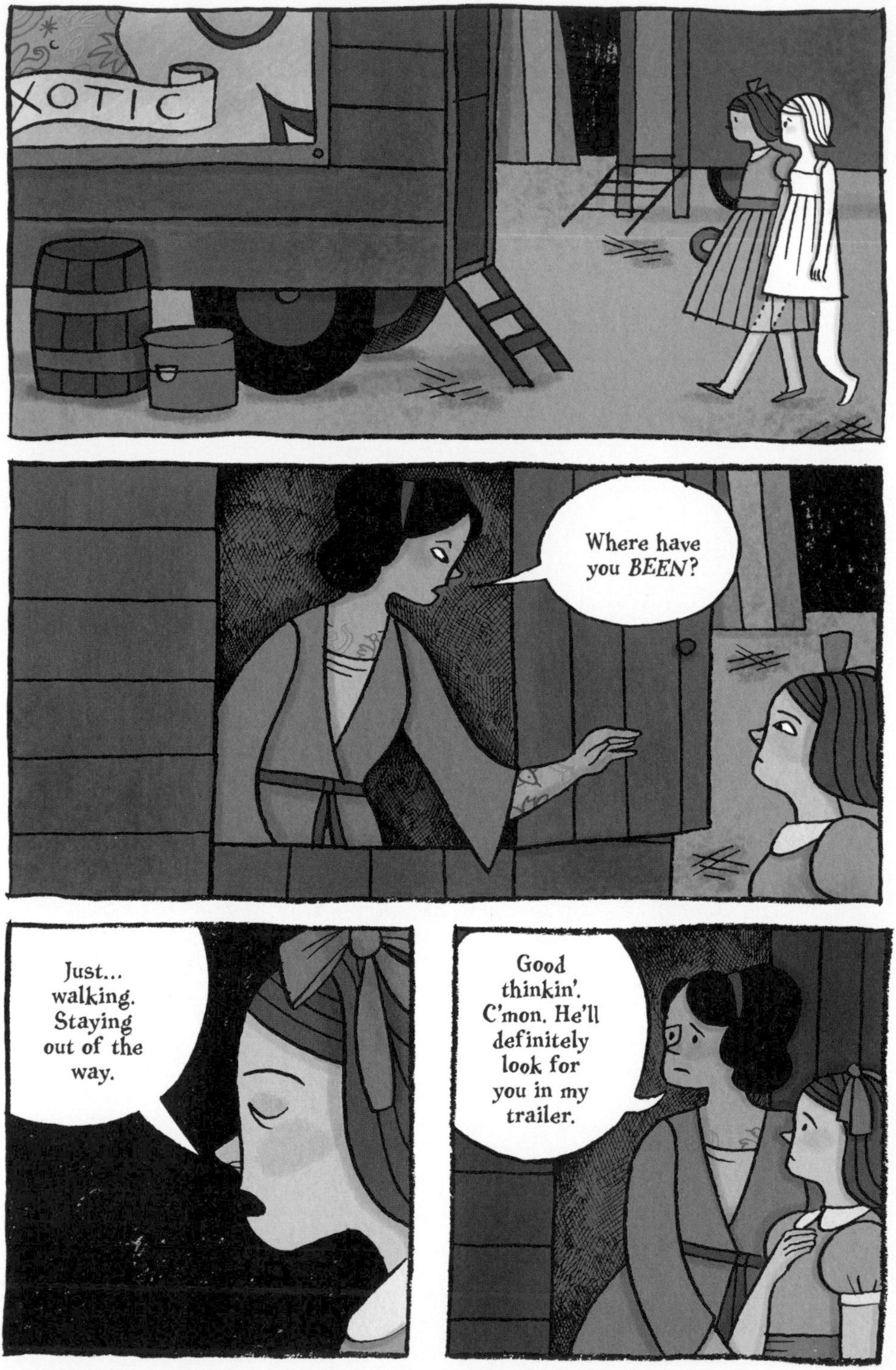
XOTIC
Where have you *BEEN*?
Just... walking. Staying out of the way.
Good thinkin'. C'mon. He'll definitely look for you in my trailer.

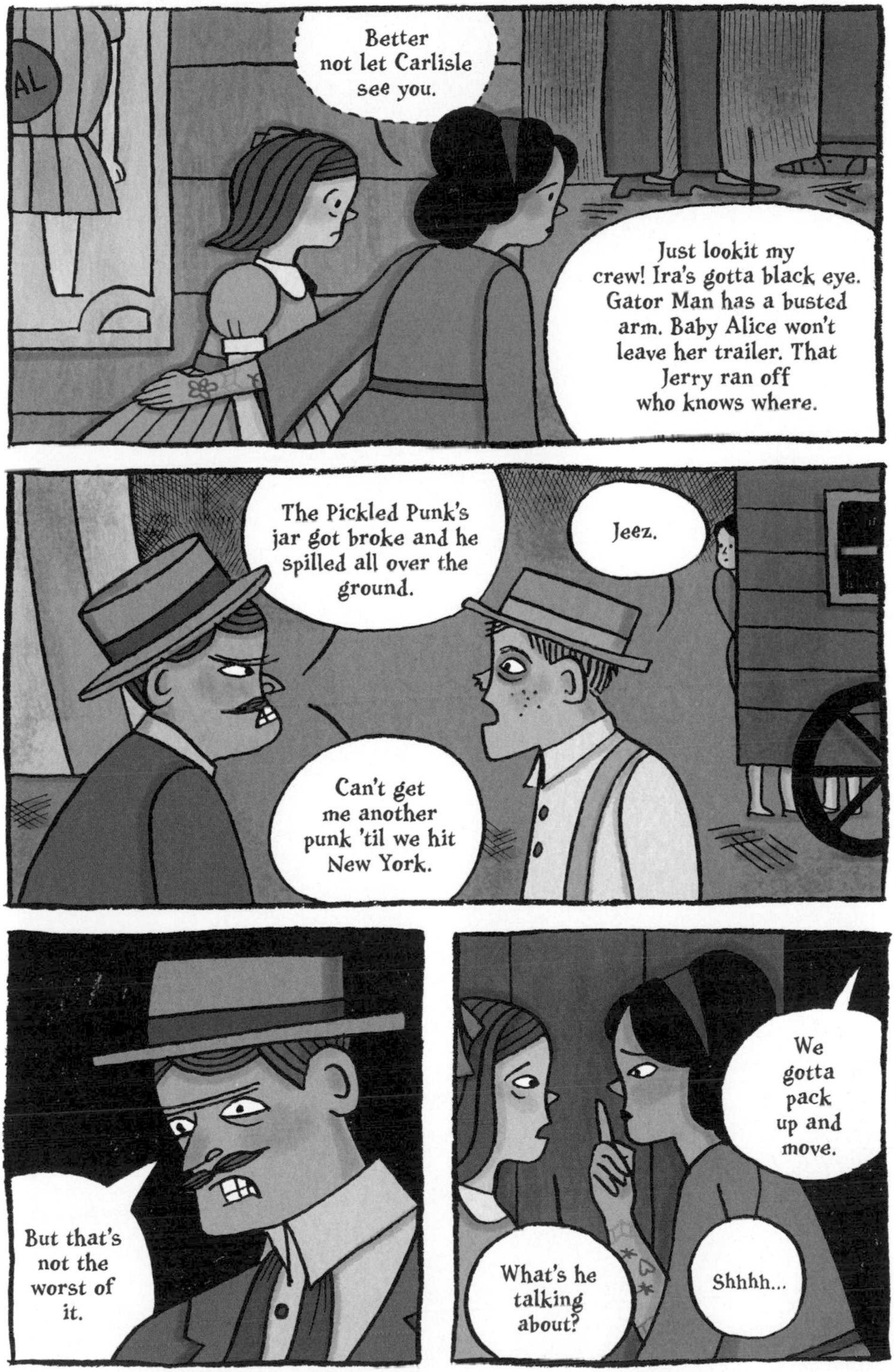
Better not let Carlisle see you.
Just lookit my crew! Ira's gotta black eye. Gator Man has a busted arm. Baby Alice won't leave her trailer. That Jerry ran off who knows where.
The Pickled Punk's jar got broke and he spilled all over the ground.
Jeez.
Can't get me another punk 'til we hit New York.
But that's not the worst of it.
We gotta pack up and move.
What's he talking about?
Shhhh...

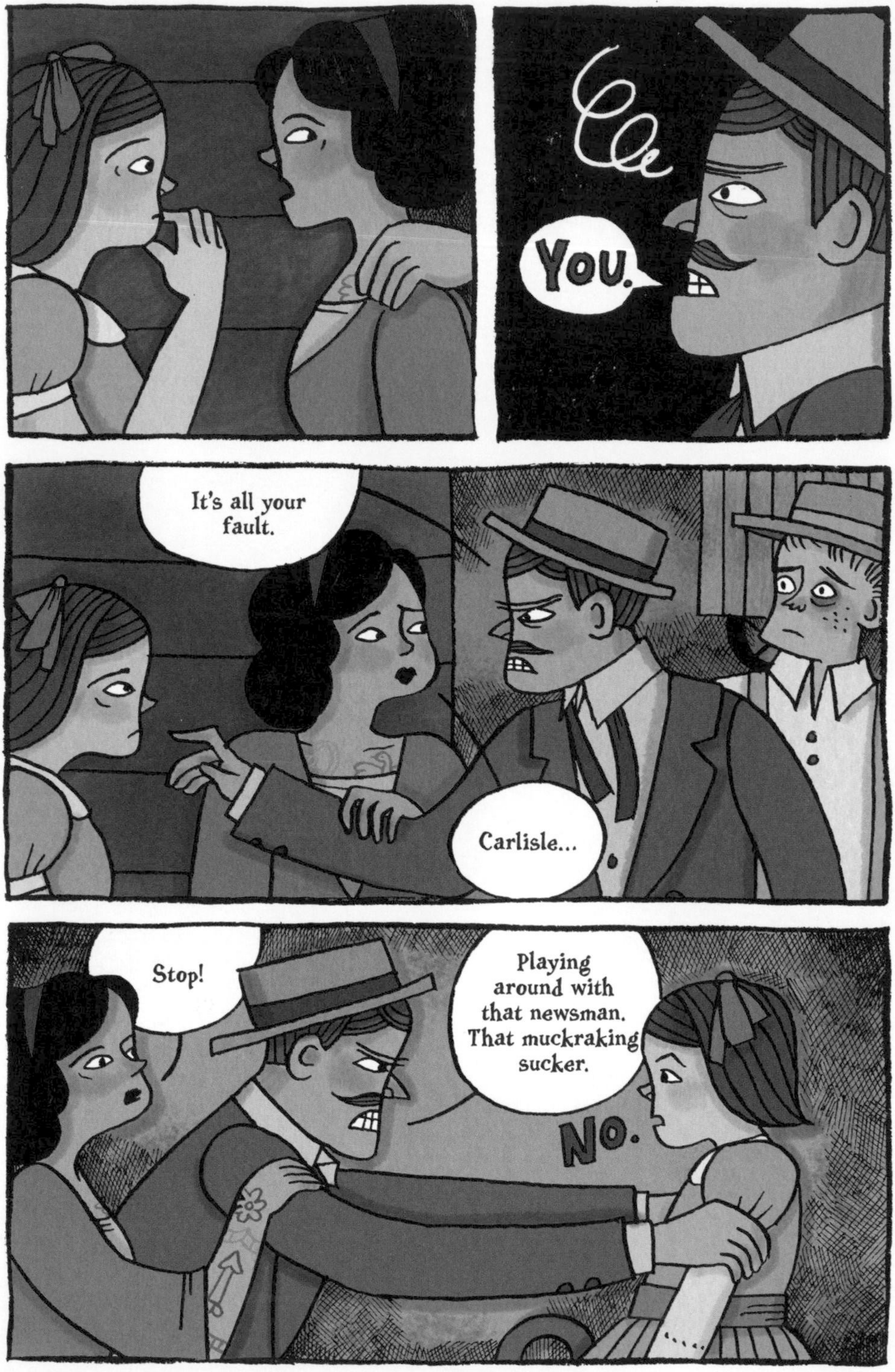
YOU.
It's all your fault.
Carlisle...
Stop!
Playing around with that newsman. That muckraking sucker.
NO.

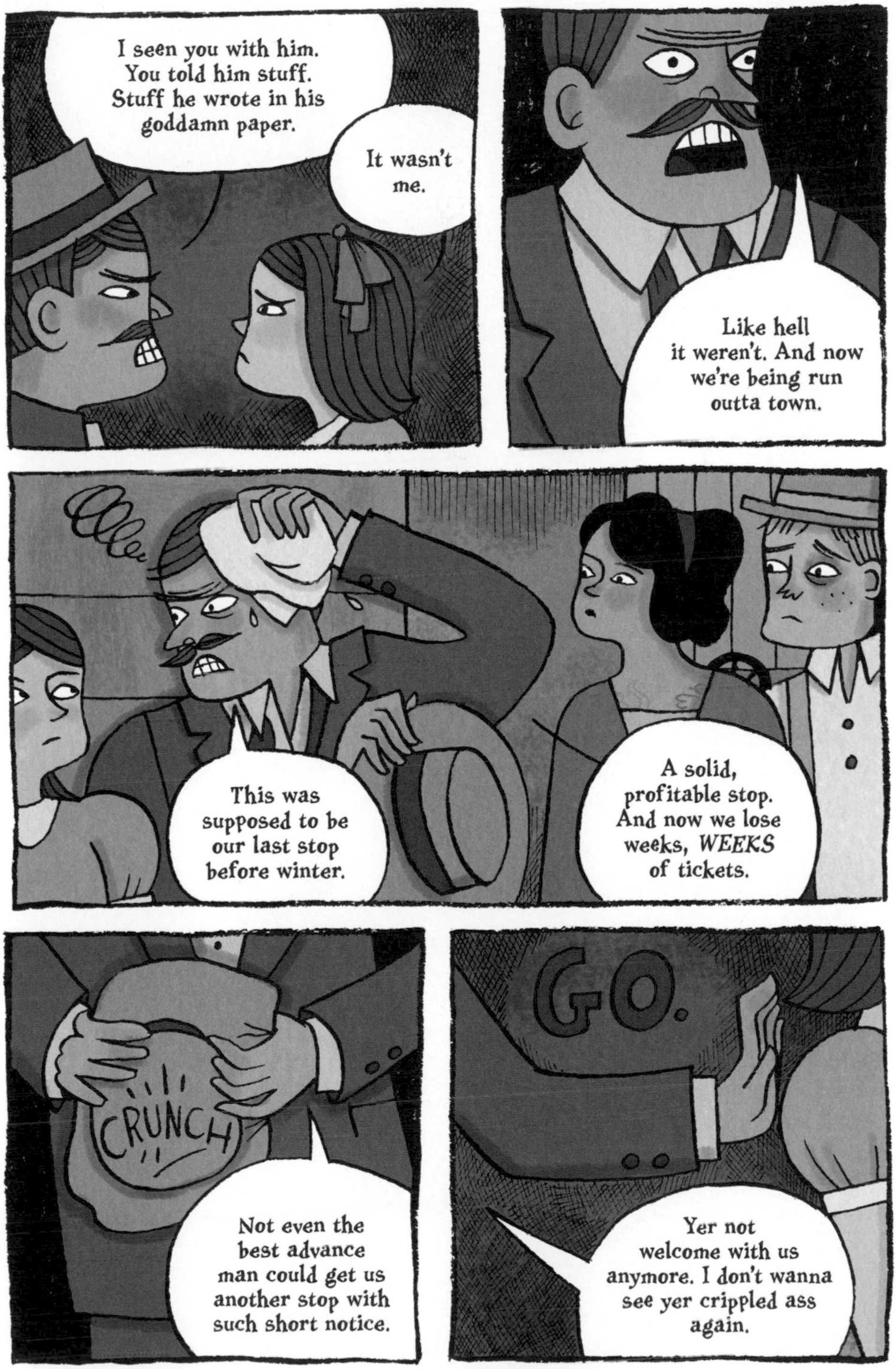
I seen you with him. You told him stuff. Stuff he wrote in his goddamn paper.
It wasn't me.
Like hell it weren't. And now we're being run outta town.
This was supposed to be our last stop before winter.
A solid, profitable stop. And now we lose weeks, *WEEKS* of tickets.
CRUNCH
Not even the best advance man could get us another stop with such short notice.
GO.
Yer not welcome with us anymore. I don't wanna see yer crippled ass again.

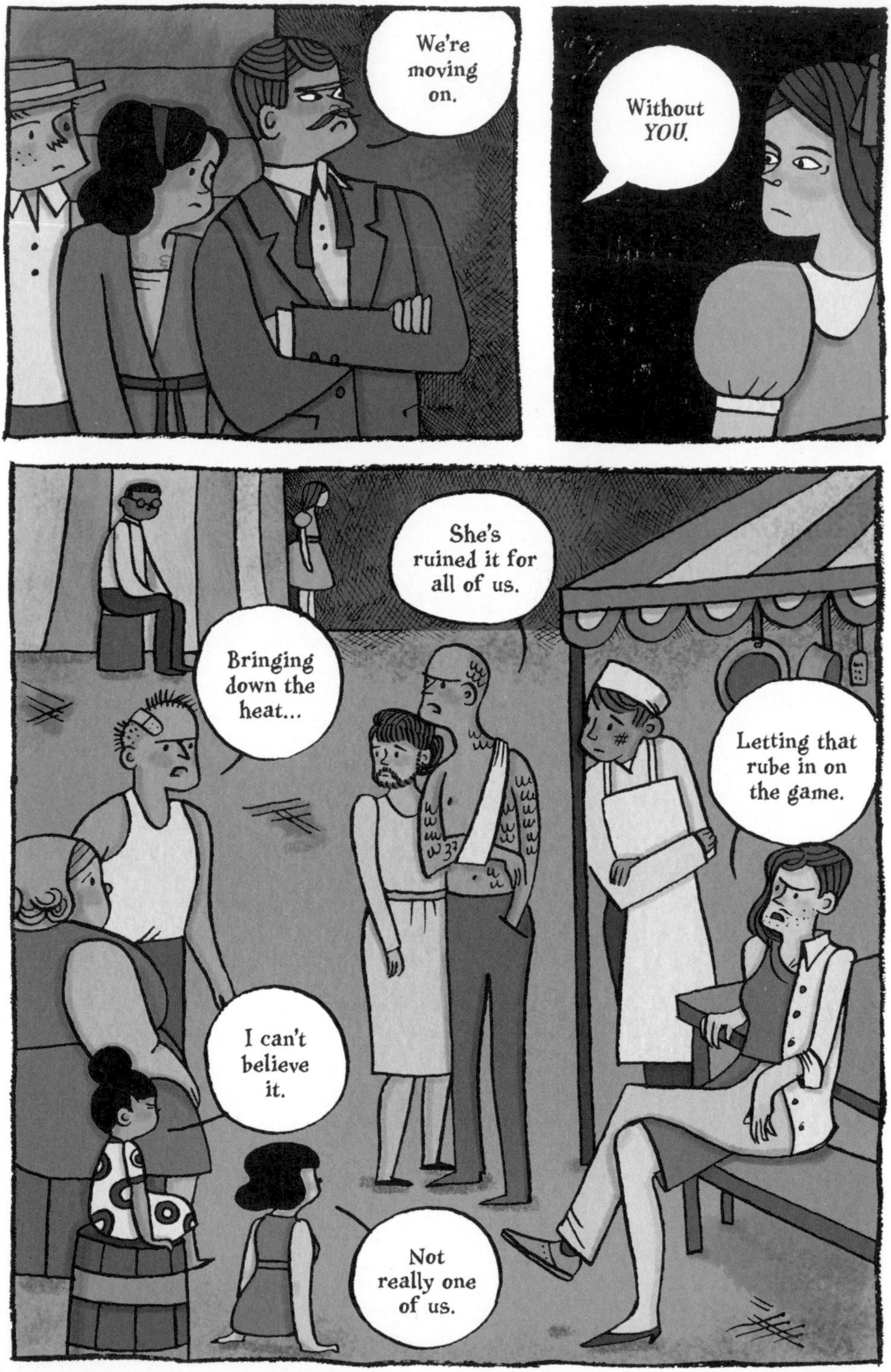
We're moving on.
Without *YOU.*
She's ruined it for all of us.
Bringing down the heat...
Letting that rube in on the game.
I can't believe it.
Not really one of us.

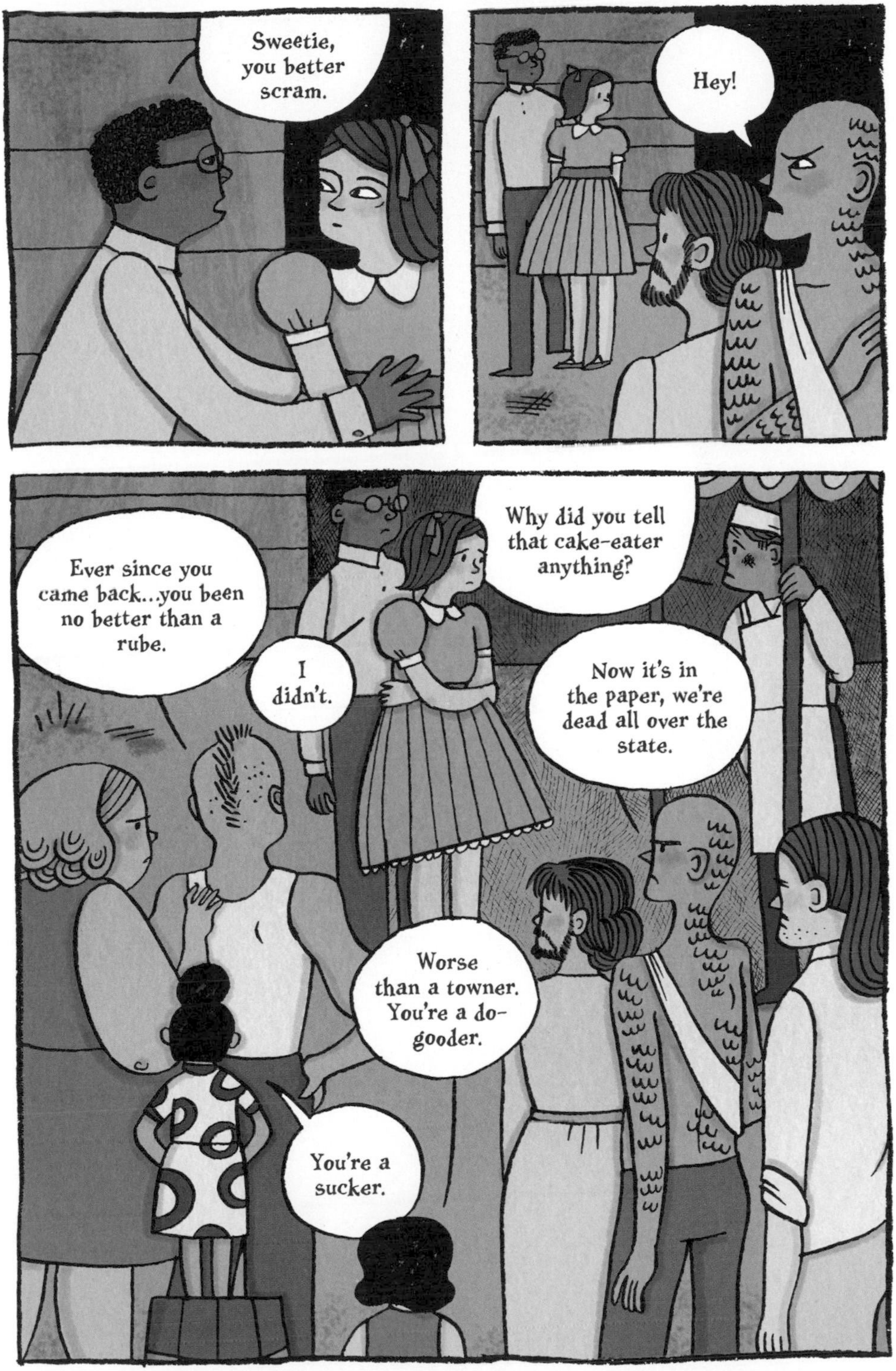

Sweetie, you better scram.
Hey!
Ever since you came back...you been no better than a rube.
I didn't.
Why did you tell that cake-eater anything?
Now it's in the paper, we're dead all over the state.
Worse than a towner. You're a do-gooder.
You're a sucker.

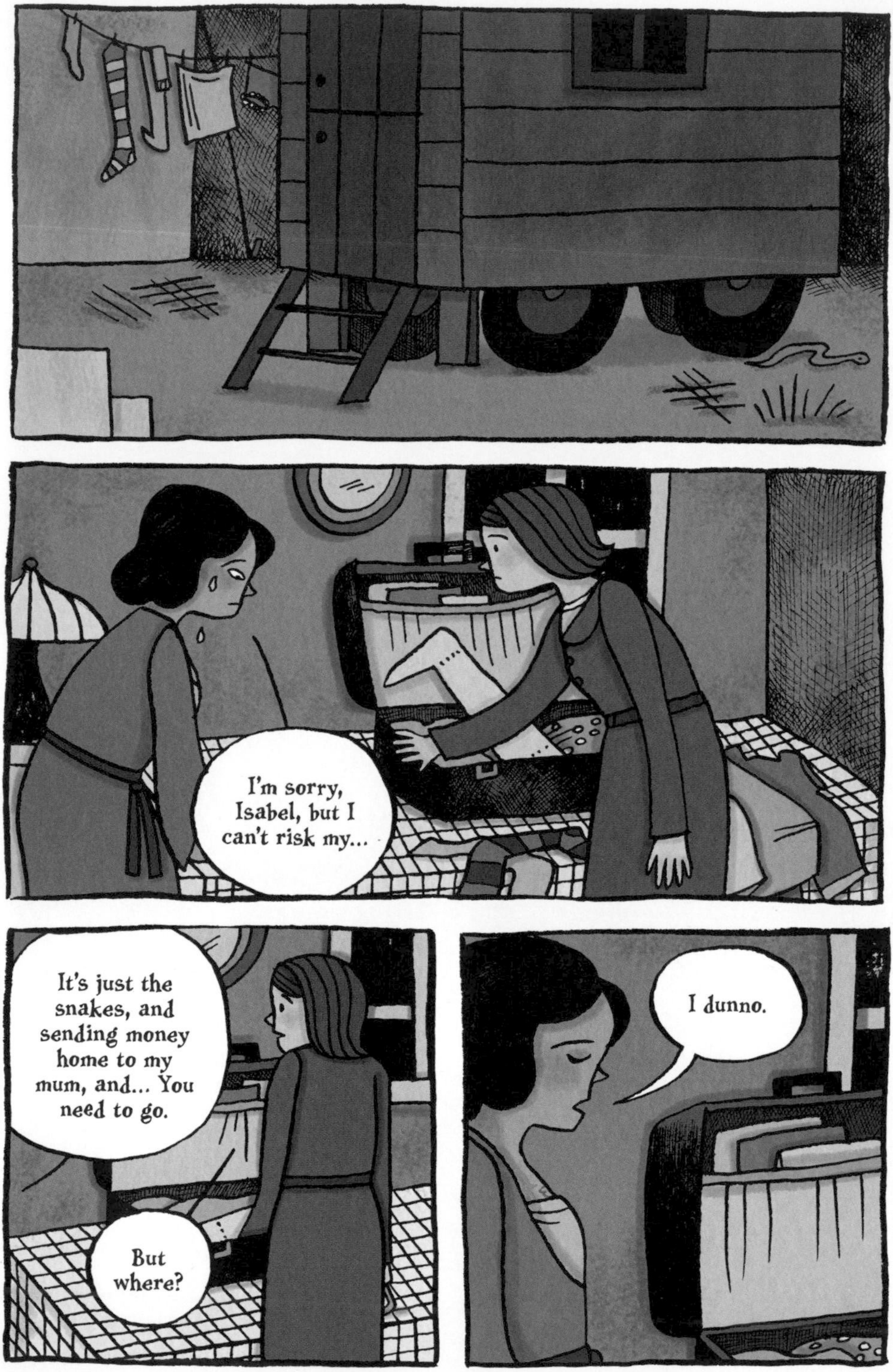
I'm sorry, Isabel, but I can't risk my...
It's just the snakes, and sending money home to my mum, and... You need to go.
But where?
I dunno.

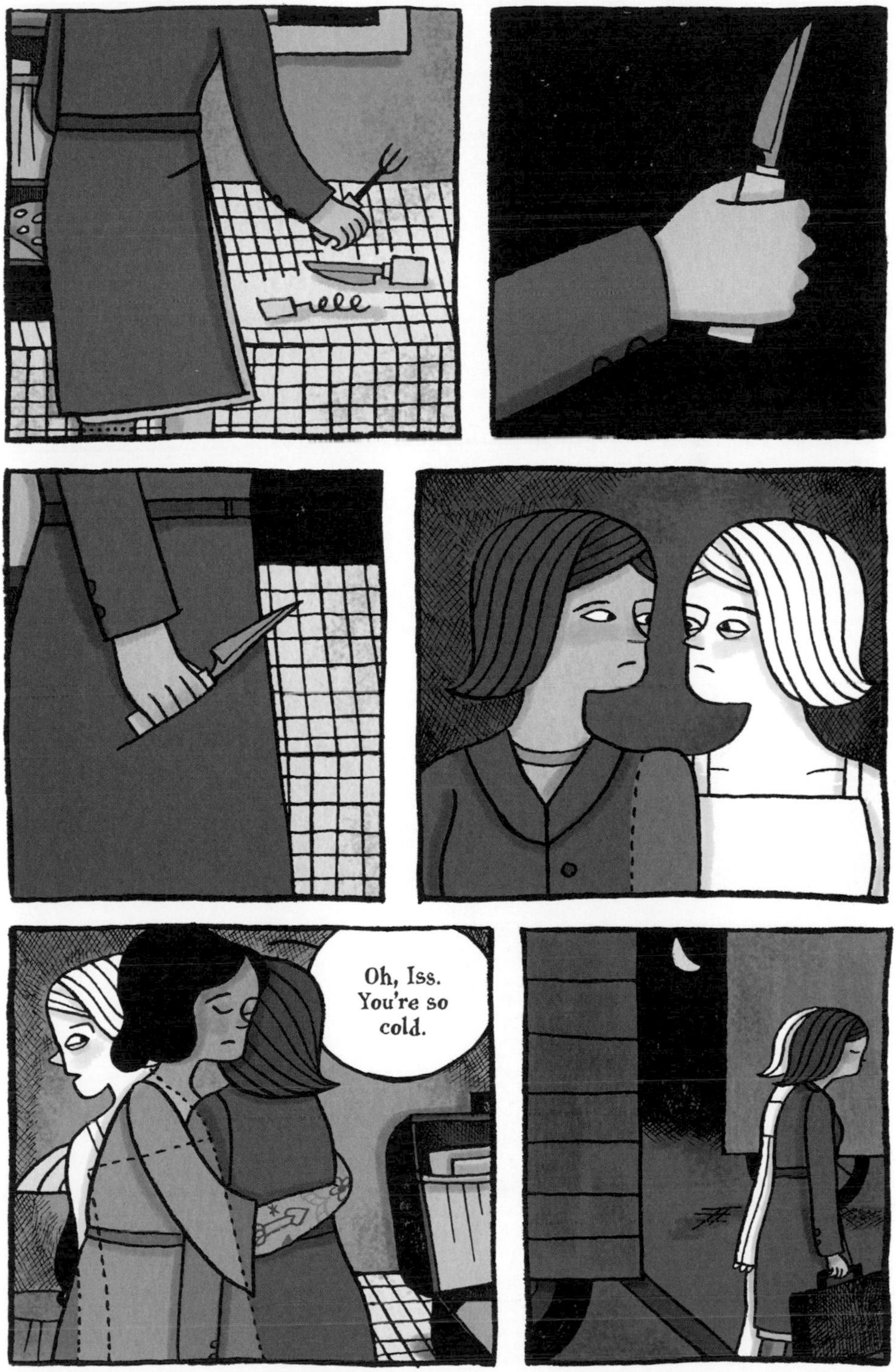
Oh, Iss. You're so cold.

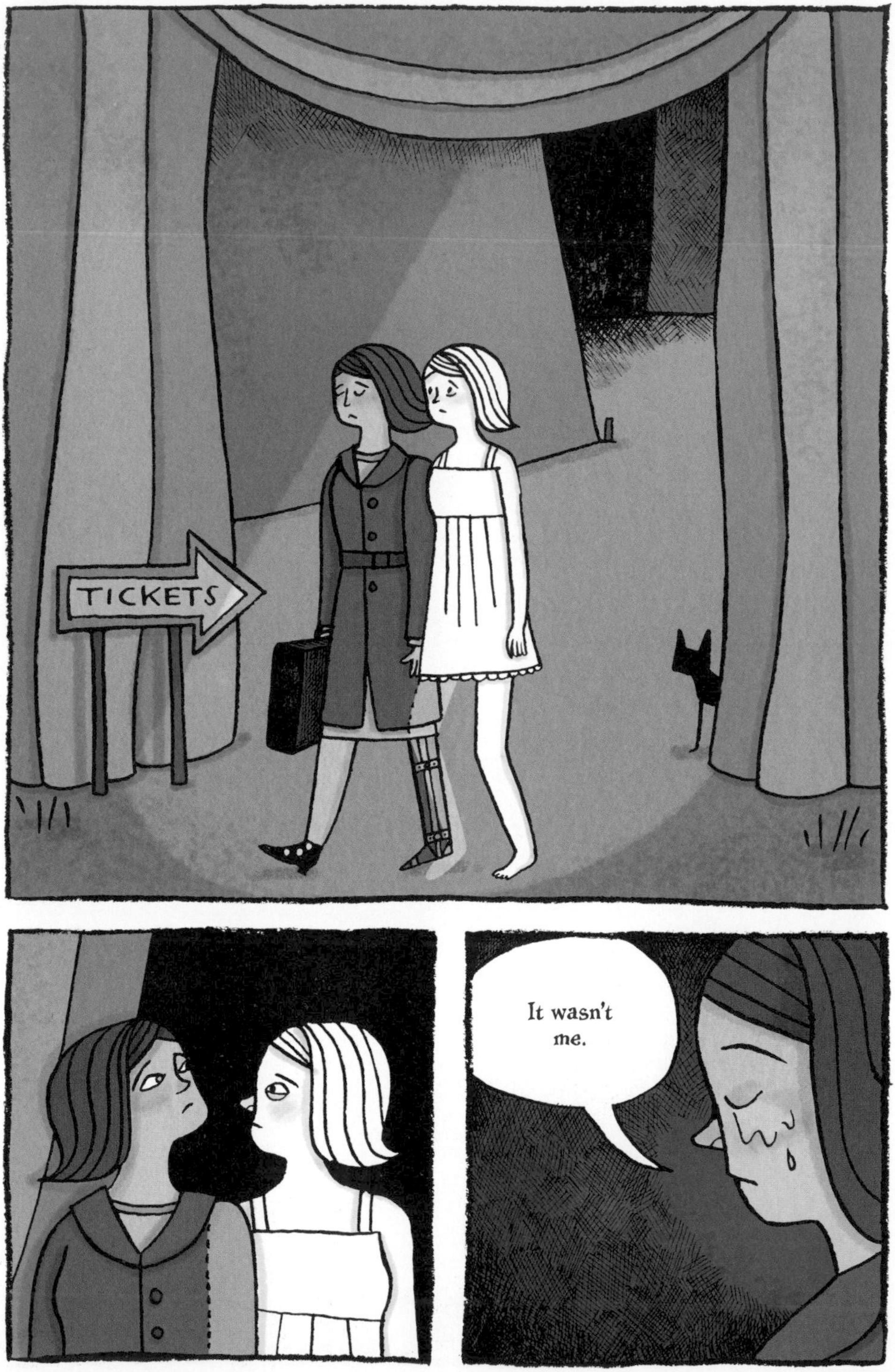
TICKETS
It wasn't me.

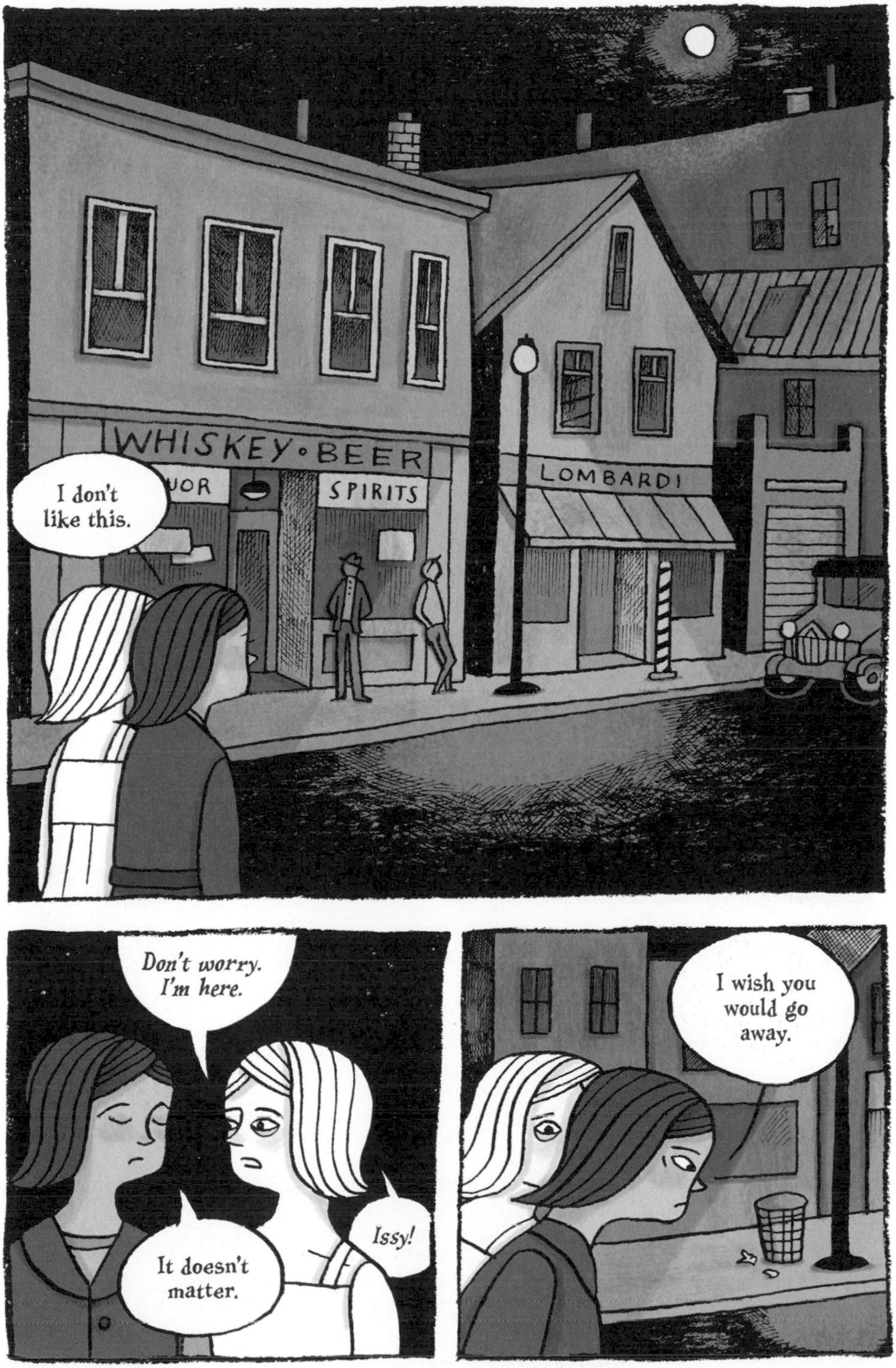
WHISKEY • BEER
UOR
SPIRITS
LOMBARDI
I don't like this.
Don't worry. I'm here.
It doesn't matter.
Issy!
I wish you would go away.

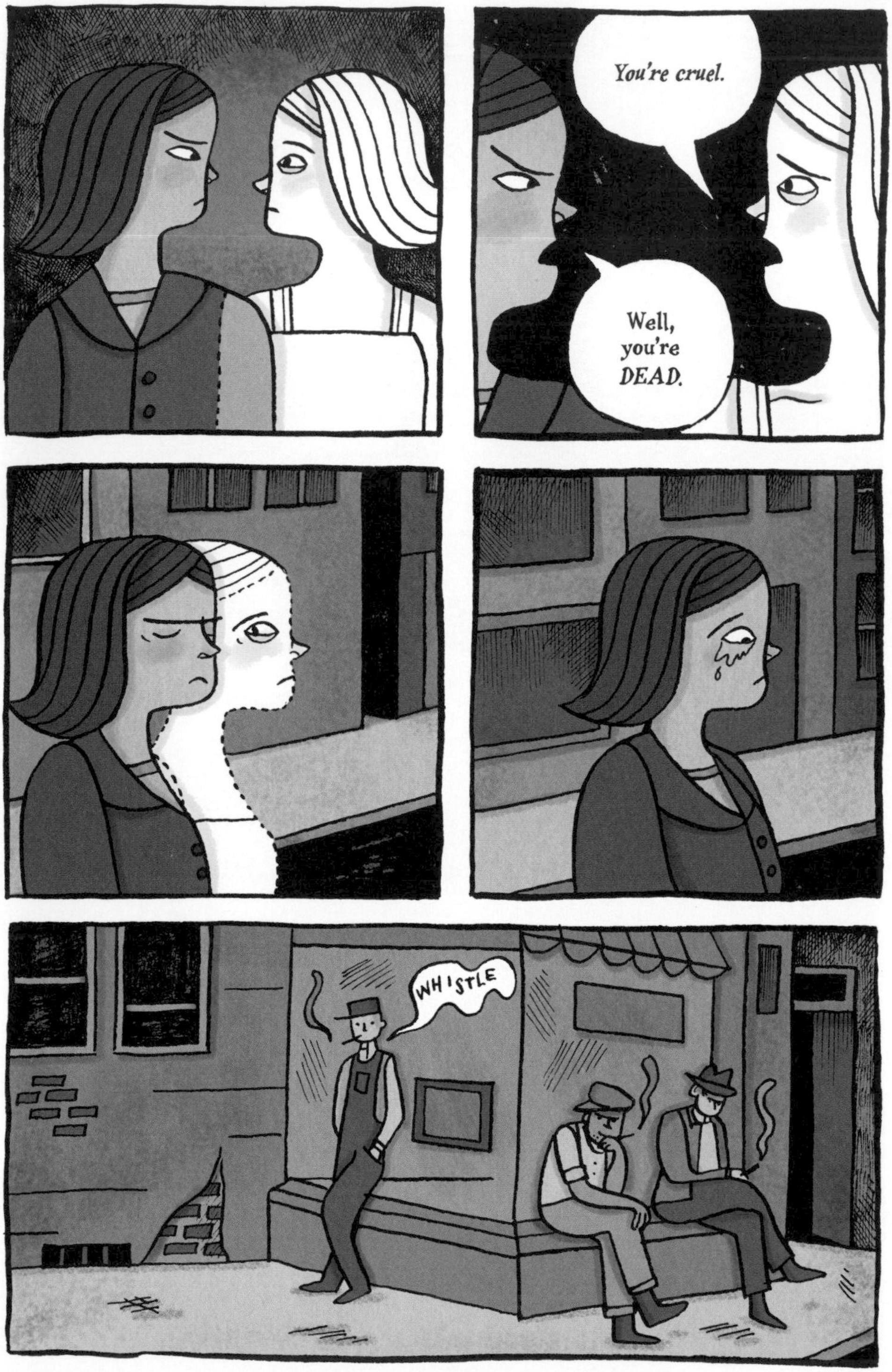
You're cruel.
Well, you're DEAD.
WHISTLE

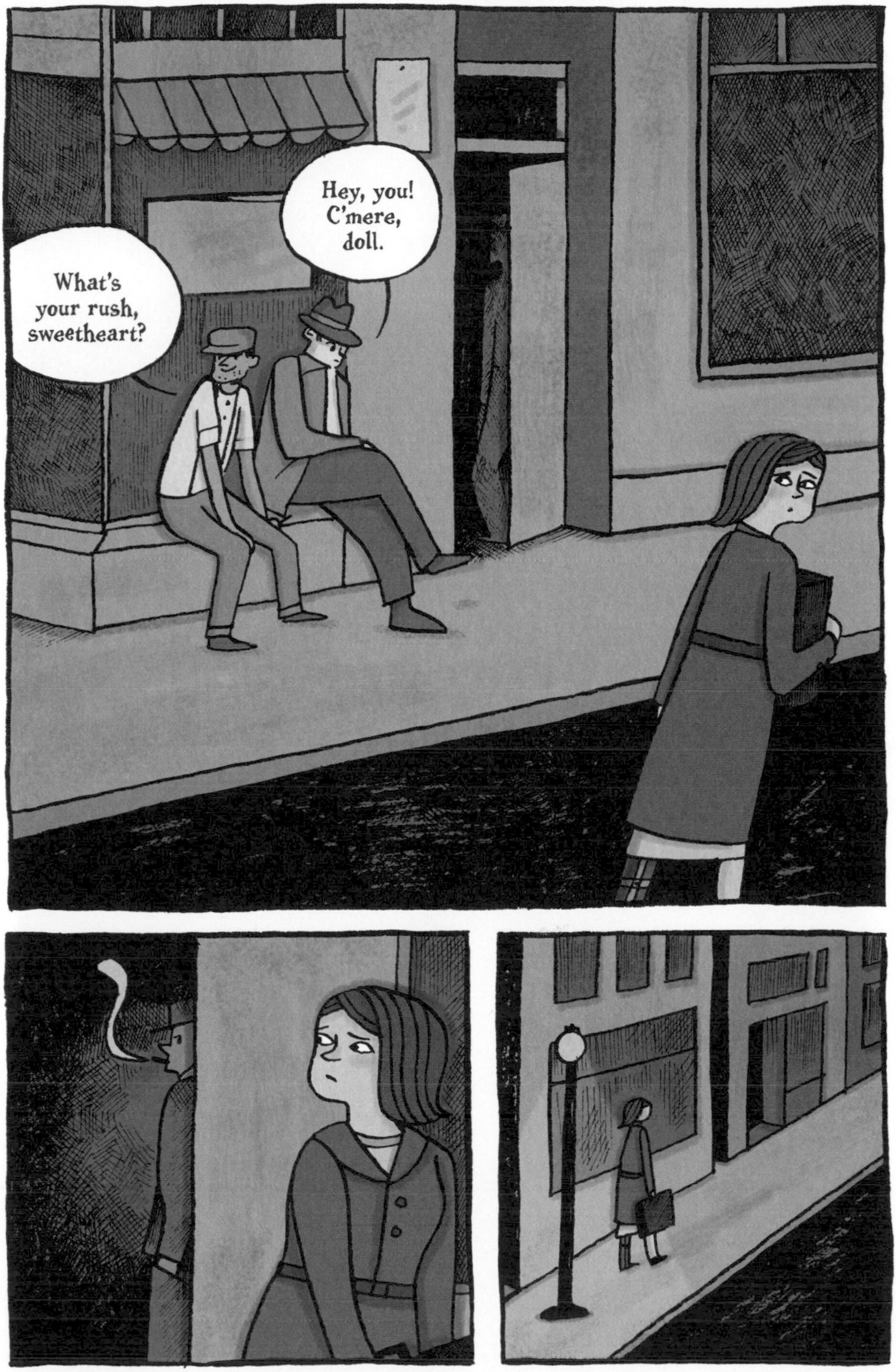
Hey, you! C'mere, doll.
What's your rush, sweetheart?

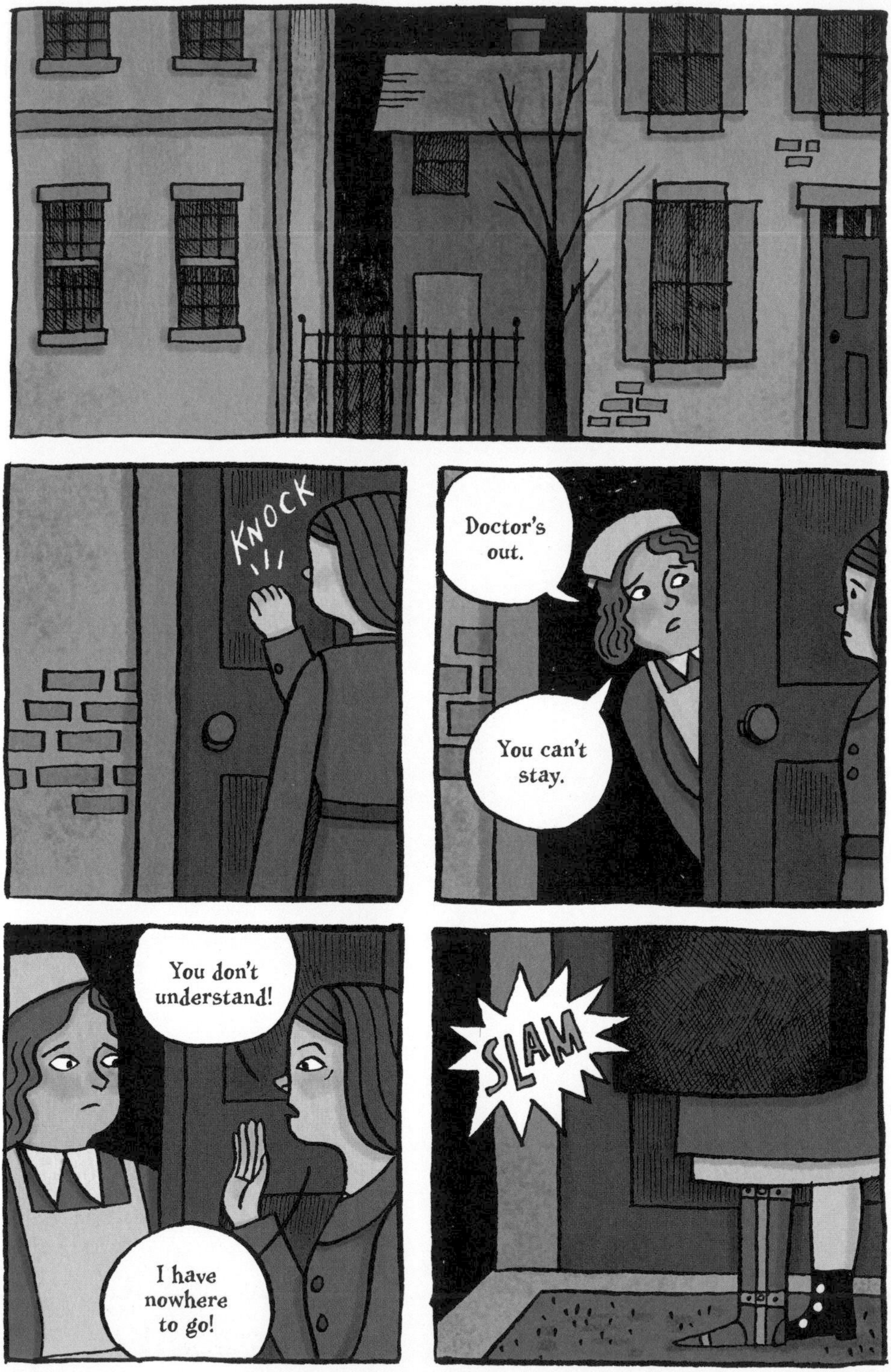
KNOCK
Doctor's out.
You can't stay.
You don't understand!
I have nowhere to go!
SLAM

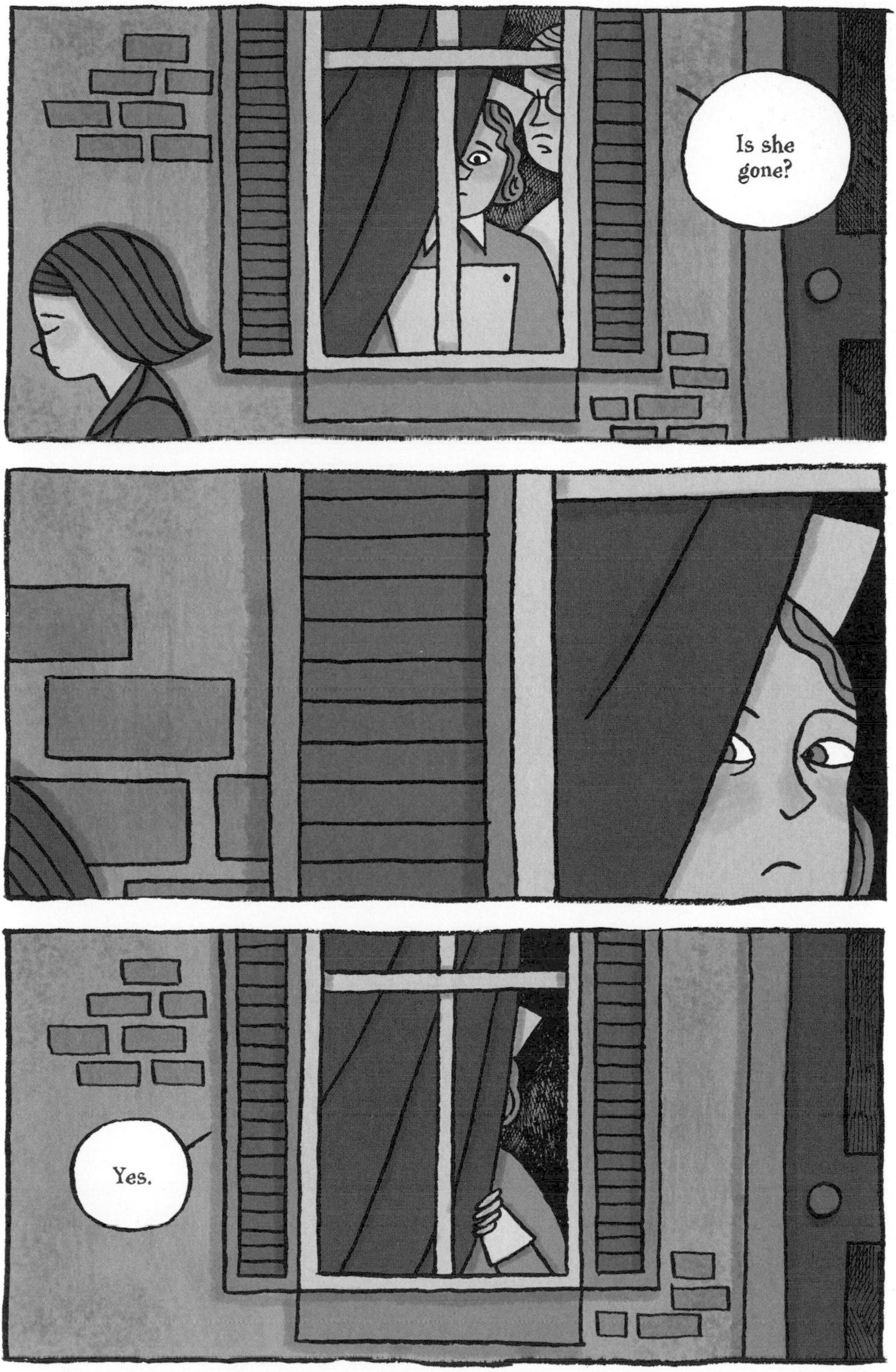
Is she gone?
Yes.

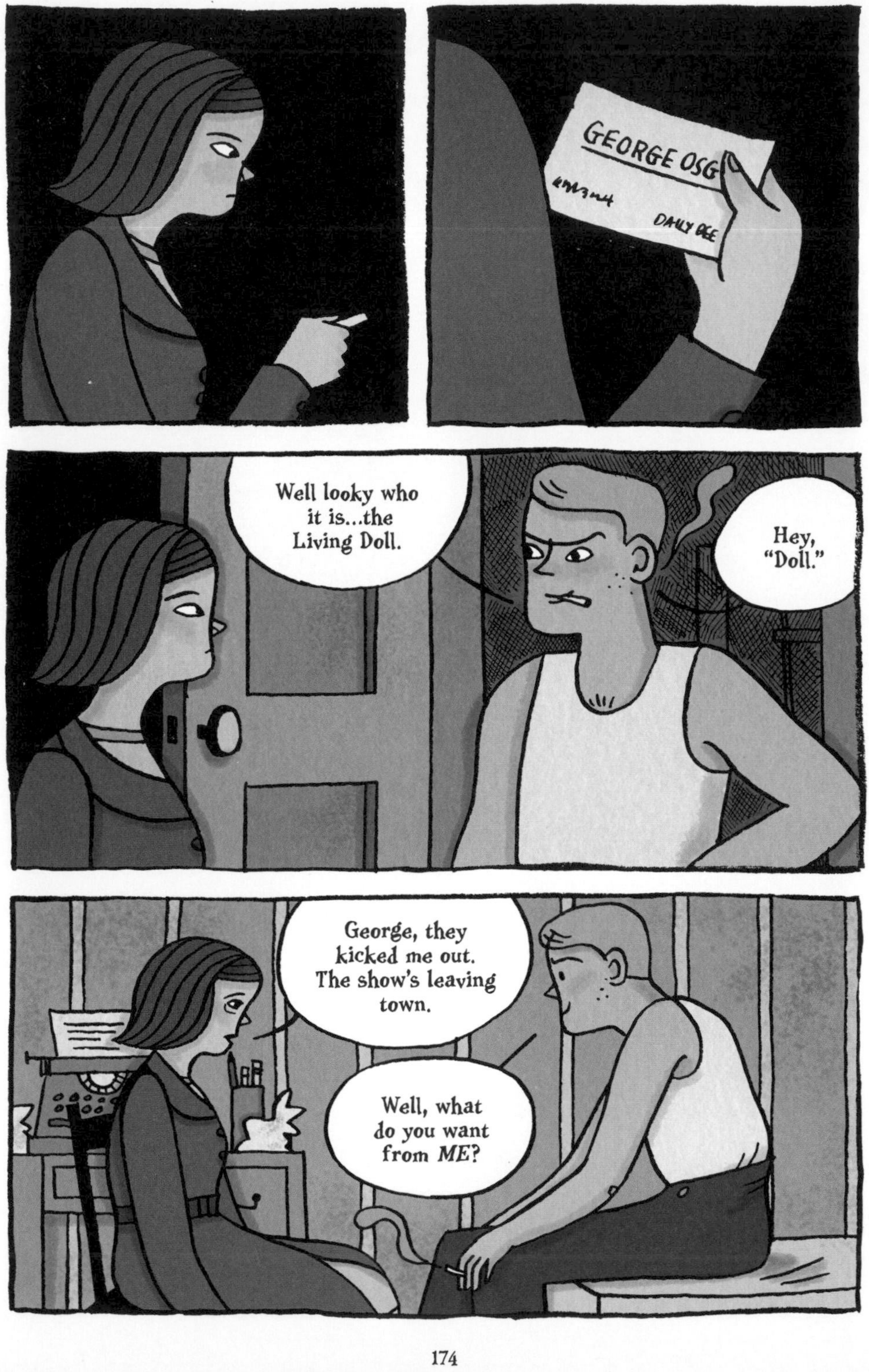
GEORGE OSG
DAILY BEE
Well looky who it is...the Living Doll.
Hey, "Doll."
George, they kicked me out. The show's leaving town.
Well, what do you want from *ME*?

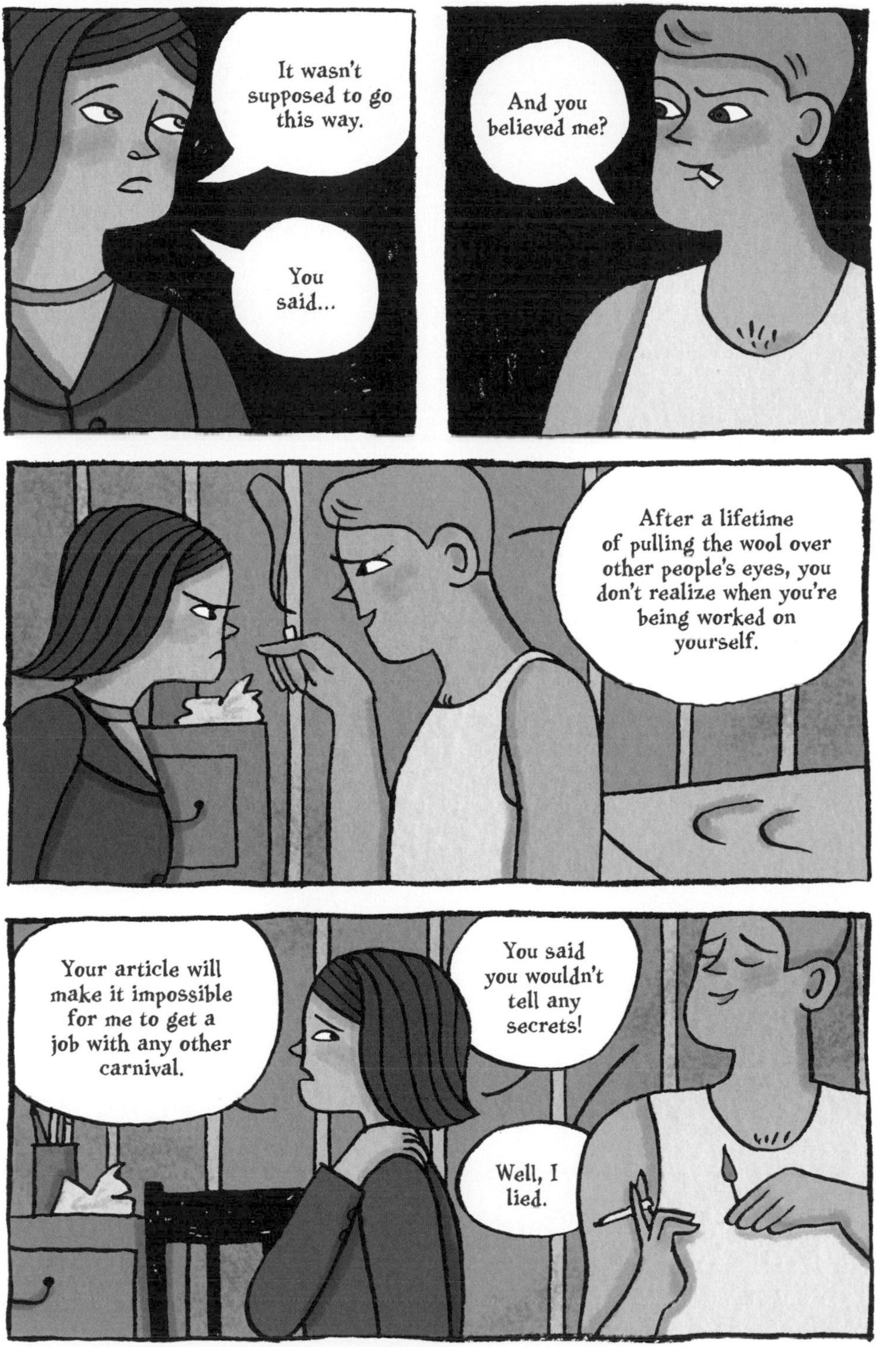
It wasn't supposed to go this way.
You said...
And you believed me?
After a lifetime of pulling the wool over other people's eyes, you don't realize when you're being worked on yourself.
Your article will make it impossible for me to get a job with any other carnival.
You said you wouldn't tell any secrets!
Well, I lied.

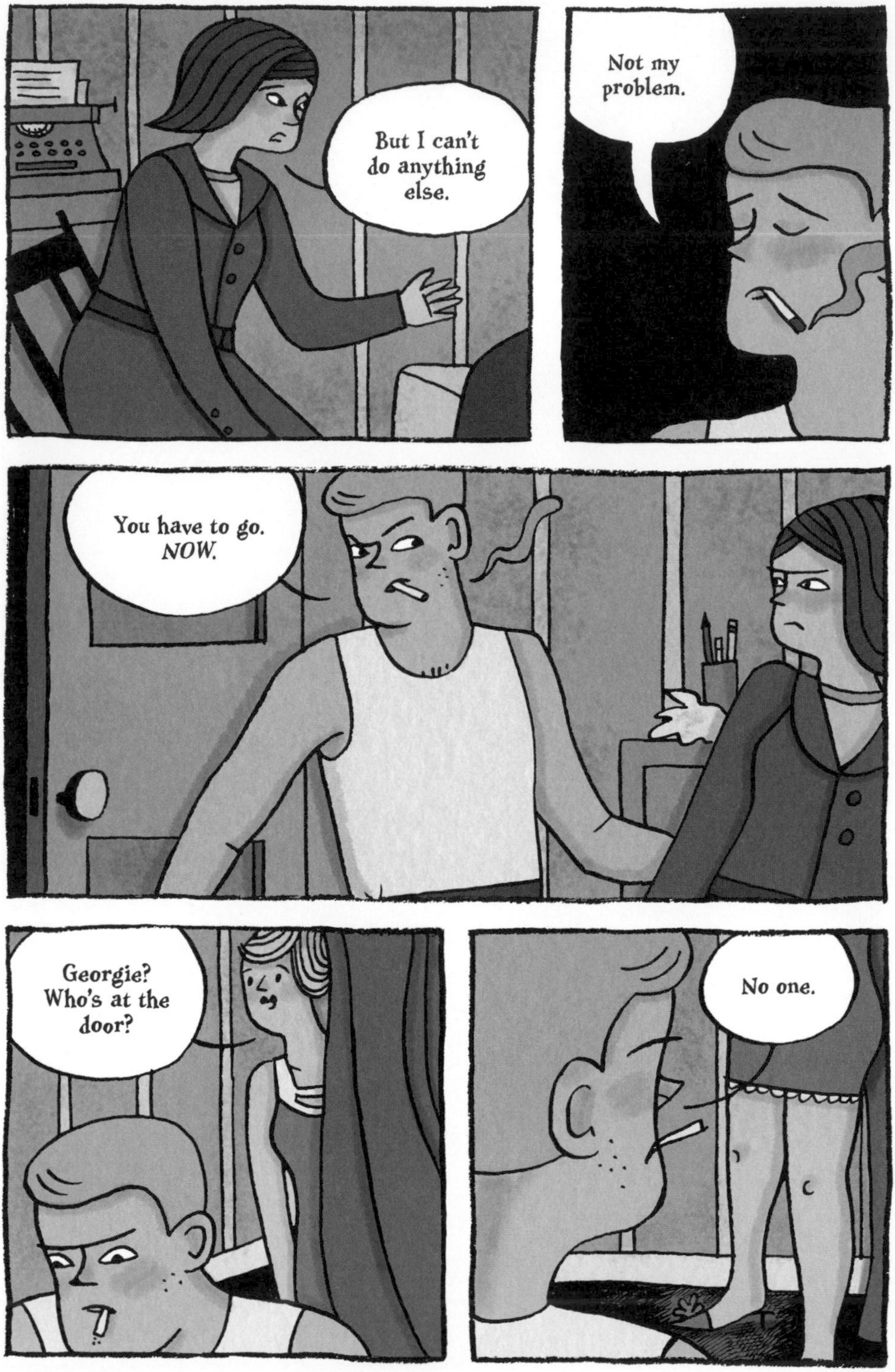
But I can't do anything else.
Not my problem.
You have to go. *NOW.*
Georgie? Who's at the door?
No one.

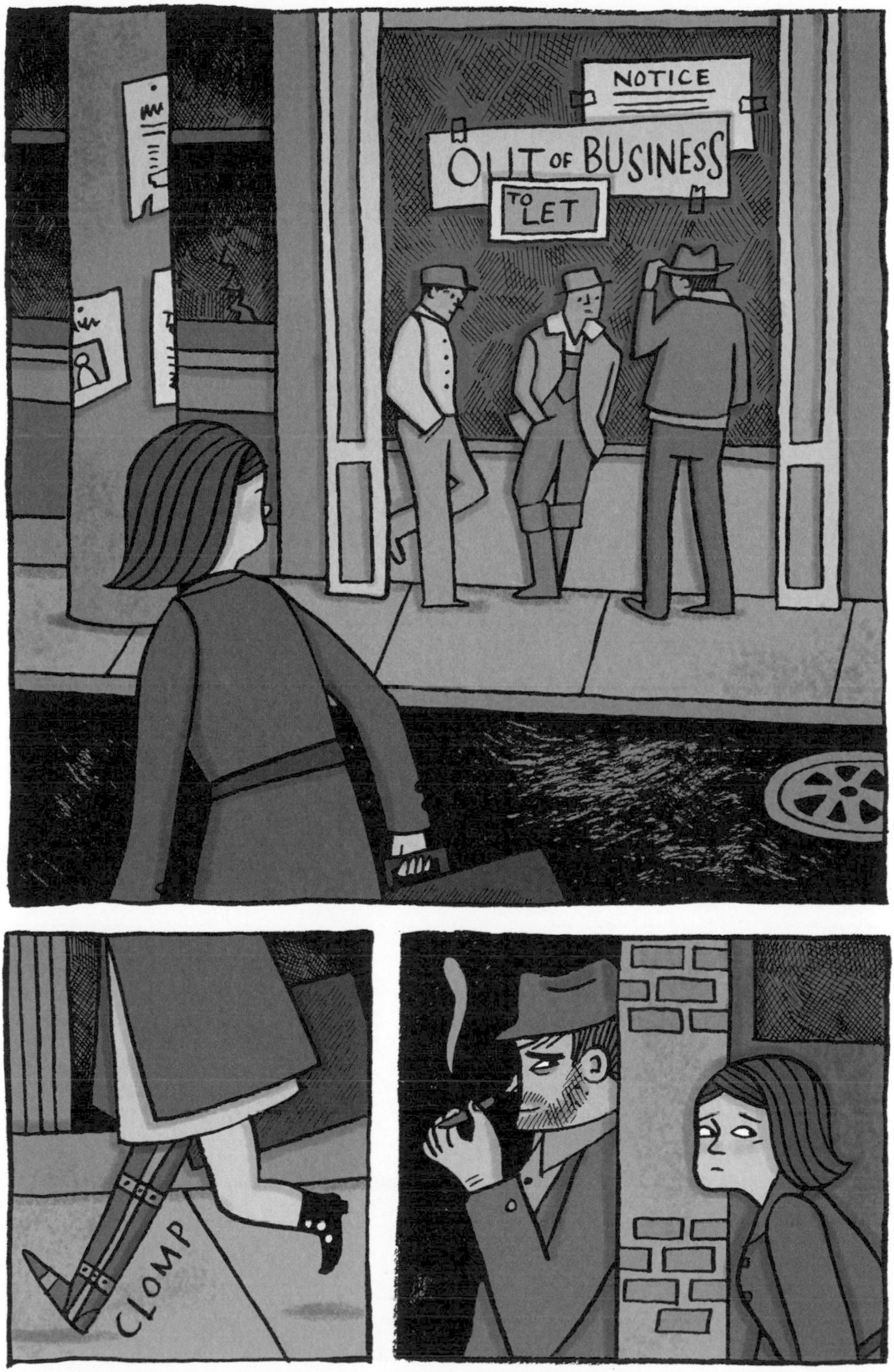
NOTICE
OUT OF BUSINESS
TO LET
CLOMP

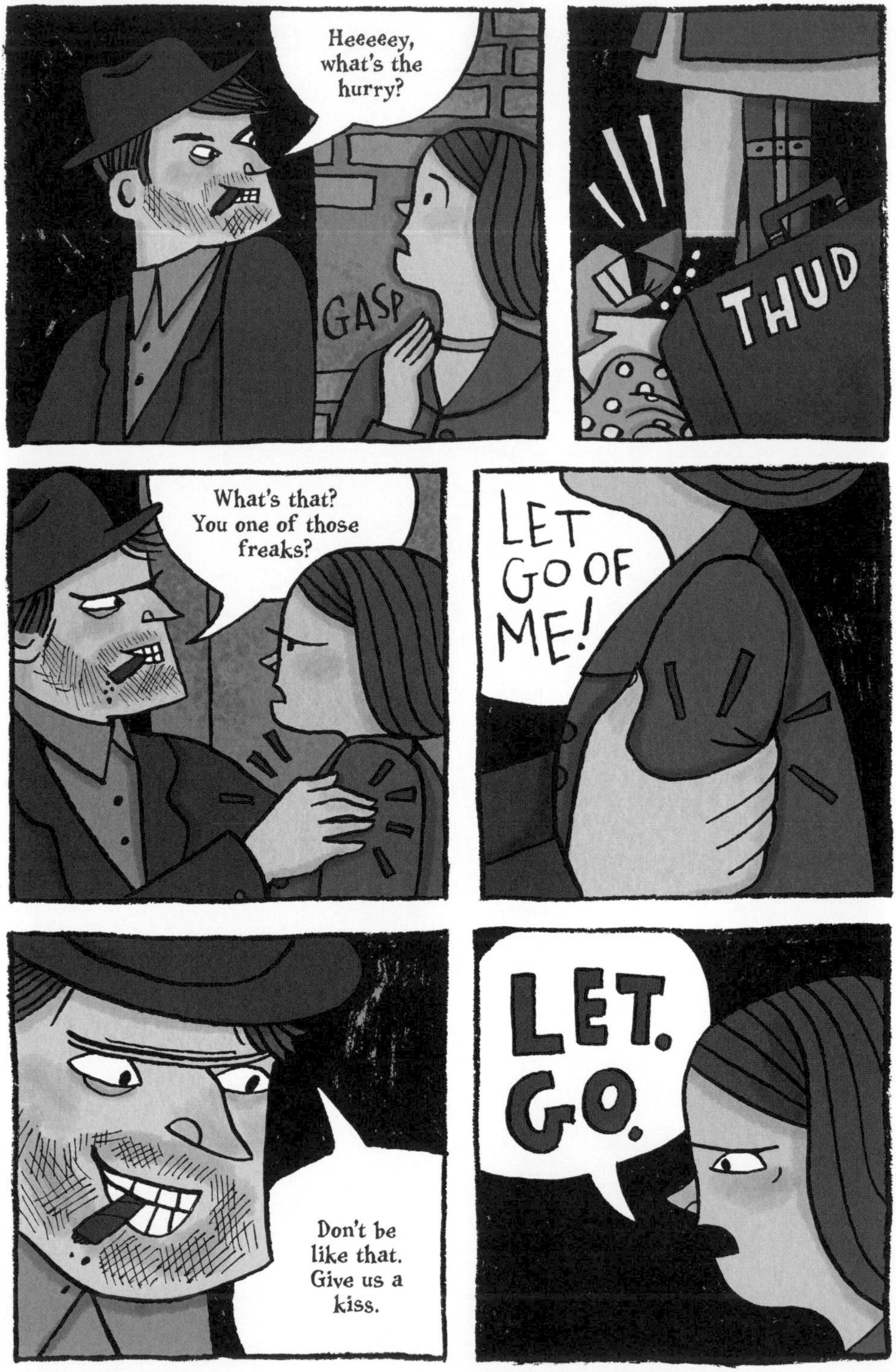
Heeeeey, what's the hurry?
GASP
THUD
What's that? You one of those freaks?
LET GO OF ME!
Don't be like that. Give us a kiss.
LET. GO.

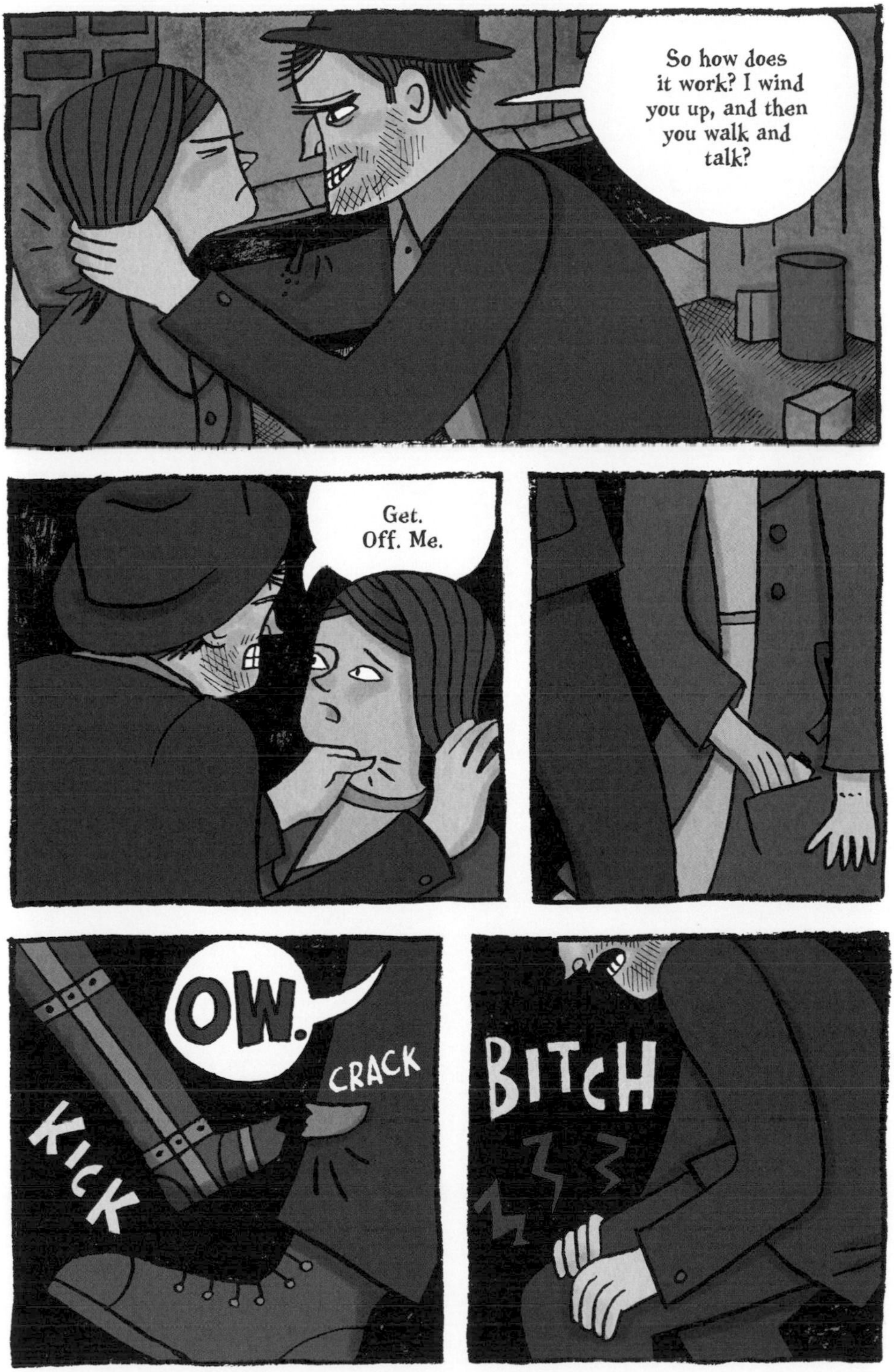
So how does it work? I wind you up, and then you walk and talk?
Get. Off. Me.
OW.
CRACK
KICK
BITCH

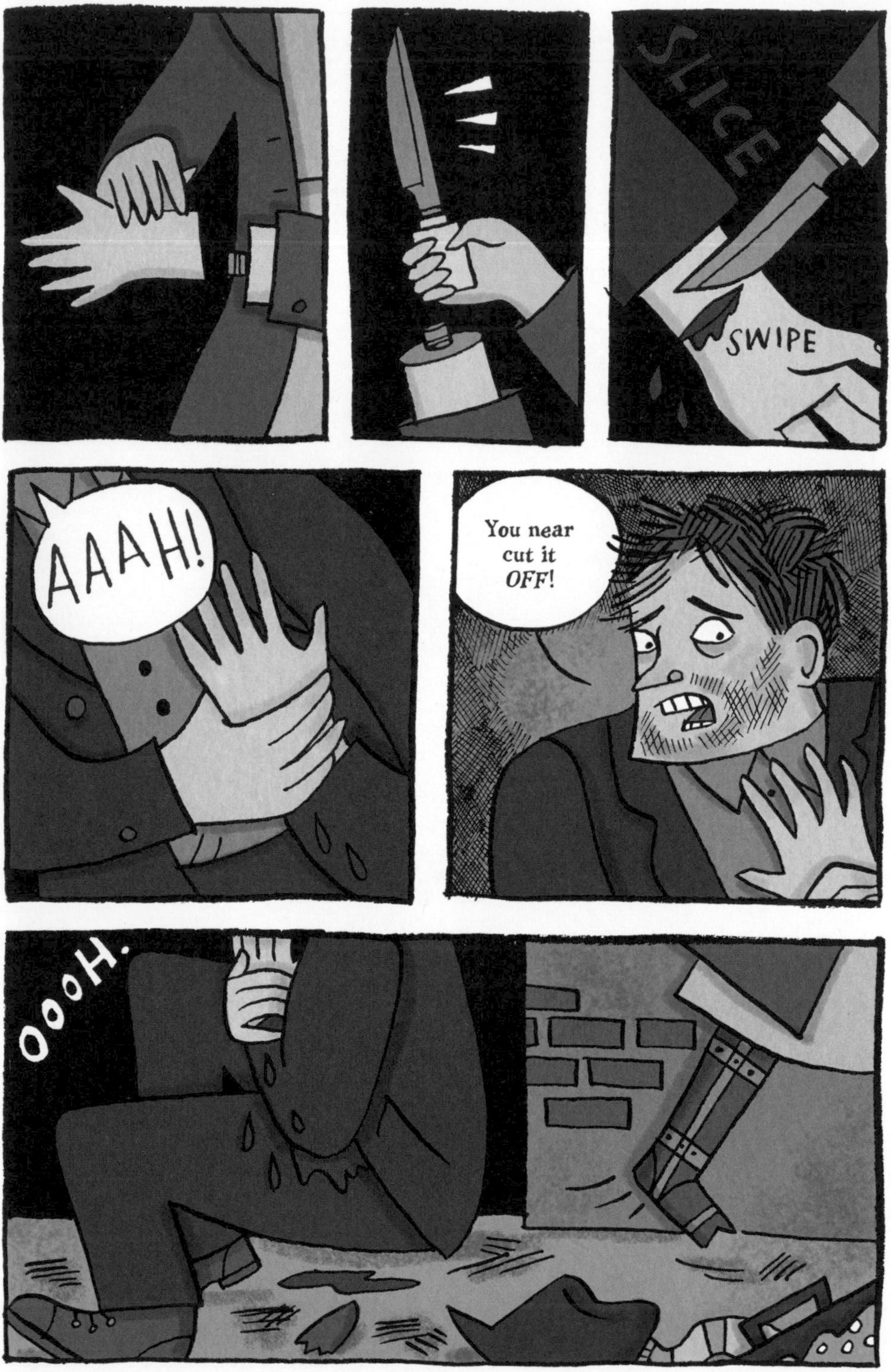
SLICE
SWIPE
AAAH!
You near cut it *OFF*!
OOOH.

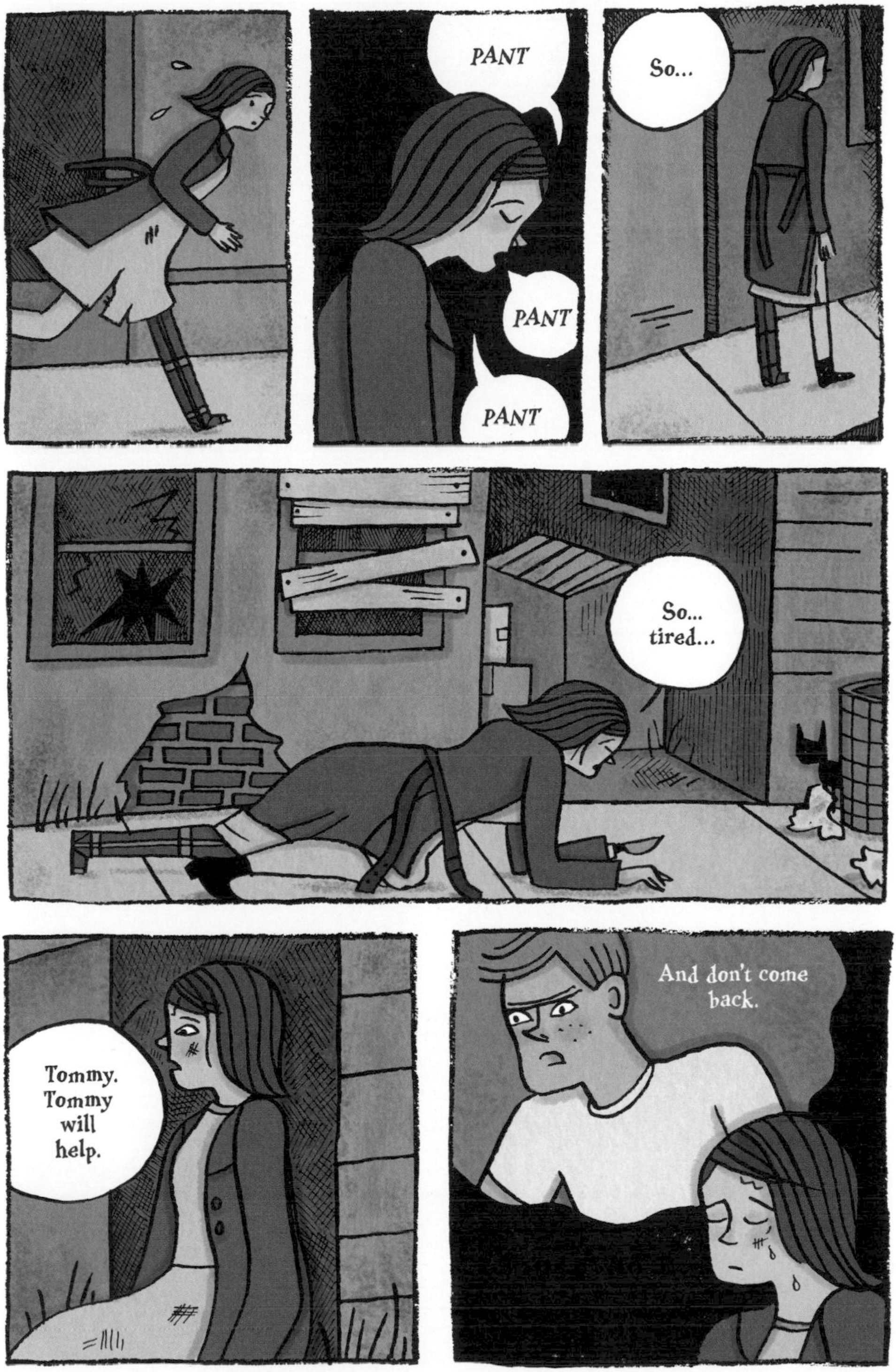
PANT
PANT
PANT
So...
So...
tired...
Tommy.
Tommy
will
help.
And don't come
back.

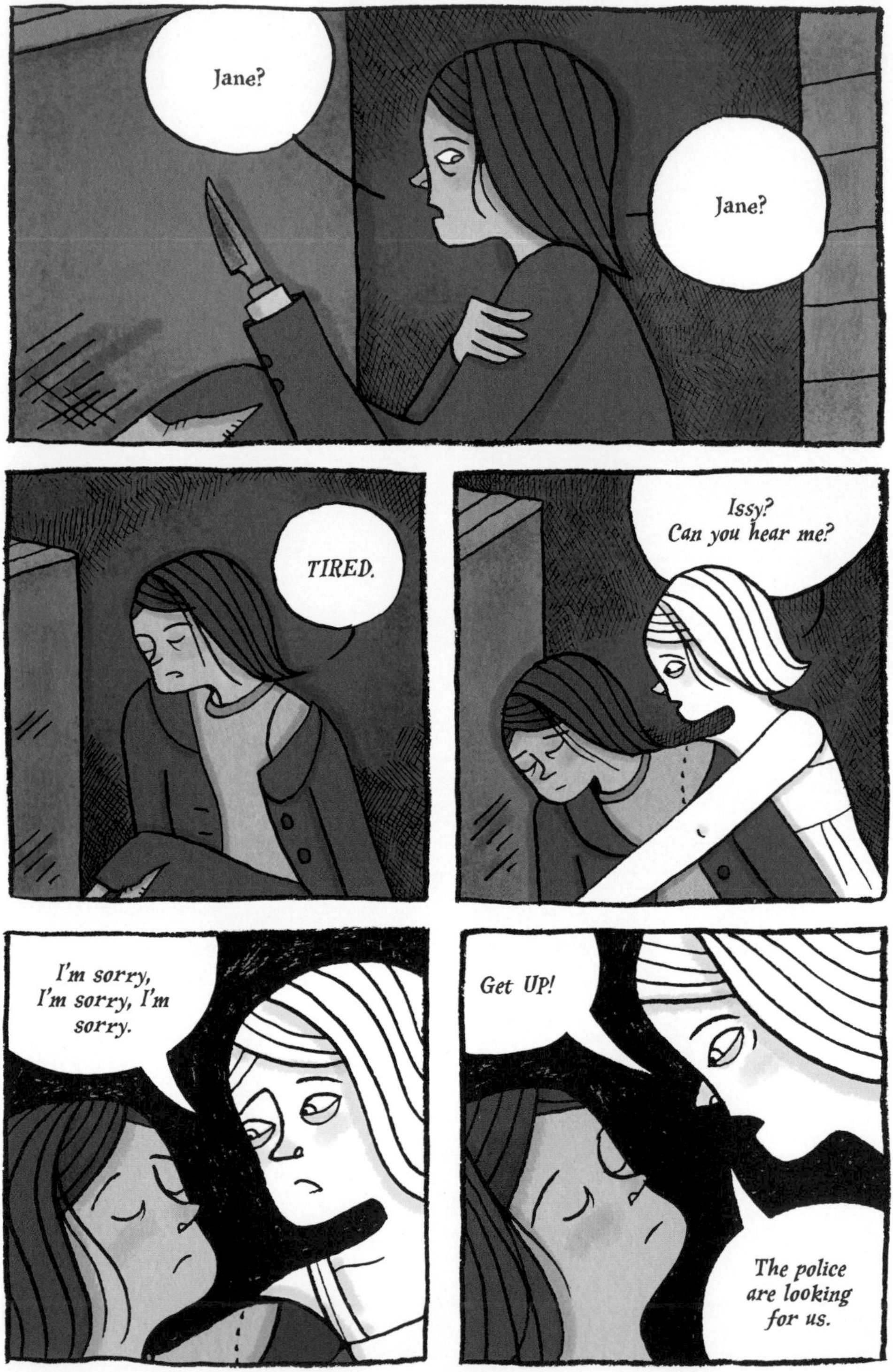
Jane?
Jane?
TIRED.
Issy?
Can you hear me?
I'm sorry,
I'm sorry, I'm
sorry.
Get UP!
The police
are looking
for us.

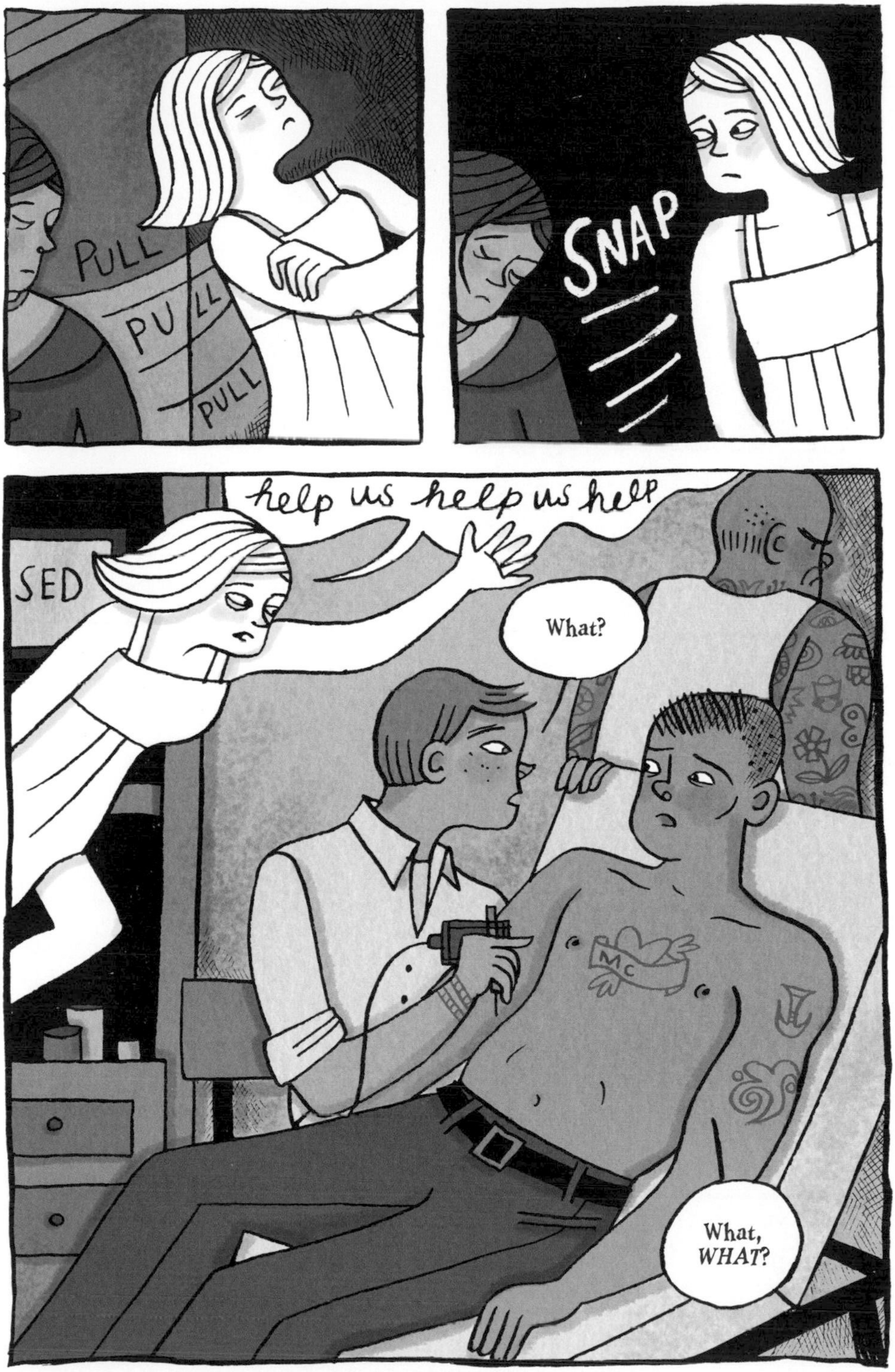
PULL
PULL
PULL
SNAP
SED
help us help us help
What?
What, *WHAT*?

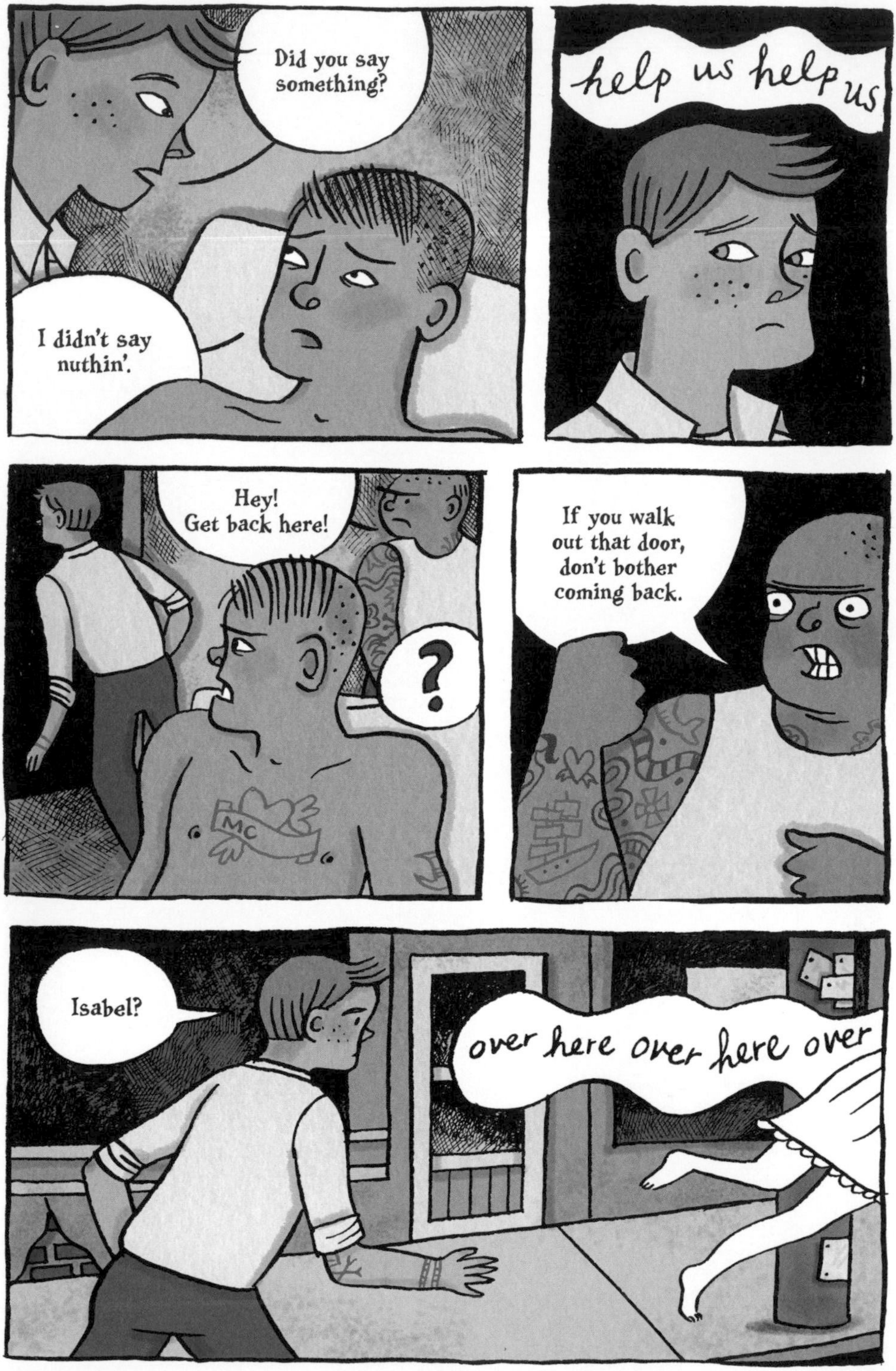

Did you say something?
I didn't say nuthin'.
help us help us
Hey! Get back here!
?
If you walk out that door, don't bother coming back.
Isabel?
over here over here over

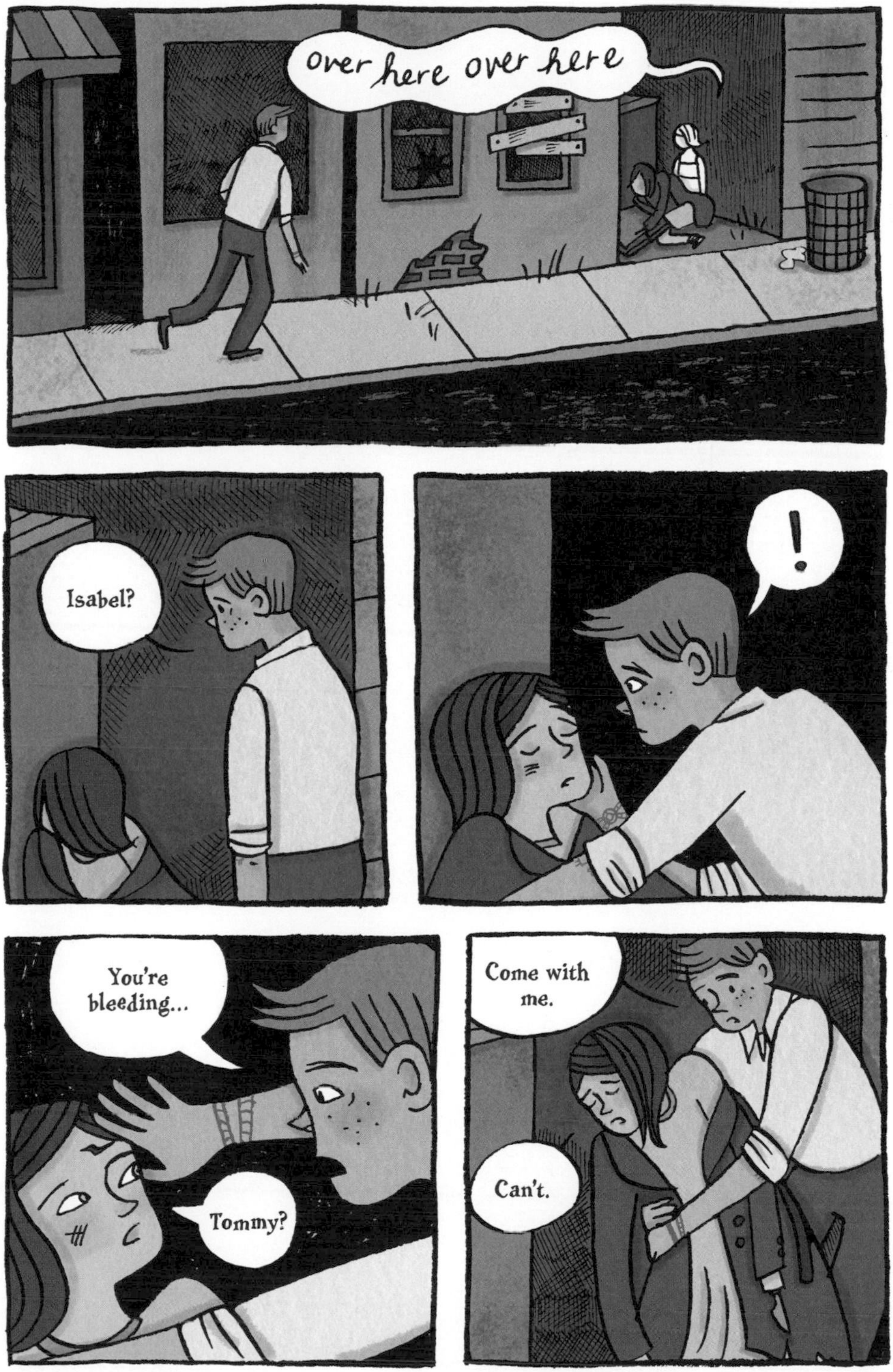
over here over here
Isabel?
!
You're bleeding...
Tommy?
Come with me.
Can't.

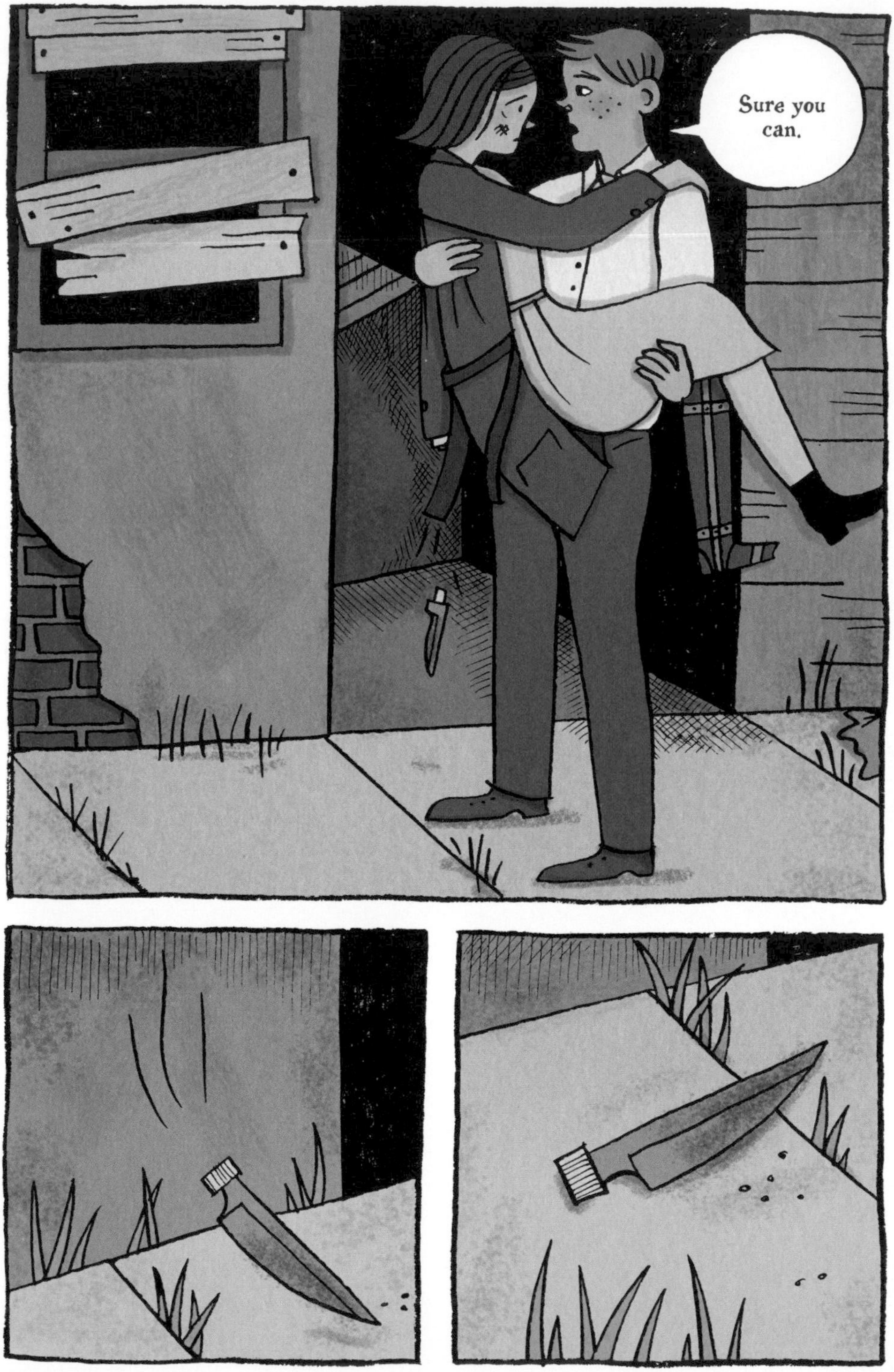
Sure you can.

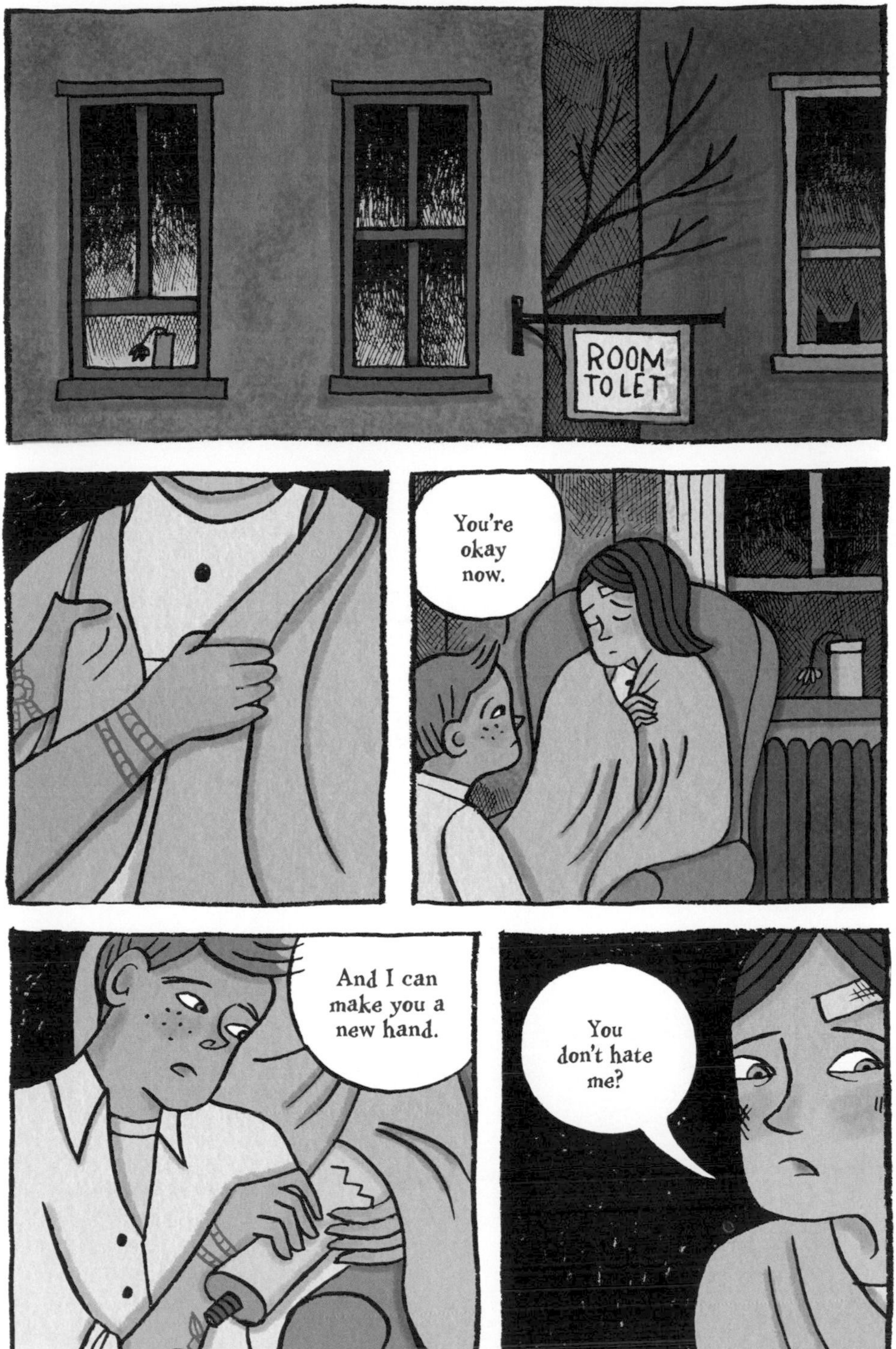
ROOM TO LET
You're okay now.
And I can make you a new hand.
You don't hate me?

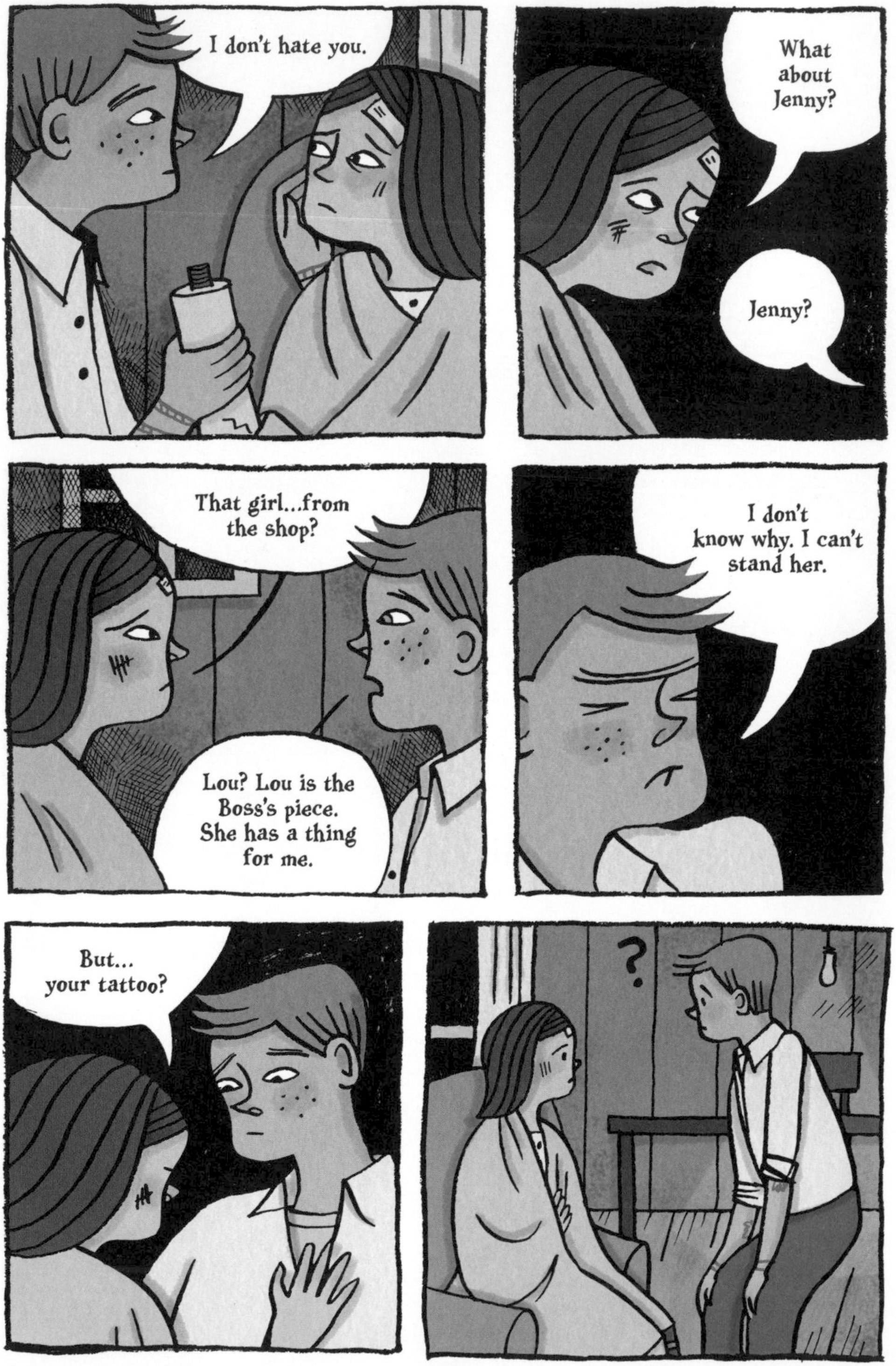
I don't hate you.
What about Jenny?
Jenny?
That girl...from the shop?
Lou? Lou is the Boss's piece. She has a thing for me.
I don't know why. I can't stand her.
But... your tattoo?
?

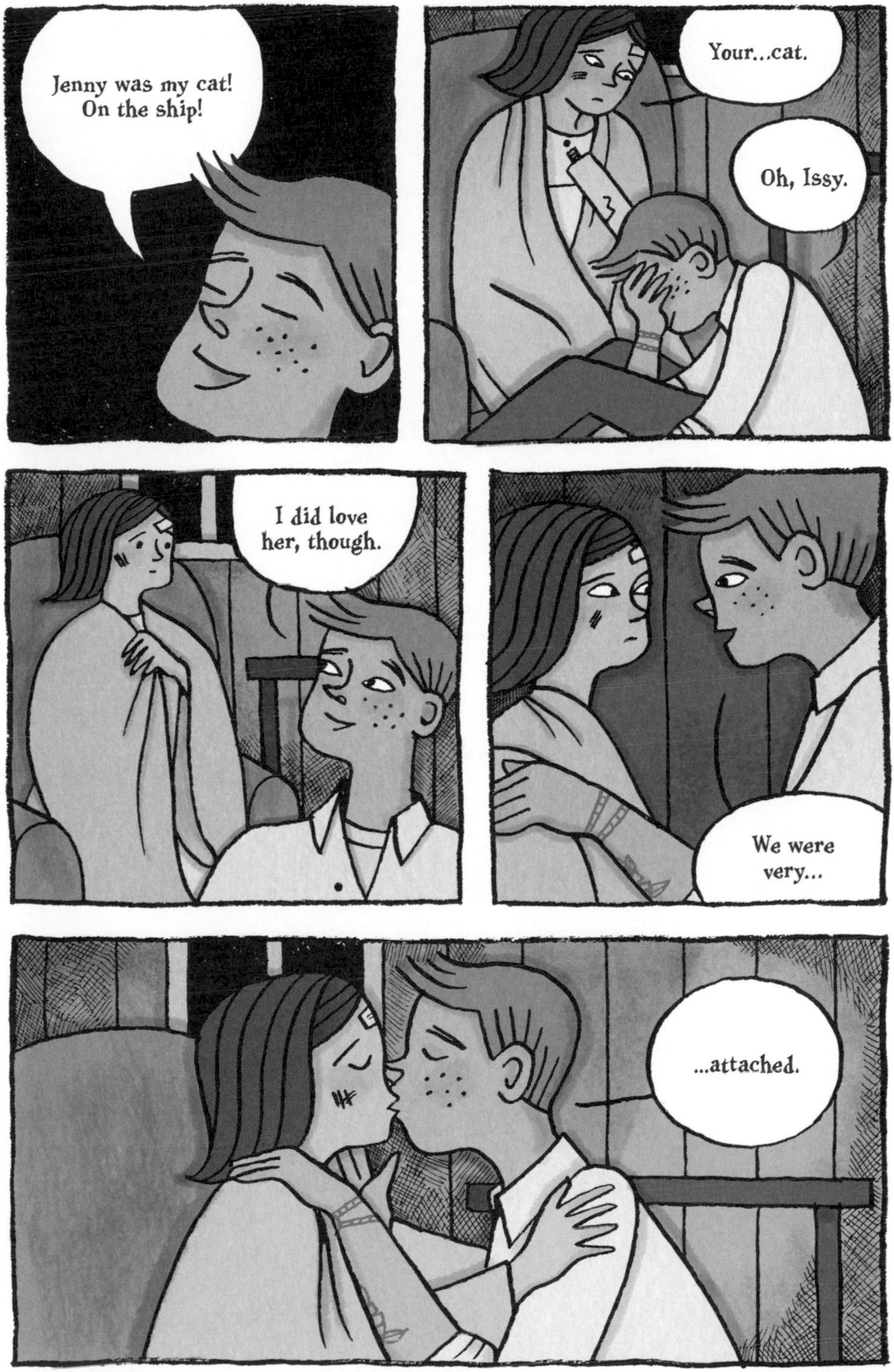
Jenny was my cat!
On the ship!
Your...cat.
Oh, Issy.
I did love
her, though.
We were
very...
...attached.

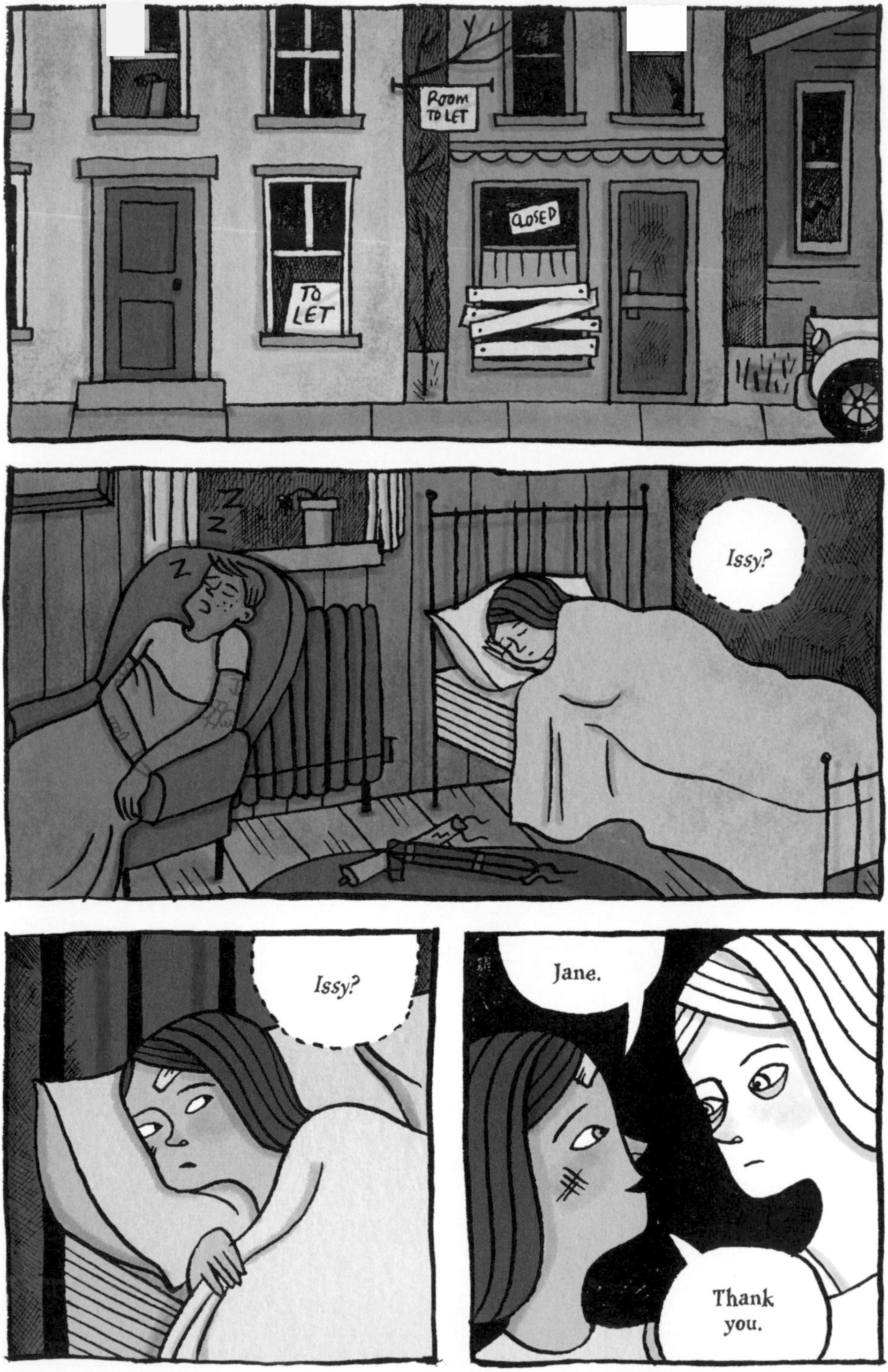
ROOM TO LET
CLOSED
TO LET
Issy?
Issy?
Jane.
Thank you.

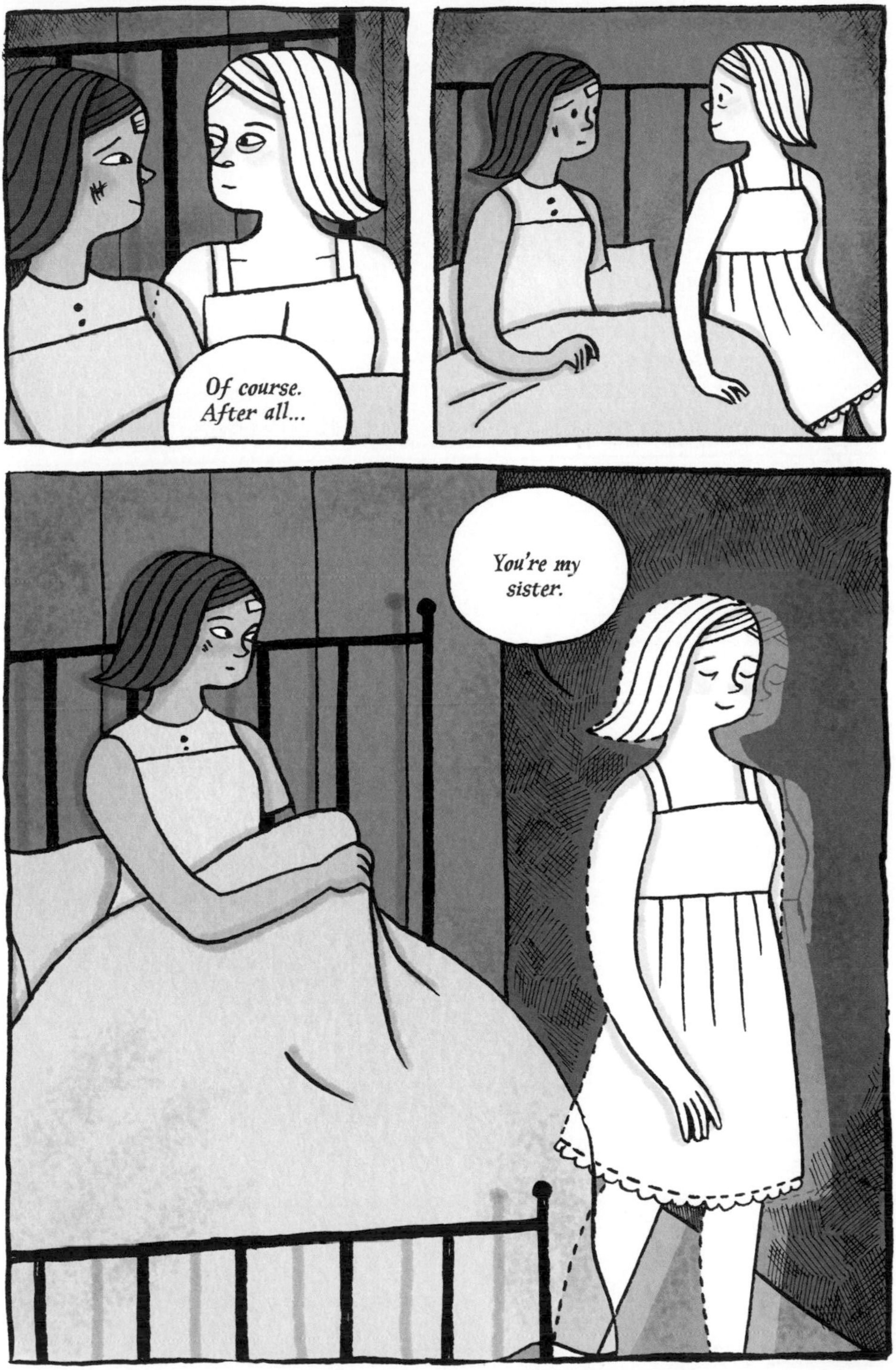
Of course. After all...
You're my sister.

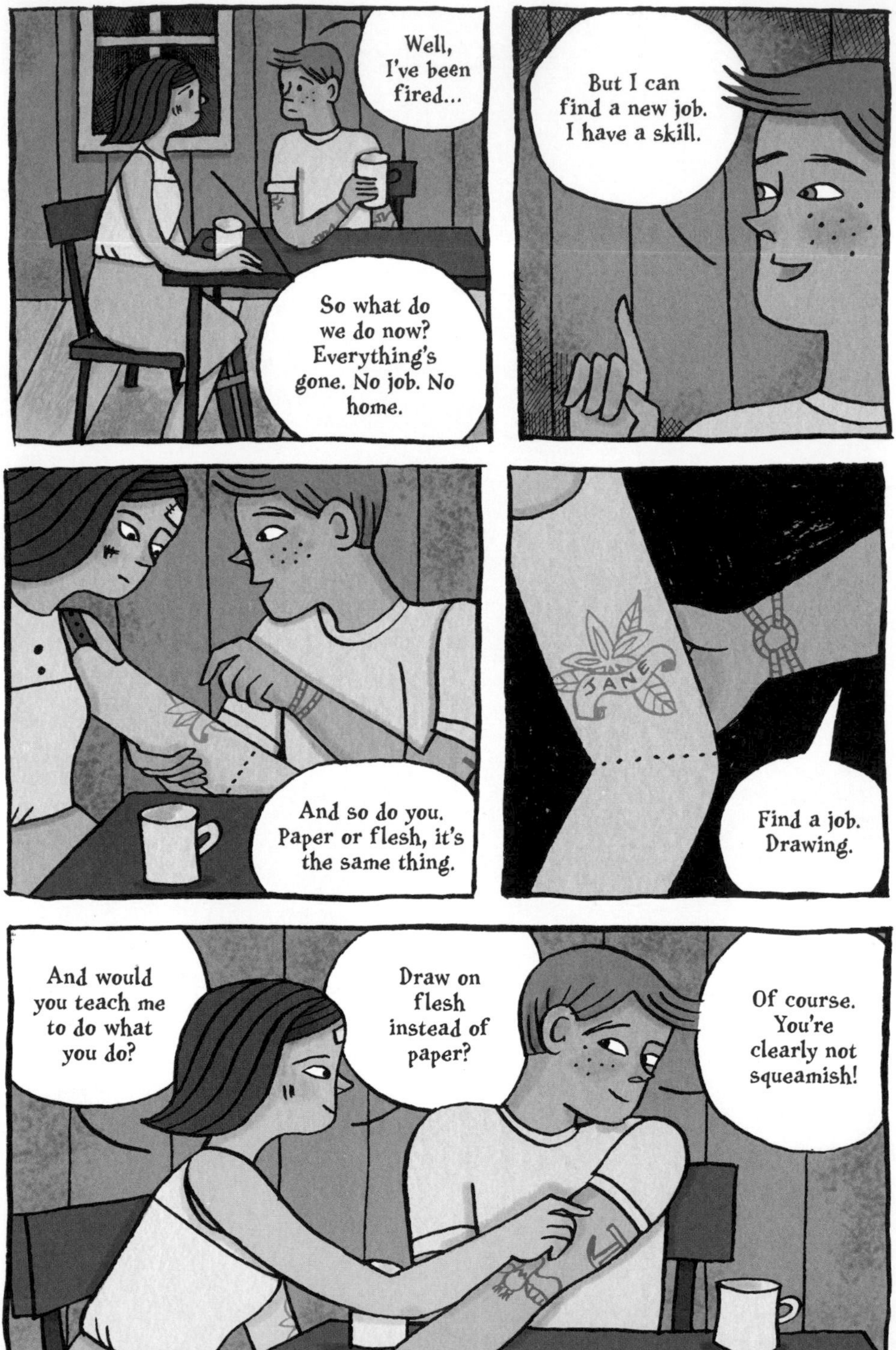
Well, I've been fired...
So what do we do now? Everything's gone. No job. No home.
But I can find a new job. I have a skill.
And so do you. Paper or flesh, it's the same thing.
JANE
Find a job. Drawing.
And would you teach me to do what you do?
Draw on flesh instead of paper?
Of course. You're clearly not squeamish!

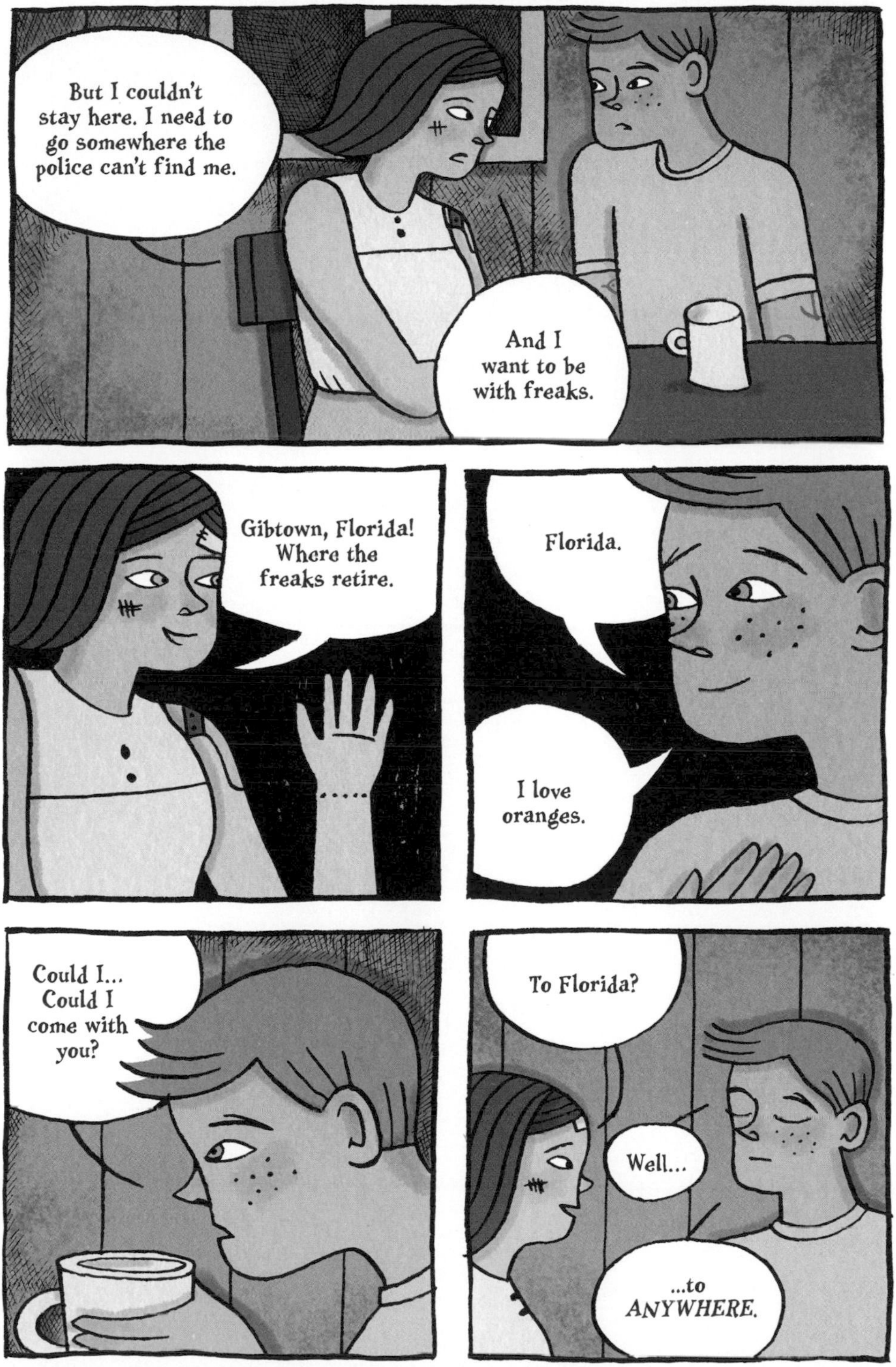
But I couldn't stay here. I need to go somewhere the police can't find me.
And I want to be with freaks.
Gibtown, Florida! Where the freaks retire.
Florida.
I love oranges.
Could I... Could I come with you?
To Florida?
Well...
...to ANYWHERE.

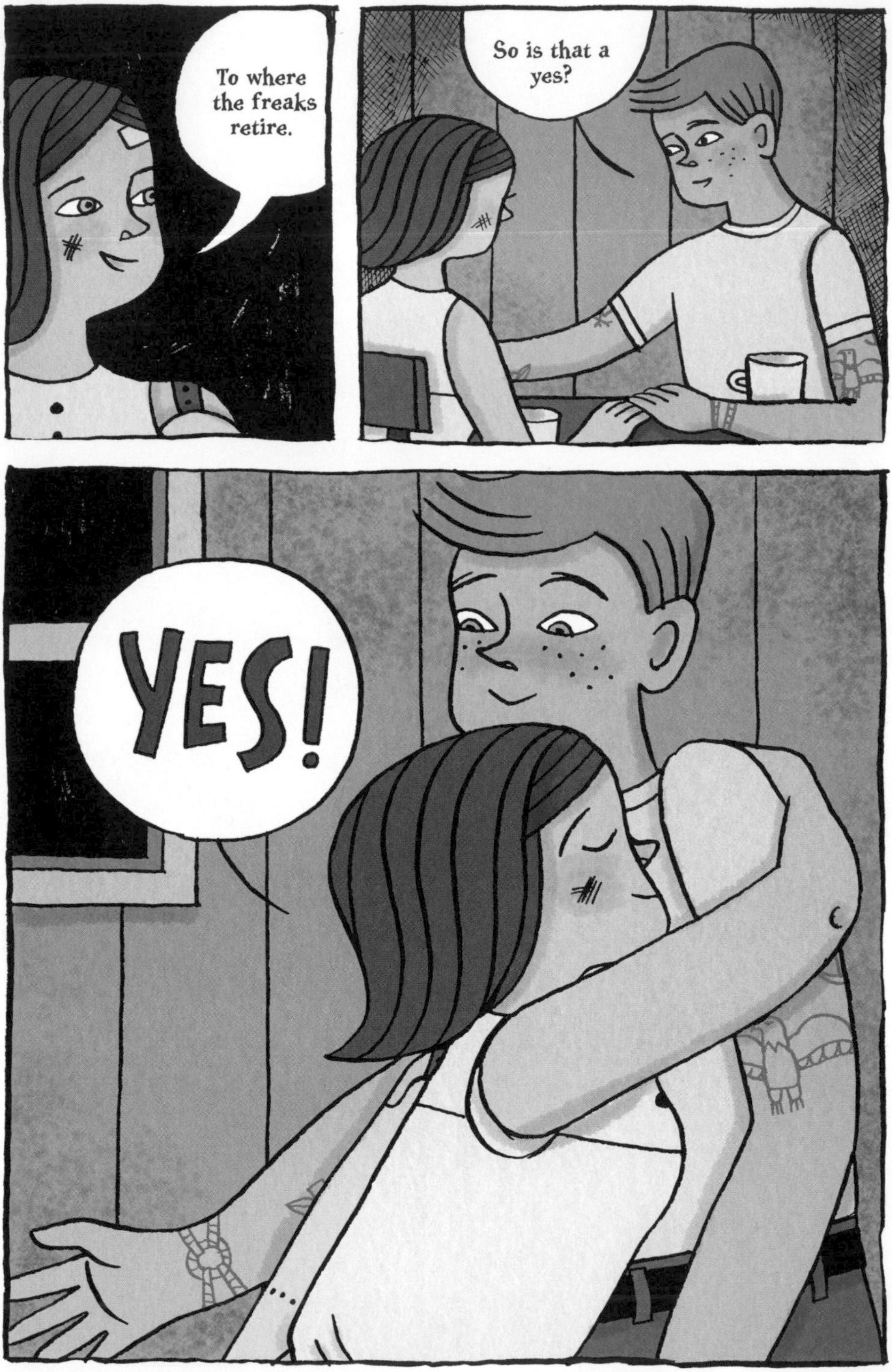
To where the freaks retire.
So is that a yes?
YES!

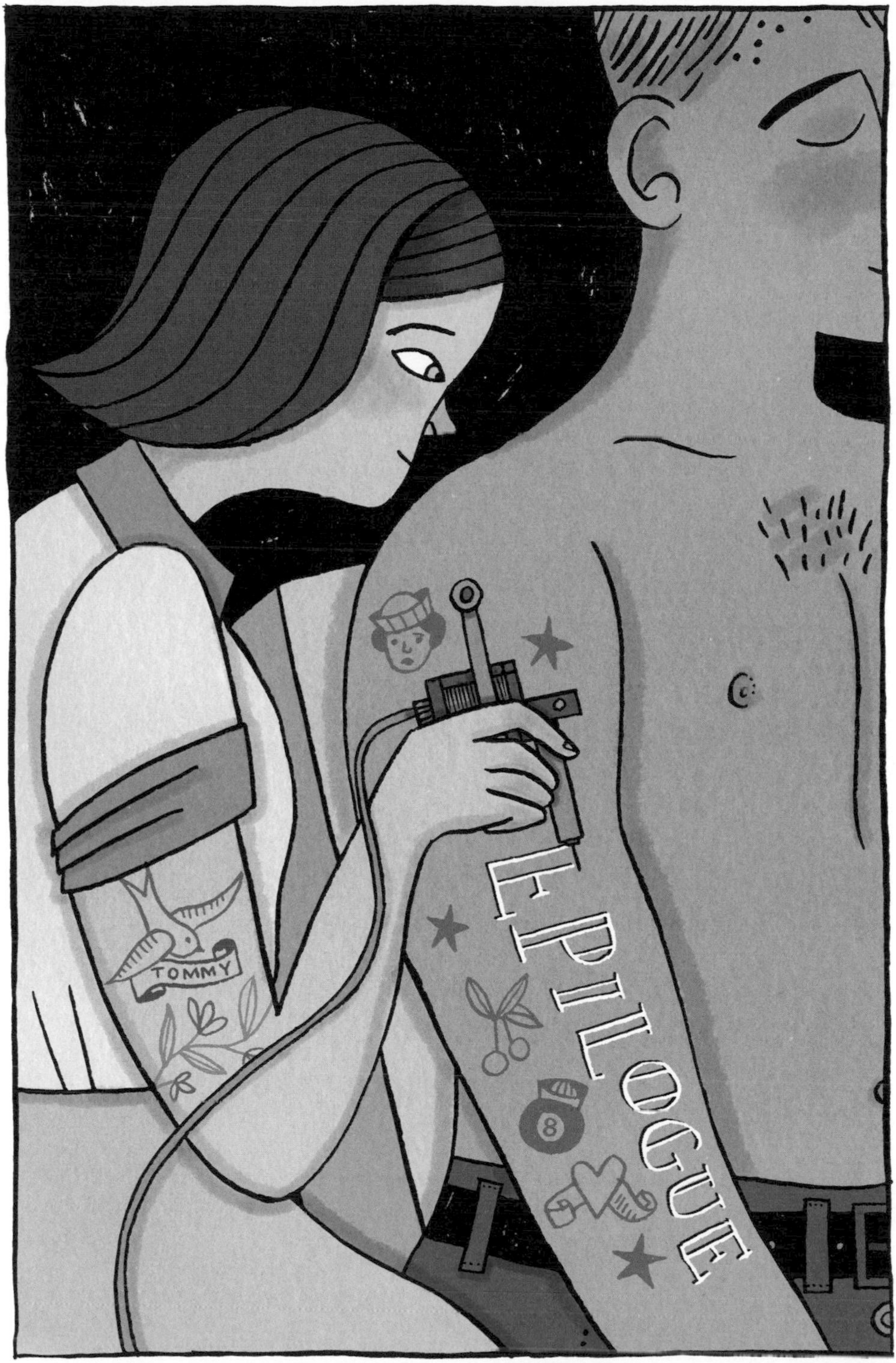
TOMMY
EPILOGUE
8

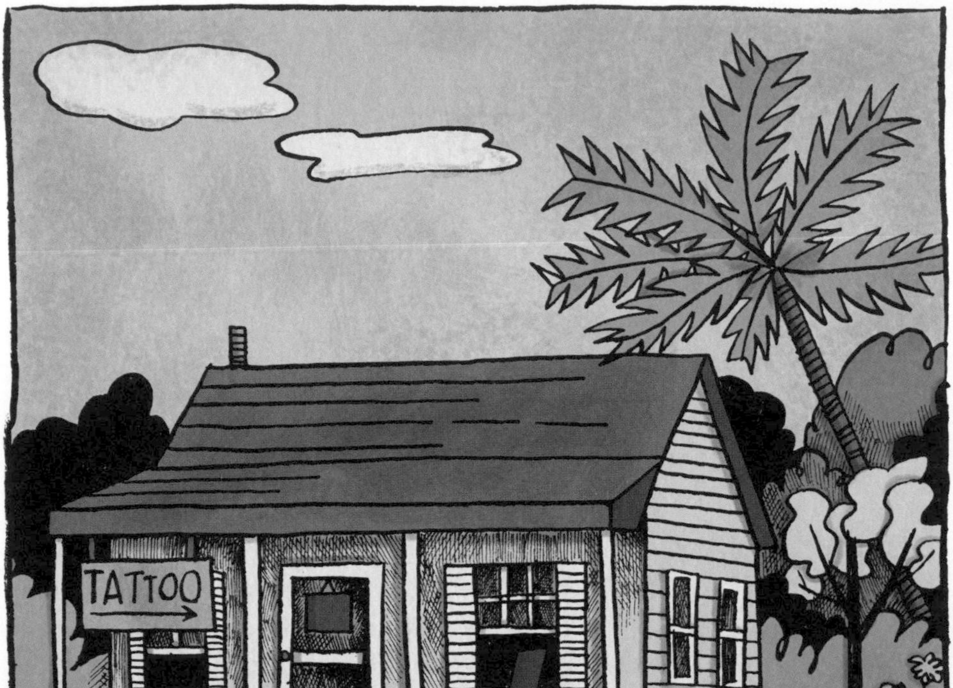
TATTOO

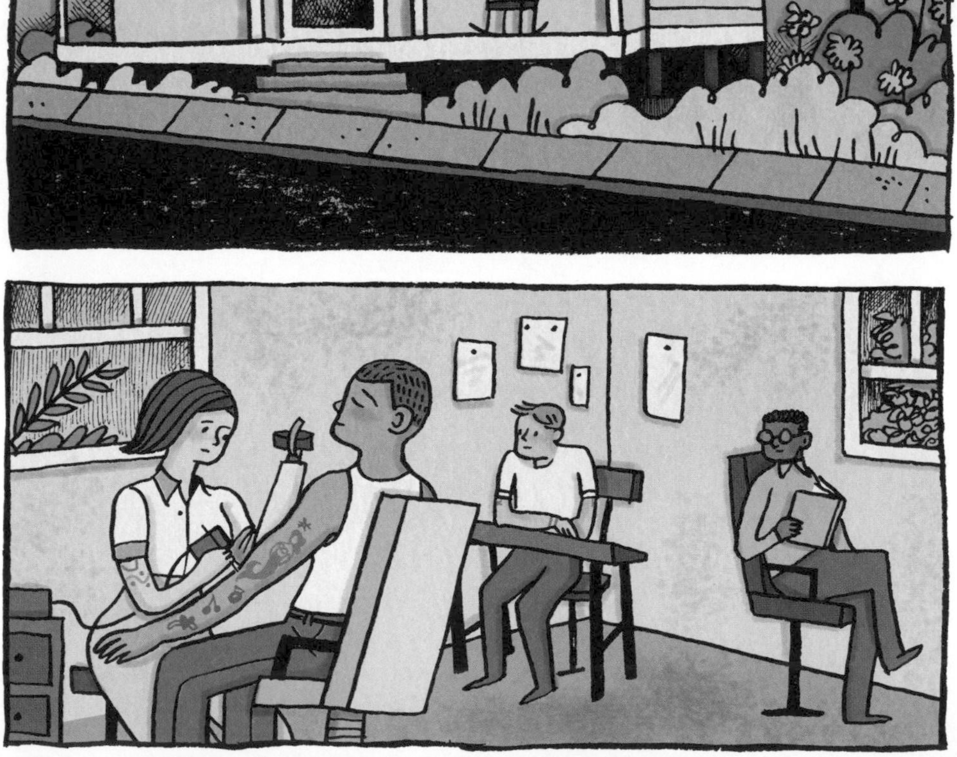

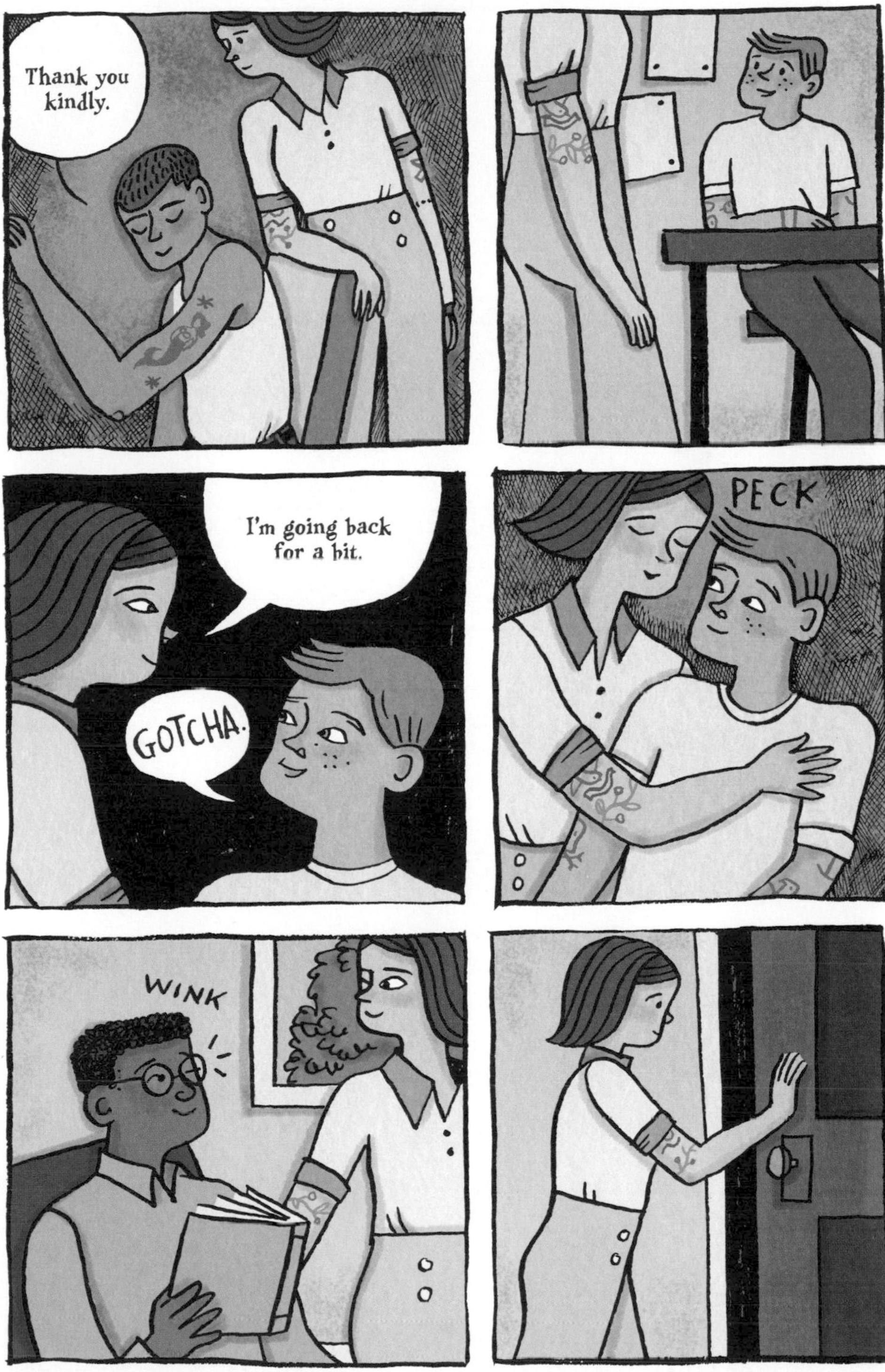
Thank you kindly.
I'm going back for a bit.
GOTCHA.
PECK
WINK

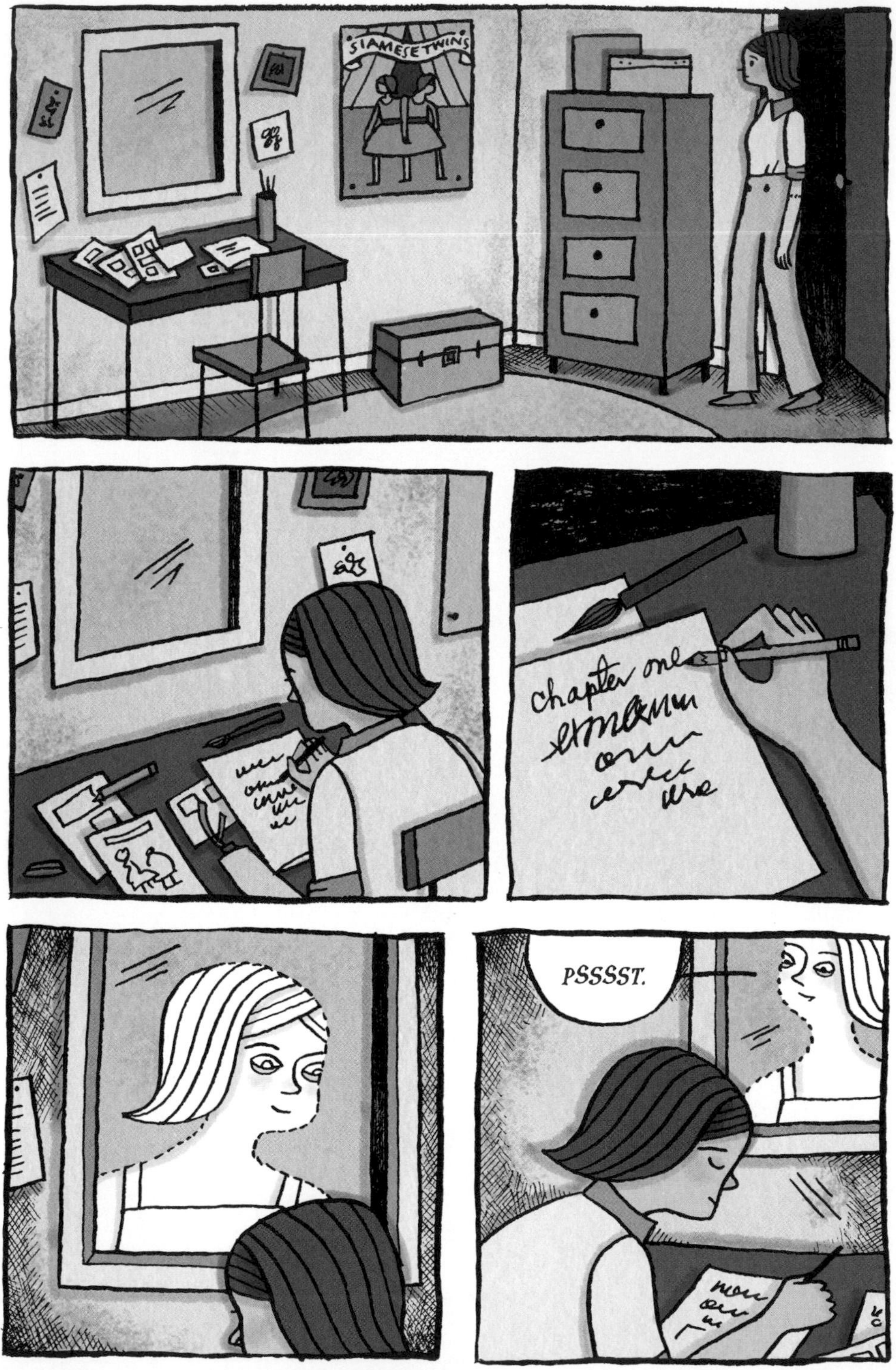
SIAMESE TWINS
chapter one
PSSSST.

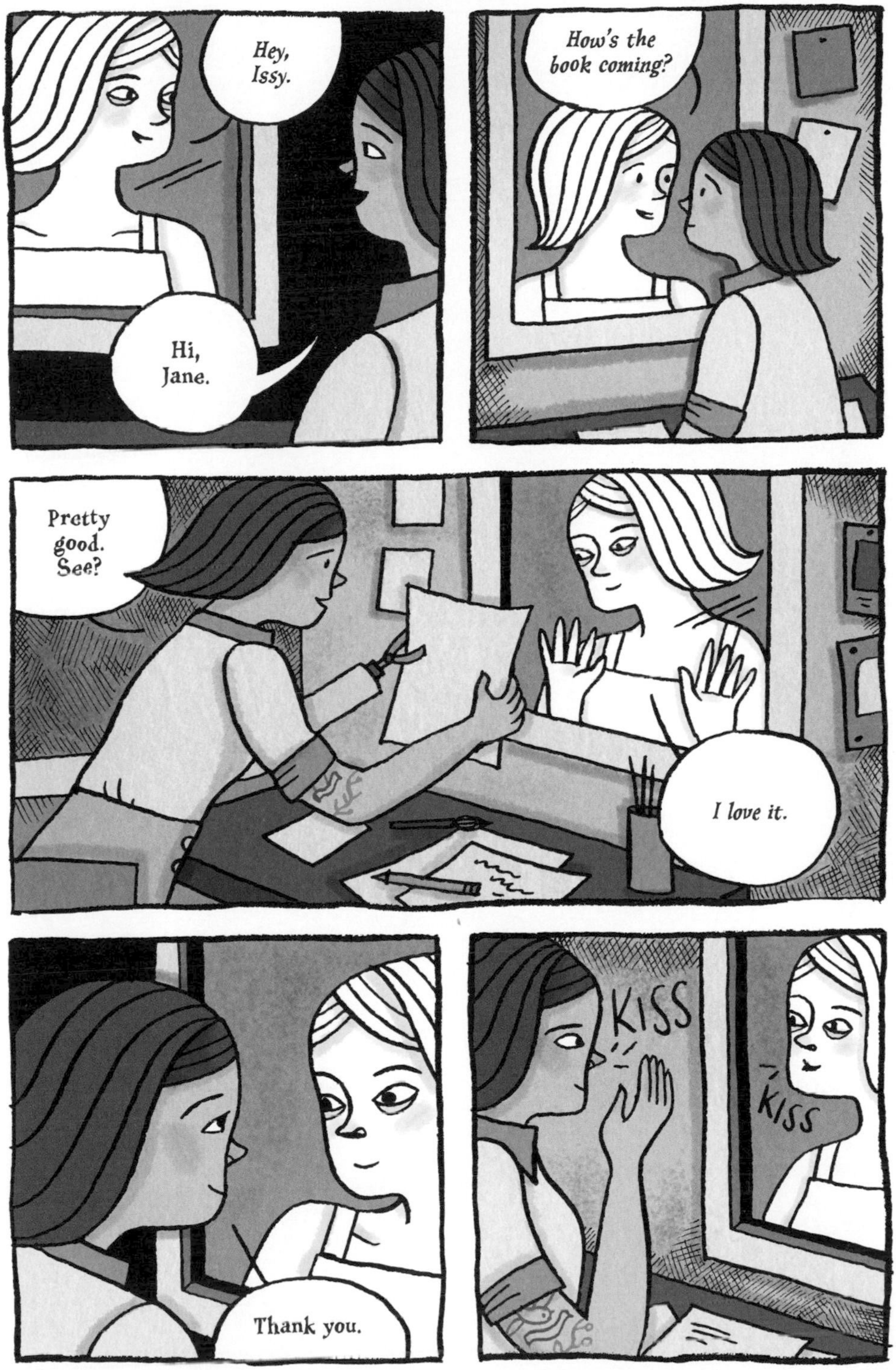
Hey, Issy.
Hi, Jane.
How's the book coming?
Pretty good. See?
I love it.
Thank you.
KISS
KISS

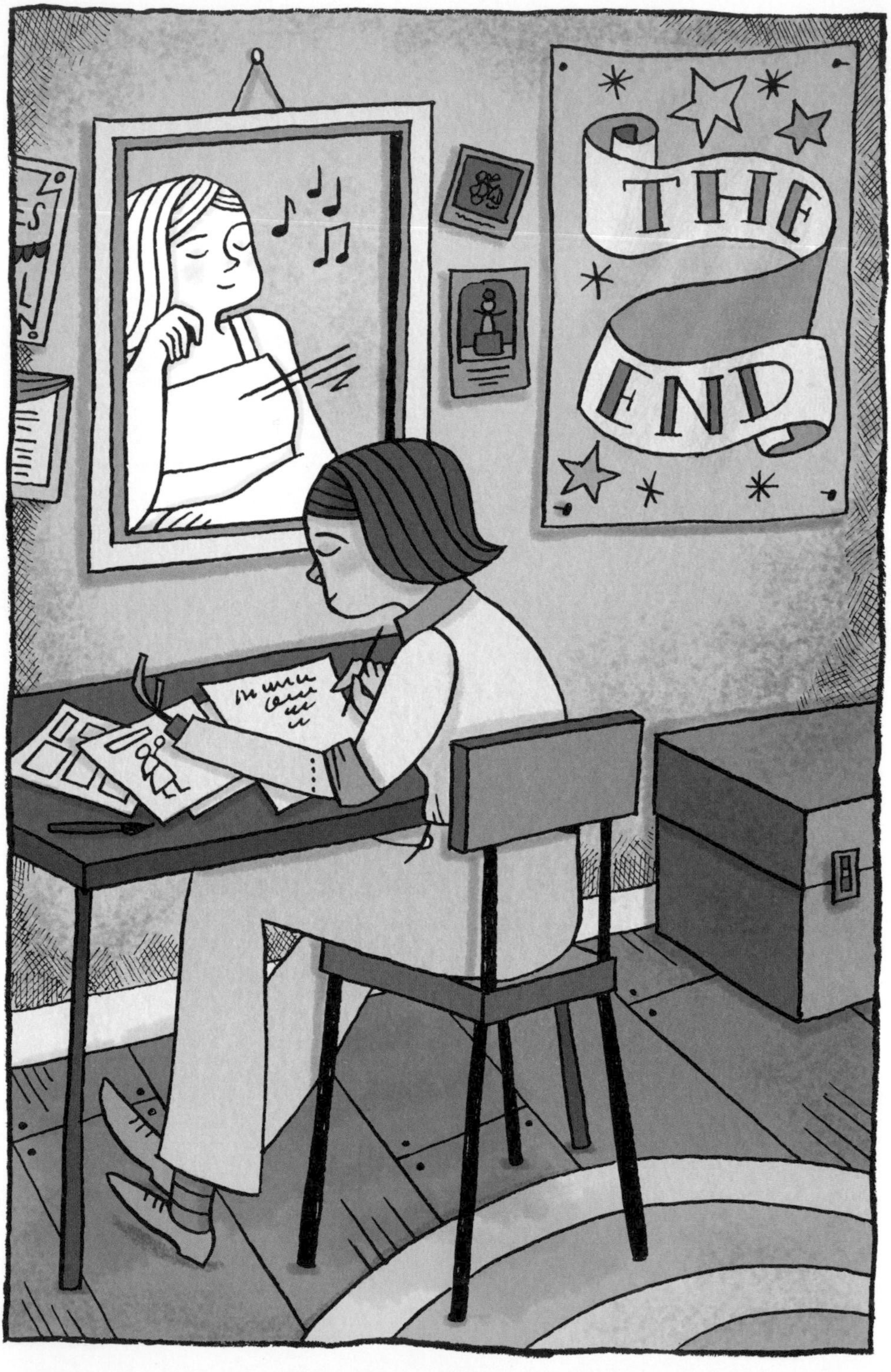
THE
END